HEIR OF THE BEAST

Heir of the Beast

F.R. Black

Fairy Godmother Inc. Novel
Book 1

F.R. BLACK
FAIRY GODMOTHER INC. SERIES

TO ALL MY READERS
WITH THIRSTY HEARTS
AND
A LOVE FOR ADVENTURE,
THIS IS FOR YOU.

CHAPTER 1

The pits of hell belch and cloud humanity with the pungent smell of rotten eggs that harbors the fiery embers of Hades.

Bleeding hearts.

What is it? Two-hundred degrees?

I wipe the beads of sweat from my brow and take a labored breath of humid air that seems to suffocate me like meaty fists gripping my dainty throat, watching in evil delight as I sputter for air, fighting for my life. If the musty air manifested into an illusion of flesh and blood, I'd be trying to gouge out its eyes, fighting like a wildcat, trying to break its firm grip on my neck.

I'm not sure what gender this musty, humid demon is, but I attempt a kick to the groin anyway. No good, this phantom creature is not fazed as we crash against the wall in a battle that I'm losing quickly.

But I don't die. The damp, nasty air lets me breathe just a little, just

enough to keep me alive to continue the torture.

The loud whine of my air conditioner seems to morph into high-pitched laughter, revealing its true self—one of the bad guys the whole time! It never meant to cool off the room.

The lies. The betrayal!

Am I dramatic?

Let's say you compare me to a first-class ~Karen~ dining at a restaurant, who just received her bill, not realizing ~ranch ~was an upcharge, then I'm perfectly normal.

Really though, I'm half tempted to turn on the news to see if the sun is due for impact. New Orleans has always been two steps from hell in the month of July. And it doesn't help that I live on the top floor of an old Victorian house either. It's almost like the old, haunted wood has a deal with the devil, to claim the souls who inhabit this furnace.

But back to the real problem at hand. This is bigger than the floating inferno currently surrounding New Orleans.

I'm holding a letter—a golden, sparkly letter, mind you—that was pushed under my door this morning. When it was still dark outside. We're talking ~early~, people!

The last time I checked, the postal service did not deliver at four in the morning under said person's door.

Why? Because that's creepy, and that's not how they conduct their professional business. They work at normal, suitable corporate hours.

Only mentally unstable people deliver letters at four in the morning by sliding letters under your front door, probably followed by heavy, excited breathing.

You know what I'm talking about. Stalkers, serial killers, rapists.

Freddy.

2

The letter would read, "~Peek-a-boo, I see you..."~ or something else alarmingly sinister, and then that would be the start of a B-budget horror movie.

I would be running, cleavage all over the place, and I would shockingly trip over nothing, resulting in my brutal death by the ax. But no, that's not what it says, not even close.

It radiates light. For a fleeting second, I'm sure that I'm being invited to Willy Wonka's Chocolate Factory, holding the golden ticket. But it's way weirder than that, trust me.

This letter is why I now doubt my ability to function in polite society.

I shift my weight as I stare down at the ghostly missive that lights my fingers and half my arm. The paper is feather-soft, and I can hear a faint jingle, like if you erratically shook Tinkerbell.

Apparently, folks, the Fairy Godmother herself felt the need to write to me and invite me on a romantic fantasy of vast proportions. A charming prince of Fate's choosing.

I place my hot hand on my burning forehead and read the letter again, to confirm my slow-boiling hysteria.

Dear Viola Del Vonsula,

Congratulations to you.

If you are standing, I might suggest you sit. You have been chosen at random to take part in the two-hundredth anniversary of Fairy Godmother Inc.

Though this is a random picking, I know much about you—possibly more than you might even know about yourself. I see you now, reading this missive, with a frown upon your beautiful little face.

But rest assured, Viola, I do have your best interest at heart, and that is quite a bit better than what you're used to.

I know you have lived a life of fear with no family, orphaned as a small child. What a poor, poor child you used to be, quite heartbreaking, having to grow up too fast.

But you were once a dreamer, full of hope and excitement, seeing the beauty in everything and giving humanity the benefit of the doubt. Indeed, a wonderful girl inside and out.

But now you wallow in paranoia. Getting mixed up with the wrong crowd can prove to be devastating to one's person.

Your innocence is leading you down a path of such darkness and despair, I fear. It does sadden me, for being the Fairy Godmother, I do despise such a tragic story.

But I have brilliant news, Viola. I, the Fairy Godmother, have an offer that may change your life forever. God knows you need it. You can only go up, dear girl.

I am giving you a chance to find a happily-ever-after.

On behalf of Fairy Godmother Incorporated, you will be able to compete against four other ladies for an opportunity to win a happily-ever-after.

4

Keep in mind that this offer is a once-in-a-lifetime opportunity full of adventure, danger, and the ultimate prize of true love.

Love is the secret to life, Viola, and it could be yours. Please take a moment to imagine falling in love with a handsome, dashing prince.

I know your first instinct is to throw this letter away, but please do not, dear girl. For Heaven's sake, this is your only chance at happiness—trust me, I've checked.

Did I mention that people want you dead? Quite disconcerting.

I'm the All-Knowing. Fate is my specialty. Destiny is my hobby. Bloody hell, child, I'm the keeper of the most powerful emotion of all...true love.

The choice is yours.

This offer will last until tomorrow night when the clock strikes twelve. If accepted, all details and answers to questions will be provided to ensure complete and total understanding.

The meeting will take place at the French Quarter past the tall, charming man in white. Please do not be late, or this fantasy will be nothing more than a rotting pumpkin.

Upon accepting this offer, you will agree to pay for this experience by handing over half of all your assets, including but not limited to bank accounts, IRA's/401K's, jewelry, vehicles, clothes, shoes, electronics, real estate, animals, and animal's belongings.

If failed, all family ties will break, and you will be alone in the world. All competitors will travel to the same kingdom; the choice of kingdom is random by a spinning wheel of destiny.

This trip is known to cause vomiting, diarrhea, nausea, dizziness, lightheadedness, drowsiness, uncontrollable tremors, fatigue, and in rare cases, death.

Everything about the Fairytale Challenge will rely solely on Fate, and all aspects will be unpredictable and potentially dangerous, even possibly resulting in your demise.

Each contestant will have their chance at the spinning wheel, where they will find out what their fate will be for the next three months of the challenge. Whether a contestant spins to be a princess or a pauper, they will have to make the best of it to catch the prince's eye and heart.

Godspeed,

Fairy Godmother

Fairy Godmother, President & CEO, Fairy Godmother Inc.

"Where dreams come true."

Do you see what I mean?!

This lady knows bits about my life, and I know for sure that I have told no one of my bad life choices. That was between me, myself, and I, mainly because I have no friends and family that I wish to claim.

Seconds pass as I stare, heart pounding with indecision. The only way this makes a little sense is if this letter invitation is genuine. Which it most definitely is not.

I laugh.

~Ok, Viola, let's not get on the bus to Crazy Town just yet.~

Let's list the facts and look at this logically:

*This letter is glowing. ~Seems impossible.~

*This letter is glowing ~and~ sparkling by an unknown source~. Seems supernatural.~

*"The Fairy Godmother" knows things she most definitely should not about my life. ~Very unsettling~.

*I hear clear sounds of sparkles.

*Fairy Godmother Inc. sounds a bit like the Hunger Games — but for the hopelessly romantic.

*I'm a secret lover of the movie ~Anastasia~, tell no one.

*A meeting at midnight to find Mr. Charming might be a red flag for a rapist~.~

I think about this.

If this is a hidden camera show or a scientific study to test dumb and gullible women, then I will be a proud statistic. Maybe they're offering to counsel us? I might benefit from that.

This could be a study approved by Dr. Phil! I always wanted to get counseling, a hidden desire, actually.

I secretly want the doctors to look at me and tell me if I really am psychotic or if I have been mistreated my whole life, and it's not my fault, and then we would cry together. I could break down the emotional walls!

I could get sent to a really nice beachfront rehab facility.

Am I doing this then?

Midnight tonight.

Well, Fairy Godmother, you can count on me. I'm just the right amount of messed up to show up and represent. I glance back at the glowing letter and can't wipe the silly smile off my face.

I have bought a ticket to Crazy Town.

Or a nice bed at a rehab center.

CHAPTER 2

11:34 p.m.

I should have already left.

Not sure what's making me delay.

I take a deep breath and glance at my reflection with a sick feeling in my stomach. Do I look mentally stable? I frown and take in my discolored gaze staring back at me in my cracker-box bathroom.

Definitely, probably, not really. Not when you really take a good long look past my cute face and long black hair.

I used to think my oh-so-blessed, exotic looks would get me far in life, but it has produced adverse effects.

Now, before you get the wrong idea of me, I do appreciate them. I do. I thank the mother who left me at the Water Crest nursing home in Houston, Texas, for them.

But, in a way, it has made me lazy in areas I should have been strong in, like common sense. Street smarts.

I would tell my younger self that getting involved with a known drug dealer's handsome son should be avoided at all costs.

Because they do not take breakups that well. They want to find you and bring you back to talk.

11:49 p.m.

"Oh noooo," I hiss to myself. My heart starts the crazy drumroll again as I run to snatch my purse and iPhone. I grab the now dim letter and stuff it into my leopard pack, saying a prayer as I run out the door.

I really hope the glowing letter is not a figment of my imagination, or I will never let myself live this down.

I am going to need help if I'm going to find this guy in eight minutes. My violet romper says that I'm cute and approachable, maybe I could find some defenseless guy to help me look.

Luckily, I live one block from the French Quarter. I should be able to find help. I'm only 5'5" for crying out loud — like, I'm adorable.

Damsel in distress.

~5 minutes later…~

Wrong.

"Excuse me —" I am aggressively shoulder checked by what appears to be a vampire in a bright purple cape and excessive costume makeup.

"Hey!" I get out and shoot him poison-death-rays out of my eyes. He will die a painful death tonight. Or maybe karma will at least grace him with explosive diarrhea.

Somebody must know something! I run up to a group of middle-aged tourists who seem to be well into their cups, all sporting tall hurricanes and loud laughter.

"Hi, could you help?!"

I try to show them my golden letter. "I need to find a charming man. I know I sound weird, but it's kind of for a game show." I wave my hand as I explain. "I would guess he would be wearing a suit—"

They push past me like ~I'm~ the crazy one. I grit my teeth in embarrassment. That man with the camera is wearing white socks with his Velcro sandals! A true crime to humanity.

Karma really has her work cut out for her tonight.

I am on my own.

Two-and-a-half strained minutes pass without luck. I see no signs saying: Over here, looney ladies! Fairy Godmother Inc.!

What the heck was I thinking, only leaving myself ten minutes to find this mystery man? What does that even mean?

I'm a horrible procrastinator, always waiting until the last minute to make up my mind. I just like to think it keeps things interesting. I'll keep telling myself that and not panic.

I'm bumping into people left and right, and I manage to step on some hot gum that now makes a sticky sound every time my black wedge heel hits the ground.

Perfect.

I check my phone.

11:59

"I'm a pumpkin!" I yell in defeat, feeling failure seep into every inch of my body. I read over the letter again, and it gives no clear directions. Son of a monkey's uncle! "I'm a rotten pumpkin," I moan to myself.

Cue crazy tears.

I'm probably going to start Mrs. Flow. I'm usually not this emotional.

Lies.

A lady with her gummy-faced child ushers him to move past me faster as if I might reach out and grab him like ~oogy boogy~!

"Oh great!" I get out as they pass. "I'm a child-scarer." I moan. I sniff. But what kind of mother keeps her kid up this late anyway?

I feel a hand touch my arm. I whip around to stare at a tall, lovely redhead, her hair cut to an A-line at her shoulders. Her white summer dress is pretty, and her smile even prettier. She looks like a Southern Belle.

"May I help you?" I say, more angrily than I want.

I'm not in a good mood, lady.

"I noticed the letter you're holding." She nods to the paper, fisted into my grasp. "It would seem that we both are having trouble finding Mr. Charming."

What?!

Relief washes over me like a waterfall. So I'm not the only idiot present tonight. "It's midnight," I say in defeat.

"Well," she begins as she glances around the busy streets, "they can't be mad if we are late with directions like that. I mean, this is silly anyway."

She laughs and looks at me as if desperately seeking to confirm her thoughts.

And really, this is silly. "I guess I feel a little ashamed even searching for Charming, curiosity got the best of me."

She giggles and blows out a big breath, starting to fan her face. "I know, and it's so hot tonight. I bet they're filming us right now. We're probably the only two who showed up."

I join in because there is nothing else to do but make fun of ourselves. We look around for maybe a hidden camera or a group of people looking our way and pointing.

What I was not expecting was to see a very handsome man dressed in a crisp

12

white suit, standing not too far from us, in the alleyway across the street. Our laughter dies as we both sober and stare at him.

I swear I looked in that direction earlier and he was not standing there with a brilliant smile directed at us. Is this him?! I'm lightheaded, and that tingling in the pit of my stomach is back, my pulse pounding.

"You see him too?" I ask hesitantly. "The man?"

"Sure do."

"What do we do?" I risk a glance at her, my pulse hammering.

"Make kissy faces at him? I have no clue," she offers breathlessly, her voice wavering.

I'm too shocked to grin. Glancing back at the man, my brain realizes that this man is incredibly handsome, standing there with one hand casually tucked into his suit pocket.

He is leaning against a door, just staring at us with an amused smirk that is utterly charming.

"You think he's into that?"

"Into what?"

"Kissy faces."

She grabs my hand and looks down at me, pulling me. "We should go over there."

I think I say something, but it's lost in the humid night air.

Walking up to him does not ease our nerves. I can tell because Tall Redhead is grabbing my hand in a death grip.

He smiles brightly at me, then to her, and shifts his weight. His gaze lands on me again, and something odd sparkles in his perfect blue eyes that makes a shiver slither down my back.

"You girls are late." His voice is smooth and lovely. His blond hair is combed back perfectly, and his face is that of a prince.

I open my mouth to speak, but nothing comes out.

My mind is flatlining.

"Please, come in. The Fairy Godmother hates to be off schedule," he says, like we were talking about the weather, something completely normal. He opens the wood door that ascends upstairs and beyond.

It's dark up there.

Are we going to a mental institution? Will men in white medical outfits seize us and place us in a padded room and shove pills down our throats?

"Hey, are you going to drug and kidnap us?" I ask, then blush. Redhead blanches beside me, then looks back to him. I just gave him the idea, didn't I?

Though, let's be honest, being taken advantage by him might not be so bad. I might play-fight at first, but then I would be totally into it.

I'm a sicko.

He turns his shocked face toward me and laughs loudly, but doesn't say anything, disappearing up the stairs. "Come on, ladies."

Redhead shrugs and proceeds after him.

"Was that a yes?" I whisper as I blindly follow them, feeling my skin prickling.

She turns to face me as we walk up the dark stairway. "I think that was a maybe."

I bet I can outrun Redhead if shit hits the fan. Hey, I have never claimed to be noble, it's a personality flaw that I'm working on.

We make it to the top, and he opens a large silver door. I tense, bracing myself. Immediately, cool, unusual, wondrous air hit us. The sight before me steals my breath clean out of my lungs.

14

What the…

The room is spacious and completely beautiful—jaw-dropping. I think I hear Redhead gasp, placing a hand over her mouth.

Everything is white and sky blue. The floors are glistening white marble with light blue glittering swirls throughout it.

The ceiling is vaulted with shimmering bits of glass, and the seating area is exquisite with blinding white couches and sapphire accents.

The whole thing doesn't look real. I take a shaky breath and try to count to ten in my mind.

"Welcome to Fairy Godmother Inc., ladies. Please check in at the front desk," Mr. Charming says in a sing-song voice. "Please make haste."

I glance at Mr. Charming, my mouth hanging open. "Check in?"

He points to a large, U-shaped desk with a beautiful woman smiling at us. She is typing away at a computer and has an earpiece in, talking to someone on the other end.

She is wearing an all-white dress fit for luncheon at the royal castle. Her golden hair bounces as she types, apparently enjoying her job with great enthusiasm. I'm getting a creepy, Stepford-wife vibe.

I tap down my hysteria, eyeing everything for a potential threat. We walk up to her, and she points at the sparkling paper and pen, then keeps talking.

"Yes, they have just arrived—uh-huh." She pauses, listening. "Of course, I know they're late." She glances up at us with a stern look.

"I will get them checked in quickly then—I understand. I will usher them back, my lady. I know time is of the essence." She glances up at us and forces a smile.

"Please sign in and take a seat over there, then Pierce will bring everyone into the arena."

Arena?

What the hell?

This place is not big enough for that, and even I'm not that gullible. I sign my name and notice five other names on the list.

Seven girls? I thought the letter said five? Hmm, fascinating. I was expecting more for an advertising stunt, though.

I walk around a corner to see five lovely women sitting on white couches, looking just as nervous as I feel. Redhead gives a little nod to them, and we sit together on the only empty couch next to a refreshment table.

Okay, this is weird.

"What is this place?" Redhead whispers.

I swallow and shrug, glancing around the beautiful sitting room. "This is getting weirder by the second," I whisper back.

Redhead speaks to the other girls. "Hi." She clears her throat. "My name is Cherie. Did you all receive a letter this morning?" Her name is Cherie—noted.

They all nod and murmur something inaudible.

A snobby, blond-haired girl sniffs and stands up to look around, her rose heels clicking on the marble. I say snobby because she has that mean-girl look about her.

Perfect blond hair, Barbie body, pink sundress, and a perfected resting-bitch-face that is even better than mine. She must have had years of practice. Bravo.

"My name is Laura Rogers. I'm sure you heard of my brother. Luke Rogers? He's the pitcher for the Red Sox," She beams, looking way too smug.

Laura examines her manicure and walks around the room, listening to everyone's praise. "I hope this is something to do with TV."

"I don't watch baseball. So boring," I blurt before my faulty filter kicks in. I feel Cherie shoot me a glance, then a grin, covering her smile with her hand.

Laura's gaze pins me and she takes her time to look me up and down. She raises a thin brow and walks over to me, lips pinched. She has very thin lips, I

16

notice, that flatten out into a line.

"And who are you? Madame Darkness?" She laughs lightly.

I resist an eye roll. "My name is Viola Spearrrr, andddd I'm here out of pure curiosity," I answer with my chin raised.

Not sure why I just gave her a bogus last name.

Maybe I'm subconsciously embarrassed to be here.

"Whatever," she shoots back. "Aren't we all?"

A Black girl who sits on the couch opposite of me leans forward. "Hi, I'm Destiny. This place gives me the creeps — too sterile. Anyone else feelin' this way?"

She adjusts her jeans and white tank top. She has on cute silver pumps. I take note.

The girl next to Destiny, with short platinum hair, nods in agreement. She raises her hand.

"I'm April. I am a little nervous about this setup. I hope there is no auditioning or anything like that. I'm not good in front of crowds — like, I will have a panic attack."

"We are in a documentary or movie set," Laura chimes in, sounding annoyed by everyone's incompetence.

A tall brunette laughs. "Let's not forget how hot Mr. Charming is," she whispers, loud enough for all of us to hear, and looks around the corner. "Oh, and I'm Ivy, a former Marine."

We all murmur something about her exceptional service to our country.

The last girl with caramel skin and a Cuban bun raises her hand to introduce herself, but Mr. Charming comes in. Everyone's mouths shut and eyes widen.

My heart pulses to life like a drunken tap dancer who just pounded five Red Bulls.

17

He grins and places a hand in his white suit pants.

"Ladies, we are ready for you all to move into the arena, where all of your questions will be answered. We are a little bit behind schedule, so please, let's not let the Fairy Godmother wait another second."

I hear a muffled giggle to my left.

He glances at all of us. A severe look crosses his handsome features as he studies us.

"Please take this seriously. What you are about to see is real. You all are chosen for a reason by Fate's hand, and before you enter, you must take a deep breath and find your inner calm."

I frown, not liking the sound of that at all.

If we walk into a sex dungeon like that girl from ~50 Shades~, I'm tripping Laura and running. Not even kidding — the survival of the fittest. I can fight like a wildcat if need be.

But here I am.

The blind leading the blind.

We all line up and proceed to follow Charming through a sliding door made of glass.

Okay, I need to explain this slowly so you understand what I see as I pass through the door.

We walk into a large, U-shaped seating area, like something you'd see at a university — a lecturing room with high seating. I calm my pounding heart as I grab the back of a chair to steady myself.

The problem is…

The problem is that where a chalkboard and wall would be, there is nothing. There is nothing behind the large white desk and podium. No, I don't mean nothing. What the hell am I saying?!

18

I might throw up.

Behind the desk was outer f-ing space.

In case you didn't understand that: Behind the desk where a wall should be is OUTER SPACE.

I am looking at the big, black abyss that is our universe. Like someone cut a spaceship in half, and we are standing on the edge. There are distant shooting stars, comets, and an enormous planet that is far off in the distance. You can see the atmosphere moving around it.

Oh, and there is this breeze. I can see little pieces of my hair flowing with the air current.

I feel Cherie's hand on my arm, squeezing, her fingers turning white as her arm shakes. I'm numb to the pain of her death grip.

I slowly look up and see Charming walking down the pale marble stairs to the bottom level, where the large desk sits. Dear goodness, even a red shiny apple lays on top of it, like we are in grade school.

"Ladies!" Charming booms with his hands outstretched. "Please have a seat wherever you like.

"I know what you are seeing does not seem real, but you'll find out soon enough that this room is the least of your worries. I say this with the deepest part of my heart. Welcome."

He eyes everyone in the room as we take seats on our shaky legs. His eyes rest on me for a second longer than everyone else.

I get a bizarre feeling that he knows something concerning me, but I'm too overwhelmed to give it any thought.

"A drink will be passed around to allow you all to take this in, in a much calmer state of mind. You may pass if you like, but I strongly suggest you take it."

He motions for two women in white clothing to come in with trays and pass around some pink, fizzy drink in flute glasses.

"This will help you, ladies, so please drink up. We do not have time for panic attacks or fainting spells."

Destiny has her head in between her legs, breathing hard, and April is feeling her pulse on her neck, looking sweaty. Laura sits in silence, her eyes wide and unbelieving.

"Viola? May I offer you a drink?" A woman leans down to hand me a flute glass without even waiting for a reply.

"Yes," I barely say, more so to myself. I am already down the rabbit hole, so I might as well fall without screaming.

I look to my right, seeing Cherie and everyone else downing the fizzy drink with desperate gulps.

"Is anyone scared of the date rape drug?" I continue, not even sure if I am saying it out loud. "It's a real thing, people."

I see a distant shooting star, probably miles and miles away, making my breathing hitch. Okay, I'm losing it fast. I feel my left eye start to tick. Bottoms up.

I down the fruity flavored drink and repress a burp from the burn of the carbonation. Welp, there is no going back now. I just took the blue pill, and it's coursing through my system.

I can feel my body humming, my muscles relaxing.

I will now enter the matrix.

Cue the electronic computer sound as I get sucked into a different reality.

"You all should be feeling calmer in about two minutes," he says as he grins at us all, his arms crossed over his chest. His shining blue eyes watch us.

"Let me know when you all feel like you can focus, and we will begin." Charming leans against the desk and lights a cigar like he is at home sitting before the fireplace. Or at a high-end lounge.

I take a breath and feel my nerves settle. A wave of warmth spreads through me like a slow-moving river of lava. I take another deep breath, and my arms stop shaking. My eye goes still.

Okay…

Okay.

I can do this. I glance around, seeing everyone else visibly relaxing, sitting up straighter in their chairs. What was in that drink? I feel great. Now I can enjoy the brilliant view before me.

This is real. Unbelievable. All this time, the letter was genuine.

"All right, I can see that all of you are ready to get started," Pierce says with a smile, and he holds out his arm toward the universe. "Ladies, may I present you to…the Fairy Godmother."

Suddenly, a door opens, and a stunning woman walks through the archway. Are the stars and planets just an illusion, then? Amazing technology.

Her midnight blue gown glitters and her silver hair is up in a bun on top of her head. She looks like a nineteen-fifties celebrity.

The dress flows out at the tight waist and stops under the knee like she is wearing petticoats. The off-the-shoulder neckline is elegant, probably the envy of every trophy housewife.

She looks like a version of Meryl Streep in the movie ~Devil Wears Prada~.

She looks just as intimidating.

Her expression as she walks is one of utter seriousness. I can't believe I'm looking at the legendary Fairy Godmother. Our reality is stranger than fiction.

There is still no smile, no happy greeting like Mr. Charming. She glances at Charming with an all-but-pleased look on her face.

"Pierce, are we ready to begin?" she asks as she scans the room, her gaze resting on mine.

I hold my breath.

Do I have something on my face?

She tilts her head, and I think I see a hint of a smile. The Fairy Godmother looks back to Charming, and he gives her a wink and blows out a trail of smoke. "The floor is yours."

The Fairy Godmother nods and takes a couple of steps toward us, her gown twinkling and her black pumps clipping. She takes a moment as if gathering her thoughts.

"I will have all of your undivided attention."

No one says a word.

We will now find out why we are here.

"I will assume you all read your letter sent to you this morning. Each one of you has been chosen to partake in the Fairytale Challenges as our agents."

She continues as we all hang on every word, "I'm afraid that this time, things are going to be a little different, due to unfortunate circumstances."

I frown.

She takes a breath and places a hand on the bridge of her nose. "I have been running Fairy Godmother Incorporated for two hundred years, always providing a happily-ever-after."

She pauses again as if she is having trouble saying what she wants.

Charming steps forward and places a hand on her shoulder, whispering something in her ear. She shakes her head and whispers something back, looking very upset.

What's going on?

I shift in my seat and look at Cherie, noticing that everyone appears concerned. Cherie shrugs and glances back at the two.

We see Pierce give her a hug, and the Fairy Godmother leaves the room with her hand over her mouth, clearly distraught. Charming walks her to the door, then he returns to us and exhales.

"I'm sorry for the delay." He saunters over to the desk and sits on the edge. "I will be leading the discussion today. The Fairy Godmother has a lot on her plate with appointments she cannot miss. I will be taking questions shortly, but for now, just listen." His blue gaze lands on me, then passes over everyone else.

"If everyone here agrees to the terms, then all of you will be transported to another world—a kingdom, if you will. And yes, ladies, we can do that.

"There are many different dimensions, with many different planets with functioning worlds like Earth. Believe it because it is very true."

He moves to stand behind the desk and starts typing, then waves his hands up in the air as 3-D images come out.

In one instant, the view of the universe changes.

I gasp.

I see some insanely technological PowerPoint display.

On the 3-D screen, I will call it, planets appear in a list from number one to a thousand-and-something. The top half is labeled in white, the middle blue, and different hues of red for the bottom.

"As you can see, these planets are currently under contract with Fairy Godmother Inc. This is not the normal speech we give our agents, and for that, I apologize.

"We need help. Desperation is an understatement here. Fairy Godmother Inc. is on the verge of being out of business. This is the best way I can describe it for you to understand.

"I will explain why, and you're the first group to hear this behind-the-scenes information.

"The entire purpose of this company is to control and maintain peace within the universe. The Fairy Godmother answers to a higher authority, who gave her the responsibility to keep a certain level of peace between all worlds."

He pauses as he gazes around. "All the planets are invisibly connected, and when one harbors evil, it affects the others like dark oppression, a chain reaction of negativity.

"This evil is not okay, and it needs to be managed. The Fairy Godmother believes that love can heal all wickedness; this has always been her slogan. She is an amazing woman, always thinking that redemption can be a part of the most corrupt." He pauses at our still-confused expressions.

"We need to keep each planet above 50 percent—evil versus good. We can never eliminate evil altogether, but we can keep it manageable with this system we have used for hundreds of years.

"We are talking about the people who inhabit them. Their souls combine for a total percentage. If we cannot do this over time, we are out of the business, and a different power will take over."

I raise my hand.

He looks at me, then nods.

All eyes are on me.

"So," I clear my throat, "I'm guessing that the Fairy Godmother is going out of business because she is having trouble with keeping evil below 50 percent?"

I am trying to understand this complex dilemma. I blush, hoping I didn't ask a stupid question.

He takes a moment. "Yes, we are having a problem with one planet. Remember that each planet is judged separately," Charming continues as he points to the 3-D screen.

"The last world on the bottom is the one in question, the one that is bright red.

As you can see, the other planets above it are being affected by it, starting to turn red as well.

"It's like an infection, spreading unless we can cure it, fast."

"I get it," Laura blurts out loudly, looking around. "You want us to make the leader of a kingdom fall in love with one of us. To cure their evil souls. How romantically heroic of us."

Her eyes are lit with excitement. "So we are like heroes — love heroes."

"To change the heart of the corrupt," I say quietly, ignoring Barbie.

"Yes." He glances at us. "This one planet is out to destroy us. We have tried three times already and failed. This has never happened before. Heroes you all will be, as these are not easy missions."

"Three groups like us?" asks April with a frown.

"Correct." He takes some steps toward us and exhales. "This is our last chance, so you can imagine how distraught the Fairy Godmother is. She will lose everything we have worked for.

"We were very close to the last mission, getting to 40 percent. But sadly, almost doesn't cut it. We need to be above half. The Fairy Council is very strict about sticking to the rules that keep this universe in balance.

"Our Fairy Godmother will be replaced with another. A fairy that I shall not name, but that does not believe in what our Fairy Godmother does. The woman is a vile creature and happens to be our Fairy Godmother's sister."

"Does our Fairy Godmother have a name?" Destiny asks. "Or are they all called Fairy Godmothers?"

Charming smiles. "Her name is Zora, and you didn't hear that from me." He leans back on the desk. "Her bitch sister is Mildred. And yes, she sounds just like her name."

I can't help but giggle. So we have a family feud filled with jealousy — how very human of them.

No pressure.

But this confuses me. What's this talk of missions? I thought we were going on an adventure to find love.

"So, what do you mean you were close? He almost fell in love with a girl in the last mission?" For some reason, that doesn't sit well with me.

He chuckles and rubs the back of his neck. "Not even close." Charming looks up at me and exhales. "The best way I can describe it, in this short period of time, is like this.

"Think of this as a video game, where certain things you do give you points. Having the main ruler fall in love for the right reasons is like a 40 percent boost. Everything else is minor.

"Like getting rid of the bad guy, solving hunger issues, slavery—the list goes on. We only have three months; that's all Fate will allow us to intervene.

"So, if you choose to solve their world issues instead of falling in love, that is a tough road to complete in three months. Not to mention dangerous.

"Don't get me wrong; falling in love is also hard, but much more plausible. And generally, when you fix the ruler, you fix all of the smaller issues as well. It's like a chain reaction of joy and happiness.

"Therefore, Zora believes so much in true love because it fixes everything else along with it."

Wow, this is complicated.

It's much different from Disney movies, but kinda of the same.

"So, on the last mission, they tried to fix the world, not their leader?" I ask, my mind spinning in all different directions.

"They had no choice, for their leader was not interested in any of the women we sent. They just tried to make the best of their time and tried to help out Zora the best they could."

He looks down like he is lost in thought.

Laura laughs and shakes her head. "This guy is picky. I like my men picky, and I like a challenge."

Charming looks up and stares at her, probably trying to determine if she is serious.

"I guess you can say that he is picky. I have a feeling he is onto us, knowing something about what we are doing." He pushes off the desk and starts clapping his hands.

"This is the time to tell you the rules. We have very little time to do this because the council gave us only today to send out another team."

I think I hear him use profanity under his breath. Pierce Charming is not happy about this.

"You each will be in the hands of Fate. That's how this works—to keep the balance, we must follow what Fate dictates for us." He holds out his hand, and the ground vibrates.

I sit up in my chair and watch as a stone…birdbath…raises out of the ground. In the bath is a metallic liquid. How very curious. What is this?

"This is simple, ladies, and again, I am sorry we are rushing through everything. You each will place your hands into the Bowl of Destiny and Fate will determine what you will be in this challenge. A princess or a pauper.

"This is crucial, for you may not change this once a title has been given to you."

My eyes widen. So it's like the Harry Potter hat.

I hear murmurs all around the room, some excited and some worried. I, myself, have very mixed emotions coursing through my body, like lunatics escaping from the institution.

But I am mostly…excited. I am glad Fate gets to pick. It makes it more exciting.

Because we all know everyone would choose to be a princess. Duh.

"After you get your title, we will talk briefly about Delorith, the world you will be traveling to. Then you will be able to change three things about yourself to help you ensnare the heart of Apollo Augustus Garthorn.

"You may choose to change appearances or to master an ability. This choice is yours and yours only."

"Wow," I whisper. Cherie turns toward me with wide eyes and whispers an OMG. I smile and glance back.

Apollo Augustus Garthorn. He sounds hot and powerful, and I am so curious to see what this dark ruler looks like. Cute? Handsome? Average? Sexy? I ponder this.

He's got to be easy on the eyes, right? Maybe he isn't, and that's why no girl has worked. Crap. That would be difficult. Maybe he is funny. I could do funny.

"All right, we will talk more after titles." He stands up just as Zora, the Fairy Godmother, walks in. She looks composed, unlike earlier.

Standing by Charming, she says, "Please, let us begin. There is no turning back now. There is the door if you wish to leave. If not, let's not waste Fate's time."

I suddenly feel very nervous—sick, even. This is real. There is no turning back. No turning back.

I swallow and stand up with everyone else, taking a nervous breath.

Well, Viola, looks like you're going to take the blue pill and escape the matrix.

Bring it on.

CHAPTER 3

I accept and sign the official Fairytale Challenge contract. I probably should worry that I didn't read every little detail, but time was apparently of the essence.

I pale. Oh my gosh. I'm like those idiot girls in horror movies who run to the creepy shed full of weapons instead of the only working truck on the property.

Hey, but I was in, baby.

Glancing around the room and watching everyone else sign their name is unnerving.

I really hope I didn't just make the biggest mistake of my life. And that would be a very big mistake considering all my other bad life choices.

Positive thoughts.

The only girl who doesn't stay is the Latino woman, whose name I never caught. She says that this is a twisted freak show. A trap, something underground and illegal.

Does she have a point?

I'm getting nervous now. Maybe she is the only one with some real sense of danger, not buying into this fairytale. The rest of us must look like dumb sheep, gullible bunnies.

Suddenly, the urge to flee is as bad as trying not to itch a mammoth-sized bug bite.

Too late. Charming is instructing everyone to line up and start the next phase— meaning the birdbath of Fate.

Taking a shaky breath, I keep repeating to myself that this is going to be a blast, and nothing terrible is going to happen. I plaster a smile on my face and get in line.

This is going to be great. Amazing. Nothing to worry about!

I am super stoked.

Am I panicking?

I wipe my forehead and clench my fist.

Destiny is going first. She looks confident and unafraid, but I don't buy it. I am willing to bet we all are freaking out on the inside.

She walks up a few short steps to the Bowl of Destiny and pauses with her hands hovering over the metallic substance. She's scared.

It doesn't help that the solar system is back on display behind her.

My equilibrium is slightly thrown off as I feel a wave of dizziness. I could compare this feeling to taking shots on an empty stomach while wearing five-inch heels. Steady…steady…

"Go ahead, Destiny. It will only take a moment," Zora says calmly behind her.

She puts her hands in the substance and gasps. "It's freezing."

We all wait quietly, our hearts in our throats. I'm even scared to take a small breath, for it might upset Fate into giving Destiny a less desirable role.

On the screen behind us, in bold letters, it magically reads: Castle of Garthorn Royal Chef.

Destiny turns around and reads it, taking a moment to register that she will be making food for Apollo and the royal family. "Well," she breathes with a smile, "food is the way to a man's heart!"

Everyone cheers, and Zora nods.

"Quickly now — next!"

April walked up next, pushing her short hair behind her ear. "Okay, here goes nothing."

The screen reads: Castle of Garthorn Royal Horse Master.

Everyone oohs and ahhs at this one. I bite my lip; I would have loved that one, horses are beautiful creatures.

That would be exciting — riding horses with a hot prince and making love on a cliffside while my hair blows in the wind. I would say something witty, and his laughter would ring in the air.

Focus.

Ivy is next and laughs before she touches the liquid. "This is crazy! I feel like Harry Potter!"

The screen reads: Ladies Maid to the Queen of Garthorn.

She didn't look too pleased with that one, but that position would put her right next to Apollo and his mother.

She needs to think outside the box. No cliff side ***, but she could bang Apollo in his mother's bed.

That's a joke.

Laura is next, and she just wears a smirk, grinning at Ivy. I hope she gets chambermaid. Please, chambermaid.

"I hope this isn't a random drawing," she complains, and rolls her eyes, putting her hands in the liquid. "Because I am an inner princess, my daddy said so."

She laughs loud like she told the cleverest joke. It's high pitched and forced. It's embarrassing to see that nobody laughs after. I am about to chuckle out of pity, and I dislike her. That's how bad it is.

Her face reddens as she clears her throat. Her hands soak in the liquid and seconds pass.

The screen reads: Royalty of a Foreign Country.

"Yes!" she screams. "What does that mean?! Does that mean princess or queen?"

Zora takes a moment as she eyes Laura. It's hard to tell what the woman is thinking, but I'd bet my poker chips that she is irritated with her.

"You will get detailed information later." She turns to the next in line. "Next!"

Cherie glances back at me with her fingers crossed. I pray she gets something decent because three months is a long time to be a slave or a toilet cleaner.

The screen reads: Royalty of a Foreign Country.

Laura whips around to Charming and the Fairy Godmother, marching up to them, her heels clicking. "That's the same thing mine said. Is it broke?"

Charming smiles at her, but it's far from reaching his azure eyes. "I assure you they're very different. These are inexplicit titles. You will get the details later, as the Fairy Godmother already explained."

She glances at me with cheeks flushed the color of a cherry ICEE. Laura plasters a smile on her face that I am sure goes against the laws of gravity.

I am the last one.

No. No. NO.

"Come along, Viola," Zora commands. "Is that your natural eye color? Or contacts?" Everyone stares at me like they are wondering the same thing.

"They're real." My fingers tingle, and my vision begins to tunnel. I take a shaky breath and walk up to the Bowl of Destiny. Please don't make me a crap emptier; I dislike bodily waste.

I look up at her and say, "I'm ready."

She nods but doesn't say anything, and her calm blue gaze is eerily mysterious. I sniff, feeling like I am some rare creature on display at a zoo. I go to stare down into the pool of metallic wonder.

So, this Fate Bowl reads palms? Maybe it reads deeper than that? A shiver slithers down my spine. ~Just do it.~

My hands slip into the cool substance, and instantly I feel sensations coursing up and down my arms. I pray, ~Please give me something I can work with, Magic Bowl. Tell Karma to back off.~

It seems like it takes forever before it says: Castle of Garthorn Slave: With a Hidden Secret.

My eyes scan over the words, and dread sinks in. I hear whispers around me, probably expressing their sympathy. A slave?!

"Are there do-overs?" My voice breaks. This is not fair. I want the Horse Master one. I feel like sitting on the ground with my arm crossed and pitching a fit.

Next to me, Charming says, "Things are not always what they seem. The part you need to focus on is the hidden secret." He starts to clap to gain attention.

"Everyone, please quiet down. I will now introduce to you your partners for the next three months—our highly trained Fairy Godmother Agents. The FGAs."

Agents?

"You will not be thrown into an unknown world without guidance. We will set you up for success, not failure.

"These worlds can be very dangerous, and I should hate for any of you to end it quickly by unknowingly eating poisonous fruits."

Zora walks over to the edge of the classroom to where outer space starts.

Where it looked before like it dropped off into space, there is now thirty feet of more room behind the white desk.

And not only is there extended square footage, but standing there are six people decked out in black army outfits with FGA on the front.

They are all petite looking women, some with odd colored eyes and abnormal hued hair. Who were these strange people? One of them looks like a small version of Sailor Moon. Are these aliens?

My eyes widen in wonder—seeing a different life-form is trippy.

Zora nods at them, then turns to us, her midnight dress sparkling brilliantly. "These agents will follow you around, disguised as whatever they need to be to fit in. They are brilliant shapeshifters.

"They will be your walking computer, advising you on the world and its inhabitants. They communicate telepathically and verbally.

"Pierce will also be keeping track of you ladies, providing clothing and the essentials. The perfect aid to make sure each one of you has the best chance at succeeding.

"You all know how important this mission is to me. But keep in mind that you all are competing against each other, and strategy is key. They will help you on your journey to ensnaring the prince."

This fantasy went from a Disney movie to me being a part of the Special Love Operations, with a dose of Survivor. I am in way too deep now. There is no turning back.

Maybe I will get lucky and get placed as Apollo's slave?

Wishful thinking never hurt anyone.

CHAPTER 4

Everything is happening very quickly, and Charming keeps apologizing for it. I hug Cherie before we are split up to go our own ways.

I keep praying he will not lead me into a drug-infested sex trade operation.

Pierce glances back at me. "How are you doing?"

"I'm excited," I deadpan. I think I would be more enthused if I didn't draw to be a slave. It might be a very long three months.

He smiles back at me. "You are going to a new world, and that right there is worth it. Delorith, though infested with evil, is very beautiful."

I can't say anything to that.

Room after room into long white hallways, I stop questioning how all of this can fit into a New Orleans historic building. Somehow, I don't think we are in Kansas anymore.

When we arrive, our destination is a large room with a very bizarre contraption sitting in the middle of it. It reminds me of an alien space pod ready to beam me down to this crazy planet.

"Viola, this is your briefing room." He pauses and opens another door on the opposite wall. It sounds like a pressurized space door. An agent walks through, and it's the one who looks like Sailor Moon.

"This is Mort, your guide to everything you need." He continues, "It's time for your preparation. Have a seat, please."

He is carrying a huge stack of papers a foot thick. He slams the stack on the little metal desk in the corner of the room.

"This is everything you need to know about Delorith and its people. It also contains relevant information about Apollo." He waves his hand in the air.

"You know — his likes and dislikes, that type of thing. Blond, redhead, brunette...

"Is he a happy drunk or aggressive one? Does he like his mother? How many people has he killed, if any? Boxers or briefs? Does he have any fetishes?"

I can't tell if he is serious, but I think he is. "That's a lot of information."

"Isn't it, though." He smiles at me. His mood seems borderline unstable.

Charming laughs, dusting something off his perfect white sleeve.

"We don't have time for anything. That is all the information you do not get to read before we thrust you into a very dangerous place. You must rely heavily on Mort as your sole lifeline."

I glance at my agent, knowing I must confirm this, in case I misheard. "Your name is Mort?"

Her big eyes narrow. "Where I'm from, it's a lovely name." She raises her small chin. "Ignorant human."

I nod and glance back at Charming's amused face, finding my composure. "So you're saying I'm screwed."

His face brightens. "Yes."

I stare at him.

"Moving on, we have thirty minutes to get you dressed and ready." He claps his hands, and the machine in the middle of the room comes to life with glowing pink and blue lights.

"You will automatically speak their language, so no worries there. But you can die in this world, so you have to be very careful."

He walks up to me and leans in very close to my face. He smells like Old Spice. I could almost hear the Old Spice jingle.

"This is important, so pay attention. You have three lifelines. Let's say you're about to be killed by a wild animal, for example. You may use your lifeline, and you will immediately transport out of harm's way.

"If you forget to use it, you will be mauled and die. If you use all three of your lifelines, on the fourth, you will be ejected from the world entirely. No ifs, and's, or buts. You're too much of a liability."

He held up his hand. "Not my rules."

I swallow and nod. "How do I use a lifeline?" I should probably know that.

"Very easy. You say, 'Lifeline activate!'" His gaze holds mirth.

"That's it?"

"It has to be simple, does it not?"

I thought about that. "Okay, let's say they capture me, and I say the lifeline, and I disappear. Won't that mess with sensibilities? Like, what the hell? She just disappeared."

"Yes."

I stare at him, waiting for him to respond. Really though, I'm about to punch him.

"Leave that to us. This is not our first rodeo, and you only use it if you're going to die. It is not permitted to use a lifeline in less-than-desirable situations."

He winks at me, then walks over to the machine, or alien-fairy-pod. He bent down like he was getting the thing to start with elaborate waves of his hand.

"You are to be a slave, congratulations."

"That's horrible," I say, wondering what I'm missing. "What kind of slave? I am not going to do sexual stuff against my will." That is a deal-breaker.

Pierce glances at me and nods.

"Pierce?" I bite out.

"Yes."

"Elaborate."

"Of course, do you think I would send you without informing you details of your position?" He has the gall to look offended. "I read over your file, and it is fascinating."

Mort steps forward. "I have read and confirmed a plan of action."

"Perfect, Mort. You can get into details once arrived." He turns toward me. "Your position is simple, except for the fact that you harbor a secret. The secret is that you are the long-lost princess of Galleon.

"Now, here's the kicker. Laura is the current princess of Galleon and an impostor, not the true birthright princess—you are. I love it when Fate creates drama!" He claps his hands.

"Now, this does not mean Laura is evil. She is not to blame for this mix-up. It's Laura's deceitful mother. You were lost as a baby, and the title has passed to your cousin, Laura.

"This is a competition. No one will know of this deceit unless you bring it to light. Which will be a task because Laura must stop you from exposing her. It can get rather cutthroat out there."

"Oh, perfect," I say, looking at them both in awe. "I'm not only a slave, but I have to expose my birthright in three months and make Apollo fall in love with me?" I'm breathing hard, about to lose my mind.

"Yes," he says, and moves his hands around. "It's not just you with obstacles. Each player will have them and must overcome them. It makes for a much better journey.

"Laura's obstacle? She is not the birthright princess. April? She is an outlaw. Destiny? Is a Galleon spy.

"Ivy? Must save her brother, who the Queen of Garthorn wants to kill. Cherie? Is promised to another prince from Mont Gallow."

My mouth hangs open. "I see."

"Enjoy this. It can get hard, but it will be an experience you will not forget." He studies me with a serious expression.

I nod.

"All right, you can pick three things to change about yourself. Look over this book, and I will be back in thirty minutes. I must see to the other ladies." He leaves.

I start flipping through all the different traits I could gain or change.

Mort sits down on the metal chair across the room and examines her pointy nails. The silence is painful as I stare at her, and I realize she is pretending to ignore me.

I clear my throat. "Any pointers?"

She looks at me like she is put out. "Get a nose job."

"Really?"

This Mort character is delightful.

She glances at me for real this time and seems to assess me. "I get a bonus if we win," she says matter-of-factly, and without emotion.

"Number one: a master at riding a horse, which always comes in handy. Two: being in the best physical shape, which gives you a killer body. For a human, that is.

"Three: being a master at archery—you need a defense. It looks like your face is okay, and you have decent-sized breasts, so no need to change any of that."

"You are very blunt."

"I will confirm that," she says without smiling.

"Is he a breast man or butt man?" I must ask.

"Very hard to say. I am unsure of that at this point." She stares at me.

Right.

Pierce finally returns and relieves us of our awkward conversation about how not to eat anything blue in this world. Especially if it has spots—severe intestine issues, gas for weeks.

A deal-breaker, according to Mort. I want to add that it might be a deal-breaker for anyone.

Charming claps his hands and stops in front of the alien pod, hands on his hips. "Okay! Not all of the ladies took the details of their position as well as you, but that is to be expected."

I can only imagine how Laura reacted to the news that she is not the true princess. "I'm ready. Mort shared her expertise and some other…interesting facts."

"Perfect. Come over here and step into the converter," he orders, smiling at me.

I do so, and I feel like a character from the movie ~Alien~ when they're in their sleep pods.

The pod shuts around me, and I feel a wave of nerves. I hear a loud pressurized sound, and I can see electronic writing on the screen in front of me.

I hear Pierce's voice come through the speaker. "All right, which is the first trait?"

I falter for a second. "Master horseback rider."

"Nice choice, and the second?"

"To be in perfect physical shape."

"Always a favorite," he says. "Lastly?"

"Master at archery."

"Very smart. Okay, just give me a second, and if I can have you close your eyes and take a deep breath…"

I don't even have time to ask if it is going to hurt! Bright lights flash before my eyes and my body feels hot and cold at the same time. I think I scream, but I can't be sure.

I let out a loud gasp when I hear loud ringing and pink lights blinking and flashing. Right before I panic everything starts to power down, leaving me breathless. I feel dizzy. My skin is tingly and weirdly hot.

The pod opens, and I walk out on shaky knees. Pierce grabs my arm for support.

"I forgot to tell you that this process can cause dizziness and hot flashes." He grins at me and looks me over. "Very nice indeed. Here's a mirror."

As I try to get my muddled thoughts together, I wonder, did Pierce just check me out? I look down at my body, and I notice I am tone in all the right places, and my skin is smooth and unblemished.

I glance in a mirror that is placed in front of me and—Holy Mother of Mary! I look amazing. No need for foundation. My skin is gorgeous and flawless. "My skin?!"

Pierce nods and beams at me. "Airbrushed is a Fairy Godmother given, a freebee. It's in your contract. Didn't you read it?" He laughs. "Here at FGI, we mean business."

I stare at him. This guy. He's teasing me.

"I feel like this is cheating. No one looks this good in real life," I say breathlessly.

"Excuse me?" he asks and tilts his head. "This is the Fairy Godmother Inc. We go big, or we go home. We can do whatever the hell we want because we can. Enjoy it.

"You look stunning," he says, and leans a hip on the desk. "Men are defenseless against our agents. We only need three months to complete FGI missions. And that is not arrogance. It's just fact."

Mort snorts. "Yes. You look wayyyy better than before."

I shoot her a look.

I think she just insulted me.

"Ok, now spin, we are five minutes out!"

"5 minutes?!"

"You both are slaves that were recently on a merchant ship carrying silks that sunk. The ship was overtaken and destroyed by pirates.

"You are traveling to the Kingdom of Garthorn, where you are employed. You both obviously survived. Apollo's ship will intersect with your raft, saving you," he says quickly.

"Raft?"

"Mort will give you more details when you're there. Don't worry. You will be just fine. Now spin." He places his hand on my shoulder.

"Spin?" I sound panicky even to my ears. I'm not sure if I'm ready for this — it's happening too fast!

"Yes, my favorite part, your dress!" He motions me to spin.

"Where do you think Cinderella got her dress? Fairy Godmother? No, it was my design. I design all the clothing here at Fairy Godmother Inc." He beams. "Now spin."

I start to spin, wondering how cute a slave's outfit could be. My body starts to tingle, and I inhale as a flash of white light blinds me.

I look up into the mirror, and I am wearing a provocative, ship-wrecked, deep purple gown. A ragged slit exposes my thigh, and my bustline is ripped, exposing my corset. Scandalous, to say the least.

The corset seems to push my breasts high, making them very tantalizing, if I must comment on them. "A slave wears this?" I ask, my heart pounding.

"No, but a ship-wrecked one does. The actual slave gown is very modest and covers everything, including the face. So this is your chance to catch his attention, which is why I placed you in this particular situation."

He turns to Mort. "You will be a very plain looking slave, nothing to draw attention. Ms. Pipper."

"You got it."

In one second, Mort is this cute little Sailor Moon creature, and the next moment, she is a very non-descriptive woman. Mousy brown hair and plain features. Clothes ripped in all the wrong places.

"Whoa," I say.

Pierce touches his earpiece. "Yes, we are a minute out. Yes, I'm aware, you idiot!" He nods and looks at me.

"Your name is Ms. Viola Luna Stark under the Kingdom of Garthorn. You will be Ms. Stark, a sector 5 slave, which is high up, like a ladies' maid or housekeeper.

"Here is proof that you are a citizen and your employment."

He hands me a bronze necklace with a falcon on it and shows me a tattoo on my wrist that I didn't see before. It's a strange symbol that I can't identify—a G with weird inscriptions.

"That is the mark of your employment at the Garthorn Castle."

"Okay," I say meekly.

"Ready, and FIVE, FOUR—"

"I am not ready!" I panic.

OH NO.

"TWO, ONE!"

Blackness overcomes me.

CHAPTER 5

When I come to, I'm confused. A lot of different sensations slam into me at once, causing total brain malfunction.

But it's when a heavy force of water crashes over my head that I really jolt out of this brain fog.

Oh noooo.

My eyes take in a vast black sea. The sheer dominance of it is knee buckling. I'm shaking, my lungs are constricting, and I feel a scream rise out of my throat.

The sound is lost.

We spawn onto the smallest F-ING raft, in the middle of the biggest F-ING sea I have ever seen! No land in sight.

The water looks dark and monstrous, probably harboring the Kraken and other horrifying sea legends. Every so often, I can feel deep vibrations that course their way up my body, heightening my panic.

What in the holy Moses was that?!

The angry sea is drenching my body, making me gasp for air as I try to hold on for dear life.

My nails are digging into the handles conveniently provided on top of this shitty raft so we won't slide off. I shall remember to thank Charming for that.

Why, this is very close to tubbing on the back of a speed boat, except for the fact that if I fall off, I most likely will drown. No lifejacket.

Do the lifelines work if I scream them underwater?

I need to know this.

This raft is the size of a king-size bed. That's not big, trust me. Mort is hissing like an alley cat, trying her best to stay in the middle of the splintery raft by pushing me dangerously to the edge.

What. The. F.

"Mort!" I swallow some water, making my throat burn from the salt. "You're pushing me off, you idiot!" I yell as a big wave brings us almost vertical.

I gasp as the water crashes upon us like a Water World ride on Crash Mountain. How I didn't fall off is a mystery. My little body is still clinging on for dear life. I impress myself sometimes.

Mort screeches and claws the splintery wood. "I H-HATE WATER!"

"Are you kidding me, agent Mort?!" I look at her in disdain, then violently push her to scoot over. "I'm not about to use my lifeline in the first t-ten minutes we are h-here!"

More waves crash on us, forcing an alarming amount of seawater up my nose. "Mother of Mike, that burns!" I gasp. "Where is this Apollo ship?! Screw you, Pierce!"

Great, I'm sure I look like a washed-up rat! Water is coming out of my nose, and my eyes are most likely bloodshot.

Perhaps Pierce thought I was immune to crashing waves and saltwater being violently forced up my nostrils.

But by pure luck, the waves die down after ten minutes, and I can shakily go on my knees to scan the dark sea around me. This is the first time my thoughts are not ~I'M GOING TO DIE!~

A couple of steady breaths and I can process coherent thoughts.

This is real.

This is happening.

I don't trust this sudden calm water, and the thought that I could die at any point scares the hell out of me.

My thigh-high, soft leather boots do nothing for traction, and my torn skirt is making me slip like a baby deer on ice. Worst case scenario times TEN.

I slowly sit up on shaking limbs and try not to freak out. Mort does the same, probably embarrassed of her un-agent-y antics.

The sky is stormy, swirls of black and gray with flickers of lighting. It is not raining yet, but I bet it's about to pour hellfire. My adrenaline is pumping, making me forget the bitter cold of being soaked.

I'm on a different planet, I remind myself.

"Big, d-deep breaths, Viola," Mort commands through chattering teeth.

I just look at her.

"Thanks, I feel much better," I respond with sarcasm. I can feel my teeth start to chatter too, and my muscles are shaking.

Mort looks like she is typing on an invisible computer with one hand and blinking her eyes like she has computer contacts.

Really though, she looks like she has mental issues. Perhaps dropped on the head as a baby.

She glances at me and nods out in front of us. "They already see us."

"What?"

"Their ship is invisible."

My gaze jerks to stare in front of me, my heart pounding. "Where? Can you see them?"

"Yes, just the negative outline of it. They're about a hundred feet to our left, trying to see who we are most likely before they show themselves and offer help."

"That's close," I whisper, seeing nothing but endless sea. ~Wild.~

"Uh-oh."

My head jerks toward her. "What does 'uh-oh' mean, Mort?" I yell, glaring at her. I am starting to shiver uncontrollably now — the wind is like ice.

"I am getting a red alert."

"Explain before I strangle you, so help me God!" I am on an alien world in the middle of the black sea — you don't just say that to someone.

Isn't that like survival code or something?

She is visibly pale. That's when I feel a hard bump on our little shit-raft. Something underneath just hit us with force, jolting me to the left. "What was that?!"

This is not happening.

"Something very large, I would say the size of a whale, but like a shark." She was typing on her invisible computer. "And more snake-like. Confirming, but I think we are in trouble.

"We might need to use a lifeline. My scale shows they're a seven on the danger scale. We probably have five minutes. It looks like it's circling us."

I just stare at her, mouth hanging open.

I can't even.

"Give me a second, this is my first mission. I'm just getting used to this computer program."

"This is your first mission?! Computer program?!" I scream so loud, my voice cracks.

Just then, like magic, the massive three-story ship is visible, cutting through the black waters like a silver blade. It takes my breath away like someone literally punched me in the gut.

It looks like a pirate ship, but it is made from silver metal and shiny bronze. This is a pirate ship on steroids and a little acid…and maybe some meth thrown in there too.

"Holy…" I trail off.

The vessel is terrifying. I can see figures on board running up and down the main deck. Apollo is supposedly on this ship. I might be the first to see him. I wonder if they saw me yet.

Then I remind myself I probably resemble a drowned rat, and my spirits fall.

"Viola!" Mort screams.

I look back and see a high dorsal fin circling us, and I gasp. "Oh, shit, that's big!" I realize I have taken my potty mouth to a whole new level.

Both of us are trying to sit in the middle of the raft as if that will save us. I think I'm screaming, but I am not sure. My brain is misfiring at a very crucial time.

I glance back to the ship and notice men on board yelling something at us, but I can't make it out. "What are they saying?!"

She blinks, then blinks again. "They are telling us not to move a muscle, or we will die—something like that. They are lowering a small boat to fetch us, I believe."

It slithers like a giant anaconda, its enormous body becoming visible on top of the water.

Oh no. What a horrid way to die.

I need to think. I try to calm my breathing to ease my shaking body. I am always good at thinking under pressure when I can calm myself. I just need a moment's clarity.

I really don't want to use a lifeline. Not this early. That is as bad as being on ~Who Wants to Be a Millionaire~ and using a lifeline on the first question.

"Mort, can you give me a bow?"

"On it." She is doing the typing and blinking thing again. "I will give you one with speed-enhancing arrows."

I look at her, shocked. A smile spreads over my lips. "Mort, you just redeemed yourself!"

She glances at me and smirks back. Holy moly, I think we just bonded.

Hopefully no one notices, but I now have a black metal bow with deadly looking arrows strapped to my back. We are still a ways away, so I doubt it. I know what I must do, and I have to do it fast.

I stand up, rocking the raft to gain balance, and ignore the yells from the men trying to make their way to us. This is suddenly awesome. I don't need Apollo's men because I forgot that I'm a badass!

The shark-snake disappears underwater for a moment, then comes back up, charging us.

Now or never.

I stare. That is one frightening-looking SOB. Its teeth look to be a foot long and tinged black. Horrifying.

"Kill the bastard," Mort hisses beside me, making me grin.

"From my calculation, your skill level is that of a sixty-year-old man/woman. That's how long it would take you to master your current skill level in archery. You should be able to hit it."

Charming hooked it uuuuuuuup.

I have my bow ready and aimed. Time slows, allowing me to aim at the rapidly moving sea monster to almost a standstill.

I can feel my whole body tingle, my mind going into an altered state of AWESOME. Aiming is easy when they barely move.

The monster is about to dive again, and when it comes back up, I'm going to shoot it.

"Mort! Where do I shoot it?"

"Between the eyes!"

Of course.

It comes back up, and the sound of the arrow slicing through the air is like a distant woman screaming. Or maybe that was Mort — can't be sure.

I hit my target in the dead center, making the massive sea monster jerk to the right as if it's shocked, then it disappears underwater.

I lower my bow, my whole body on an adrenaline high.

I did it.

Mort stands up. "Like them apples, bitch?!" she screams, spit flying from her mouth, staring at the black sea with murderous intent.

"Shhhhh," I whisper, and try to suppress my laughter. "We have company."

She blushes, and whispers close to me, "Isn't that how you express victory, being a human?"

I didn't have time to respond as I'm face to face with a petrifying-looking man in metal and black armor. He looks like a superhero or something from the future.

The armor has pale blue lights coursing through it like Iron Man. The giant of a man has a beard and a massive white scar gracing the left side of his face. His gaze is dark and menacing.

"Ye' are lucky ye' are a straight shot," his gruff voice yells as he pulls up next to us. The small boat is powered by an unknown source. I do not hear a motor. Odd. What do they have here? Atlantis power?

"Jump on. The lipers travel 'n packs, there will be more with'n minutes." He stretches out his large, gloved hand to us. "You just shot a pregnant mum, that is na' good."

More lipers?

We take his hand and jump into the small boat just as we see more dorsal fins heading our way. The rugged man controls the boat with a series of buttons and interesting small levers.

I glance back and see the lipers surrounding the raft we just left. Safe. For now. I look back at the man driving the small boat and study him. Is this Apollo?

I frown. I am not attracted to him, but he does have a rugged charm. I shouldn't be so vain—he is probably a teddy bear on the inside.

"Mort," I whisper. She glances at me, her face pale, her body shivering. Mort probably hates being human.

~Is that Apollo?~ I mouth to her, and nod my head in his direction.

He looks at me, and I smile, blushing a little bit. Drat. He narrows his dark eyes at me then continues to anchor the boat next to the massive ship.

Mort looks at me and scowls, shaking her head no.

I don't have time to feel relief. They hoist us up like we are rag dolls and force us up the ladder.

Minutes later, I find myself dumped on a hard surface, water puddling around me. I am dripping, breathing hard, and scared to look up.

I feel the tension like a cloud of thick smog, my nerves making my body shake like a scared rabbit. I have lifelines, I remind myself.

I feel Mort beside me, pinching my leg and whispering for me to get off my ass. Since when is Mort such a bossy potty mouth?

I hear murmurs and grumbles everywhere.

"Stand, woman," the man who saved us orders, and jerks me up by the arm, hurting me. I bite my lip, keeping the hiss of pain to myself.

When I look up from under my soaked hair, I realize they are bringing other prisoners out, who are shackled at the neck and ankles. They look skinny and beaten down, and bruises mar their dirty skin.

I shiver, wondering what kind of hell they must have endured. Mort stands on her own, and soon there is a long line of us.

Dear God, am I considered a prisoner? Is a slave any different here?

I swallow a moan back down my throat and will myself to stand firm. I flinch as I gaze at all the men in front of me, with their muscular forms and armored bodies.

On their uniforms is a large G with a pointed line down the middle. Simple but strong—intimidating. They do not look like a friendly lot. Wouldn't want to golf with them on a Sunday afternoon.

A look of scorned indifference graces everyone's features, their eyes seemingly focused on ME. I quickly look down and take another shaky breath.

I'm wet, my clothes torn—thanks to Charming—and breasts on display to a bunch of heathens who probably have not seen a woman in a long-ass time.

If rape is on their menu, I will happily use my lifeline with no complaints. When I get back, I will knee Charming in the groin, and then I will have my happily-ever-after.

The ship's deck is massive with tall poles that carry sky-scraping masts, catching the wind with each violent whip.

I glance back up and can see a large, two-story staircase that leads into a three-story glass cabin. Or whatever they call this metal creation on water.

I would not want to run into this warship on the black sea; this rig probably never saw a loss.

I look closer and see machine guns with strange sapphire lights glowing within a place where you'd think cannon balls would go. Yeah, these guys mean business.

A tall man with a long, narrow face stands a couple of feet in front of me with a clipboard. He looks ratty, and his nose twitches as he stares at me. My heart stops.

"Snake eyes," he says in a condemning tone. "Where are you from? To whom do you owe your allegiance?"

My arms move, thankfully. I show him my necklace and wrist tattoo, and Mort does the same. He stares at it for a while, then glances back at me with a leering grin, eyes traveling down my body, licking his thin lips.

"Very nice," he whispers. "Were you on the McDon's merchant ship, then?"

I nod.

"Any other survivors?" he snaps.

"Not that I'm aware of."

"Keep your eyes down, slave!" he commands, making me jump.

"His Highness will not like this news." He whips around and speaks to the short, portly man to his right.

"I believe this is worthy of Prince Apollo's attention. Sirona Bandits strike again in the same week. Will you go and inform him that his presence is needed?"

The ratty man turns to look in the direction of the glass cabin.

A flash of nerves courses through me like lightning.

Why am I so nervous?!

I barely glance up and see three men at the top of the stairs, and I stop breathing. They're swiftly heading our way, and I can tell you that I might need medical help myself.

The man in the middle is undoubtedly Apollo, walking as though he is a Greek god.

I always read that in romance books—you know, the dashing hero being compared to Greek gods. Now I completely understand.

He is all that is power and beauty, garbed in all-black armor save for the midnight blue cape with silver clasps at his broad shoulders. A slow shiver licks its way down my spine.

The two men with him also wear the same color and cape. I faintly wonder if it's a sign of royalty. He looks like Thor, but with an extra dash of sexy and darkness.

I feel my face flush with hot lava as he nears.

His arresting dark gaze homes in on me and me alone. I'm not used to this intensity — my ovaries, I think, explode.

His skin is beautifully bronzed, with perfect high cheekbones and the most delicious law line my hungry eyes have ever beheld.

I desperately want to put my face in his neck and inhale, and maybe a little tongue action. I bet he smells and tastes glorious.

He has beautiful golden hair. Some pieces look white-bleached, probably due to the adoring sun making sweet love to his hair. You think I'm being dramatic? I assure you I'm not!

I was never boy crazy as a girl, not being interested in anyone that I can recall. I might have been too picky. But now, I am reeling, entirely off-balance. I can't even catch my breath.

Apollo's almost-black, hot-as-hell gaze contrasts with his light hair and tanned skin. He should have sparkling blue eyes, but no, the glittering darkness of his eyes gives me hot flashes.

I feel Mort bump me.

I flush as I give myself a mental shake. I'm too busy in my fantasy to realize Apollo is asking me a question. Embarrassment stains my cheeks and chest.

Apollo arches a brow and glances at Ratman with the clipboard. "Does the slave speak? Is she mute?"

My eyes widen.

Oh, great first impression.

The ratty man swallows, then glares at me. "Yes, she does. Answer His Grace! How did you learn to shoot the arrow like that?! And where did you find such a fine weapon being just a slave?"

My heart is about to give out. I take a steady breath and glance at Prince Apollo, willing my voice to work. Apollo is quite tall, way over six feet, and I feel like a little girl being scolded.

"I was taught by someone well qualified. I'm a fast learner. I guess it is a gift I was born with, taking to archery quicker than others."

I have no idea if that makes sense. I'm still killing Charming for no back story and for making me look like an idiot.

Apollo frowns, his dark gaze seeming to flicker as he crosses his arms over his muscular chest.

"Are you deliberately being vague? Because if you are," he slowly looks me up and down, "a night with my men will make you talk."

He is rude. My cheeks heat at his crudeness. "Yes, I'm being vague."

I hear Mort groan.

Fail.

"Only because I suffer from amnesia. I fell off a horse a few years back and I have no recollection who I am or how I became good at archery. It sounds a little far-fetched, but that's the truth."

I want to slap my forehead. I told you I was a fan of Anastasia.

"Is that so?" He nods and turns to another man. "Have someone look into her situation. If she is lying, her pretty little head will look good in a noose. I have no room for spies, nor the patience."

56

His glittering gaze holds me prisoner. "She does not act nor talk like a slave, which concerns me."

The good news is, he thinks I have a pretty head. The bad news is that if he finds out I'm lying, I will be hung. I need to talk to Pierce to clean this up ASAP.

"Bring them to the servant's quarters and put them to work." He pauses as his eyes linger over my body. My skin heats to overdrive.

"Give these women something proper to wear. I don't need my men distracted." He turns to leave.

I blow out a long breath, not realizing I was holding it.

This is not going to be easy.

Now that I see what this man looks like, I'm afraid that this competition might get ugly in a hurry.

CHAPTER 6

This is bad.

We are not treated well, and they stuff us into a room that not even my shoes from home would fit into. It smells like the essence of wet dog and spoiled fish were used to wash the floors.

Our ankles are shackled, and we are wearing an outfit that would belong perfectly on the set of ~The Handmaid's Tale~. Not even exaggerating.

We are wearing bonnets with long brims to shield our faces and nothing short of a nun's cloak to cover our ripped clothing.

"This is bad," I say, crouching in the corner. There is no room to lie down or stretch our legs, and they told us we should be lucky we are not bunked with the other slaves.

Well, I guess I will agree with that assessment. I desperately do not want to be with the other stinky men and watch them stare at us like we're lunch.

My ego is not so big that I can't recognize that this could be much worse. I have an excellent imagination.

"What are you doing?" I glance at Mort in the dim lighting.

"Talking to Pierce." She is typing and blinking.

"On your imaginary computer?"

She huffs. "It's not imaginary, and yes. Pierce is always online, keeping track of us. I'm talking to him about your backstory. Pierce says he is working out references for your amnesia case."

"That's a relief."

Mort nods. "He also says quick thinking on your part. It will fit in nicely with the lost princess scenario."

"Yes," I deadpan. "It's starting to sound like a Disney classic already."

Not.

"He is apologizing for the liper attack," she says without looking at me. "And says he will make it up to you. But Pierce says that the outfit he made for you seemed to do the trick."

"How so?"

Mort winks at me.

"What does that mean?" I say dryly. "You mean you think Apollo fancied me?"

She giggles. "Oh yeah, Apollo liked what he saw."

"You don't think it had anything to do with me being half-naked and any hot-blooded male would do the same? Nothing special about me, per-say."

"Maybe," she says.

I narrow my gaze at her.

"But," she continues, "you're a slave, and Pierce says normally Apollo does not openly show signs of interest, especially not directed at a slave. We don't know for sure, but it's a good sign.

"Your wardrobe is going to be an obstacle, but nothing Pierce can't handle. He says he has some tricks up his sleeve."

I glance down at my attire. I have no clue how I'm going to make this work being a slave. I might not ever get a glimpse of Apollo again. And if I do, he will not recognize me in this getup.

That thought makes my tummy turn, imagining all the other girls getting ample time with him.

I shift uncomfortably. "Man, I wonder what the girls will think when they see him."

Drool. Smacking their faces and jumping up and down like cartoon characters.

Mort glances at me. "I will admit, for a human, he is very striking if you like the alpha-male-with-gorgeous-hair type. I prefer more of a beta male, myself."

"He did have gorgeous hair." The bleach-blonde mixed with golden locks would be the envy of every California male ever born.

Then there is his beautiful tan skin, not pale like most fair-haired people, which contrasts with his hair so exotically. His animalistic dark gaze.

I want to groan. I feel a wave of jealousy, wondering who will be the first to kiss him. That would be an experience no girl will forget. A man of his caliber probably ruins every other man for any woman.

I now feel for the poor girls on ~The Bachelor~ when they had to watch the hunky dude kiss all the women. I can say that I feel genuine rage, and I have only caught a glimpse of him.

I need to calm down, or this will get very unhealthy.

"Is Apollo even looking for female companionship that's long term?" I ask.

Mort nods. "New development. Yes. His father is very sick and is dying. Apollo will most likely be king very soon and needs a queen quickly, in fact. This will help us. Finally, some good news."

"Oh great, that probably means every girl in the kingdom will be after him." My situation keeps on getting worse. All I need is more competition.

The sound of the door opening makes us both jump. Nerves flash through my body when I hear male voices. The rusted metal door opens with a groan, and two large men stand there looking at us with frowns.

"Get up, slaves. We ar' in Garthorn!"

The next thirty minutes, we're jerked here and there, placed in a long line of Garthorn slaves. My ankle shacks almost make me fall, but luckily the guard yelling at me grabs me by the neck, steading me.

It is dark outside and chilly, and the sky flickers with blinding flashes of light, giving it an evil appeal. A shiver licks its way down my spine as nerves crash my senses.

At this point, if I can make it without using all three of my lifelines, I'm winning. The thought of Apollo falling in love with me seems to drift further and further away.

A large man is shouting something at us that I can't make out, then the line starts to move once again. We are descending from the ship onto a massive drawbridge.

A large crowd is present on the dock, along with carriages and massive horses. Big puffs of breath are seen as the monstrous black stallions stomp the ground impatiently.

I can hear yells and chants, and it sounds like chaos. Raising my head slightly to take in the distant city and castle,   my breath hitches.

Oh, wow.

In the darkness, the city reflects deep blues and silvers, giving the whole landscape a daunting appearance. At this point, I feel like I'm way in over my head.

Garthorn looks like something out of the Lord of The Rings.

Towering buildings disappear into the mist-like clouds with sharp edges and some that end in long, spear-like points. As if the buildings were not human made, but carved out of the jagged mountain structures.

Breathtaking

Overwhelming.

I risk a glance to where Apollo stands with his men some distance away from the slaves. My tummy tightens. He looks like a superhero.

The lightning from the dark sky flashes behind him, giving his powerful form an unnatural allure. His sapphire cape flaps with the gentle wind, and his shiny black armor reflects every vein of lightning.

Apollo's face is a stone mask, carved from granite, as if he cares not that the people are chanting his name. I can hear women scream like we are at a boy band concert, for Pete's sake.

Talk about looking desperate. Someone should tell these women men like the chase. Not to be chased.

He nods to someone in the crowd, and then my heart jumps to life as he points to Mort and me.

I gaze to where he points in the crowd, and it's to a very stern looking woman with men standing behind her. High bun, thin lips, with an outfit fit for an eighteenth-century royal governess.

"That is the headmaster, in charge of the female servants, divisions one through five. We call her Headmaster, pretty simple." Mort whispers behind me.

"Pierce placed vague memories of us in their brains. So our story checks out if Apollo should ask, which it looks like he is now." She pauses.

"It seems like Apollo is an impatient human. Good thing Pierce is a fast worker."

I'm not sure if I should feel excited or dismayed that the first thing Apollo does is ask about us.

I bite my lip as the severe headmaster bows in front of Apollo, and they're no doubt talking about us. I see the woman glance over in our direction then back to Apollo, nodding.

"You must always keep your head down and do not talk unless you are spoken to. No eye contact whatsoever," Mort murmurs behind me.

Good to know.

I hear a man yell, and apparently, Apollo has given orders for us to go to them. I feel a jab in my back to start walking toward them, who are standing at the base of the draw bridge.

My heart is beating so hard it almost hurts. I feel so out of my element, and I hate not being in control. I keep my head down and fist my cloak to hide my hands shaking.

We arrive, and all I can see is my feet.

I gasp as the headmaster grabs my chin, jerking it upward and ripping off my bonnet.

My dark hair is a wild curly mass, flipping in all directions. Apparently, my hair dried in a fashion like if I stuck my finger in a light socket.

She is inspecting me to see if I am who I say I am. I can feel eyes on me as she examines every inch of my face, tilting it to the left and right rather aggressively.

She jerks my chin to the right again, and my gaze clashes with Apollo's.

I don't breathe.

Apollo has his hand over his mouth as if in serious thought. His black gaze is zoned in on me, the intensity of his stare scattering my brain waves.

It's hard to tell where exactly he is looking due to the darkness of his eyes, but I will guess it's my hair.

And now, my eyes.

He is rubbing his chin slightly as his gaze immobilizes me.

Mercy.

My cheeks heat to boiling point, and I look away, trying to calm the frantic beat of my pulse. Pull it together, woman!

I would bet my cards that he saw the reddening of my face even in the dark. Hell, for all I know, the prince is nocturnal.

I'm not prepared to deal with a force like him. Maybe the others will have better luck. I feel like a little bug next to a lion. The two can't relate.

That thought unnerves me.

I look back to the headmaster to see if any recognition lies in her gaze. Come on, Pierce, make her remember! I need out of here STAT.

"Yes, the amnesia girl with the discolored eyes. Level five, if I'm not mistaken," she says, and grabs my wrist to confirm. "Yes, she is one of us."

Thank you, Pierce!

The headmaster inspects Mort and confirms we both are Garthorn, Sector 5 slaves. I risk a glance at Apollo and bite my lip. I'm such a coward.

His expression is unreadable as he stares, and the attention he is showing me is starting to draw more stares.

"Well then," he murmurs. "Welcome back."

My skin prickles and alarms are ringing in my head. The way he said it didn't seem like a ~welcome back~, but rather a ~don't get comfortable~.

I hear Mort's breathy giggle behind me as we are dragged off.

And this is only day one.

CHAPTER 7

The hallways are towering and forbidding. The Gothic craftsmanship seems impossible to construct, but I also don't know what kind of technology inhabits this place.

A thrill shoots through me, and even though I am a servant, I will admit that this is still awesome. Seriously, when we go into room after room, I must make sure my mouth is not hanging open.

I feel like I'm starring in my own movie, and all this scenery should be bright green in the large green room, with the complex special effects to be added later.

The walls look like they're made from a dark, organic material that reminds me of granite or marble. I don't think a bomb could take out this place.

I have so many questions. My curiosity is banging on all cylinders now. But I'm not dumb enough to ask the headmaster, ~"These walls are fabulous. What are they made out of?"~

Yeah right.

And then, ~"What's your favorite color? I'm a purple person, myself."~

The headmaster does not strike me as a chatty sort.

With heads lowered, nobody talks—ever. We all follow the headmaster to our next duties. We have already beaten the carpets in some of the spare bedrooms and replaced all the linens.

Apparently, kingdoms from all over are coming for the Garthorn festivities.

Rumor has it that grand balls will be held because Prince Apollo needs to find a dearly betrothed. King Augustus's last dying wish is to see his eldest son married.

Mort confirmed earlier that she thought the king's sudden health decline was caused by foul play, and Apollo could be next.

Someone wants the throne, and I would assume they do not want to see Apollo be king. Perhaps a younger brother? An uncle? Hard to say.

I can't find out much being a slave, so maybe the other girls are having better luck. Ivy is the spy, and I wonder what dirt she is uncovering being next to the Queen.

The footman caught up with us on our cleaning spree and ran up to the headmaster. After a few words, the headmaster claps her hands.

"Attention! The House of Galleon has just arrived. Split up into pairs and see to their needs right away!" She points at two girls to my left. "You two go to the queen and the princess immediately."

~Galleon.~

Apparently, I'm their lost princess.

"Mort," I whisper as we scurry off to help the royal family.

"Yes?"

"I am assuming Pierce put memories of me in the family of Galleon?"

"Yes, and it's complicated."

We pass a couple of guards, and I lower my head, not wanting to draw attention. "How is Laura the princess?"

"She does not have royal blood. The second Queen of Galleon had an affair without the King knowing."

We turn a sharp corner and stop, waiting till the coast is clear. If we are caught talking, I'm assuming there will be hell to pay.

"Go on," I whisper, impatient.

"Your mother Alexandria had you with the King, Bel De Monte, then she was murdered. She fell off a cliff and was declared that she committed suicide.

"I do not think that's what happened, and you can probably guess the same. The King remarried Laura's mother, Irena. Irena then had an affair with one of the King's advisers, and I'm not sure which one.

"But Laura does not have royal blood, and I believe whoever disposed of your mother also got rid of you," Mort whispers quickly, then glances around.

Oh wow.

Is it weird that I feel pain at not knowing my fake mother? Probably because I never had parents of my own.

"I'm placing a bet on Queen Irena, and if I'm right, I am going to bring that bitch down." How dare that woman kill my fake mother?! And then sell me to the highest bidder, no doubt.

"What did they say happened to me? How old?"

"You were four. Your family picture is still hanging in the Galleon Castle."

"How will they know it's me?"

I'm so confused at this point.

"Your eye color," Mort continues. "Among other proof, like a DNA test. But you are the only other person to possess snake eyes besides the lost princess of Galleon. Your real name, if it gets to that, is Ursula."

"Ursula?"

"I picked it out. Pierce let me."

"That's the name you picked out?" I ask in horror.

She looks genuinely offended. "It's a beautiful name!"

"Shhh!" I place my hand over her mouth. "You want people to hear us? Fine, it's a lovely name."

We hear voices, then they fade again.

"Is this what happened? Or is this all made up by Fairy Godmother Inc?"

Mort nods. "Mostly. The real princess of Galleon also possessed snake eyes, weirdly enough, but we cannot use her name because she ended up dying. So, you can avenge her death.

"Irena's affair led to Laura. Fate works it out somehow to where it does not upset the shift in the universe but benefits it. But everything is pretty dead on."

"I'm starting to see, sort of."

No wonder Pierce and Fairy Godmother were giving me weird looks—my ~eye color~.

Mort is typing and blinking now. "The plan of action I came up with is to get Laura's DNA. Not sure how, maybe off a glass or napkin."

"They have DNA tests?"

"Of course. Garthorn is very advanced. Just no one ever thought Queen Irena would cheat, leading to an illegitimate child. Or if someone knew I'm sure they were silenced."

Mort is still typing. "Update. Pierce just said all players are at Garthorn Castle."

A wave of panic hit me. "We better leave and go to our duties. That means the House of Mont Gallow just arrived, and the headmaster is probably having a cow!"

***

Another day passes.

I don't think I have worked so hard in my life.

On my only hour break, I sleep hardcore. My body aches, and my feet are still throbbing from going up flights of stairs for hours. I have not seen Apollo since our time on the ship, just like I feared.

I spotted Cherie from a distance, but I could not say hi, being a slave in all. Must keep our heads down and averted from our betters.

Slaves know our place.

Envy washes through me upon seeing what gown Pierce made for her. It is dazzling emerald-green with cream lace — a vision.

But she is also on the arm of her soon-to-be-husband. He is a handsome fellow but didn't hold a candle to Apollo Augustus Garthorn, the third.

Still, though, she is better off than I am. I feel like all she must do is tell Apollo she dislikes her betrothed and wants out.

Eye roll.

My plight is quite desolate.

"Get up!" Mort yells in my ear.

"No."

I have no enthusiasm. All hope is lost for me. I just pray someone else gets Apollo over entitled Laura. Barf.

Mort smiles. "We have to go wash up a mess that was made by the royal hounds, mud, and water."

I barely look at her, wondering if she's also lost her mind.

70

"The mess is right next to the drawing room where Laura is, and I believe Apollo is there with his brothers."

I jump out of bed so fast I think I upset the planet's gravitational pull. I must see them out of curiosity, in my defense.

We both power walk toward the main wing of the castle like it's an Olympic race. It takes us fifteen minutes, but we arrive in the main hall.

The hall is gigantic with ceilings so high I can barely see the top of their splendor. People are everywhere, servants and royalty in the massive mix. We keep our heads down as I follow Mort toward the dog mess.

The grand hall thins out and breaks off into two large rooms, the drawing room and the Grand Library.

There are not very many people down this far, and I immediately spot the muddy mess by a back entrance to the royal kitchen. My heart starts to pound when I hear laughter coming from the drawing room.

"Look from over here," Mort whispers and jerks her head. "You can see inside."

I get down on my hands and knees and pretend I'm cleaning along with Mort. ~Don't mind us, just poor little servants~. I inch forward and slightly turn my long brim bonnet to the left.

That's when I see Apollo Augustus Garthorn.

I have to say his full name because I don't know him.

Cue pity party.

But goodness, that man is handsome. He's finely dressed in an all-black dress coat and tight black pants showcasing the thick muscle of his thighs. I keep my mouth shut so I don't drool.

The style is very eighteenth-century Europe but with its own futuristic twist.

Apollo's sleek boots go up to his knees, and the crisp white shirt is tied together at the neck. The necktie looks like it's woven from pure gold, matching the undertones of his hair.

He smiles at something, and I realize he is leaning up against a large black piano. The color drains from my face as I hear a lovely opera voice drift out of the room.

"I guess we know what talent Laura requested," Mort whispers next to me, rolling her eyes.

A beautiful voice.

Her blond hair is piled up high on her head, and she is wearing a lovely lilac gown. ~Thanks a lot, Pierce,~ way to make my life miserable.

Apollo is watching her, and I can't see his expression. But I can see that Laura is closing her eyes as she hits a high note, making me want to vomit.

"Her breasts are bigger too," Mort confirms, to my dismay.

I'm sunk.

"We need a diversion."

My head whips to hers. "What?"

Mort looks pissed. "~Ohhhh~. I hate her agent, Leenie."

I glance back and see the plain maid by Laura's side with a smile on her face.

"At this rate, they both will win." She gets up and leaves me, disappearing through to the kitchen.

"Mort!" I hiss.

Great.

I start scrubbing the floor in case anyone glances over, my nerves in a jumble.

Minutes later, Mort reappears and throws a piece of meat at me, bits of steak littering my basic gray gown. "What in the hell?!" I stare up at her and frown at her wicked smile.

"Trust me."

Panic hits me. "No, Mort! Whatever you're thinking — don't!"

I suddenly hear dogs. Lots of them.

~Oh, for the love of everything that's holy.~

It happens so fast I don't have time to run. Three large and slobbery bloodhounds are trampling me. I scream.

I hear fabric ripping from somewhere on my person, and I make out distant shouts to my left. I cover my head as I'm crushed by hyper and hungry canines.

I feel a sharp pain in my leg, and I gasp in agony.

Make it stop!

Mort will pay.

Vengeance will be mine.

I scream again as I suddenly feel myself being lifted and my whole body being thrown off-kilter. Panic rises in my chest as I realize I'm being carried like a sack of potatoes!

I hear a loud male voice yelling something, causing me to tense.

My hair is tangled around my head, preventing me from seeing straight, but I know that voice. My heart leaps to life, and fright sets in.

Seconds later, I'm dumped on something hard, and it's not until I can get the hair out of my face that my world comes into focus.

Apollo's face is right in front of mine, and his dark eyes widen when we make contact. The impact of his stare feels like someone took a bat to my head.

I slowly glance around to see that he carried me into the back entrance of the kitchen. I'm sitting on a table, Apollo's face in line with my chest.

"You," he accuses. He glances past me at all the kitchen staff, who are frozen in shock by the incident. "Everyone leave, now. Tell someone to fetch the healer."

Then Apollo leaves!

He leaves me sitting here on the table, and I hear voices talking outside the door. I don't think my pulse has slowed down even a hint from ramming speed. What am I to do?

My cheeks stain red in embarrassment. I wince, and I try to move off the table right when Apollo returns.

He points at me. "Don't move."

I freeze.

He comes to stand right in front of me for several seconds, and then his arms brace on either side of me.

Oh. My. Goodness. He. Is. ~Close.~

I swallow and try to breathe. "Thanks for saving me," I whisper, not knowing what else to say.

His dark gaze glitters as the light catches his eyes. He says nothing as his stare travels down my neck and lowers to my ripped gown. "You're hurt."

"Not bad," I get out, still scared to move.

Apollo's hands move to my torn dress and yank it open, making me gasp.

My thighs are exposed, and my ugly nylons are ripped. I have a gash on the side of my leg, but I am too focused on my exposed thighs.

I take steady breaths as I watch Apollo stare down at me, his chest taking a deep breath.

His hand feathers across my knee, then higher to my exposed thigh, causing an army of butterflies to take flight in the pit of my stomach.

"Your skin is soft, perfect," he says, almost to himself.

Thank you, Fairy Godmother Inc, for that one. I'm very grateful for that at this moment, because my legs do look killer.

He raises his black gaze, and a shiver runs down my spine. "Amnesia, you say? I had my people investigate your situation further, and I can't find anything. Why is that?"

I shrug and glance away, not being able to hold his stare. "That's the thing with amnesia. You can't remember."

"Uh-huh," he murmurs, and nods. He looks back down to my legs, and I can see his jaw flex. Then he grabs both of my thighs, making me yelp.

I'm helpless as he spreads my legs and steps in between them, bringing us very close. I can't breathe. I feel his heat. I can smell the intoxicating scent of him, and it makes me dizzy.

The position is scandalous, I would assume, for this time period. Right?!

But I don't move. I look up at Apollo and narrow my eyes. "You think you can manhandle me because I am a slave?"

~Atta girl.~

His face is mere inches from mine. "Absolutely. But you should already know that from being a slave," he murmurs back, and shifts his weight, hands tightening on my thighs.

I bite my lip as he leans closer. I feel his breath on my jawline. "Maybe I was not a slave beforehand."

Apollo laughs. "I think that's a safe bet."

"You're so sure?"

"Absolutely."

I must ease into this lost princess thing. It's time to stop acting like a slave and find some courage.

"Then help me find out who I am," I offer and force a grin, making Apollo raise a brow. "And you should let go of me. Seeing how we both know what I'm not."

I jerk my legs and kick him hard in the stomach.

That shocks him, but I can see something in his black gaze as a dark grin spreads over his lips. There is excitement in his eyes, or possibly something equally as alarming.

My heart pounds as he grabs my thighs again, his hands firm.

"Try that again, and I will have you restrained," he whispers and leans into me, his mouth right next to my ear. A part of me cannot comprehend that this has turned sexual, the tension crackling.

I feel him grab my hair and pull it back, making my head fall back and exposing my neck. A thrill shoots through me as I feel him pull my hair harder.

His breath is hot, and the slight feel of his lips on my skin unleashes an army of butterflies to take flight.

"I would watch yourself, Angel, because I have the power to make your life a living hell."

He lifts back from me and walks to the door without a second glance. I'm left here, breathing hard, and a smile spreads over my face.

Mort deserves a medal for this one.

I still have a silly smile on my face as the medical help arrives.

Game changer.

CHAPTER 8

I'm having the greatest dream, featuring a particular alpha male.

~Cough.~

It is delicious while it lasts, but I don't even get to see Dream-Apollo bare his chest! He is in the middle of unbuttoning his shirt when I'm ripped out of the dream.

I wake to guards bursting into our small bed chamber.

I scream as they grab Mort and me, dragging us out of our beds like fugitives. Exclamation marks fire off in my head, and complete confusion overwhelms me.

It isn't until we are taken to a dark and spine-chilling room that we are chained to the wall.

"What is happening?!" I yell, eyes welling up with tears.

They hurt me as they lock chains around our ankles, jerking us around like ragdolls. Mort hisses at them, and then suddenly, the guards laugh, leaving without a single motive as to why they did this to us.

This is bad. It smells like urine, and the ground is cold and wet. I glance at Mort, breathing hard.

"What happened?!" I yell, and look around the obvious dungeon. There are bars on the tiny window and there is a bowl sitting in the corner, probably a chamber pot.

Disgusting.

I start to panic.

"I am finding out right now," she says, eyes narrowed in anger. Mort starts to blink, and she is still able to type in her invisible computer with her left hand. She growls. "I knew it."

"Knew what? What happened? Did we do something wrong?!" I ask impatiently.

"Yes," she sighs. "Leenie, Laura's agent, knew it was us and feels threatened. I guess she can sense Apollo's infatuation with you."

It takes me a second for my brain to get up to speed. "Wait, slow down. You think Apollo is infatuated with me? And how is that related to this?"

I'm smart enough to know he thinks I'm cute, but infatuated?

"I do. He has been since the moment he saw you," she says, and keeps typing. "You had Pierce singing hallelujah in my earpiece, and by the way, that man has a horrible voice. So, thanks for that."

"Not that I would ever botch a mission just so Pierce would shut up, but I thought about it."

I raised a brow at her. "Focus."

"But Apollo's attraction for you is a red alert for Leenie. She is a very sore loser; trust me. When she plays, she is out for blood.

"In our world, it's a very big deal when our team wins. A showcase of talent and rank. If I were to guess, this has something to do with that, which is not good."

"Oh please, we did not do anything bad." I continue, "For crying out loud, I was attacked by dogs! What could they possibly say to get us in trouble?"

78

I feel my anger boil.

Mort gives me a dry look. "Clearly, you lack a sufficient imagination."

I didn't want my mind to go there. "What did Pierce say?"

Mort shrugs and tilts her head back against the cold wall. "He is unable to tell that confidential information about another player. But he did say it does not bid well for us."

"Isn't competing against each other like this making things worse? Going against Fairy Godmother's cause? Like, if Apollo really is into me, wouldn't this tamper with that?"

"No," Mort says flatly, and starts to blink again.

"Fairy Godmother Inc. believes in competition, and that pushing someone to their limit will produce the best version of themselves — or the worst. They want to see true colors."

I frown.

"They want the one person who rises above the challenge to be a worthy individual who has what it takes to rule beside an alpha-male figure. She must overcome obstacles and fight back."

She glances at me. "We learned that in our training."

"Well, geez, if you put it like that."

If Fairy Godmother Inc. likes the competition, then I need to up my game. I was an athlete in high school, so I understand how a little competition can bring out the superhero in you.

We both tense as we hear footsteps coming down the stone stairs, followed by the clear sounds of the metal door being unlocked. I grab Mort's hand, and she squeezes it.

The headmaster, of all people, saunters in, her long dark gown looking malevolent with all the shadows it casts. She must be here to tell me what world of hurt I'm in for.

"Aw, there they are," she says, and I am surprised acid is not dripping from her lips. She looks like a wolf and is followed by gruff-looking guards

"What have we done, headmaster, to deserve this?" I ask meekly, head lowered.

I can hear the swish of her skirts, and she kneels in front of us. "Raise your head, slave."

I do, and I am greeted with pure revulsion in her dark gaze, her lips chapped and pale.

"I knew from the moment I saw you that something was off, but I just could not figure it out. I have very respected sources that say they caught you multiple times pining for His Grace's attention.

"That reason alone is why I rarely keep slaves as comely as yourself here at the castle." She continues as she glances around the room.

"Eye contact with the royal family is forbidden on the highest level, and this you should know already! I should have seen the red flag sooner. A beautiful girl without a past?"

She laughs, her eyes seeming to bulge out of their sockets. "If you are a spy, then you will be dealt with lethally.

"I shall inform His Grace of our allegations. His Grace is very sensitive to Infiltrators, seeing how His Majesty has fallen ill."

"I am not a spy—"

Speckled blackness clouds my vision as pain erupts on the side of my face. I glance back at the headmaster in shock.

She is still holding up her leather whip like she will do it again, and she does, even harder this time. I scream as my neck jerks so hard to the left that I feel it crack.

I feel warm liquid run from my nose down to my chin.

"Speak again without being asked and I will crush it," she hisses with a smile.

If she didn't already.

She stands, and I think I hear her saying that I cannot leave this place until Prince Apollo returns from his raid on outlaws on the outskirts of Garthorn. I could be in here for weeks.

My vision swims and my head pounds in fury. The pain is so great I feel numb. I hear Mort calling my name, but it's no good. I pass out cold.

Light as a feather.

***

It has been four days, and I feel weak.

Defeated.

Thirsty—starved.

I have been consuming barely enough questionable water and stale bread to stay alive. The ground is cold, and I have been laying in murky water for a while now.

I think I hear dripping coming from my left, though I am too tired to raise my head and look. This Fairy Godmother adventure has turned into something I'd rather not be a part of.

But I am still too proud to use a lifeline. I will not give Laura the satisfaction that she got to me.

I'm just dying on the ground from hypothermia and starvation, no biggie. I probably have some virus from the murky water I'm lying in, but I will not give up just yet.

I am made from thicker stuff than that.

Mort has been doing her best with her shapeshifting abilities, morphing into random bugs to see what is happening outside this dungeon cell. She has been gone for hours now, and I am about to lose my mind.

I just keep running scenarios of payback, revenge. Maybe I will out her birthright in front of everyone, pointing and shouting. I don't see that plan going wrong at all.

~Vengeance~, I repeat to myself.

Mort finally returns. I can see the little butterfly fit under the metal door and flutter in. "Mort!" My voice cracks.

She materializes next to me, her face pale and out of breath. "I was almost eaten by a cat."

"Oh geez," I whisper, feeling dizzy as I try to sit up, water dripping from my tangled hair.

"It's nuts out there. The castle staff is preparing for a grand masquerade in honor of Apollo's safe return and victory," Mort says, and smiles at me.

I jerk toward her with a slight burst of energy. "He's back?! He's back!"

"Yes. For a few hours now, and I happened to be there when the headmaster told him about your situation. Which led me to almost being eaten by the cat.

"I was not paying attention because I was listening to the conversation, and I didn't want to miss anything." Mort looks sick again and shivers.

"Do you know how big cats look when you're this big?" She holds up her fingers to show me the size of the butterfly she was.

"Mort," I moan. "What did he saaaaay?!"

She's killing me softly.

"Well, he pushed past the headmaster pretty aggressively and is headed here, I think. I had to fly through shortcuts to get here this fast.

"I was having trouble with the coordination of my wings, kept flying into the wall. I also flew into a window, which actually really hurt.

"Because, you know, it would be bad if he beat me here and I was still a butterfly." She gives me a pointed look.

82

I shake my head. "He is coming here now?!"

My heart kicks to life.

I didn't know I mattered that much to him.

We both gasp as the door is forcefully thrown open, and Apollo's figure fills the doorway. My heart stops at the sight of him. I always forget what a striking force he is.

I can see his eyes widen even in the darkness. He slowly walks in, his chest rising and falling at a rapid rate. That's when I notice myself and what I must look like.

I am lying on the ground with my hair splayed everywhere, soaking wet. I stopped caring yesterday, or was it the day before?

Apollo kneels down next to me and glances up at Mort. "Are you hurt?"

She shakes her head no.

"I can see the same isn't so for her," he says grimly, his jaw flexing.

I barely peek up and see two guards come running in along with the headmaster. Apollo turns, and the look he gives the headmaster makes her clutch the cloth at her neck.

"Unchain them now," he orders.

I can see the confusion written on the headmaster's face. "Your Grace, she is supposed to be a spy!"

"From now on, you do nothing unless you consult with my advisers or me," he commands. "I will decide what her intentions are, not you. You have no authority."

I would have swooned if I was not already on the ground lying in muck.

He glances back, and I feel his hand softly touch the bruise on my cheek. He is looking at me like I am a delicate little flower that was dropped in the mud.

He lifts me off the ground, and I am carried, my memory fading in and out.

I'm safe, though.

His body heat warms mine, and I never want him to let me go. I can smell the spicy scent of him. Yum.

I almost moan in protest when he hands me off to the medical staff to clean me up and see to my wounds yet again.

Though I do see him watching me until I'm out of view.

I think that's a good sign.

CHAPTER 9

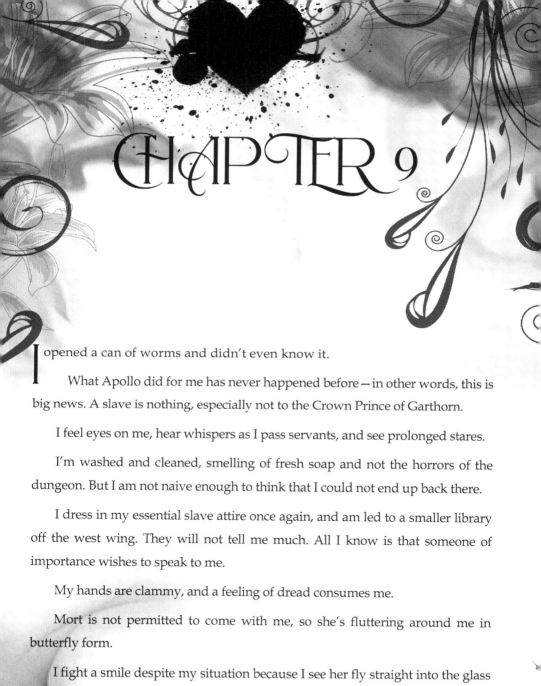

I opened a can of worms and didn't even know it.

What Apollo did for me has never happened before — in other words, this is big news. A slave is nothing, especially not to the Crown Prince of Garthorn.

I feel eyes on me, hear whispers as I pass servants, and see prolonged stares.

I'm washed and cleaned, smelling of fresh soap and not the horrors of the dungeon. But I am not naive enough to think that I could not end up back there.

I dress in my essential slave attire once again, and am led to a smaller library off the west wing. They will not tell me much. All I know is that someone of importance wishes to speak to me.

My hands are clammy, and a feeling of dread consumes me.

Mort is not permitted to come with me, so she's fluttering around me in butterfly form.

I fight a smile despite my situation because I see her fly straight into the glass of a massive Grandfather Clock. Not sure how she didn't see that, but practice makes perfect, I suppose.

I'll be sure to tell her that — then have to escape her fist immediately.

This library is very masculine, not like the Grand Garthorn Library, which is adorned in   silver and sapphire splendor.

This one is decorated with rich woods and dark marble that catches the glowing light and illuminates the two-story library. I wonder if this is Apollo's study.

I am seated on a somewhat oversized leather couch and left by myself. I take a steadying breath and tell myself everything will be okay.

Five minutes pass as I watch Mort flutter over the large desk in the corner. Maybe she sees something?

She manifests as herself and peers over a letter on his desk.

"Mort!" I hiss. "You're going to get caught!"

She glances up. "I will only be here a second. Chill."

"Chill?!"

"I see a letter from the House of Galleon." She continues with narrowed eyes, "It's a thank you letter and mentions prospects of joining the Garthorn house with Galleon."

I stand up.

"They're offering Laura as his potential betrothed, in so many words," Mort says, confirming my fears.

"Do you think he is entertaining it?"

"It's the only thing on his desk."

"Maybe this is not his desk."

"It is."

I take a breath. "You don't know."

Mort frowns at me. "You know another Apollo Augustus Garthorn?"

The sound of footsteps approaches the door, and Mort instantly morphs into her signature white butterfly. I sit down and swallow the lump in my throat, willing my hands to stop shaking.

A woman walks in, followed by guards wearing scarlet red. These are not Garthorn uniforms, so I'm making a wild guess that this is Galleon.

The lady is older but still quite beautiful. Her golden hair is piled high with a red and silver crown. Her elaborate gown flows around her like she is an Egyptian queen wearing gold and crimson.

Then it dawns on me. This is Queen Irena.

My pulse jumps to life.

"Forgive me for keeping you waiting," she says, motioning her guards to leave. I pick up on her sarcastic note, as I'm not so dumb to think that a queen is sorry for anything, especially for keeping a slave waiting.

I'm immediately on guard.

I keep my head down and my mouth shut.

"I asked you here out of pure curiosity." She laughs. "I heard of this slave who is creating quite the commotion."

I say nothing and bite my lip, not sure where this is going.

I hear her walk toward me as she sits in the chair opposite me. Her skirts are taking up most of the couch. "You may look at me, slave."

I raise my head and stare into frigid, cold eyes. The blue is the color of the polar ice caps, devoid of all warmth. I can see the wrinkles around her mouth and eyes, and her neck tells me she is most likely in her fifties.

"I see that your eye color is shocking." She narrows her gaze at me. "I hope you can understand my surprise upon hearing a simple slave possessed discolored eyes."

"Why is that a shock, if you do not mind me asking?" I ask quietly, genuinely curious.

She laughs like I said the funniest thing ever. "I forget that slaves do not know much about worldly things. Well, my husband, the King of Galleon, lost his daughter long ago.

"She was said to be the only one to possess this rare eye color, you see. The King was devastated, calling all witches and sorcerers to make it so that no one shall possess that rare eye color again.

"Ridiculous, if you ask me, but that's what he wanted. That uniqueness was saved for his poor, precious daughter."

"What happened to his daughter?" I stare at her, wondering what the witch really did.

"That does not concern someone like you. But, if you must know, she died at a very young age. Stolen in the middle of the night, never to be seen again.

"Later, her shoes were found drifting in the Galleon Great Lake, the very lake where her mother jumped to her death. It's all very tragic and a very touchy subject." She tilts her head at me.

"In Galleon, many have claimed to be the missing princess, faking the eye color and such. Some even went to great lengths by invoking the dark arts to change their eye color."

I think about that, noting this sounds very similar to ~Anastasia~. Weird, though, that the movie is my favorite of Disney's. I wonder if ~Anastasia~ is originally a Fairy Godmother tale. I

will ask Mort when I get a chance.

"I assure you this is my natural eye color." I narrow my gaze at her. Queen Irena arches a brow and thins her lips. "I also do not remember my past, having hit my head, resulting in amnesia."

I hold her gaze, my implication evident.

She looks as though I slapped her in the face. "Do you dare to imply you could be my stepchild? Because if you do, you are overstepping your bounds, slave.

"My husband's late daughter is deceased, and I will make your life a living hell if you do not back off." She leans forward.

"I see that you have a face that some men might find desirable, and I can also see now why you are trying to ensnare the affections of Prince Apollo, which I find laughable.

"If anything, he is only interested in a quick toss, and I might say you are in the wrong profession then. As a prostitute, you could make a lot of money." She laughs and smooths out her skirts.

"You are very bold. If you aim to escape slavery and con your way into my family, you have another thing coming.

"You do not know what you're up against if I catch wind of anything to do with my husband's late daughter. Do I make myself clear, slave?" Her face is flushed with rage.

I keep my anger in check. Sounds like the witch needs to get laid more than I do. The grumpy old coon.

Oh, wait, she is — by the King's adviser.

How could I forget that juicy little tidbit?

"Very clear," I continue, "though I do at least want to conduct a DNA test, if I can get approval from the Garthorn Royal family, seeing how I answer to them, not you.

"And I know Prince Apollo is also curious about my origins, so I don't think this will be a problem. There will be no deceit." I smile.

"His Grace is now out with my daughter, Princess Laura of Galleon. I believe that she will soon become your queen, so I would watch your ignorant mouth, you slave!

"I will have a word with Apollo about your request and express my displeasure.

He will not want to offend the King of Galleon and start a war with the House of Garthorn, after we have been allies for so long."

I keep my mouth shut.

Hardball.

She stands, and before she leaves, she adds, "Apollo is falling in love with my daughter, and if I catch wind of your boldness again, I will not show you mercy." '

I take a large breath when I hear the heavy door shut.

Mort is now in human form. "Extortion. She is nervous. That's obvious."

I stand and glance at the seat Queen Irena just occupied. "If the King finds out about her infidelity, what happens?"

"She would be beheaded."

***

I thought I would be able to see Apollo again, but I was wrong. Mort believes he is keeping his distance because of all the rumors.

Earlier, I was questioned by Apollo's advisers, and I asked if I could get a DNA test. I never received a clear response, which was disheartening. But at least I am not placed back in the dungeon.

I am cleared for now to do my regular responsibilities — clean and clean some more. The headmaster gives me the worst jobs, I swear.

I really would like to fight her. Put on some boxing gloves and have at it.

I walk alone because the headmaster wanted to borrow Mort and another slave to clean the central chimney. She had no choice but to go, which makes me nervous.

I don't like being by myself. I have my lifelines, which makes me feel a little better.

I keep walking down the long, busy hallway, keeping my head down. I barely glance up, and I nearly gasp.

Apollo is talking to what looks like high-ranking officials. He looks powerful like he just came from riding his mighty stallion.

His hair is wild and up in a man bun, but not in a metro-sexual way, like a ninja warrior way or a samurai master.

Apollo seems to be out of breath and is having a heated conversation. They must have just come in from outside. He shakes his head and puts his hands on his hips right as he glances at me.

I yank my head down and turn a corner as fast as I can. My heart is pounding. I am not sure if he saw me, but my heart beats anyway.

I'm also not sure why I don't want to see him. Maybe deep down he intimidates me to crazy levels.

My whole body tenses when I hear footsteps behind me; they sound heavy and fast. I turn another corner, and thankfully it's empty, without prying eyes seeing me almost run. That would look very suspicious.

As I walk at a reckless pace, I hear the footsteps still behind me. I take a deep breath.

It could be anyone.

The footfalls are closer, and I have no choice but to glance behind me. My eyes widen when I see Apollo with a grin on his face.

"Angel, there is no way you're out-walking me," he says, catching me by the shoulder and spinning me around.

I gaze up into his graveyard eyes, and my tummy starts doing backflips. Apollo tilts his head at me as his eyes search my face. "How are you?" he says in a soft and very sexy way.

His voice is like melted chocolate—the hottest thing I have ever heard.

"That good?" he grins.

I shake my head and glance away. "I am doing much better, thank you."

"Good," he says, before he yanks me into a room and shuts the door. I can't move or talk when he puts both his muscled arms on either side of me.

He stares at me for a second, then smiles again like he is genuinely happy to see me. "You smell nice." He winks. Trust me, he smells better.

This boyish side of him is going to be my undoing.

I blush and look down. "Yes, I'm sure my fragrance is much better now than the last time you saw me."

He makes a sound. "Trying to pinpoint you in this getup is exhausting. You all look the same," he huffs, then rips off my hat, making me yelp. My black hair falls down my back, and our eyes clash.

Has he been looking for me then? My cheeks heat.

The air changes and the boyish light in his gaze turns into something primal. No one should trust a gaze that dark, and I can almost feel its intensity.

His eyes lower to my lips then back up. His chest is rising and falling, and his jaw is flexed like he is trying to hold back.

"What are you thinking?" I whisper, almost feeling scared.

"You don't want to know, Angel," he rasps, and lowers his head to my neck. I quickly inhale from the shock as I feel his hot lips move over my skin.

~Mercy!~

My eyes close, and my head falls back, unable to process what's happening. Is he sick in the head?!

He must take that as a green light because in the next second, he picks me up and is pressing me harder into the door, hungrily kissing my neck and jawline.

I moan and wrap my arms around his neck, wanting more of everything. I arch into him, feeling a massive surge of raw desire. This is insane and unexpected.

The crush of his lips over mine makes the pulse in my neck jump as if electrocuted.

The delicious feel of his mouth , as it moves over my lips, makes my head spin. His lips are hot and aggressive, taking every breath that I have.

"Open," he rasps into my mouth.

I open, and his tongue thrusts into mine, Apollo is taking over this kiss forcefully. He is drinking me and sucking my lips like a starved man in search of water.

I barely have time to breathe as his mouth devours mine. I feel his hand in my hair, pushing my head closer to his assault, his tongue plunging into my mouth repeatedly.

I have never in my life been kissed like this—with so much lust and passion, heated fever.

I gasp as I feel him yank my head back by my hair, and his mouth trails hot kisses down my neck. I feel his teeth like he wants to bite me. Then I hear him curse, not wanting to rip my conservative gown.

I can feel the urgency, impatience, irritation. There is something wild in him that thrills me beyond measure. He lifts me higher and starts kissing me through my clothing.

His hand grips my breast through the material, making my toes tingle, and a hiss escapes my lips. This is getting out of hand in a hurry.

I cannot even see straight at this point. My brain can't even compute what is happening to me. Apollo is whispering things that I can't make out over our rushed breathing.

Then his mouth closes over my nipple, and I can feel the heat of his breath through the clothing.

Frustrated, he starts kissing my neck again as he raises my skirts. My pulse is pounding in my lady parts, and I feel like a wild animal.

He groans again in my neck as he finds the skin of my thighs. He shifts me in his arms, so his free hand has better access.

"Angel," he pants.

I think I moan when his hand brushes over me there. My clothing is still a nuisance.

Then the unthinkable.

Voices.

I can see the pain and anger in his face as he drops me, his chest still rising fast. I hear female voices mixed with male ones. It's a group.

We cannot be caught.

Apollo grabs my face before he leaves, his breath fanning mine. "You're mine, Angel," he declares, not caring what I have to say about it.

It is scandalous to hear something like that from Apollo, with me being a slave. "I want more," he says with a wicked wink, then leaves.

I put my hand on my forehead and take steady breaths. What on Earth just happened? Apollo just made it to second base with me, is what happened. I bite my lip to make sure I'm not dreaming again.

"I want more," he said

I place a hand on my trembling lips and expel a harsh breath.

Down the rabbit hole I go.

CHAPTER 10

That make-out session changes everything.

We were intimate.

Holy moly.

It was hot, and I'm still getting flushed cheeks just thinking about it.

Apollo knows how to kiss a woman, which is a fact. It should be printed in every history book. Apollo's name should be in the dictionary under the adjective kissing.

I walk with my head down in the long line of servants, mulling over my thoughts. Maybe things didn't change for him, but they sure changed for me.

You can't be kissed by a man of his caliber and not be altered forever.

He said I was all his. But does he just tell women what they want to hear so they will just give it up? I don't know. I pray not, but I am also not stupid.

I am a slave. He is the Crown Prince of Garthorn. Maybe I am the flavor-of-the-month slave. A man that kisses that well has had plenty of experience. ~Believe me~, in Donald's Trump's voice.

I frown as we turn a corner, in deep thought.

Mort was so enthusiastic that he made it to second base, saying we needed to go forward with our plan to get Laura's DNA and bring down Queen Irena.

It will prove her infidelity and her betrayal of the House of Galleon. I wish I knew her lover, and we could just catch them in the act.

A grand feast is being held tonight, and we have been in the kitchen all day. Level five slaves will be the servers — lucky me. I get to serve two-hundred people. That's a lot.

I used to be a waitress at an underground strip joint, and let's just say it was a very low-key, under-the-radar type thing. Not to reflect on my bad life choices, but I have no experience serving this amount of people.

There are only fifty sector-five slaves, so you can do the math. I am still an oddball, though, always getting stared at. They treat me like I am a rare beast, a human with three eyes.

Was it that odd that Apollo had shown me attention? Slaves are considered less than human, so maybe.

We are an hour out for the ten-course meal to start, and the headmaster is giving Hitler a run for his money. If our heads are slightly tilted the wrong way, we get our ankles whipped.

It's a pain worse than stubbing your toe, and I thought that was impossible. Thought nothing was worse than stubbing your toe? Wrong. Ankle whips are worse, trust me on this.

The headmaster's father oversees the male staff, and I am not kidding when I say he moves at the speed of smell. He must be over a hundred years old, for Pete's sake.

My right eye twitches as I watch him pick up a fallen napkin off the marble floor.

This scene needs epic soundtrack music as his hand nears the napkin, heightening the dramatic tension that is sure to unfold.

The choir voices singing loud in the air as the climax approaches and tension rises to full capacity.

My eyes widen, bulge even when he snatches at it and misses it completely, producing a sheen of sweat on my forehead. He goes for another try and promptly side-steps to the left, off-balance.

Alas.

I bite my lip.

He comes in hot this time, but oversteps the cloth by a foot, making me hiss in frustration. What in the ever-loving-shit. Just grab it! Please. Please…

At this point, it's almost worth an ankle whip to jump out of line and help the poor bastard. This madness needs to stop. I can't take the stress anymore.

Lifeline activate! #jesustakethewheel.

A commotion to my left thankfully gains my attention. Dancers exit from the massive dining hall—finished with their exciting performance, no doubt.

I look wistfully at them, wishing I was a performer rather than a slave in an ugly black gown even a nun would deny. And this is our nice gown. I look like a pregnant penguin.

At least I was able to hang out with Destiny earlier, her being the head chef. She told me she had zero luck with Apollo, but she didn't seem too worried about it.

I wondered why until I saw her with the tall butcher's son Antangeo. He is handsome, but not on Apollo's level, according to me.

I wonder if you can stay if you fall in love with someone else. I didn't get to read the fine print, but that would be super cool.

Destiny comes out in total command, giving each one of us trays of mouthwatering food to serve. She looks like she is enjoying her situation.

But really, though, I can't be completely ungrateful of my horrid position. I did have a hot make-out session with Apollo, so... maybe this slave thing is working for me.

The next thirty minutes are insane. I pass out so many dishes that I don't have time to think or even to take in my surroundings. If I spill anything on anyone, the headmaster will open a gateway to hell and push me in.

Laughter is loud, the clinking of wine glasses rings in the air, and the performers blow fire from their mouths.

I glance up and notice that the massive seating hall is elevated, with an open space at the bottom where all the dancers and performers do their thing.

In the middle section, we have most of the House of Garthorn, with the House of Mont Gallow to the right and then Galleon to the left. Quite extravagant.

The low lighting makes all the crystal dinnerware sparkle and twinkle. The music is exotic, almost having an Egyptian/Middle Eastern feel.

The vaulted ceilings are magnificent—there is no other way to describe the twenty-story high masterpiece. Gold and silver were everywhere, from the walls to the decor, displaying the great wealth of the House of Garthorn.

It's hard to spot people when you have to keep your head down, but I spy Cherie and Laura, and jealousy comes to life inside me.

They look like they're having the time of their life, laughing and eating with royalty. Their evening gowns are gorgeous.

The only thing Pierce could do for me was blow out my long hair, a nice wax, and a moisturized body. You know, so if Apollo takes my bun out in a fit of passion, I will have fantastic hair. Eye roll.

As I carry the third course, I'm ushered to the middle toward Garthorn royalty.

I bite my lip, not wanting to go this way and encounter Apollo.

I don't know how to act now that he has kissed me. Does he think about it? A thrill shoots down my spine.

I see him now that I'm close, and I groan inwardly. I try to keep my head down, but I can't.

He looks unnaturally handsome tonight with the low lighting. His platinum ringlets are pulled back in a messy manner, probably making every female secretly throw their panties at him.

How could such an alpha-male warrior have such glorious hair? Because he is a god, that's why. He's probably the real Apollo the Greeks wrote about. I can't believe that creature kissed me the other day.

Then a thought occurs. Maybe I imagined the whole thing? I start to panic, hoping I'm not so infatuated that I could do such a thing.

I carry wine, filling up glasses, until I get to him and hold my breath.

He is talking to a man sitting to his right, seemingly in a deep conversation, the candlelight flickering over his muscled forearms. His tan skin looks rich, and smooth, thick veins grace his taut skin.

My hands are shaking as I fill up his half-full goblet. Don't mess up, and please don't breathe, be still my heart. I do it, and the glass is full without a single drop spilled on the silver tablecloth.

As I stand up straight, his hand snatches my wrist, preventing me from standing fully.

I gasp.

His dark gaze meets mine, and I am lost. Everything falls away.

Apollo pulls me closer. "Tell me," he says in my ear, in that accent that turns me into a wild animal. "What if there's nothing on the menu I am interested in?"

I take a harsh breath. "I-I can talk to the cook," I whisper.

"No good, I doubt they have what I'm looking for," he murmurs, his thumb moving over the pulse in my wrist.

I glance up and see that no one is paying attention to us. Drunken laughter pierces the air. "Then, I'm sorry, Your Grace, but I'm not sure what you want."

He clicks his tongue and licks his bottom lip. "I think you do, and I want it now."

I feel lightheaded and note that he appears to be a bit drunk with his heavy-lidded allure. "I don't," I lie.

I cannot believe he is coming onto me in front of everyone. I could get punished for this.

I am just glad the lights are down low, and the wine flows like water here. I don't need to be accused of being a tart by the headmaster and whipped later.

"Liar."

"You're going to cause a scene," I say desperately. "Stop."

He frowns and tilts his head looking adorable. "I believe you're the first female to tell me that."

I whisper close to his ear with a grin, making him tighten his grip on me, "I'm glad I am your first for something. Now dry your eyes." I rise to leave before we start gaining looks.

He jerks me back down. "I want you."

I suck in a quick breath, not knowing what to say to something like that.

"Tonight."

My stomach flips, and I feel dizzy. "Why?"

"Because I can think of nothing else, and it's driving me half-mad," he hisses in my neck, and pulls me closer.

"I want to lick every inch of your body until you scream my name. I want you in every way possible," he confesses with an erotic glimmer in his black gaze.

I can say nothing.

My brain is misfiring.

Crash and burn.

Someone calls for Apollo, making him loosen his grip on me. I yank my wrist free and speed away, face hot as lava, extremely bothered. I almost trip, but right as I raise my eyes, they clash with Laura's.

She saw the whole conversation with Apollo and me.

Laura raises a brow and sips her wine, smiling into it. I don't like that look, and I lower my head and keep going.

Somehow, I make it to the bottom and stand in line with the others, waiting for anyone who needs a refill.

I think I black out, actually, because an hour passes that feels like a minute. Voices sound far away.

Apollo wants me.

Like, bad.

The amount of desire in his gaze scares me. It is exhilarating.

Mort is suddenly beside me, jabbing me in the side. "This is not good."

I shake my head and look up with a frown. The King of Galleon, my fairytale father, is toasting to Laura, who is standing, and Apollo, who is also standing. I'm confused.

The King speaks, and I try to follow the conversation.

An engagement announcement.

I frown in confusion.

Apollo just offered to do very bad things to me, knowing he is to be engaged tonight? Pain erupts through me, confirming my worst fears.

I am nothing more than a sex object to him. Slam bam, thank you mam! I'm nothing more than a whore to him, a slave he can have fun with until he is married to Laura.

Laura wins. Fairy Godmother wins. I should just back down and let it happen.

I swallow the lump in my throat and will the tears away. I'm such a silly girl. "Does that mean Fairy Godmother wins?"

Mort barely looks at me. "If it's true love."

"She wins," I murmur.

"That's noble of you, but he does not look at her like he does you."

I nod. "That's only because he wants to sleep with me, then leave me."

I look up and see them seated together now, Laura whispering something in his ear. Probably loving the way he smells, and the rock-hard arm she is hanging onto.

Apollo is looking down and nodding at something she is saying, with an expression that is hard to read. He looks up then, and his gaze finds mine.

I would like to think the glare I gave him yells a thousand words at him.

~I hate you. You prick. I am not a whore. How dare you tell me those things when you're engaged? I am declining your invitation for tonight, you arrogant ass.~

But now that I think about it, I still need to expose Queen Irena, or I fear the evil will not heal like it should. Laura, the spoiled brat, can still have Apollo because he is dead to me, even if my lady parts disagree.

It's not up to them anyway.

Laura spills her wine glass, making a loud shattering sound. She looks shocked, then points to me, as if it is a random selection, to clean it. I feel my back being nudged, and I walk forward feeling humiliated.

I keep my head down as I stand before them both, kneeling before them to clean up the mess. It looks innocent enough, but Laura just started something with me that she will regret.

I glance up, and our gazes clash.

I ignore Apollo's intense stare, which is hard. I don't want to see his pathetic reasoning for choosing Laura. So what if it will bring the peace of your kingdom, I couldn't care less right now.

Laura and I share a little special bond at that moment, and I hope she reads this loud and clear.

It's on, bitch.

I'm going to make it hurt.

CHAPTER 11

I
f I could put black football lines under each eye, I would. The urge to chest pound someone and scream in the air like a rugby player is intense.

"Mort."

She is sitting in the corner of our tiny room, talking to Pierce. "Yes, insufferable human?"

I take a breath. "We will be able to pull this off, right?" I glance at her, biting my lip. Why did something tell me that this decision would change everything?

"I sure hope so. Pierce seems to think this is your chance to turn the tables, as Laura did to you last night." She glances at me with a little smile and eye roll.

"I think Pierce is just excited to finally make you a dress. He said he has been up all night with the design. I helped some. I think you'll like the heels I pick out."

I grin like a feline with a yellow bird in her paw.

Laura and Queen Irena made the request that I do not attend any more royal functions for fear it would upset the King of Galleon. My eye color is offensive, apparently.

Laura is playing hardball, but I'm a very good batter. I keep my eye on the ball.

I'm going to smash it out of the park tonight.

I know you're wondering what we're up to, and I will get to that in a second. I told Charming to do his worst—meaning his best, of course. If I go down tonight, I want it to be in flames of glory.

We are locked in our room tonight, but no biggie. My roommate can fit through the keyhole and unlock it from the drunk guard.

Well, Mort will put create-barb in his drink. Apparently, the plant's essence will put a horse to sleep. Mort has a lot on her plate as well as me. If one messes up, the plan fails.

We have spent the last three hours preparing for this scheme. I could get ejected from the game entirely if I become publicly executed—lifeline activated and ejection from the challenge.

Bringing scandal to light is very dangerous because there are a lot of evil people who need it hidden. Somehow, I feel like Laura will fight to the death/ejection because Apollo seems to bring the crazy out in females.

It's the eyes and hair.

I'm not fighting for Apollo, though. Not anymore. I am here to help Zora and Fairy Godmother Inc., and to bring Laura down with explosions and fairy dust.

When this is all finished, I want to look like one of those marathon runners who throw all of the crazy amounts of colorful powder. A hot mess, Fairy-Godmother-style.

Then I will find a microphone somewhere and drop it while a bomb explodes behind me. It's always good to have lofty goals on a risky mission like this.

The goal is to get Laura's champagne glass tonight at the Garthorn Royal Masquerade.

Yes, I said masquerade, ladies. (I talk to an invisible audience sometimes. It's fine. I am aware that it's not healthy, but I don't care).

We are infiltrating the system. I will be unstoppable, and vengeance will be mine, for all I see is the color red.

I just pray Pierce did not construct me a gown in pink. I'm not in a pink mood, no offense to the color. Hard to be a badass in light pink, in my personal opinion.

Mort will then give Laura's glass to Destiny, who will have access to the medical sector. Mort had a chance to speak to her this morning when I was cleaning the toilets.

The headmaster hates me, but Destiny is the real infiltrator and is willing to help on behalf of Fairy Godmother Inc.

She has gotten to know Apollo, being around his family, and says she will do anything for him because he's a remarkable guy.

Eye roll.

But if she is helping us out, then that makes my job easier. I'm getting the impression that no one cares for Laura, which will hopefully be her downfall.

"We are two hours out," Mort says and looks up at me, getting off the ground. "I will be back in an hour, I hope. Destiny's agent should have the create-barb for me."

I feel like a captain saying goodbye to my most trusted soldier. We look each other in the eye and nod. "Don't get caught—and stay away from cats."

She salutes me and sings, "Float like a butterfly, sting like a bee."

***

I am sweating, pacing. I wish I had a clock. This waiting is not good for my blood pressure, and it is starting to become a health concern. I know it's been over an hour and the party has begun.

I can hear the rush and commotion among the servants outside my door and on the floor above me. I can even feel the deep vibrations of music penetrating the cold ground.

"Mort," I plead with my eyes squeezed closed, "please hurry."

Another thirty minutes or so passes and I start to panic, praying nothing has happened to Mort. Why is it taking so long? Was she caught? Eaten by a cat? I don't know what to think at this point.

Right when I am about to lose my shit, I see a white butterfly fluttering from the door.

"Mort!" I jump off the bed so fast I almost twist my ankle.

She appears and sits down on the ground, out of breath.

Pale.

"What happened?!"

"I did i-it," she gets out between breaths.

"Take a deep breath and tell me what happened," I try to say calmly.

"They put twelve guards watching your door. We did not have enough sedation for them all. Laura really does not want you out." She breathes and leans her head back against the wall. "So I had to improvise."

I feel like something always happens to Mort. "How?"

"I had to sting like a bee."

My eyes widened. "Why didn't we think of that before? That's brilliant! You stung them all?"

She lifts her head and glares. "You owe me, human."

I tilt my head and bite my inner cheek so as not to grin. "Why? Was it hard?" I ask innocently.

"I shape-shifted into a wild Sirona bee. They inject poison—no stinger, more like a scorpion." She continues, "The first two were not hard, but they all started swatting and trying to hit me with their weapons."

"Oh."

That sounds dangerous.

"I was almost squashed like ten times," she hisses and levels her gaze at me.

"The only downfall is that we have to hurry, they will only be out for thirty minutes," she says, sitting down and starting to type. "I am logging on. Pierce is ready for our cue."

I stand up, nerves hitting me hard.

"Okay, start turning. Pierce has your position. He also says you're welcome. This is payback for us almost getting eaten by those shark-whale things." She is blinking and rapidly tying.

I turn, and my skin starts to heat and tingle, making me gasp. Even my scalp is alive with sensation, and in the next moment, all I see is a white flash.

I stand there, breathing hard, scared to move a muscle.

Holy…

"I need a mirror," I barely say.

Mort's eyes are wide as she stares at me, nodding without words. "I will ask Pierce." In the next second, it is like Star Trek Enterprise beams down a full-body mirror.

I stand in front of it and gawk.

"Mort," I say.

"Look at your shoes, that was me," she murmurs. "Pierce is pretty good, I will admit."

What I am staring at is a woman that is not real—maybe an illusion. I thought Charming might put me in red or purple. What I was not expecting was to be transformed into Queen Bee.

Black lace and yellow satin. The yellow is not like the lovely sunlight but intense fire. Like when you catch a rare glimpse of stark yellow in a river of flowing lava—that yellow.

The shimmer to the silk seems almost enchanted, lit from within. My waist appears to be insanely tiny, and my breasts are pushed up in a way that doesn't seem possible without ten rolls of tape.

The yellow silk is like a second skin on my body until it reaches my curvy hips, then it flares out dramatically. White and black stripes adorn the petticoats, and I even see a layer of black and yellow polka dots.

It is beyond stunning with an old gangster, mob-ish feel to it. My long black gloves match my sparkly half-mask with bright yellow and black feathers.

I take a steady breath, loving the style of this alternate world. Pierce does not mess around, and he means business.

My hair is up and piled artfully. The raven locks almost resemble plastic. My blood-red lips look bee-stung, and my smoky eyes under my mask make my one gold eye appear stark yellow.

I see why Charming picked yellow now.

I look like a feline.

Pierce also included a short, black lace veil, if I choose to shield my eye color and still want to be able to see—brilliant. That is a must.

I smile and laugh, looking at Mort with wide, unbelieving eyes. "How the heck am I going to wear this?!" I am already shaking, and I have not even left the room yet.

I will have to dodge Apollo and Laura like the plague, but hey, when in Rome.

Mort holds out her fist to pound, and we both laugh.

"Float like a butterfly, sting like a bee."

CHAPTER 12

W e finally make it to the last hallway that will lead us to the royal ballroom in our dark cloaks. My heart is pounding, and my knees feel weak.

This is not the time to get cold feet.

"Mort, are you sure people will not ask who I am? My dress is an eye-catcher, to put it mildly. I would hate for the royal guard to be called," I say dryly.

"Five hundred people are in attendance tonight. I think you will be fine. Tonight is about mystery anyway, and I think it's rude to ask someone's name."

"That's a lot of people," I whisper with a frown.

It might be a little harder than I initially thought to get close to Laura's glass. I bite my lip as I watch Mort take off her cloak and toss it to the side.

She is in a dark blue gown resembling a peacock with feathers everywhere. It isn't horrible, and it isn't great either. Very neutral, like always.

"Game face," Mort says, urging me to get going with her raised brows.

"I will go around the side to see if I can get a clear view of Laura. Destiny stated that she is very careful to not let any of her DNA be left around, probably guessing that we desperately want it.

"I will hold up my fist when I can get a clear view of her, which means you need to keep me in your eyesight and vice versa."

"Very German soldier of you," I say, and take a calming breath. Tonight, I am not myself. I am a woman who is seeking revenge.

Nobody likes a blonde, stuck-up bully.

I slowly take off my cloak, exposing the stunning gown of glistening yellow and black onyx. My skin looks like perfect ivory, contrasting with my stark black locks.

I'm wearing so many black and white striped petticoats, I doubt I will be able to find my own legs, and the corset is so tight it leaves little to the imagination.

My breasts look glorious.   T   hey really do. Perfect ivory globes, if I were to compare them to something. I'm proud of the girls, and I'm allowed to be without any judging.

Charming did a fantastic job, and I can see why he is Zora's right-hand man. Using the ladies' room will be a challenge, though, so I need to keep my champagne intake to one glass.

I lower my black lace veil and whip out my yellow fan.

Eyes narrowed, we make our way to the grand entrance, which is magnificent in height. The silver doors must be two stories high, their splendor something I have never seen before.

Masses of people swarm everywhere in all different vibrant shades and styles, taking my breath away. I have never been permitted to go into the royal ballroom, and the sheer size of it would be a world wonder on Earth.

The lighting is low and exotic, the many chandeliers emitting a sensuous glow that makes a shiver slide down my spine.

Deep sapphire and silver adorn the elaborate decor, and the dark marble floor sparkles and glistens in the dim lighting.

When you first enter, an enormous staircase leads you down into the ballroom floor. A grand entrance is an understatement here.

The most exquisite sapphire velvet is draped down the center of the stairs, completing the masterpiece. As my eyes scan the majesty of the ballroom, I almost have to pinch myself.

It is incredible. Intoxicating.

The music seems to weave its way around your soul, transforming you into someone else entirely.

It's the manifestation of something seemingly sinful that tantalizes and tickles your senses, whether you're ready for it or not. The vibrations are mysterious and romantic, all at the same time.

I stand now at the top of the staircase, gazing down at the fantasy, a world that I never thought existed.

I suddenly smile, feeling a surge of adrenaline.

I pick up my glittering gown and begin my descent to the main level. A server runs into a pillar to my left, the crash of glass lost in the buzz of the ballroom.

~Maybe the yellow of my gown blinded him~, I think, with a nervous smile. This is thrilling—a body high I have never experienced.

I glance to my left and see men in dark masks gawking at me, so I lift my lace veil and wink at them. One of their mouths drops open as I pass, feeling spirited.

It's like you take me out of my slave attire, and I am a wild woman. I think I'm experiencing cabin fever being a slave, for now I feel free.

Even if it's just for tonight.

I ignore people's stares and whispers and grab a champagne glass from a passing server, and search for Mort. I down the contents, needing all the help I can get, and dispose of it on another passing tray.

I spy Mort and she shakes her head at me, then I lose her as groups of people block my view. It's rather hard to see, but I spot the throne seating down on the far end of the ballroom.

If I were to bet, Laura and Apollo will be seated there. There are curtains around a luxurious lounge area, almost like it is the V.I.P area at a club.

I bite my lip, praying she is getting a little drunk and leaves her glass unattended. This is the perfect setting to catch Laura off guard.

I'm hoping this can be a quick mission so I can enjoy the rest of the night. She still thinks I am locked away—licking my wounds, no doubt.

I also want to be out of Apollo's view.

He will not know it's me, so I doubt I will draw his attention for more than a minute or two. There are tons of women here, and more importantly, he is an engaged man now. That makes me want to vomit.

I wonder, as I make my way down to the throne seating, what dress Charming made for Laura. Hopefully, a brown gown with an itchy turtleneck. A little wishful thinking never hurt.

"Excuse me, madam," a male voice says next to me as I still. "You are a vision in yellow. Please allow me a dance."

I turn to see an average-height male with a purple feathered mask on.

His black-and-plum finery is appealing enough, and I do a quick glance at the dance floor, which happens to be right in front of the throne seating.

That will give me a great view of Laura—if she is there, that is.

Perfect.

I smile at him and hold out my hand for him to kiss.

He raises his blue eyes up to mine and sighs. "We were trying to guess what kingdom you belong to, for I don't remember seeing you at the feast."

Oh, I was there, cleaning up your messy dishes.

I wave my hand. "There are so many people. You must have just overlooked me."

He laughs and tucks my arm in his. "Impossible."

"Oh." I laugh, feeling nervous, and glance around for a sign of Mort.

"You flatter me, sir. I would absolutely love a dance with a gentleman as charming as you," I say playfully, hoping I sound like a well-bred woman.

Actually, I have no idea what the hell I'm doing.

He looks a bit intoxicated as he peers down at me with heavy lids, his gaze drifting to my chest.

"I will be the envy of every male here. You honor me. You look so exquisite, I almost forgot to breathe when I caught sight of you." He laughs and leans in like he is going to tell a secret.

"And, my dear, there is no such thing as a gentleman. Just a patient wolf." He leers at me, and I catch his meaning loud and clear.

He's going to have to be very patient then.

Indeterminately.

He talks about the vast estate he holds in Mont Gallow like that should make me swoon or something. I just nod with the occasional giggle as he leads me to the dance floor.

My gown is sparkling beautifully as I twirl and get into position. Now I must say that I know how to dance perfectly. My knowledge is on point.

I guess along with the language we also know the customs like dancing. Thank goodness, or this would be a very awkward encounter.

Their style of dance is a little like the classic ballroom but with added spice. A little tango here and a little close dancing there.

There are a lot of people on the dance floor, but as we start to move to a waltz-like dance, I begin to move closer to see the occupants in the elevated lounge.

I only have a few seconds with every turn to get as much detail as possible.

With another spin, I am close enough to see people in masks talking, drinking, and laughing. I bite my lip when I am twirled again. At this rate, I will need to dance all night to get a clear view.

I spin again and see Laura in a gorgeous lavender gown, of course. Charming doesn't do anything that is not breathtaking. But, I will say, mine is better.

In my humble opinion.

She is walking on the arm of a masked man who is definitely not Apollo—maybe a cousin? Looks like he is leading her to the large dance floor.

My heart skips a beat when I see a wine glass just sitting on a glass table where she came from. Is it hers?

I would have to get closer for a better look. I pray it has lipstick on the glass that matches the pink on Laura's lips.

I also see almost all the occupants of the royal family's box descending to the dance floor.

The dance stops.

I frown as I glance around.

Everyone, including my dance partner, starts clapping. I glance in front of me and see Laura laughing and clapping, and to her left is the magnificent Apollo Augustus Garthorn.

I suck in a harsh breath, realizing I'm close—too close.

I happen to be at the front of the dance crowd by chance, which is not ideal. I'm terrified Laura will recognize me and call me out in front of everyone.

115

And with that thought, I try to scoot back as best as I can but to no avail. It is drawing more attention to me.

Apparently, the royal families will participate in a dance, and everyone is honoring them, from what I gather. My mind is in panic mode.

My eyes take in Apollo, who is laughing at what someone said.

He looks like a version of Zorro with his plain metal mask and dark attire. The buttons at his neck are undone, and his billowy back dress shirt is making me feel lightheaded.

Did Apollo ever look bad?! Never in his life probably.

I feel bad for the other normal looking men standing around Apollo. It is like seeing Jason Momoa standing next to Zack from ~Saved by the Bell~.

His muscled thighs are well displayed in his tight gray pants, showing every bulge, ehem, of muscle.

My cheeks heat, and I curse, looking away, not wanting my gaze to travel to the family jewels, which appear to be quite impressive.

~Get a grip, Viola.~

When I glance back, my whole body freezes. Apollo's dark gaze is currently inspecting my yellow gown with an expression I can't read. ~It's normal~, I tell myself. The gown is, in fact, stunning.

I take a big breath and shift, looking away like I don't notice. I most likely just drew attention to my impressive cleavage — no more big breaths, idiot.

La-la-la-la, just another average girl with an amazing dressmaker. Nothing to see here.

I feel my dance partner put my arm in his like he is staking claim from Apollo. ~Please~.

I roll my eyes and slowly glance back to find Apollo still staring at me. He can't see my eyes, but I can see his, and they are definitely homed in on me.

He raises his chin and tilts his head a little, expression somewhat stony and indifferent. It's so hard to tell with him in that silver mask. I'm sick with nerves, wondering desperately what he is thinking.

Why on Earth did Pierce put me in such a bright dress?! Now I'm regretting wearing this masterpiece of a gown. I need to get out of here, or at least out of Apollo's view, before I blow my cover.

I feel like I can't breathe. Suffocation.

I mentally slap myself. I need to stay calm and stop being awkward.

Apollo is just being a typical man and merely admiring female beauty, nothing more. He's engaged, for Pete's sake. I am overreacting like normal.

I hiss under my breath because the dance is starting, and to my horror, it's an interchanging dance. Of course, it is.

The music is exotic and enthralling, precisely what I do not want. I am just thankful for the low lighting and masks.

Laura is now paired with Apollo—good. She looks completely infatuated with him, pursing her lips and standing too close. This dance is not fast, but you do change partners throughout it.

I grab my partner's hand and curtesy, and he bows.

We dance, and I feel like I'm in some sort of twilight zone, where my body is moving, but my brain is in a fog. I can only hear the seductive notes of the symphony and my beating heart.

I must dance my way to the edge and make a clean escape without being detected. I'm in the danger zone.

We are intertwining now, and I spin and raise my arms as a new gentleman takes my hand. This continues as I near the edge of the dance floor as I'm twirled again. Just a couple more twirls and I'm free.

I make it to the edge, and I feel a strong hand take mine and yank me back into the dance floor, spinning me forcefully.

Somewhere in the depths of my panicking mind, I know I'm screwed. I know who I will see when this twirl stops.

Dark, glittering eyes gazing down at me, leaving me little clue about his thoughts. My whole body tenses up, and I forget to breathe.

Just act natural, please.

I feel his hand low on my hips, much lower than the other men's hands, and too low for an engaged man.

As he spins me, his fingers trail over my midsection and lower, applying pressure here and there. Seems deliberate, but I can't be sure. I hate this tension, this panic.

As I spin again, I come face to face with him, and it's so unnerving that his expression has not changed.

Does he know?!

It is time to change partners, but he doesn't move. He just grabs my hand again and spins me.

Uhh…He might know.

Apollo does not change partners, and I am petrified to ask why. ~Maybe it is a mistake on his part~, I think quickly. I don't want to jump to conclusions quite yet. Surely this is all my paranoia, my demented thinking.

I suddenly feel the heat of his body against my back as his hand presses me hard to him. I feel every inch of his rigid body against mine, and we are no longer dancing.

Luckily the crowded dance floor and low lighting almost hides us in the swarm.

My heart pounds in my chest.

I feel like the little mouse being caught under the lion's paw.

His hand, which is splayed over my stomach, moves upward, applying more pressure as his palm ascends. I try to move, but his free hand grabs the glittering fabric of my gown and yanks it back.

Okay, I'm in trouble. Warning sirens are ringing in my head. Escape now! Red alert!

My adrenaline is flowing through my veins, and I gasp when I feel his hand under my breasts.

Apollo's mouth is hot against my ear as he lets go of my gown to rip off my mask, tossing it somewhere to my left.

I try to move again, but his hand grabs my neck, squeezing it just enough for me to panic. His fingers under my breasts move up, feathering over my impressive cleavage.

Butterflies scatter in my stomach as I feel him boldly caress me. Under different circumstances, I would be considered the luckiest girl in the kingdom.

He is provoking me.

His mouth on my neck almost makes me groan. I feel his fingers dip below my lace corset to cup my breast fully, but somewhere in the back of my mind, I find my senses.

I whip around to slap him. He barely flinches as he catches my wrist midair. Our gazes clash like the mighty Titians. His dark gaze is hard, and his jaw is flexed.

He looks slightly manic. Unstable. Unpredictable. He is breathing hard, and I can tell the beast inside him has awoken.

Apollo moves so fast the only thing I can do is yelp as he holds me forcefully to him.

I pray no one is witnessing this.

His mouth hisses into my ear, "I will give you a five-minute head start."

I jerk my head up to his. "For what? Until you force yourself on me?" I spit back, feeling almost dizzy from my adrenaline.

He throws off his mask, and the look he gives me makes my knees buckle. He is still breathing hard as his gaze drifts over my yellow glory, and he licks his lips. I shiver, seeing the desire flair to life in his eyes.

"Unfortunately, not Angel. I will give you five minutes before I call the royal guard for your arrest."

I gasp. "They w-will kill me."

He tilts his head and holds up his five fingers and whispers. "Five." His eyes seem too dark, and the grin that spreads over his lips makes me want to scream.

This is a side of Apollo I have never seen before.

Abort mission!

I back up and turn to run!

CHAPTER 13

I run blindly.

My heart is beating like an ancient war drum, echoing loudly in my ears.

I glance behind me just in time to see Apollo whistle loud in the air and hold up his powerful arm, his dark eyes focused on me. He looks ominous, his tall frame gaining everyone's attention.

This is bad.

I think I scream and body-check a half-dozen people on my mad dash out of the ballroom. A waiter is carrying a tray of sparkling champagne that I manage to crash into, shattering glass everywhere.

I have tunnel vision as I hurry as best as I can in this elaborate gown. I hear gasps and yells as I run past people.

Apollo didn't even give me five minutes.

I'm in shock.

I hate him with a passion.

Taking off down a long, dark hallway, I try to remember how to get out of this damn castle. There is a fork in the hallway, so I stop, out of breath, and desperately try to remember. ~Which way?!~

Cursing, I take a left and force myself into several different corridors and rooms. I hear the deep rumble of guards, heightening my panic.

I end in a large storage room and pause to gain my thoughts and wits. ~Focus,~ I need to operate on a higher level than I am right now.

"Viola!"

I tense, then turn around to see Mort materialize before me.

"Mort!" I scream, relief washing through me. "We are screwed—he knows!"

She runs up to me and starts typing quickly. "Not quite yet," Mort says as she glances around the room. "I was scared this was going to happen. I will find us transportation.

"But you need to get out ASAP, seeing how you are limited to only your human form. Go through that far door and take your immediate left, then up the small stairs and to your right.

"After you go to your right, climb the servant's ladder and sneak into the laundry shafts. You will want to take a sharp left then right, then another left, but not the sharp left.

"Go down that long hallway and proceed to take your left three more times and keep going straight. That should bring you to the servant's exit."

I give Mort an ~are you shitting me?!~ look.

She exhales and frowns.

I squeeze my eyes shut. "I will make it to the bottom floor and jump out the freaking window, in the old library in the east wing that is barely occupied. I know how to get there, I think.

"I did, after all, clean the chimney there for two days straight. Meet me on the

122

outside of the window. It's a bay window." This is probably a horrid idea, but it's the best I can come up with.

She bites her lip, then nods. "You go quickly. Stay in the shadows."

I look down at my sparkling yellow gown. "I need a cloak."

"On it."

Mort leaves in killer bee form, and I stand here mentally preparing myself. My black cloak hides my gown, giving me more confidence. ~Now or never.~

I take off, being sure to stay in the shadows. I am thankful that the castle is dark due to being nighttime. Going through that many doors without being seen by anyone could not have been repeated.

I am sure I don't breathe for a good three minutes as I run past the Grand Library.

Really though, it is not some secret ninja talent that I possess that gets me to the east wing undetected, but pure dumb luck. I hide in the shadows while a group of guards runs past me.

Closing my eyes, I jump out of hiding and turn a sharp corner, then gasp, clasping a hand over my mouth to keep in a scream. My heart is pounding as I look at a statue of a Garthorn warrior.

Just a statue.

Madness.

I hear voices, and my whole body stiffens. ~Code red~. I can literally see the east wing library from where I stand. Should I make a mad dash for the door?

Before I can decide, my legs are already sprinting to the library. It's like when you choose to go for it when the traffic light is yellow, praying there are no cops around. It's more instinct than anything.

If my heart beats any harder, it's going to break my ribs.

As I turn the golden knob, in the back of my mind, I realize that I do not hear any more voices. I shut the door and take in a laboring breath, trying not to hyperventilate. I want to scream in relief.

I made it.

I am breathing hard as I survey the room~—empty~. I push myself off the door and run over to the large bay window. Mort must be there by now.

Jumping on the couch, I peer through the glass, the pane fogging with my rapid breaths. As my eyes scan, I suddenly hear distant whistling.

I pause with a frown, listening.

Tilting my head, I realize it's coming from down the hallway where I just came from.

As the eerie whistling becomes louder, my whole body freezes in dread. The little hairs on the back of my neck rise, and my breathing escalates.

It sounds too calm, too self-assured for the frenzy of the castle.

~It can't be.~

I stand slowly as the whistling stops right in front of the door. I don't even move. I can't. I am in a state of shock when the door is thrust open—and there in all his glory stands Apollo.

What in the ever-loving—

"There you are," he says, with a smile that seems a little on the wild side. Apollo has lost his marbles, it would seem.

"How did you find me?" I whisper harshly.

He leans a hip on the large black piano and looks offended, his dark eyes glittering. "I thought you'd give me more credit than that, Angel."

He clicks his tongue, and the look in his gaze reminds me of a feral animal. Wild. Unpredictable.

I just stare at him, pulse hammering in my neck.

I have no idea what his intentions are at this point. I feel like a cornered animal—if I choose to bolt, he would have me in his jaws in seconds. So I stand as still as I can.

"Don't feel like talking?" He tilts his head and looks concerned.

"How did you know I was in here?" I ask again, taking a little step back.

"I'm like a bloodhound. I can smell you a mile away," he murmurs with a twinkle in his graveyard eyes. He crosses his arms, making his biceps appear gigantic.

A chill runs down my spine, and I'm not entirely sure if he is serious. But a part of me thinks he's very serious. The man does have abnormally weird eyes, which puts me on edge.

I really have no idea what Apollo is capable of.

His pale hair catches the moonlight. "And I can see in the night. A warning, should   you decide to run into the darkness."

"What are you?" I say before I can stop.

He better not say vampire.

But Apollo chuckles like I'm...cute?

And why is his voice so sensual for the love of everything holy? It's deep enough to command armies into battle but still beautiful enough to tempt any woman into delicious seduction.

I grit my teeth, mentally slapping myself. I feel like I'm going to jump out of my skin. I'm drawing blanks here, and this guy has me on a whole new level of messed up.

"Take off your cloak."

My eyes widen. Something flashes to my left before I tell him to go to hell. I swiftly glance over and see a silver bow behind the desk out of Apollo's view.

That was not there before, which means Mort is in here! She must have had

Pierce beam me down a bow.

I'll be damned.

I quickly glance back to Apollo, and he frowns like he can sense a shift in me. I take a couple of breaths and move to the side, toward the bow. He pushes himself off the piano and steps forward.

~Now.~

I immediately jump and dive and grab the bow. It all happens so fast that I forget to breathe.

I'm breathing hard as I aim right at Apollo. "Don't...move..." I get out through panting breaths.

He looks genuinely shocked. Apollo holds his hands up, and a slow smile spreads over his lips. "I was not expecting that, Angel. Bravo."

"I want you to back up."

"I'm afraid I can't do that."

I swallow. "I will shoot, and I will remind you that I have very good aim."

He narrows his dark eyes and tilts his head. "I bet you do."

"Last warning."

Apollo whips out a long blade that catches the firelight. It looks lethal. He twirls it and winks at me. "Fire away, Angel."

He ~is~ crazy.

I bite my lip and aim for his thigh—I really don't want to kill him. "I'm sorry," I say as I let the arrow fly through the air.

Time stands still.

I have never seen a human move so fast. Apollo jumps to the left so quickly that he dodges the damn arrow. ~Double damn~. ~Impossible.~

I fire another one and aim for his arm. He looks focused, the perfect form of a ninja warrior as he takes his knife and slices the arrow in half. My eyes widen. This might be harder than I thought.

My pulse is hammering as I watch him, just as arrogant as ever.

He twirls the knife again and grins at me like he's ready for more. "I'm starting to think you're not an angel at all."

"I am going easy on you."

That makes him laugh. "So am I, Angel." He pauses as he flips his knife again. "I want that cloak off."

"In your dreams."

~I've always wanted to say that.~

"You have no idea," he murmurs.

In the next second, he throws his knife at me, making me scream. I was not ready for that.

The force of the throw is powerful, piercing my cloak at my side, and before I know it, I'm pinned to the wall behind me. The knife is embedded deep into the wall and my cloak.

The blade is centimeters from my skin—he could have killed me.

"You're lucky I have very good aim as well," he says, and walks toward me slowly.

My stomach flips, trying not to notice how insanely good looking he is. His shirt is unbuttoned at the neck, showcasing his golden skin.

~Focus, woman!~

The irony does not escape me that I must free myself from the cloak to escape. I yank the cloak off.

This man is either insanely clever or mad. "You're mad," I say, deciding to voice my deep thoughts. I run to the other side of the room, my yellow gown glittering.

"That would depend on who you ask," he says as he continues to follow me. "And where did you get such a gown?"

"I'm resourceful."

"So many lies from your pretty mouth," he murmurs, clicking his tongue. Apollo wipes a blonde lock out of his face as his dark gaze consumes my body.

He shakes his head as his gaze rests on my cleavage. "Maybe I shouldn't have removed the cloak. Quite distracting."

"Why do you think I wore it?" I wink at him and step around the large desk

I'm baiting him for some reason.

"Not smart."

I stare at him.

"I am going to make you pay in more ways than one," he says darkly, continuing to walk toward me, slowly stalking me.

A thrill shoots up my spine, and I must look away. Apollo's sinful eyes are going to be my downfall. They are so deliciously abnormal, a wicked gleam dancing in their mysterious depths.

I continue to circle around the desk, hoping I can get close to my bow that I stupidly left by my cloak. I have to end this little thing we have going on here before it goes somewhere I don't want it to.

Well, in these particular circumstances anyway, where Apollo wants to throw me in prison.

Apollo pulls out another knife from his boot, the silver flashing. "Who do you work for, Angel?"

I swallow. "No one of consequence."

He raises his brows mockingly. "Well, that's a relief."

I'm in trouble without my bow. My heart is pounding in my chest. I slowly make my way toward it as he watches me with an amused smirk.

He holds up his finger and shakes it at me like I'm a naughty kid. "I don't think so," he barely says as he chucks his knife at me with speed and accuracy.

~Duck!~

~Move!~

I squeeze my eyes shut as I try to dodge it, but it pierces the vibrant yellow skirts. I scream in frustration as I am once again pinned to the wall. I am on the ground, trapped like an idiot.

This guy throws a knife with such force it is entirely unnatural. What do they feed the men in this world? Steroids? Steroids for breakfast lunch and dinner? I try to yank my dress free, but it's no use.

Unbelievable.

"If you want to escape, you can take the dress off," he offers with a shrug and a tilt of his head.

I glare at him.

He chuckles as he makes his way to me, making me panic. I'm so screwed. Where is Mort? Did she leave? She must have! "Are you going to call the guards then?"

Apollo kneels in front of me, his eyes traveling over my body like a starved tiger. I think I hear him make a sound in the back of his throat, but I am not certain.

I look away because I don't want him to see what his desire does to me. He is purely erotic; his smell alone is making me dizzy. I can feel his heat, his energy like electricity.

My pulse is thrashing against my neck, and I try to take a steady breath without success. I feel his gaze on me, and it's making me senseless.

"You wore the dress for me?"

I try to shift into a different position, slightly yanking on my skirt again. I hear a ripping sound, to my quiet relief. "No."

I gasp as I feel him grab my hair, forcing me to look up at him. "Try again, Angel." He is removing the pins from my hair, and his grip tightens.

"No, I did not wear this gown for you."

~Why am I provoking him?!~

"I'll stop as soon as you tell me the truth," he murmurs as he leans his head down to my breasts, which are on brilliant display. He jerks my head back for better access to my neck and chest.

His hot breath fans over my cleavage, making my skin ignite into flames. When his lips touch my skin, I am nearly undone.

~I need a cigarette.

~I need a firetruck.~

~I need something!~

He shifts his position as his arm circles around my back, lifting me, giving him better access. The feel of his scorching mouth on my sensitive flesh makes my lady parts come alive with alarming force.

Apollo moans into my breasts, and the sound makes my toes curl. I feel so much power around him that I feel completely weak, vulnerable. He could probably snap me like a twig if he wants.

"Angel," he whispers. He drops his knife on the floor and grabs my right breast to massage and caress through my corset.

~He dropped his knife~, my brain whispers through heated desire.

For a fleeting second, I don't care. The feel of Apollo worshipping me is so intoxicating that it wipes out my sane thoughts. I feel him licking, sucking, caressing.

He is losing control in the most delicious way, for his breathing is escalating and his kisses are becoming frantic.

Apollo takes a harsh breath as he uncontrollably lifts my skirts, knocking the knife next to my hand.

~Oh, mercy.~

I don't want this to stop.

But I grab the knife as I feel him reach my thighs, then dangerously higher. My mind is now in fragments, shattered glass. My head falls back as I feel his fingers rub me ~there. ~Just a little bit longer…

I can barely breathe; my skin is on fire. My neck muscles are no longer working.

I hear fabric rip, then his hand is on my bare flesh. I scream in pleasure as he starts to work me into a wild animal with each deep plunge.

He is maneuvering his fingers as I have ~never ~felt before. I can't even think. I feel his hot mouth on my neck, breasts, shoulder, jaw, and ear as he works me harder.

He is unrelenting, not allowing me to think for one second. His fingers swirl over my most sensitive parts, my core hot and throbbing.

I feel him smile into my neck as the pressure builds, and I let out a moan, moving my hips in sync with his hand.

The only thing I can do is moan and writhe.

I scream, biting my lip to quiet my voice. I know nothing. I see stars, fireworks, and an atomic bomb exploding with the mushroom cloud.

After the waves of sensation leave, my brain returns.

Holy moly, what did we just do? I suddenly feel him kissing his way up my leg and red alerts ring loud.

I close my eyes, wanting this so bad, but I know if I let him and he returns to his senses, realizing I have his knife, I will not escape. This is my only chance to catch him off guard.

I feel him grip my thighs hard, and I must shove the erotic thrill back down. I need to hurry, because if he reaches his destination, I'm gone with the wind.

I feel his tongue licking his way to my core, and his moan sends lightning streaks through my body.

I f-ing hate to do this.

I use the sharp knife to slash my pinned dress free. I feel him instantly react, but it's too late as I drive the sharpened blade into his thigh.

He will not die, and it should heal nicely.

Tunnel vision sets in as I get up, hearing him yell in agony. This is a ~dick~ move, but I have no other choice. I'm sorry.

I want to yell, "Thank you for the amazing experience we just had!" but that might come off wrong.

Everything seems like I'm in a dream now as I run toward the bay window. Slow motion.

Somehow, I find something heavy on the desk and throw it at the large pane. It shatters into a million pieces.

I'm outside now, and it's raining hard. I have blood on my arm, probably from the jagged window.

I'm dizzy.

Very disoriented.

"Viola!"

Mort is running up to me, soaked from the rain. "What took you so long?!"

I might not expound on that.

I glance back at the window, expecting to see Apollo cursing me to hell, but I do not. All I hear is a loud siren. The eerie sound is ringing loudly in the night air. "What's that?!"

Mort wipes the rain out of her eyes. "Similar to when an inmate escapes!"

Apollo.

He must be livid.

"How do we get out of here?" I ask desperately, flinching at a crack of lightning.

"Too many guards! I could not find a horse!"

I grab her shoulders. "You be a horse!"

She looks horrified. "Hell no!"

"You have too!"

Mort closes her eyes, then nods. She shapeshifts into a powerful gray horse, and I don't have time to be impressed.

I jump on her back from pure adrenaline, my dress making it challenging to feel confident. But I have an amazing horseback talent, thanks to one of my three wishes.

"All right, Mort! Let's outrun Apollo's men!"

I squeeze my eyes shut and find my inner badass.

CHAPTER 14

This is insanity.

It's not quite what I was picturing when I was offered the once-in-a-lifetime chance at being a part of a fairytale romance.

Disney princess fantasy, I think not.

This is freaking Braveheart.

"Mort, I sure hope you're fast!" I scream as I see the massive gate of the Garthorn Castle open.

The loud siren reminds me of something from ~Silence Hill~. Goosebumps litter my body as I try to tap down my hysteria at the situation.

Mort nervously pounds the ground with her massive hooves, jumping to the left then right. The rain is relentless, making it hard to see clearly through the night.

What in the world have I gotten myself into?!

I am not sure if it's the thunder rumbling or the dark riders that are emerging from the castle, but I do know we need to move fast!

Mort also seems to see them and jumps into a dead sprint, hammering the ground in mighty strides. I grab her mane and lean down low, my thighs holding on for dear life.

A part of my brain can't believe Apollo is going to this great length to bring me back. Is there something I do not know? Maybe they think I carry valuable information back to my evil superiors.

But really, Mort should get a medal for this. Best agent ever.

"Faster, Mort!"

She takes us down a road that leads to what looks like a giant forest. My adrenaline is racing through my veins as we cover ground quickly.

I risk a glance back, my long hair temporarily blinding me, but I see dark riders following us.

I gasp at the sight.

The night appears ghostly, the rain and thunder creating an ominous scene.

As we near the forest's edge, a low level of mist covers the ground that is highlighted by three giant moons. I have no time to marvel at how fantastical this all is because we now are engulfed in the dense forest.

It's dark and scary. The towering trees loom over us as Mort tries to weave her way through without a head-on collision with a tree.

I scream as I am hit in the face with a wet branch, nearly knocking me off Mort. I regain control and crouch low, urging Mort on, praying my nose is not broken.

"I sure hope you know where you're going!" My voice is most likely lost in the rain and wind.

I know Mort was talking to Pierce earlier, so maybe they have a plan.

I see something to my left and gasp—a dark Garthorn rider. "Mort! We have company!" Mort makes a sharp left athletically, jumping over an impressively large fallen tree.

I lean low, feeling airborne as Mort clears it with shocking skill. Mort lands and presses on, finding a wide path to accelerate her speed.

My triumph is short-lived as I see another dark rider to our right deep in the forest. This one is close and is making a beeline toward us.

I look to my left and start to panic when I spot the other Garthorn soldier we just ditched. We are going to be sandwiched!

"Mort!"

The rider to our left is right beside us on the narrow path, and I risk a glance at him. He is gruff and wearing Garthorn armor with a bow on his back.

I see him whip out his long sword, and I freeze, wondering wildly if this is the moment to scream, "~lifeline activate!"~

I brace myself for impact.

I can tell Mort sees the threat, and she aggressively moves to her right.

I only have seconds to move my leg and sit side-saddle before Mort crazily rams the rider. The impact makes me lose my unstable seating, and I fall.

By the grace of God, I manage to grab onto her mane, and I'm able to boost myself up on her back like a circus rider. I groan loudly and exhaust all my muscles to gain back position.

I am so thankful that Mort told me to pick being a master rider, or I would have already used all three of my lifelines in a matter of five minutes.

I glance back to see that the rider we slammed into is nowhere to be found.

Mort slows, breathing heavily.

The wind and rain whip me in the face as we stop in the middle of the path. Mort pounds the ground, and large puffs of air emit from her nose. She jolts me, and I think she wants me to get off, so I do.

My legs are wobbly, and my dress most likely weighs two-hundred tons from being soaked.

Mort materializes back into human form and is breathing so hard on the ground I'm actually concerned.

"Mort!" I kneel beside her. "Talk to me!"

She takes another breath and sits up. "I have a r-red alert."

I start to panic. "Something worse than this?!" I wave my hands around at the insanity of this.

"Pierce is obligated to send any player a red alert no matter what," she says, and regains her breath.

I glance around the spooky dark forest. "Where is the other rider?!"

"Queen Irena wants you dead. She sees Apollo's infatuation with you and knows that Laura will never get to marry him. This is what me and Pierce talked about earlier."

She continues at my stunned expression, "Now I'm not definitely saying he is madly in love with you, because we don't know. He still could be crazy enough to kill you for lying to him.

"He seems wildly unpredictable."

I swallow, wiping the rain from my face.

"But Irena is an evil witch and knows you are the lost daughter of the King of Galleon. And if her infidelity is found out, she will be publicly executed. So you see why she would want you dead—and fast."

"Ok." I look around, feeling spooked. "So what's the red alert? And why is there no one around us?"

Without answering me, she takes off into a sprint. "What in the hell?!" I call after her, following her, my skirts almost making me trip.

We stop at an unconscious soldier that apparently was slammed into the tree by Mort. She turns him over and takes off his bow, tossing it to me.

"You will need this."

I glance up, seeing the sky reflecting a deep purple, and the ground rumbles as if the gates of hate opened. "Talk to me!"

"We have to make it to the village of Demour, which is not far, but we can hide out there until we can come up with a plan of action. I have to talk to Pierce ASAP when we get there."

My eyes widen, and I see dark shadows darting in the trees around us. "Mort?! What are those?"

I whip around to my left then to my right, my breathing harsh and frantic. I hear branches breaking, and I look to Mort, who is backing up, wide-eyed.

"I'm not sure! I'm not logged in, but I think that they are a very dangerous animal. Some wolf breed brought on by Irena. Use your bow!" And with that, she becomes the gray horse, stomping about nervously.

Right!

Awesome sauce.

~Please don't freak out.~

I hear a deep growl that is so low it almost sounds like vibrations, for the human ear is most likely unable to pick up octaves that deep. Mort rears up on her hind legs and neighs loudly.

I swallow and turn slowly to see a wolf-type animal—except that it's not. It's not at all a wolf. Maybe if a wolf had a baby with a grizzly bear.

It is mere feet from me, eyes glowing yellow and long trails of saliva falling from its knife-like teeth. I stop breathing, too scared to move, for it may make it come after me.

I hear Mort making lots of noise, but the creature is crouched low and homed in on me. The ground is rumbling again, but I am locked eye to eye.

I slowly try to take a step back, but that only makes the low rumble from its throat become louder.

I'm so screwed.

~Don't cry.~

Be brave.

I am trembling, ready to yell my lifeline, as it crouches even lower, the beast snarling louder. This is it.

Time stands still as I see it lunge at me. My heartbeat is echoing through my head, and my erratic breathing is all I can manage.

I jolt backward and yell, "Lifeline act — "

An arrow pierces the head of the beast right through the skull.

I fall to the ground in shock, utterly numb to the core. Eyes wide, I glance to my left, seeing Apollo on a magnificent black mount with riders behind him.

He is standing in his stirrups with his bow aimed at three more to my right, firing at them with a skill that exceeds mine.

His long black coat flaps in the wind, and his face is like stone, jaw flexed, and eyes intense.

I watch him kill more as he yells something over his shoulder to his men, touching his chest plate as blue light flickers under his soaked coat. He is magnificent.

I watch in awe on the ground like an ogling schoolgirl.

That's when I notice the bandage on his muscular thigh as he stands. He jerks his stallion to the left, trying to calm the massive horse, the black hair reflecting the moonlight in the pouring rain.

Suddenly our gazes lock, and I suck in a harsh breath.

He looks livid.

I scramble to my feet and back up, almost falling again. Apollo sits in his saddle and holds up his fist to stop his men from coming at me.

He stares at me, then glances at Mort as if he is reading my mind. Lightning flashes behind him as he shakes his head ~no~.

I ignore him and mount Mort, feeling every muscle in my body protest. Apollo gallops up to me, controlling his wild stallion with ease.

"You cannot outrun me, Angel!" he yells over the wind and rain.

I have zero plans now, and I also doubt I can outrun him either. ~This man has mad skills~. I need to think of something fast that will save my cold freezing ass.

"I will not go to the dungeon!"

Great.

I'm in no position to give orders.

His hair is tied back, and being wet, it appears much darker, giving him a very dangerous appeal. Apollo in the rain and being nothing short of a superhero is a little much for the female brain to take in.

I am breathing hard as my eyes go to his lips and I remember how well he can use them.

Be still, my heart.

Apollo tilts his head, and a grin spreads over his lips. "Do I have a choice? You did, after all, assault the Crown Prince of Garthorn," he says, and kicks his mount even closer to mine.

~Oh, right, his thigh.~ His eyes travel over my soaked body then back up to my face.

"You need to come with me or you will catch your death out here. And I'm not just talking about the cold. Evil is out tonight, and you will get killed without me!"

"Isn't that what you want anyway? I'm confused!" I yell back at him, griping Mort's mane even tighter.

He is perplexing. First he wants to lock me up, then protect me, and the next ravish me?

"Who are you?!" he yells, jerking to control his mount.

"I am the lost princess of Galleon! Look at my eye color for Pete's sake!"

There I said it.

A claim like that could get me hung, but who cares.

I wait. Did he hear me? His eyes are narrowed, and he stares like I have grown two heads and five boobs. I swallow, waiting for him to speak, but he doesn't.

Then dread sinks in. He must not believe me and thinks I am a looney. I didn't exactly pick the best time to tell him, I get that! The ground abruptly rumbles, and Apollo looks to his left.

"We have to move now!"

He jerks his stallion around and yells orders to his men, then turns back to me, extending his gloved hand to me. "Come with me!"

I'm not idiot enough to say no to that.

I go to reach for him, but all I can see is blinding white light. The crack of lightning is so great that my ears are ringing.

This spooks Mort, and she takes off into a mad sprint, trying to get away from the loud cracks of lightning.

"Mort!" I yell. "Calm down! Stop!"

I hold on for dear life, praying not to fall to my death. I have no idea where she is going, and I don't even know if Apollo is following.

I hear yells from behind me, and it sounds like him. I glance back and see him right behind us as another flash of light almost blinds me.

His mount nudges Mort to the side, making room for Apollo's stallion to gallop beside us. He stands up in his stirrups and leans far over to grab Mort's mane—something that looks extremely dangerous.

Apollo forcefully pulls Mort, changing her direction, which almost made Apollo slam into a tree if he hadn't jerked his horse to the left.

After a few terrifying moments, Mort stops, and I nearly yell in relief.

As my eyes adjust, I see that we stand on the very edge of the cliff. Like, ~right~ on the edge, making me gasp. My situation keeps getting worse and worse!

"Oh shit!" I yell in alarm. "Mort, back up slowly, for the love of God!"

As Mort slowly backs up, pieces of the cliff start to break off and fall.

"Get off the horse!"

I look behind me and see Apollo and his men. He stands out in front, not coming any closer, about twenty feet away.

"You are on an overhang. It cannot support your weight!" he yells with his hands up. He throws off his big overcoat, revealing his black billowy shirt from the masquerade. "Get off the damned horse now!"

He slowly inches forward.

I nod, carefully easing myself off Mort. I whisper, "We can do this. Just back up slowly."

"Gently!" I hear Apollo's panicked voice.

I am off, and I tiptoe my way from Mort, barely breathing. ~Be strong, little cliff~, I plead. I swallow and glance back at Mort. "Slowly…Easy does it."

She takes a step back, and that's when I hear the crack, and everything happens so fast.

The edge of the cliff breaks off, and I jump.

I land on the new edge of the cliff, but when I glance back, I realize Mort was not so lucky.

"Mort!" I scream, and I feel my eyes well up with horror. "Mort!"

No.

No.

She is fine.

My body is shaking. My mind is malfunctioning. Of course, she is fine. She's a freaking agent! I'm sure she had excellent training.

"Angel!"

Apollo apparently has been screaming my name for some time. I glance at him to see him on his knees, face pale.

"Focus! You must get off the cliff now. I can't come to get you because I'm too heavy! You have to come now before another lightning strike!" He motions with his hands like I am dumb.

Apollo looks petrified.

Through the haze of my mind, I'm touched. I look at his rain-soaked face and see genuine fear for me, and I would almost say he is two seconds from a full-fledged freakout.

I will have to reflect on this later, I decide, as I look at the jagged cliff I am laying on.

"Oh shit."

If I fall, I can scream my lifeline, but Apollo does not know that. Hence the absolute terror etched into his features.

"Crawl!"

I nod and slowly start to crawl, and I can feel the cliff cracking. I look up, heart pounding. "It's cracking!"

~Oh no.~

Apollo's chest is heaving, and it looks like he enters a state of extreme focus. He stands and yells to his men, and I watch as they bring him a lime green rope.

Apollo works so fast it almost takes my mind off the fact I will be airborne in a matter of seconds. He takes out his arrow, which is tied to the rope, and aims into the forest and shoots.

He is talking to his men as he wraps a belt around his trim hips and fastens the rope to it.

I feel another crack and can now see it on the surface. "Apollo!" I scream.

I look up to see Apollo sprinting at me right as the edge gives under my weight. I try to move, but it's no use. The cliff is just too fragile.

I scream, grabbing at nothing but air, seeing the mountain edge slowly becoming out of my reach.

Seconds feel like minutes as I fall, looking up for any signs of hope.

I then see Apollo swan dive off the cliff after me, and in a matter of moments, I feel his body collide with mine. I feel his arms around me, and I grab onto him desperately, my legs wrapping around him.

The rope has a little give to it, but nothing to lessen the pain Apollo must feel when the rope goes rigid, stopping us from our descent. We jerk to a standstill rather violently.

I hear him yell and groan in pain as he tries to get a better grip on me.

"Wrap your legs around my waist!"

I am hanging on him as best as I can in my billion-pound skirts.

"Son of a bitch! No wonder the cliff broke!" Apollo hisses as he grabs the rope with both hands, steadying us upright. His arm muscles are bulging, and the veins in his neck are protruding with his effort.

"Take off the fucking skirts!"

"How?!"

"My knife," he gets out. "Belt buckle."

I reach down to the front of his pants and feel around his belt, coming dangerously close to his manhood. I have a dirty mind even when I'm about to die, apparently.

I find the knife and pull it out so fast I make Apollo gasp in fear. His dark eyes meet mine, only inches away.

"Be a little more careful," he struggles to get a better grip, "around that area, would you? If I pass out, we are both dead."

I try not to smile and start ripping away at my skirts with one hand, stabbing myself in the process. "Mother f—"

Apollo rips the knife out of my hand and cuts a few strings in back, and my skirts fall, the weight sliding right off my legs as Apollo holds me up. I'm left with my tattered black lace slip and my thin underwear.

My heart is still beating erratically. Of course Apollo is good at removing women's clothing. I guess now is not the time to be a prude.

I hear him groan in relief at the release of weight. He uses the rock wall to help him climb up, little by little. "You never said where you acquired your dress," he whispers in my ear.

My arms are wrapped tightly around his neck, pressed to him as close as one can get. I still can't believe he just dove off a cliff to save me. "I will have to kill you if I tell."

Hey. That's a classic one-liner.

No judging—he has never heard it before.

He chuckles, and I can feel his hot breath on me. "You claim to be Princess Ursula? That is quite the claim," he grunts as he pulls us up and up.

"Yes."

"That changes everything."

I glance at him. "You're not throwing me in the dungeon?"

"No."

"Where then?"

"My bedroom."

CHAPTER 15

This is my Cinderella moment.

I am the lost daughter of Galleon.

It didn't take them long to do blood work and to prove that I have the royal blood of the King, my~ father~.

I wonder if I would have saved myself a lot of pain if I had brought it up in the beginning. Maybe, and maybe not.

I am feeling a little numb now.

You must understand that I have never had a family before, being an orphan and all. So meeting the King was a lot to take in emotionally. I get that he is not my birth father, but this experience is very real to me.

He cried, tears of joy in his hazel eyes as they searched my face and kissed me. Saying I look just like my mother, that I have her beautiful soul and eyes. He made my heart clench.

I have never had someone look at me that way before, and it makes me yearn for more. Is this what it's like to have a loving parent?

King Alistair Zorne Lowthe of Galleon is my father.

And Laura is my ~evil~ stepsister.

I smile.~ How do you like them apples?~

Mort has informed me that Irena is furious, and I'm sure Laura is no different. I am on an equal playing field now. But Queen Irena does not know I'm aware of her affair, and it needs to stay that way.

Laura knows I know. That will give me a bit of leverage. Blackmail, if you will.

It feels so good to be on top for once. I glance around my beautiful room as I take in a large breath, and I can't believe it. The room is stunning. A chamber fit for a princess, not a slave.

The large four-poster bed is rose-colored, with cream satin. Flowers are everywhere, making the room smell heavenly.

A large window with a deck is to my left and a vanity that might be made from pure silver is to my right. I was bathed in lavender scented water and had my hair combed by four servants. I'm receiving the royal treatment. I was able to bring Mort along with me as my personal maid — my ~father~ didn't let me forget that I shall have anything I want.

"Ursula!"

I turn around at Mort's musical voice and grin. "I guess I will get used to that name eventually."

"I thought we were done for back there in the woods, but Apollo is proving that where you're concerned, nothing else matters. You should have seen the outrage on Irena's face when they were doing the blood test," she says, and glances around the beautiful room.

I sit on the edge of the bed, the rose silk glimmering in the sunlight. "I bet, which means she might try to get rid of me once and for all."

Mort plops down beside me and sighs. "This is comfy."

I lay back. "I know. Heaven."

"No bumpy mattress."

"Or bed bugs."

Mort grunts. "Or freezing mornings trying to pee in that bucket that kept tipping over."

We both lay in silence, thoughts running through our heads.

"Did Apollo cancel his engagement?"

Mort looks over at me. "The banners are still up, so I don't think so."

"That's confusing."

"I bet he takes them down—like, everyone knows he's obsessed with you. Never has a crown prince sent out a royal search party for a mere servant. And you stabbed him and did not hang for it."

She continues, "But you're a princess now, so I don't see a problem with him switching his choice. He would be just switching sisters."

"So he is not obligated to stay true to his word?"

"You know," Mort sits up, "I am not sure, actually." She starts typing and blinking with a frown. "I should probably find out."

I sit up too.

"Oh," she says, scowling. "Pierce says nice job, by the way, but he is telling me that an engagement like this is very serious.

"To break it would mean dishonor to Laura and her family, even though you are of the ~same~ family." She looks at me and expels a breath.

"Shit. That might complicate things yet again."

One step forward and two steps back.

"Unless you can prove that Laura is not of royal blood," Mort says. "Then that would be bound to break the engagement."

I stand up and look out the balcony door, walking out into the warm sunlight.

"Well, that means we still need her DNA."

Damnit.

"You might try and tell Apollo that you think Irena is having an affair," Mort suggests.

"But how would I know that? I don't know who with. I can't just say because she looks like a whore." I give Mort a pointed look.

Mort shrugs and stands beside me. "We can watch her and see who she is sweet on. I have been too focused on Laura."

I nod. Tonight, they're having a ball in my honor. The King of Galleon is overjoyed and wants to celebrate.

I don't blame him, for it's not every day your dead daughter comes back from the grave. A princess, no less.

I will admit that it's going to be awkward seeing Apollo with Laura. And seeing Laura and Irena will be an icy reunion, but something I might enjoy.

I declined to see them earlier, saying I was too full of emotion and needed to take baby steps.

I can't decline tonight.

Tonight, I have to be Princess Ursula of Galleon.

I spend the entire day visiting with the House of Galleon's royal family, getting reacquainted with my lost family members. It's pleasant; everyone stares at me like I am a ghost.

And really, how I got here is weirder than being a ghost. What they don't know will not hurt them. I think.

"No yellow gown, please. I think that color is bad luck," I say with a frown, picturing myself running through the forest with it.

Mort is typing as I stand, ready to spin like Cinderella.

"Pierce says he thinks you will love this dress. It's fit for a princess. And he also adds that the yellow dress saved your ass. It made Apollo go bonkers, so he wants you to apologize," Mort says, and looks up at me.

"He can hear me?"

"When I'm logged on, yes."

I bit my lip. "Sorry, Pierce!" I think for a second. "Apollo did seem to love it." Visions of us in that library light up my brain like a bonfire.

My cheeks heat—just the thought of Apollo gives me hot flashes. His golden skin and sinful lips...But his eyes are a drug, and once they have you in their possession, you're done for.

"You," she types more, "can spin now."

I turn and gasp, still not used to the tingling sensation. My scalp feels hot, and my body hums. After the flash of white light, I'm still breathing hard. That was fast.

I glance down and suck in a breath.

Mort says, "That might make Apollo feel a little uncomfortable if you know what I mean."

I give her a look then walk over to the full-body mirror. Oh, baby. Charming did me a solid yet again.

I am in a shimmering pearl-colored gown, the shade almost the same as my skin. If you saw me from a distance, you might think I was topless, save for the pearlized splendor.

It reminds me of a glistening opal.

It's beyond stunning.

My breasts look remarkable in the snug-fitting corset and the long sleeves are transparent, shimmering fabric. I look like a goddess—or an angel, perhaps.

The gown flows out at the waist like a waterfall of airy sparkles. It almost has me entranced with its beauty. Every move I make, I glitter like a rare diamond.

In this dress I feel like flowers will bloom where I walk. It's that enchanting.

My glossy hair is plaited and hanging down my back like a fairy princess.

"Pierce says your silence is all he needs." Mort stands and smiles. "This should be interesting. All I'm missing is popcorn."

***

I am about to be announced. Everyone will finally see the lost princess revealed and I'm all nerves—my palms are sweaty. I think I need to be featured in ~Eight Mile~, like a remake.

I take a shaky breath when I see the King~, my father~, ready to escort me down the grand staircase. He comes to me and takes my hand, tears in his eyes.

"You look just like your mother," he says in a gruff accent. The King is a handsome man, but a bit on the rough side.

He is decked out in his golden finery, and his gray hair is combed back perfectly to fit his ruby crown. His eyes are kind that crinkle on the sides when he smiles.

"Thank you, your highness." I curtsey, trying not to fall over.

"Ursula, my darling, please call me father." His large hands grip mine again, eyes round with emotion.

I swallow the lump in my throat.

Don't cry.

Don't.

"Of course~, Father."~ I smile up at him, and he laughs.

"Good girl!" He puts my arm in his and leads me to the entrance. "Now, let everyone see my lovely daughter who has come back to me!"

My heart jumps as I hear someone announcing my arrival to a crowded ballroom. My first thought is of Apollo. He would be on the hand of Laura, the happy couple.

I try to shove my jealousy down, and it tastes like acid in my mouth. She still has time to win him over, and he might not care that her mother cheated if he loves her.

I feel sick.

My father leans into my ear.

"Apollo's cousin, Tarren Somon of Garthorn, will escort you to the ballroom. A fine fellow. Owns three large estates in the west region. Your mother and I spent our honeymoon at West Lyth Falls."

His eyes glitter with pride, and we walk. I glance at him and smile. Matchmaking already? But I only have a month and a half! And there is this guy named Apollo that I have to get over...

We enter at the top of the stairs, and the once-buzzing ballroom quiets. You could hear a pin drop — and my rapid breathing.

"Do not be nervous," he whispers, and pats my arm like a good father.

I nod and begin my descent with him, one marble step at a time. There are a lot more people here than I thought.

My gown sparkles even more in the dim ballroom, making me want to pinch myself quickly to make sure I'm not hallucinating. Everything is so romantic — like straight out of a children's fairy tale.

It's then I see the Garthorn royal family lined up at the bottom of the stairs to greet me in honor of their alliance. Everyone is looking up at me in awe, smiles on their faces, except for one.

My heart dips.

Apollo is absolutely striking, as always.

I glance at him for only a moment, but I take everything in like a starved

152

animal.

He is in black and white, crisp and elegant. His black pants hug his thighs, and his black dress coat is stretched tautly over his muscular torso.

He has some sort of shiny armor on under that intensifies his superhero appeal. The stark white necktie contrasts with his bronzed skin, and his cupid hair is tied back.

My knees almost buckle, and I can feel my father grip me a little tighter to steady me.

I have tunnel vision.

Other than Apollo, I can't tell who is there, my brain giving me only vague descriptions. But what I do know is that everyone is looking at me ~except~ for him, for he stares straight ahead.

I am halfway down the stairs, and I can tell that his jaw is rigid, like he is clenching it and grinding his teeth.

His gaze hits me hard, and I feel immediately self-conscious—~naked~.

I look away for a second to regain my composure, but I can still feel my skin tingling. I glance back, and he is almost frowning, but not quite. Just very intense as his dark gaze travels up my body to my face.

A thrill shoots down my back and explodes in my stomach when I see his mouth drop slightly. The look would send a nun into fits of hot flashes.

A man suddenly gains my attention when he steps forward and bows in front of me. I am breathing hard as I realize this must be his cousin Tarren.

He is handsome, with dark hair and eyes, but irritation rises in me when I start comparing him to Apollo immediately. I don't feel the same erotic pull I do with Apollo.

And...I ~feel~ Apollo—his energy, his magnetism—even when I'm not looking at him.

My skin tingles because I can feel his dark eyes on me, not because the man before me is looking at me like I am the prettiest thing he's ever seen.

He kisses my hand, and I smile to be polite, taking a shaky breath. I curtsy, feeling the hairs on the back of my neck rise. If I were to bet, I'd bet Apollo is not happy about this, because I can almost feel the tension intensify. But I can't care too much.

He is engaged. I repeat that to myself to stop myself from crumbling under his powers.

Tarren is introducing himself and everyone in the line as I smile and nod, feeling a bit overwhelmed by one person.

When he gets to Apollo, our gazes clash again, and I can't tell what he's thinking. His gaze glitters. It's the only indication that I get that he's a real person and not a statue.

He bows without a word.

I frown slightly, wanting to stomp on his foot for not calling off the engagement and whisking me off into the sunset.~ As if it's my fault he's engaged?!~

He tilts his head slightly as if sensing my troubled thoughts. I see something in his gaze now, an emotion. It's amusement.

I don't get to look at him for long, for I am ushered away toward the royal lounge area.

We walk through a multitude of guests and ignore their wide stares and whispers.

"You are more stunning than the rumors said," Tarren says as we sit on plush seating minutes later.

"And to think you were the long-lost daughter of Galleon all along. A slave at that—astounding tale if you ask me. When my aunt, the Queen, told me the tale, I will have to admit I didn't believe it."

154

~You have an idea.~

"Yes, quite the tale," I murmur, trying to hide my shaking hands as I glance out over to the swarm of guests. I need to get my shit together.

He leans in closer to me. "I came here from the country because of Apollo's engagement, you see." He pauses as he follows my gaze.

"They seem like they are a great fit, on the outside anyway. I never thought I'd see the day that he proposed. I was utterly shocked. Princess Laura of Galleon is quite easy on the eyes.

"I am sure this engagement will help our kingdoms stay at peace. The House of Galleon are not people you want on your bad side, for they are very brutal, and ancient in their ways."

He chuckles to himself and takes a moment to sip his drink. "But strangely, there is this rumor that Apollo has lost his mind over you." I feel him looking at me in question.

I stiffen just a bit and glance at him. "Rumors are rumors."

He smiles and grabs my hand, turning it over to my wrist, and starts to tickle it slowly. I let him, eyeing him suspiciously. He looks up at me, studying my face.

"I never believe rumors, but I can't help but get lost in the romance of this. The beautiful slave girl who catches the eye of the prince, and just happens to be a princess?"

He clicks his tongue. "Now that's a rumor worth believing in."

I chuckle at his serious expression.

That can only come from Fairy Godmother Inc.

He sits up straighter and nods his chin to Laura and the women she is walking with. She will not make eye contact with me, and I think I know why.

She may have the engagement, but I have Apollo's interest. For now, anyway.

I know for a fact Laura has not given up yet. I can tell by the determination in her eyes when she is with Apollo—hanging on his arm, seductive looks whenever he gives her attention.

"Do you think you two will be friends now that you're sisters?"

I snort, causing him to smile wide. I probably should not be so openly hateful.

He sighs. "I don't blame you."

I look at him, shifting my weight as I sip on my champagne. "You are very observant."

Tarren sits up straighter and glances at me. "I am a writer, my lady. I have to be. It's in my blood." He pretends to think then winks at me.

"When Apollo and I were younger, he always made me do the negotiating. Well, you know, to convince the cooks to give us extra cakes and chocolates. That sort of thing.

"I could always read people very well, and it worked to my benefit almost always."

I smile, thinking of the two young boys getting into trouble.

"Apollo always looked innocent, and me not so much. I had to convince my way out of everything, whereas Apollo just had to smile." He chuckles again.

Tarren adjusts his white necktie, his broad shoulders similar to Apollo's. I can tell they are related.

"Well, you developed lifelong skills it would seem," I say, and take a sip, deciding I like Tarren.

"I keep telling myself that." He smiles.

I laugh.

He glances at me, and I feel my cheeks heat as his eyes travel over me. "I know Apollo, and I can see why you have him hot and bothered. He always liked the dark and mysterious women."

"And what do you like?"

He tilts his head. "We have the same tastes, which led to a lot of black eyes and brawls in our teenage years."

I think for a second, trying to figure out Tarren and his motives.

He leans his head into my neck, lips barely grazing my skin, making me tense.

"If Apollo is such an idiot not to see what's at stake here, allow me to court you. I, for one, am not daft, and I can try to erase whatever my idiot cousin has done to you."

I doubt that, but I'm flattered. Tarren is handsome, but not on the level of Apollo.

Now, don't yell at me yet. I do understand it's not all about looks. But I also feel alive when next to Apollo, like electricity courses through my body and soul. I don't get that with Tarren.

It's hard to explain, but I light up by just thinking of Apollo. I have it bad, and the fever is not going away anytime soon.

"Tarren."

My whole body stiffens.

Tarren pulls his head away from my neck and smiles up at Apollo. It is a smile you would see on a wolf.

"Apollo!" He stands and claps his hands. "Congratulations on the engagement, cousin! She is stunning, really."

Apollo's expression could have turned Medusa into stone. I swallow, watching the two in a silent battle. I think Tarren's presence here might be the crazy I need to tip the boat.

I sip my champagne and stand, placing my arm in Tarren's. Two can play this game, and I can play very dirty when I want something.

Apollo's heated gaze shoots to my hand on Tarren's arm, and the gauntlet is down.

I never claimed to be a good person.

Sue me.

CHAPTER 16

I need a drink.

Tarren and Apollo stare at each other, the tension so thick you can almost feel the intense vibrations.

Apollo shifts as he grins, looking at my hand on Tarren's arm then up at me. "Ursula, is it?"

I take a steady breath. "Yes, Your Grace. Princess Ursula." I smile as fake as I can.

"Forgive me for being so informal," he says politely, but his eyes are hard as steel. The man is beyond furious. I can see the dark depths of his gaze pinning me with needles. "~Princess~ Ursula."

Tarren places his hand over mine and glances at me. "I must say, that gown you are wearing makes you look more like a goddess than a mere princess."

I smile at him like it is the cleverest compliment I have ever heard. "I don't know about that," I murmur. "You flatter me."

Barf. I sound so fake even to my ears that I must tone down the smiling. "Lord Tar—"

"Please call me Tarren."

I ignore Apollo's slight eye roll and tilt my head beautifully. "Tarren," I say with vigor, "would you like to dance?"

He places his hand on his heart and chuckles at Apollo. "Beautiful and ~brave~?" He glances at me and leans in. "Let's let Apollo and his lovely fiancé have alone time up here," he says.

He nods to Laura, who is glaring at her champagne glass some feet away. Her rose-colored gown almost resembles a wilting flower with her sour demeanor.

I don't blame her. Apollo seems on a different agenda tonight than to impress his lonely fiancé. A woman ignored is worse than a starving, raging beast.

I just made that up. Words of wisdom by Viola, a.k.a. Princess Ursula.

Apollo makes a sound, reaches out, and grabs my arm, startling me. Apollo looks down at his hand on my wrist, almost as shocked as I am.

"Tarren is the worst dancer on this half of the fucking planet." He shoots Tarren a murderous glance. "Allow me to take you. It's the least I can do after what happened."

Tarren clicks his tongue. "Such foul language in front of the Princess of Galleon."

Apollo's black gaze seems to flicker unnaturally. "Careful, cousin," he hisses. "Watch out. She will chew you up and spit you out."

And with that loaded statement, he turns to leave, leaving a cold chill in his wake.

I don't realize I am holding my breath until I let it out, my pulse hammering. I glance at Tarren's intense expression. "What is he?" I blurt.

Tarren exhales and looks at me, and it seems like forever before he says,

"Come with me."

I'm sure I am breaking every good princess rule, but I follow him as curiosity overcomes me. He takes my hand and leads me out of the ballroom, through the royal gardens, and into the west wing of the castle.

"Where are we going?"

He looks back at me. "Just to the library."

I frown.

Actually, I don't think I have ever been to the royal library. As a slave, I was never permitted.

We walk through long, towering hallways, and the only sound I hear is the swishing of my extravagant skirts and my heels.

Finally, we walk into a three-story-high library, and I suck in a breath. Books as far as the eye can see, it seems like, and massive pillars accenting the brilliant architecture. This is a museum, not a library.

"Over here." His voice echoes off the towering walls.

I follow, only to come face to face with a high wall full of massive portraits. They are amazing in detail and are clearly the family's royal line on the display. "Oh wow," I murmur.

Tarren nods. "This is the House of Garthorn royal family, and a few others."

He points to a high picture of a man in a dark cloak with a sapphire crown in his hand. His eyes are a brilliant green and the long, snowy beard gives him a wizard's appeal.

"Who is he?"

"He is the legend of Garthorn."

I glance at him to expound.

Tarren takes a moment to stare at it. "He was the start of the rule of the

161

Garthorn family centuries ago, a blessing and a curse.

"As legends have it, our Garthorn ancestor made a deal with a powerful warlock. Aloin Xadalf was said to be so powerful he could grant whatever the heart desired if you wanted it badly enough.

"So Hayden Garthorn, a mere peasant at the time, sought him out in the dark of the night. He pleaded with Xadalf to grant his family riches beyond imagination.

"He would do anything for this, and Xadalf saw his raw desire," Tarren says, and glances at me.

"Is that true?"

"If it is," he spreads his arms wide to showcase the castle, "it definitely worked, eh?

"But the legend also says that with this great gift came great responsibility — always a catch. Aloin Xadalf does nothing for free or without meaning."

I swallow.

"Every firstborn will inherit the power of the beast, or so the legend states. Great power will run through the blood of this child and fester if not treated with care.

"Now this power will either be a blessing or a curse to the chosen king, the next in line. The child must overcome such darkness to keep this," he waves his hands around again, "alive.

"Once the beast inside is tamed, it will blossom into the great power only a king should possess."

I glance back up to the picture and note the sly grin on Aloin's face. "So you're saying every king up here has had the curse?"

Tarren shrugs. "That would be a correct assessment, seeing how we are all still here."

"And they all had to overcome the beast within?" I'm trying to understand.

"Well, yes. Once the born leader transforms himself in a positive light, I guess it breaks the curse for that generation.

"That is why every firstborn is carefully looked after with the utmost care. Teaching them right from wrong, preparing them to overcome the darkness. Our Garthorn heritage depends on it."

~Beauty and the beast, anyone?~

"Interesting," I murmur. "So Apollo is next in line."

"Yes," he says, and looks at me.

I take a breath. "And he is not doing so well, I take it?"

"No."

I look at him, feeling almost panicked. Now I understand why this ~world~ is in the red on the Fairy Godmother charts.

"It's not Apollo's fault, per se. I believe over the generations the teachings have become lazy, forgetting what we were founded on and what could be at stake. Now the King is sick, and I fear Apollo is not ready.

"For a long time, this legend was kept a secret, but I'm afraid not any longer. Every kingdom knows what it means when Apollo finally creates an heir.

"The child will be powerful, just as Apollo is. The child can either be good or evil, and unfortunately, there are a lot of unsavory people who would love his seed."

"They want his child," I say to myself.

"Correct. That is why I nearly fell off my chair when I heard of the engagement. This is huge, and everyone knows it. His wife must be pure of heart, without evil intentions, or this will be the downfall of Garthorn."

I see now why this engagement is a big deal. "That's a lot to take in."

He tilts his head at me. "I would have thought this was common knowledge by now. I'm actually shocked you have not heard of this. Usually slaves know everything, despite their position."

~Yeah.~ It would have been nice if Pierce had filled me in on this little tidbit. Mort is probably wondering where the hell I'm at.

"We have to stop the engagement," I say, and glance up at him.

He looks at me. "We do?"

I try to think fast. "I do not get good vibes from the Queen of Galleon."

"Queen Irena?" he asks. "She has always been lovely with me, but I am not around enough to know for sure."

"Just a hunch. I think it's worth looking into. I mean, this is serious!" I might be panicking. I do not want a poor, innocent child to be taken and created into a monster, especially not Apollo's child.

The boy would probably have curly blonde hair and golden skin like his father. Innocent. My heart clenches at the thought.

He chuckles. "Yes, I agree, but I do like the House of Galleon. They have always been righteous and fair. I'm surprised you would find your newfound family not to your liking."

The dad's great. Not his whore of a wife.

"My father seems like a great man, but it's just his wife that I am wary of. I am usually a really good judge of character."

Actually, that's a lie. I am the worst judge of character. I would probably let a rapist into my house because he just ~needed~ to use the phone. After all, his car broke down.

I would probably ignore his flannel shirt and blood-stained jeans. Who am I to judge?

He nods and stares at me. "Well, good thing he is not marrying her but your stepsister."

I bite my lip. "True, but you know Irena can have much influence." I dislike

Laura, but I do not think she is evil. She just wants to win Apollo.

Technically we are all on the same team, but I fear that Laura will not be bold enough to stand up to Irena. Laura should turn her own mother in as a fraud for the good of Fairy Godmother Inc.

But Laura is vain, meaning she would no longer be a princess. I need to find Ivy. She might have an idea who Queen Irena is sweet on, being a spy and all.

"So you see why I taunt Apollo."

That pulled me out of my thoughts. "I don't understand."

"I am fine with Apollo marrying Laura if that's what he wants. But I have a hunch that he feels something deeper for you," he says, and reaches out to touch a silky black strand of my hair.

"You are quite an eye-catcher — mouthwatering, in fact. And, not to sound too forward, I would love a chance to win your heart if Apollo chooses Laura."

I blush, not sure what to say.

"I am taunting Apollo into jealousy, hoping he will make the right decision in the end. Apollo is a very selfless person despite his privileged position.

"Hence marrying a woman, he does not love for the better of the kingdom. Well, I'm assuming anyway. Apollo has always made sure my family was well taken care of, and for that, I own him a debt.

"He will not let me repay him or say thank you simply. He takes care of his family, even extended, without any praise for it. So this is my silent way of saying thank you, even if he does not see it now."

He sighs as his eyes travel over me. "He owes me a big one after this, though. I am showing him a little tough love, hoping in the end he will see what I was trying to accomplish.

"Apollo needs to change his heart to be free of the beast, and true love might just do that."

I took a second to regain my thoughts. "You think he loves me?"

"I don't know, but he is acting very out of character." He glances back to the royal family on display. "Allow me to take you on a carriage ride tomorrow morning as if I'm courting you."

"But you're not."

He wipes his hand down his face as he groans. "I wish I was, my lady. I wish I was. Like I said, if Apollo chooses wrong, please allow me a chance to win your heart for real." He looks very serious.

I smile at him. "Of course."

His handsome features brighten. "Perfect. Plan A: Make Apollo jealous beyond reason. Plan B: If all fails, you have me."

I laugh, despite the conversation. "Agreed."

We chuckle together like we are little kids.

"Cousin," comes a booming voice.

We both tense.

I turn to see Apollo leaning against the entrance frame.

His shirt is unbuttoned at the neck, and his hair is tousled like he was running his hands through his hair like a mad man. To be frank, he looks drunk.

"Apollo!" Tarren shouts and winks at me, looking a little nervous. "I was just leaving. I have an appointment. Do you think you can escort Princess Ursula back to the ballroom?"

Apollo tilts his head and chuckles. The sound is cold. "I'm sure I can manage that."

"Great." Tarren moves to leave. "Until tomorrow morning." He bows and kisses my hand.

It feels like forever watching Tarren leave, each step an eternity. Now, I am here alone with Apollo, staring at me with an expression I can't read but still makes me shiver.

"You fancy him?" he asks suddenly.

I look down, then back up. "That's none of your concern."

He pushes off the doorway and walks toward me, making me back up. My pulse jumps as I feel my back hit the wall behind me.

"Are you attempting to make me jealous?" he asks, stopping right in front of me.

"The thought never occurred to me. I find Tarren charming and handsome." I raise my chin. I hope he can't see the pulse beating against my neck.

Apollo glances away then back to me with a grin. "You're joking?"

"No, and that's rude that you think so."

Apollo's dark gaze lowers to my neck then to my cleavage. "Tarren would not know what to do with a woman like you."

I laugh. "Oh really, and you do? You're extremely arrogant."

Is it getting hot in here?

"I would barely have to touch you to get you on fire," he murmurs, his black gaze devouring my body.

I take a steady breath. "Are you just proving the fact that you have an enlarged ego?"

"You calling my bluff?"

I am already hot, and he has not even touched me yet.

No, I do not call his bluff.

I dart out of his reach, standing behind the large desk like a lunatic.

"What are you doing?" he asks with a frown.

"Keeping arm's length between us."

He chuckles like he knows why, and graces me with a look that would make any female with hormones faint. His messed-up hair and his beautiful golden skin exposed is making me lightheaded.

I just want to inhale his scent and kiss his smooth jawline. And maybe unbutton his shirt and kiss all the way down to his belt buckle and…

My cheeks are flushed.

~Get a grip.~

I shake my head. "You're engaged, Apollo. We can't be a thing when you're promised to another, and you know that," I say.

Am I out of breath? I can't seem to get enough oxygen.

"I can do what I want," he says, and walks toward me.

"I know nothing about you."

He raises a brow and stands in front of the desk. "What would you like to know?"

"What's your favorite color?"

Apollo tilts his head. "I want payment for your questions."

I narrow my eyes.

"You must undo a button for every question." He shrugs like it's no big deal.

"I don't need to know your favorite color that bad," I shoot back.

"I am going to get you out of your clothes anyway, so you may as well get some questions out of it. My favorite color is green." He flicks his hand in my direction. "Unbutton or remove something."

I laugh, never having seen a more arrogant male in my life. I think for a second and bite my lip. I will play for a short time — not enough to get myself into trouble.

Those are not famous last words.

I take a large pin out of my hair, and the top half comes tumbling down my back. My hair is long, reaching to my butt. I have always been proud of it.

"I'll take that," he groans as his eyes seem to come to life, making me nervous. It's like preparing fresh meat in front of a hungry lion. The way he is looking at me, I might as well be naked.

"Your turn."

He smiles wide. "I'd love to play. What are you hiding still?"

I roll my eyes. "Try again."

He leans up against a large leather sofa, and he thinks. "How far back can you remember from your life?"

I stop and ponder that. In my real life, my memories start late for some reason, maybe I had trauma? But my earliest memory is about six years old, and I do not know why.

I can't remember my mother or anything to do with my youngest years. It's probably not a big deal, but it does bother me that I cannot remember anything from when I was four or five.

"Angel?"

"Oh," I laugh, "I can't remember much, just my time being a slave. Maybe it will come back to me someday."

"Maybe," he says suspiciously.

"Take something off," I order. This is probably—most likely—not a good idea, my brain warns. But I'm not listening at the moment. Please leave a message after the ~beeeeeep~.

Apollo stands up straight, and with one swift movement, he removes his dress shirt. He stands in a tight black body-armor undergarment that hugs every ripple and bulge of his torso. I swallow.

He is insanely beautiful. Like, if GQ and Sports Illustrated had a magazine baby, he'd be their cover star.

He is grinning again. "Your turn, Angel."

I lick my lips, my mouth dry. "What is your favorite childhood memory?"

His eyes widen. "Childhood memory?"

I grin. "Yes, Apollo. You were once a non-jaded little boy, weren't you?"

He leans back against the couch, his muscles bulging as he crosses his arms.

"My mother became ill when I was about twelve or so. So my father and I set out on an epic journey to find the rare flower that only blossoms at the top of mount Urnon. It was just us two, no guards.

"We camped under the open stars, cooked food by the fire, and he shared stories of our ancestors. It was the best adventure for a young lad to experience, something I have not thought of in a long while."

He stares at his feet as if he is reliving the precious memory.

"How long?"

"It took us seven days, and my mother returned to her full health," he says, and looks up at me. "Take off two things, my lady."

"Two?!"

He smiles, and I can almost see the young boy he used to be. "You asked two questions."

I huff, making him chuckle. If he weren't so insanely sexy, I would tell him to go to hell, but seeing how I'm affected by my vain womanly parts, I will oblige. "I need help."

Apollo jumps up and is behind me faster than I can process what I'm doing. I feel his fingers on the back of my neck, and I close my eyes.

I feel him unbutton one, then two.

"You are so beautiful, I can barely think when I'm around you," he whispers into my skin. A part of me is unsure if I am mentally ready to hear Apollo speak this way. It messes me up.

"I feel like you have infected me with something that I cannot purge. As much as I try to fight it, I can't. It's driving me mad. I don't even recognize myself."

I swallow.

Is he being serious? Or just telling me what I want to hear?

"Cancel the engagement then."

"Done."

I whip around and back up, staring up at his handsome face. "Done?"

"Done."

I take a breath. "You're canceling the engagement?"

"I want you, and if that's how I get you, then I will," he admits, taking a step forward. "I'll be damned if I let my cousin have what's mine. I want to be selfish for once."

"But I'm not yours."

Should I pull a princess Jasmine? ~I am not a prize to be won!~

"Not yet, Angel, but you will be."

A thrill shoots up my spine, and my skin ignites. Somehow, I can't disagree with him, and my brain is doing a sexy tango right now with the image of Apollo. Should I trust him?

Fool me once, shame on you. Fool me twice, shame on me. Fool me a third time?

He must be really hot, and it's not your fault.

~There, there.~

CHAPTER 17

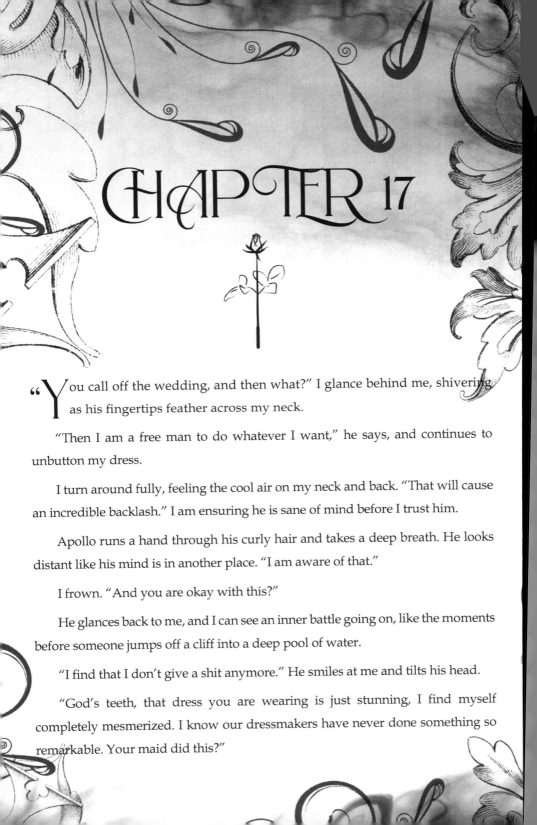

"You call off the wedding, and then what?" I glance behind me, shivering as his fingertips feather across my neck.

"Then I am a free man to do whatever I want," he says, and continues to unbutton my dress.

I turn around fully, feeling the cool air on my neck and back. "That will cause an incredible backlash." I am ensuring he is sane of mind before I trust him.

Apollo runs a hand through his curly hair and takes a deep breath. He looks distant like his mind is in another place. "I am aware of that."

I frown. "And you are okay with this?"

He glances back to me, and I can see an inner battle going on, like the moments before someone jumps off a cliff into a deep pool of water.

"I find that I don't give a shit anymore." He smiles at me and tilts his head.

"God's teeth, that dress you are wearing is just stunning, I find myself completely mesmerized. I know our dressmakers have never done something so remarkable. Your maid did this?"

I swallow. "Yes, quite the talent she has."

He nods, his dark gaze seeing too much.

I am nervous all of a sudden. It seems like he is still wary of me.

Which I guess I do not blame him for—the gown really looks like it's made from magic, let's be honest. I might have to tell Pierce to tone it down a bit.

I have no idea what Apollo's intentions are. I thought I did, but now I am second-guessing myself. I feel like he is baiting me or trying to trap me.

Here I thought he wanted a quick lay, but now I am not sure.

"You're wondering what I'm thinking?" He smiles and leans back against the wall casually.

I bite my lip, trying to ignore how hot he is. "I would say that I am curious."

He holds up his finger. "One. I want you naked." He holds up two fingers. "Two. I want you to tell me who the hell you are."

I stare at him.

"It does not matter in what order." He grins again.

"I am a princess now, you cannot threaten me like before," I hiss, and narrow my eyes.

"I can if you want to be my wife."

That takes me off guard. I think my mouth is hanging open. "Excuse me?"

He looks like he is having a great time. "I want to know what I'm marrying. I think that is understandable."

"You don't know if I even want to marry you!" I think my face is red. "You are even more arrogant than I thought!"

~I do want to marry you, but that's not the point!~

He laughs. "You're glorious when you're mad."

I take a deep breath, a calming breath. "I am not mad. I am just shocked by
173

how sure of yourself you are."

He raises a brow. "I am very," he pauses as if thinking for the right word, "observant. You want me, Angel."

I roll my eyes. "Yes, you are quite handsome—"

"Thank you," he says, smiling.

"I was not finished," I say. "I know you're handsome, but that does not mean I want to marry an overconfident ass."

Whoops.

I clamp my mouth shut.

He looks hurt, in a mocking way. "Well then. What is it that you want in a husband? Please enlighten me."

"Smart, funny, compassionate." I pause with a grin. "Humble."

"You think I'm not humble?"

I pause. "I am actually not sure, but around me, no."

He walks up to me and lifts my chin. His dark gaze glitters in the dim lighting. "That's because I'm not."

I frown.

"Or maybe I just like to see you lose control," he says with a wink.

"You taunt me then?"

He makes a guilty face. "I will neither confirm nor deny."

I fight a smile.

He is so charming with this innocent act that my defenses start to fall. He is teasing me in the most addicting way.

"Can we continue our game?"

I laugh. "Why do you want me as a wife?"

174

Apollo walks over to the couch and sits down, his large frame taking up most of it. "Why do I want you? That's a loaded question." He tilts his head as he looks me up and down.

"Because you're different from the others. Mysterious, passionate, with the most seductive eyes I have ever beheld. I know you have secrets, that there is more to you than you're letting on, but I still want you as my wife."

He pauses and smiles. "I always want the best. I am the best at everything, and that will never change. I need a woman to match me in every way."

"You're taunting me."

His eyes are alight with mischief.

I try to glare at him, not wanting to get caught in his snare. "I see."

He sits up on the couch. "You need help undressing?"

I bite my lip to keep from grinning. "No."

He groans. "Hurry, woman."

I sit down on the couch across from him and hike up my sparkling skirts. He watches my hands like I'm defusing a bomb.

I expose my thighs, where my lace stockings show, and I think I hear him say something.

"Higher."

I raise a brow, my pulse jumping.

"Let me help," he suggests with a gruff tone.

I think I nod.

Apollo is in front of me before I can even blink my eyes. His large frame is now pushing my legs apart, and he is kneeling between my thighs.

"I think you're cheating," I say breathlessly.

His platinum hair is in wild disarray, and mixed with his abnormal eyes, it's lethal. A dangerous concoction for the female libido.

He is so close I can smell the wild scent of him. The heat from his body is almost burning me. I take a shaky breath, and somewhere in the back of my mind, I know this is checkmate.

I suck in a sharp breath when I feel his lips on my neck, jaw, then down to my cleavage. My head falls back, and I am in a different time and place — a place where only intense bliss is felt.

Apollo grabs the back of my head, and his hot mouth claims mine aggressively. I don't back down, and I meet every sweep of his tongue in my mouth. He tastes delicious, like dark red wine.

Our mouths mold and move in a seductive dance that has me out of my mind with desire. I hear him groan into my mouth as he pulls me closer to him.

"Shirt!" I pull back and shout before his mouth scorches a trail down my neck. "Take y-your shirt off."

I hear him laugh. "So bossy," he whispers. "You owe me a question, Angel," he breathes into my neck as his tongue swirls around my pulse.

I can barely think, let alone answer a question.

If I didn't know any better, I would say he's taking advantage of me.

"Where did you come from?" he whispers into my ear. "Tell me, Angel." His hand traces up to my thigh and squeezes my butt cheek hard, urging me to answer. "I want the truth."

"I am the lost princess. Now kiss me," I moan.

I feel his gaze on me, and I refuse to look at him, or he will see that I'm full of shit. I feel his hand moving, and I gasp when he touches me ~there. ~I sigh when I feel his lips back on my neck.

He starts to work me like the man does this for a living. His fingers are deep within me, and again he presses me.

"Tell me where you came from," he says with force, his harsh breaths burning my skin.

I barely hear him as my body hums with such intense sensations that I think he is using some sort of black magic. No man can be that good with his hands, right? I thought that sort of thing was only in romance books.

"Where are you from?"

I feel the pressure build, and my thoughts are disconnected. At this point, I'm not even sure where I am right now, much less before.

I feel Apollo's tongue on my neck as his hand works me, and that seems to do the trick. I am going to have an orgasm close to an atomic bomb, ladies and gentlemen. Don't be jealous.

But then…

He stops.

How dare he!

"Where are you from, Angel?!"

"What does it matter? I'm here now!" I clamp my mouth shut, my breathing still harsh and uneven.

"What does it matter?! I think it matters a lot," he says, his gaze seeming to change. A wave of fear breaks through the haze of lust.

I try to move, but he holds me in place.

"Answer."

I lift my chin. "Get away from me."

He smiles, but it's cold. "Will you tell me if I do this?"

He leans his blonde head down and licks up my calf through my lace hose, lifting my leg. My breathing catches, and I feel his hot tongue caress its way up my leg. I don't stop him. I can't.

"I know what you're doing!" I pant in pleasure. "It won't work!"

~It might work.~

"We will see," he breathes into my inner thigh. "You're exquisite."

I think I scream when I feel his mouth on my lady bits, and let me tell you, his tongue is better than his fingers, something I didn't think was possible.

The ABCs are for amateurs, because this man is licking in different ancient languages — lost Egyptian hieroglyphs.

Nope. I'm not lasting long.

This man is going in for the kill this time.

Pleasure explodes inside my body, and I'm transported to a new dimension. Lights and fireworks explode in my belly, and I am left limp as a rag doll.

He is amazing — no denying that he is probably good at everything he does.

"Tell me."

"I can't." I barely move my mouth.

My eyes shoot open. I'm such an idiot. Moron! I just basically told him I am not what I seem by my idiot response.

~I can't?! ~Why could I not have said, "~I can't because there is nothing to tell?"~ But it was the way I said it like I wanted to…but couldn't.

"You admit you're hiding something then?" He is staring down at me, his chest rising and falling.

"No, it means I can't because there is nothing to tell."

Worth a shot.

"Liar."

I jerk my legs away, but he grabs me again. He licks his lips and tilts his head. "My little Angel, you're not going anywhere."

"You can't always get what you want, Apollo," I say, still coming off my high.

178

He chuckles. "Oh, yes I can."

"How?"

Not sure why I asked that.

"I will not marry you until you tell me who you are. I must have all honesty, and I think you know why. Or I will be forced to choose another." He is not smiling anymore.

This is not fair.

I need to talk to Mort.

I don't think I am able to tell Apollo that I am an agent for Fairy Godmother Inc. And, if I did, I think he would lock me up in a mental intuition.

"So I take it that you're not taking off your shirt?" I say with a pout.

He gives me a look I cannot not read, but his gaze is intense. "If you tell me who you are, I will make it worth it."

He leans back to show me his insane protruding package through his black pants. I swallow hard~. This is so not fair~. I think I'm getting hot flashes. Early signs of a stroke?

Apollo, naked in all his glory, is ~a lot~.

I think I lose my voice.

He adjusts himself with a smirk. "Tell me, Angel, and I'm yours."

~I'm yours~, he says.

I feel anger.

I don't even know what to tell him that won't get me into trouble. I squeeze my eyes shut and bite my lip, drawing blood. I can taste the copper tinge lacing through my mouth.

I want him so bad it hurts, and there is nothing I can do about it.

I feel his lips on mine, making my eyes snap open. "Don't draw blood, Angel,

179

just tell me. You can trust me. I want you just as bad as you want me," he whispers into my mouth.

I sit up, and he laces his arms around my waist, as if scared I will flee.

"I need time," I whisper.

He is breathing deeply. "You're scared to tell me?"

I stare at him.

"Are you in trouble?" His tone is turning forceful.

"No."

"Are you against the House of Garthorn or are you for us?" he asks carefully.

He is really fishing for answers, though I don't blame him one bit.

"I am not against anyone."

He frowns. "Then why not tell me?"

I look away. "I just need time, Apollo."

I feel his energy. He is holding back. "All right. But I will not cancel the engagement until you confide in me. The woman I marry will have zero secrets from me."

I cringe. Don't marry Laura then.

"Apollo," I say. He gets up, and I look up at him. "I am harmless, if that means anything."

He huffs. "I will be the judge of that, Angel."

"You're leaving?"

He walks to the door and glances over his shoulder, adjusting his pants and hair. "If I stay here any longer, I will not be able to keep my warning. Tell your dressmaker to have mercy on me."

And with that, he left.

Well shit. Don't mind me while I cry myself to sleep tonight.

I sit up and tap my chin. Time to find Mort and figure this backstory out. I need to know my options before I can play my cards.

Apollo will not stop, he will press me for answers again, and I'm not sure if I'm strong enough to withstand his seduction tactics.

Time to put on some big girl panties.

Well, like cute boy shorts that are sexy and strong simultaneously. You know, the ones that make your butt cheeks look great without looking too girly.

Maybe, I don't know, Wonder Woman Marvel comic ones.

Yea, those ones.

CHAPTER 18

"**Y**ou bitch!"

I wake up to a glass being thrown at my headboard. The crash vibrates through my disconnected thoughts as I jerk awake, heart pounding.

Mort left my room late last night, saying she needed to talk to Pierce about my dire situation. So I have no one around me to shield me from Ms. Crazy.

"Laura! What in the hell are you—"

A large vase is hurled at my bed, barely missing me and shattering into a million pieces. "You little whore!"

I sit up in bed and hold my arms out. "Laura, calm down. What happened?!" I ask, making her laugh hysterically.

"I love him! You do not!" she shouts, her blueberry gown not complimenting her flushed features.

"You are messing up my life! I am a princess here about to marry the man of my dreams! My other life back home sucked and I won't let you take this away from me!"

A maid comes rushing in, and I think it's her agent. Laura looks like a bull who is ready to charge at the slightest flash of red.

"Laura," her agent says. "Come with me and we will figure out a plan."

"A plan?" I ask as I look from Laura to her agent. "Can someone tell me what's going on?!"

Laura takes a loud inhale and exhale, adjusting her dress and hair.

"I know what you did with Apollo last night—with an engaged man! I have won, Viola! We are to be married and you are messing it up!" She takes steps toward me.

"We are in love, and I don't need you trying to break us up!"

"Laura, this is a competition for three months. We are almost in our last month here! Just because you have an engagement doesn't mean you've won," I say through gritted teeth.

She shakes her head. "I know men. He is in love with me. But men are all hot-blooded, and when you flaunt yourself in front of him, he goes with his animal instincts. Any man would!

"You're just a whore! Fairy Godmother Inc. needs to stop hiring sluts and they might finish a lot more missions! Any sweet words he might tell you to get into your panties are lies.

"That's why I still have the marriage proposal. You are only good enough to get his lust, not love!" She is turning an alarming shade of purple.

I am getting pissed now. Her ego is surpassing her pink, sparkly brain.

Mort comes charging into the room and glares at Laura, then the other agent. "Leenie. Pierce says break it up, this is a violation of code B-5." Mort glares at the agent.

"You should know this. Laura, if you cannot contain yourself, you will be ejected from the game. This is a competition, and if you cannot handle that, then you may use all of your lifelines and leave Delorith."

Mort smiles. "You may not under any circumstance bring the Fairy Godmother into any heated discussion. Pierce says this is a warning."

Mort glances at the agent. "Leenie, you need to log on and Pierce will have a word with you."

She hisses at Mort and leaves.

Laura is mentally slaughtering Mort to pieces with her death stare. "Of course," she grits out. Laughter bubbles out of her throat as she glances back at me.

"If this is competition, then I'm your worst nightmare," she threatens. "If you do not back down from my~ fiancé~ then I will make your life a living hell."

"Laura," Mort warns.

"Goodbye, Viola. I have a lovely carriage ride with ~MY ~fiancé this morning." She beams. "He found me and presented me with gorgeous flowers.

"It shocks me how beautiful this world is, so different from our own. It was all quite romantic—I am even blushing thinking about it.

"He is just so strong and handsome, and when he kissed me, I felt an electric current between us. I really think he is taking things slow with us, trying to do it right.

"We are really getting to know one another before we make the physical connection. I think this next month we will take the relationship to the next level." She laughs as if she is reliving the bliss of it.

"So, I am sorry for the drama I caused, but I just want to warn you that he only sees you for your body, as any hot-blooded male would.

"He wants more from me, and I don't want you hurt, despite how much I dislike you. Men will say anything to get under a woman's skirts. It's just a means to an end for them—it means nothing."

My mouth is hanging open.

Mort walks up to her. "Leave."

Laura nods and dusts something off her puffed sleeve. "Heed my warning, Viola," she whispers, pausing at the door. "Breasts are just breasts, and a vagina is just that, but the heart is so much more."

After she leaves, deafening silence drifts around us.

Mort sighs. "That's a horrible saying."

"I know," I say as I frown. "Breasts are just breasts? And what about the vagina?"

Mort smiles. "I think she said the heart is more than a vagina."

We both have a good laugh, then lay back on the bed. I look over to Mort and exhale. "Laura made some points that are bugging me."

Mort bites her lip. "Can you trust her though? She is clearly threatened."

"Are they going for a carriage ride?"

Mort sits up and starts typing. "I can see if Leenie has logged it in. She does not have to log activities, but some do to rub it onto other agent's faces on their progress. I am willing to bet she will be logging this."

Mort is silent for a few more seconds then, "Yes, they are."

"That asshole!"

What is Apollo up to?!

Mort glances at me slyly. "Didn't Tarren say he wanted to have a carriage ride with you this morning? Apollo could be trying to blackmail you into revealing your secret. Just a hunch."

I smile. "Blackmail? I think you mean taunt me into a jealous rage and tell him everything. And yes, Tarren did."

Mort types more. "Pierce says you are not allowed to talk about Fairy

Godmother Inc. until the end."

"What?" I glance at her.

"We normally do not disclose this information until the end, but this is a unique situation.

"At the end of the three months, we tell the man in question the truth. And on the last day, if he comes for you, it is a testament of his love and happily-ever-after.

"If he does not, we fail. We cannot have lies in the end, so we always reveal everything." Mort looks at me.

"Wait—so in the past, this has worked? You tell the prince the woman he has fallen in love with is from a different planet? And he is cool with that?" I ask, disbelieving. It's a recipe for disaster.

"In most cases, it has worked out perfectly, but in some cases, it was a little more difficult. But when the man truly loves the woman, he does not care where she comes from, and that's how we know it's true love."

She gets up and walks to the window.

"Huh," is all I say.

"Yeah, so you will tell him eventually, just not right now," she says, still staring out the large bay window.

"Sure is a pretty day today. A great day to make Apollo Augustus Garthorn jealous out of his mind. The prick."

I smile at Mort.

Apollo asked Laura for a carriage ride? Not sure what he is trying to do but I know I am not going to fall prey to the jealousy game without a battle.

I will fight fire with fire.

"Mort, send a message to Tarren. I would love a carriage ride."

***

"Pierce, do your worst."

Mort is typing and nodding while eating a cheese pastry, crumbs falling as she works.

"Pierce says he has a stunning riding habit he has constructed for you." She swallows painfully. "I helped with the hat."

"Awesome," I say, and nod to her pastry. "Drink something, you look like you're going to choke."

"Yeah, these are a little dry." Mort's plain features contort into something thoughtful. "I was sure these were the fresh ones, but now that I think about it, I might have grabbed this off the throw-away tray.

"Destiny usually perfects these things. The cake she made the other day was out of this world." She shrugs and takes the last bite, looking like a squirrel. "Okay, you know the drill. Spin."

I am excited. It's like a fantasy dress-up game to seduce an insanely hot prince. Only this is real life and there is no guarantee that the prince will love me in the end.

There is no assurance that everything will work itself out like a romantic movie. But like most girls, I want my fairy tale ending, and I'm willing to go out of my comfort zone to do it.

I spin and feel that familiar tingle coursing through my body — the excitement.

Mort had a lot of fabric delivered to her quarters. Questions were being asked about the stunning dresses that she was seemingly making. So she had to make it believable, saying she exclusively designed for me.

I'm sure Apollo will be looking into anything concerning me, trying to find a rip in my perfect storyline.

I glance in the body-length mirror and suck in a breath. I could probably do this every second and always be shocked like this. Pierce is a master at what he does, plain and simple.

I stand in the most beautiful, form-fitting riding attire I have ever seen.

My tailored coat is the color of smooth cream in a shiny fabric, almost like silk but durable. My long skirts are also a glistening cream, elegant and exquisite.

But what brings a splash of romance is the accents of bright red lace. The two together make a stunning couple, one bringing out the other.

My red lace gloves are to die for, and my deep scarlet corset under my riding coat will have Apollo's head spinning.

I grin.

My shadowed eyes seemed to glow under the wide brim of the blood-red hat with a large cream bow tilted to the side impeccably. ~My, my.~ I look like Madam Viola, Sin City mob wife.

"I would have never picked these colors out myself," I say.

Mort nods and stands next to me. "If you let Pierce do his thing, you will be the belle of the ball.

"From what I hear, Laura instructs Pierce on what to make. I'm not surprised," she continues with a pointed look. "You cannot tell an artist what to do, they do not thrive in boxes."

"Did you just make that up?"

"Yes." She glances at me. "It sounded better in my head."

I nod.

A knock at the door makes me tense. Mort runs over and opens the large double doors to find a letter addressed to me. The footman hands it to Mort.

I try to snatch it out of her hands, but she darts out of the way, opening it. "Mort! Bad Mort!"

"It's a letter from Tarren saying you all are double dating with Apollo and

Laura," she gets out before I snatch the letter.

"Double date? Perfect!" I laugh and high-five Mort. "What is Laura wearing?"

Mort rolled her eyes. "I saw it—it's not as good as yours! She made Pierce make her a baby-blue and pink riding habit. Looks pretty, but almost overkill. Yours is sexy, hers is pretty."

"You think that's what she is trying to go for? Respectable? Not slutty?" I ask. Mine is not slutty, but I will say it will get the blood pumping.

Mort laughs. "Since when did plain pretty ever get the guy? I think you will have every man from a hundred-mile radius trying to get your attention.

"Laura is not playing her cards right. We don't have a year to win him over but a month!"

"You sure?"

"Blondes do not get all the fun, that's a myth."

"Thanks, Mort."

"You're welcome, human."

Once I leave my room, I am followed by six guards and five maids, including Mort. All eyes are on me, and I faintly wonder if this was Queen Irena's doing.

I might as well be queen for all the fuss over me.

Whatever.

I look killer in my riding outfit, and I am going to play the part despite Laura. I walk with my head held high and descend the massive staircase as I pull up half of my shimmering skirts.

As I round a large pillar that the stairs wrap around, I suddenly see two incredible male specimens at the bottom.

I feel a bit lightheaded when I see Apollo's magnificent figure come into focus. I do not linger though and focus my attention on Tarren who is looking handsome

189

in light gray riding finery.

I feel my skin prickle as I near them, and my heart misses beats with every shaky breath.

Why do I always do this when Apollo is present?

I can see Tarren's eyes widen when his gaze travels over my body. Another one knocked out of the ballpark for Pierce. I hear Laura's voice and I can't look just yet; I just focus on Tarren.

If I look at Apollo, I might make a fool of myself and stutter or something. I would not put it past me to yell something incoherent.

I hear Apollo murmur pleasantries with Laura, and my smile just widens as I stare at Tarren. He takes my scarlet glove and brings his lips to it.

"You are jaw-dropping," he says with a wink.

I can't say anything, feeling eyes on us.

"Sister," I hear Laura say from behind me.

It takes everything I have in my body to turn my head in her direction.

~Smile, idiot.~

I force a smile and see Laura's innocent blue eyes, all doe-like.

She is hanging on Apollo's arm like they have been lovers for forever. Apollo is leaning slightly against the wall looking amused, a ghost of a smirk on his handsome features.

Gosh, he is sexy. There is no other way to describe him with his easy swagger and arrogance. The expression on his face says, ~Tell me your secrets and this all stops, Angel...~

His gorgeous hair is tied back save for a few tantalizing curly strands, and his dark, forbidden gaze sears me. I feel his intensity as his gaze lowers, sweeping over my body.

My cheeks heat as I look at Laura's narrowed eyes. "Sister."

"What lovely riding habit," she says, "but I wonder if it is practical." She laughs lightly, but I can see jealousy in her eyes.

Tarren says, as he touches the tight fabric at my arm, "Stunning. Feels very durable to me." He tugs at the material jokingly.

I laugh and slap his hand. "My Lord, you'll rip it!"

"If it rips that easily, I will have to thank the dressmaker personally." He winks at me, the meaning well understood.

"Let us go before Tarren embarrasses himself anymore," says Apollo in a clipped tone.

Tarren laughs as we all make our way outside to see a magnificent open carriage fit for a king. Silver and sapphire adorn the carriage with glowing lights.

My adrenaline starts pumping when I see the six black horses pounding their hooves in anticipation.

"I take it last night went well?" Tarren whispers in my ear.

I slightly glance at him while Apollo helps Laura into the ride. I try not to blush under his stare. "I'm not sure, actually."

"Well," he nods at the driver as he passes by, "I only ask because I found Apollo drunk at four in the morning, pounding on my door."

My eyes widen. "You're kidding," I hiss.

"No. He was out of his mind, to put it mildly. And threatened that if I ever touched you. he would cut out my tongue. It was all very charming.

"So it makes me wonder if you're really that ~good~, and if I should risk getting my tongue cut out for you."

I stare at him.

"I'll take your silence that it went very well." He continues with a whisper,

"Apollo has never done that, by the way. Atta girl."

Apollo jumps down from the carriage, his black attire giving him a sinister appeal, like the villain rather than the hero. His black-gloved hand urges Tarren to hurry.

"Are you waiting for me to help you up, Tarren?"

He laughs. "I thought you would never ask."

Apollo rolls his eyes and glances at me.

~His eyes.~

The wind blows his hair, and the sunlight kisses the side of his face perfectly. He is Adonis in the flesh. It is almost hard to pinpoint where he is looking due to his dark eyes making me shiver.

His lids lower , then raise with a slight tilt of his head. "Ready, Angel?" he barely says, I almost didn't hear him. I think I read his lips more than I heard him.

I walk up to him, and I feel the air around us crackle and spark. I look away and pretend to be indifferent. "Please, Your Grace, I do not need your assistance."

He smells delicious. A wild man musk that drives women to madness.

"Please, allow me. It would be my honor," he says, his voice like melted honey.

I glance up at Laura's pinched face.

"Do hurry up, dear sister. I think you have stolen enough time from my fiancé." She laughs, but her eyes are as sharp as a knife.

I raise a brow at Apollo, and he meets me with an expression I find hard to read. "Of course, I would not want to take up too much time."

Apollo grabs my hand, and it's rough. He lifts me up, and I feel his other hand much too low on my lower back. Well, on my butt, technically speaking.

I shoot him a murderous glance, and I catch a glimpse of humor before he sits next to Laura. He takes her hand in his and pats it, saying something to her, making her laugh.

Won't this be fun?

I keep my eyes away from Apollo and focus on Tarren, who looks like he is having the time of his life. Tarren grabs my hand and kisses it also in a mocking way.

"Don't they make such the splendid couple? I'm so happy to see the famed Apollo settle down finally."

I almost cringe.

I laugh and glance at the two, smiling my best feline smile. This smile is something I have worked on for a long time. Apollo sits up a little straighter, looking like he would love to strangle me.

"Yes, stunning," I say with a sweetness I'm sure will make Apollo vomit later.

Laura beams and grabs Apollo's muscled forearm through his fitted black coat. "Looks do not matter to me. It's what's on the inside that matters."

Tarren's mouth drops open. "Never have truer words been spoken, my dear."

I hold back a grin. And here I thought Laura would be competition. Does she not know how to ensnare a man? Though she is right in her thinking, voicing it out loud like this is a little much.

I think too much lovey-dovey emotional stuff seems to scare men off.

Just from observing couples throughout my life, the man always strays to the one that is hard to catch. Laura would benefit from not acting so submitted with him. Just my opinion, though.

But I will not be the one to point that out. Let her dig her own grave.

The large carriage lurches forward and a real smile spreads over my face. "Can we go fast?" I ask Tarren with a sheepish grin. I bet these horses can haul ass.

"Danger seeker?" comes Apollo's voice. I keep forgetting he has abnormal hearing.

I glance at him. "I like to go fast."

Apollo tilts his head and licks his lips, almost making me blush. "I'll keep that in mind," he says softly.

Laura frowns at him. "I would also like to go fast, for I am quite the horseman."

So Laura also has a talent for horseback riding. I mentally tally what I know — she has voice, boobs, and horseback riding. Well done, Laura.

Apollo glances at her. "I do not trust the driver. I will take over and show you some speed when we pull over."

"Apollo does not trust anyone," Tarren says matter-of-factly.

Apollo's gaze flickers to mine. "I have no choice."

Tarren nods.

Laura leans into him. "You can trust me."

My eyes widen.

Apparently, her agent did not tell her that she will have to tell Apollo the truth at the end of all of this. She will regret those words later. Well, if she wins, that is.

Apollo's jaw clenches, but he doesn't say anything.

After about an hour of riding around the city, I realize this place is out of a dream or a fantasy. It's like old-world beauty paired with some sort of supernatural power.

I will admit there is a certain darkness that surrounds this place. But I am surprised when we stop at a massive graveyard/garden maze.

I stand up to see it better — massive above-ground gravesites are spectacular and remind me of the famous graves in New Orleans.

"The royal graveyard of Garthorn," says Tarren.

"Is that a maze?" I ask in awe, my mouth hanging open. It looks like it's a few miles long! Towering green vines and walls of overgrown garden growth make a remarkable display.

Apollo stands up to help Laura down. "Yes, it's centuries old."

Laura's eyes are wide. "Are we going to go into the maze?"

Apollo grins. "Of course."

I let Apollo help me down after Laura, and my eyes fix on the massive maze in all its glory. "Are we going in pairs?"

Apollo grins down at me. "Alone."

CHAPTER 19

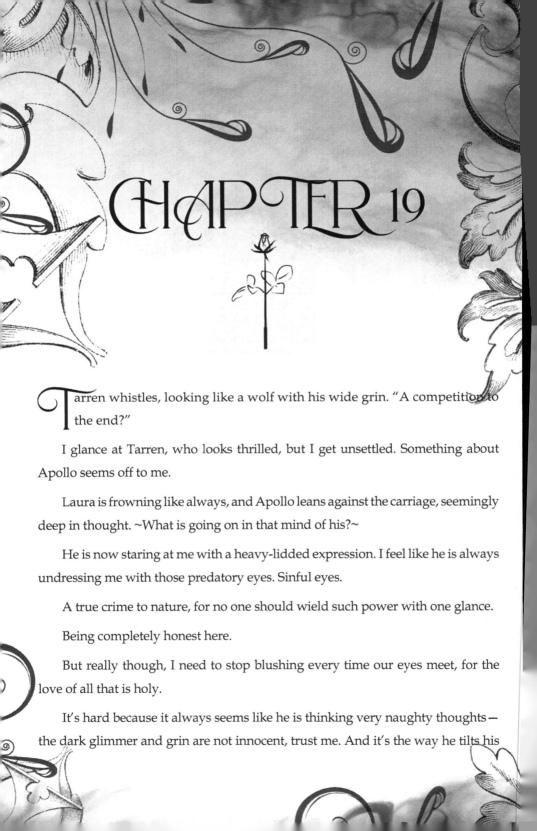

Tarren whistles, looking like a wolf with his wide grin. "A competition to the end?"

I glance at Tarren, who looks thrilled, but I get unsettled. Something about Apollo seems off to me.

Laura is frowning like always, and Apollo leans against the carriage, seemingly deep in thought. ~What is going on in that mind of his?~

He is now staring at me with a heavy-lidded expression. I feel like he is always undressing me with those predatory eyes. Sinful eyes.

A true crime to nature, for no one should wield such power with one glance.

Being completely honest here.

But really though, I need to stop blushing every time our eyes meet, for the love of all that is holy.

It's hard because it always seems like he is thinking very naughty thoughts — the dark glimmer and grin are not innocent, trust me. And it's the way he tilts his head and slightly licks his lower lip.

I mean, ~come on~.

Maybe if I picture him with a beer belly and a double chin.

Nope. Still hot.

"Ladies against men," Apollo says suddenly, gaining everyone's attention.

I take a shaky breath and fan my face. He needs to stop staring at me like I'm his next meal. Laura might stab me in my sleep tonight—one-hundred-plus wounds in a crazy stabbing frenzy. Bad blood.

She is trying hard not to look pissed, but her cheeks are flushed.

"Do we have to get split up?" Laura groans out, making Apollo break his stare on me. Apollo smiles at her and she falters, hands tying knots in her skirts.

~Uhhhh.~

I hate when he grins like that. I actually feel bad for Laura. Innocent victim. Laura looks like he just told her he loved her and wants her to have his babies.

"Are you not up for a little game, ~Laura~?" he asks and holds her prisoner with that dark stare.

I have to bite my lip and look the other way. Oh, he is ~good~. Apollo knows what he is doing, and she is absolute putty in his hands.

All he has to do is show her a little attention and she will jump as high as he says. It's like a bug flying toward the blinding light only to get brutally shocked to death.

She looks flustered. "Oh, well, I am actually very competitive."

Apollo stares at her. "Are you really?"

She laughs and places an awkward hand on her hip, probably not used to this much attention from Apollo. "Oh yes, by nature."

Tarren saves her by stepping forward, and the look on her face is pure relief.

"Perfect, Apollo. What are the rules to this devious little competition?"

"Simple." He shrugs. "We give the women a head start."

"Seems easy enough," Tarren says with a wicked smile. "If we catch the girls, do we get a kiss?"

Laura giggles. "I like the sound of that."

Meanwhile, Apollo's gaze is locked with Tarren's, and it does not look good from where I'm standing.

Tarren is taunting him, and it gives me a thrill that Apollo is acting that possessively over me. I will bet a thousand pounds this silent feud is not over Laura.

"I think that is fair," Apollo says carefully, still holding Tarren prisoner with his stare.

Tarren holds his gaze with a nod. "Perfect."

I clear my throat, trying to break up this alpha-male energy. "We just enter through there?" I point to the massive stone wall entrance with overgrown vines.

Laura glares at me and takes off her coat, throwing it on the ground. "We don't have to stick together, do we?"

Apollo unties his necktie like he is getting ready for a chase. "You can do what you want, my dear."

I see her shoot me a look before walking to the entrance. "May the best lady win then."

My heart starts to pound when I see Apollo take off his black coat and start cuffing up his white dress shirt, exposing his muscled forearms. "I will give you twenty minutes," he says in a breathy tone.

I look away, feeling lightheaded, and walk to the entrance, feeling a bit threatened. It is thrilling and a little terrifying. My lady parts are behaving like escaped lunatics in a lightning storm.

I peek back, and he mouths, "Run fast, Angel."

I glare at him, and he raises an arrogant brow. "Maybe I will let Tarren catch me," I say in a stupid taunt and turn fast, not wanting to see his expression.

A shiver licks its way down my back, but I refuse to look at Apollo.

Heart pounding, I glance at Laura. "Ready?"

She glances back and smiles. "Don't follow me." And she takes off into the entrance, taking a sharp right.

I hear Tarren's laughter as I run through the entrance in the opposite direction. I am running blind. I will be damned if Laura beats me to the end. I just hope this direction will not screw me.

The walls are towering with overgrown vegetation everywhere. Immediately I am transported to the ancient Mayan ruins of Mexico. A lot of stone and weird engravings carved into the walls.

Panic hits me.

Someone could really get lost in this place.

I keep running, turning left and right without pause. I jump over a large crack in the stone floor and keep up my pace.

The thought that Apollo will soon be on my tail makes me go faster. I would hate to see the arrogant smirk on his face.

I do not want him to catch me.

I want to catch him.

Breathing hard, I stop and think. Apollo is inhumanly strong and smart and probably knows this maze by heart.

"Shit," I mutter. He will catch me. There is no way I am outsmarting him in his territory, let alone anywhere at all.

I glance around at my surroundings, trying to think fast.

Here's an idea. I have always been quite the actress and could probably talk my way out of death row. I walk over to the stone wall and grab a vine, testing out the sturdiness of them.

"Oh crap," I say as I try to break one. These are probably stronger than a rope, which gives me a brilliant idea.

A thrill shoots up my spine as I work out my plan in my head. This is either stupid or very smart, though I think I know which one it is.

Smart, duh.

I quickly work the vines, getting a nice little pile ready.

Yes.

I will restrain Apollo, have a little fun, and make a clean break. I will finish and outsmart the amazing Apollo. Nothing can go wrong. I have it all worked out.

Famous last words? Nope.

I saw the carnal look in Apollo's gaze. He is hot and bothered. Off his game.

I hide the vines underneath me, like so.

You're probably wondering what in the hell I have planned. I have not worked it all out, but essentially, I will pretend my wrist is caught in the vines.

I am lying on my side and wait and wait for what feels like forever. I yell in the air like I'm in pain, and I know he is close. I can almost sense it.

There is a rock in my side and a stick poking my ass. He'd better hurry.

I am nervous now, my pulse hammering.

This will not work.

Yes, it will!

I tense when I hear something behind me, and I can't help but hold my breath.

"What do we have here?" Apollo's voice is smooth and low.

"Wipe the smile off your face and throw me a knife, my wrist is caught," I say like I'm upset. I should be nominated for an Emmy.

"Stuck?" he says, confusion lacing his voice. I hear him come closer and feel his knee beside me. "Let me see." He laughs.

"No, my pride will only allow me to free myself," I shoot back.

"Oh, forgive me, Your Highness." He is chuckling now, completely buying my unfortunate circumstance. "Don't cut yourself."

I reach behind me with one free hand. "Thank you."

"And to think Princess Laura is still making her way through the maze unscathed. I believe I lost a bet here," he taunts. "I thought you would demolish her."

I grit my teeth.

~You just wait, buddy.~

"Come closer. I am having trouble." I grab the vines with my hidden hand. "Ow!"

And just like that, I jump up and have his blade to his neck. He is up against the wall, breathing hard as his own knife presses to his neck. ~I can't believe that worked. I really can't!~

I laugh, drawing a little blood from my awkward movements. ~Shit.~

"Angel, you have five seconds to lower the blade," he warns.

"I give the orders!" I yell, getting into the part, feeling a bit insane. "Hands behind your back—now!"

He stares at me, then he does, holding up his hands then putting them behind his back. I make quick work of the vines, tying an impressive army knot that some stripper taught me who was really into S&M.

Long story. I think she is in jail now after being sued for wrongful slavery or something like that. Super sketch.

I step back and laugh, clapping my hands. "Now, I will finish without you being there to stop me!"

"You little minx," he whispers.

His muscles flex as he tries to break the vines with a series of aggressive movements.

I notice he is really trying hard to break free, and it makes me nervous. His veins in his neck show as he exhales, trying again with more power.

I need to distract him fast.

"I'm hot."

He raises his head to see me slowly unbuttoning my cream riding jacket. His dark gaze turns animalistic as he slightly grins. "You'd better hope I do not get free, Angel."

I swallow as my heart pounds and continue to take off my coat, revealing my sexy scarlet corset.

"I have a lot of running to do, and I'm hot, forgive me. I will send someone after you when I make it to the end. Don't worry, dear prince."

Apollo's gaze widens when he sees my corset fully.

I look down and bite my lip.

The back and sides are see-through, I'll be damned. Pierce, that dirty dog, made me a very scandalous corset. My breasts are pushed up, and I look like a vixen, ready to seduce.

I did want to have a little fun, didn't I? It is exhilarating to have this power over him. This god-like man is at ~my~ mercy.

I walk up to him slowly and take off my hat and throw it aside, then take out my hairpins one by one. My glossy locks fall down my back gloriously, and I give him a very feline smile.

I know exactly what ~I'm~ doing now. Let's see how he likes it.

He closes his eyes and says something.

I stop right in front of him, skin tingling and adrenaline pounding. "Do you want me to touch you, Apollo?"

"No," comes his raspy voice.

I click my tongue. "Too bad." My hand shakes as it unbuttons his white crisp shirt and under-armor, unzipping the contraption.

My goodness, he is glorious. His golden skin feels like granite but smooth as silk. I trail my hand over his large pecs and over his taut nipples, seeing him tense. I lick my lips and hear him groan, the sound deep and carnal.

"Untie me," he whispers harshly.

I take a shaky breath. "No."

He laughs and tries again to break the binds, almost scaring me. At this rate, he will do the impossible and break the damn vines.

I lean into him again and breathe into his neck, and almost groan myself. He smells so good, wild, untamed, hot. He tilts his head back, and I can't help but taste him.

I feel him still trying to break the binds, but I don't care. I just want to taste him for just a second. I mean, it's only fair.

I suck on his neck and hear a rumble in his throat, spurring me on. I kiss down his chest, over every deep ripple and delicious dip.

His abs are out of this world, and I lick over every sharp ridge until I get to his pants—the man V.

I glance up, and he is breathing hard, his massive chest rising and falling rapidly. Apollo's eyes squeeze shut as if he is in pain, but I know better.

I stand up and whisper in his ear, my tongue licking him. "You look uncomfortable." My hand touches him through his tight pants, and he groans again, opening his eyes.

"Untie me," he barely says.

I swallow, never having seen so much desire in someone's gaze. A few strands of hair are in his face, and he is breathing hard.

"I will send someone back for you," I say, feeling like I poked the lion a bit too hard this time.

He chuckles.

I frown.

"I have to leave. Thank you for being a good sport," I say and stumble a bit over a rock. I am losing my firm grip here.

"Is that so?"

I grab my jacket and put it on with shaky hands. "Yes."

"You get me harder than steel, and you're going to leave me?"

I blush.

I was very bold—even shocking myself.

He clicks his tongue this time. "Not happening, Angel." He slowly raises his hands, revealing the broken vines over angry red wrists.

~Oh my...~

I back up slowly. "I get that you're mad, and I want to apologize."

He laughs as he rubs his wrists. Apollo looks tall and powerful—standing there, gazing at me the way he is.

"I'm not mad, Angel, quite the opposite. In fact, I don't think I have ever been more turned on in my life."

I stare at him with my mouth open.

His lips are on mine, and I didn't even see him move. I'm crushed to the stone wall behind me, both of my arms held over my head by his hand. He surrounds me, he is everywhere.

Apollo lifts me, and my legs wrap around his waist as he grinds himself into me. His hot mouth sucks my neck as I feel his free hand grab my breast, molding it aggressively.

I don't know where he begins, and I end.

He is moaning my name, and I don't even know what's coming out of my mouth. Screams, pants, rushed breaths?

"You want me, Angel?!" he rasps in my ear as his hips roll into mine.

I feel him grabbing me here and there, ripping things. Somehow his shirt is off and mine as well. This is absolutely crazy. My brain is functioning in tunnel-vision spurts.

All I can register is his mouth in my skin, his hard erection thrusting against my lady bits, intense pleasure, my screams, skin on skin, and flashes of us tangled together.

I have never felt this amount of frenzied passion before—read about it, but never experienced it.

His mouth is everywhere, kissing, sucking, and licking. My head falls back as I scratch his back, bite his shoulder, and pant his name.

"I want you now," he rasps. "Please."

"Yes," I moan. "Now!"

I faintly feel him doing something to his pants, and then my hand is on the long length of him. ~Holy moly~…

I hear him hiss and say things I can't understand or make out as I explore his velvety splendor. My gosh, he may not fit, and I mean that.

"It will fit." He smiles into my neck.

But my thoughts are scattered as my arms wrap around his neck to hold on for dear life. He thrusts against my entrance over and over. I gasp, and the rest is history.

He pounds me into oblivion, not slowing for a second. It is a pure raw passion, our bodies moving as one. My brain is on fire as I reach my climax for the third time—or fourth? I lost count.

I feel him come, and both of our bodies go limp, exhausted. It felt like a whirlwind, and I want more.

This was the most erotic experience of my life. Hands down.

Apollo's forehead is resting on mine as we try and catch our breaths. I feel him smile more than I can see him, and he lowers me to the ground.

"You bewitched me," he breathes. "How am I to be the same after this?"

What we just did still doesn't register as he fixes my corset and skirts.

"Apollo," I whisper, a little dizzy, dreamy in fact. Apollo is amazing, and all I want is more of him.

He lifts my chin, dark eyes glittering down at me. "You say my name like that and I will have you up against this wall again."

"Something is touching my leg."

He frowns.

We both look down and see a black snake coiling around my ankle. Apollo's eyes widen, and his whole body tenses. "Don't. Move," he hisses.

Panic hits me hard.

"You move, and you die."

"Apollo," I whimper.

"Tell me something, Angel. Does someone want you dead?" he asks, his body still as a statue.

"Why?!" I ask in panic.

His jaw flexes. "Well, because this snake is extremely rare—and it is not a snake at all. It's a machine, and someone sent it out for you. Now, let me ask again.

Does someone want you dead?"

I look down, then back up innocently. "Now that you mention it...maybe?"

CHAPTER 20

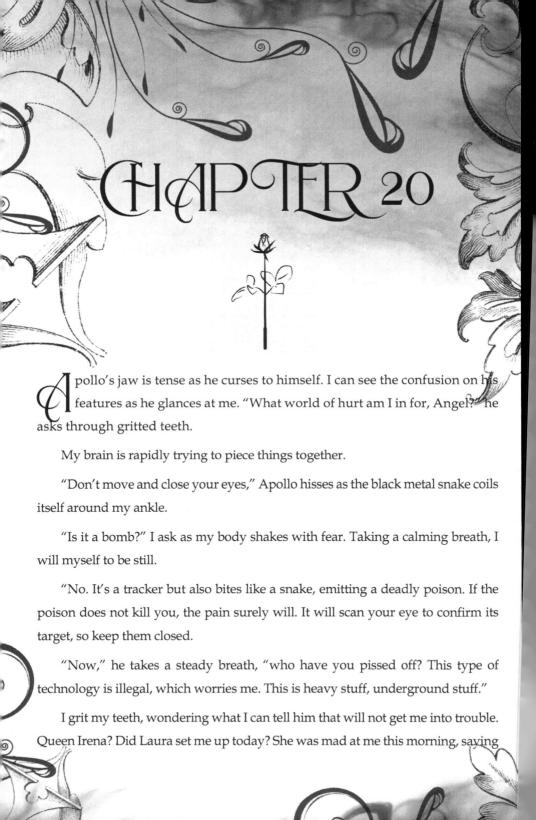

pollo's jaw is tense as he curses to himself. I can see the confusion on his features as he glances at me. "What world of hurt am I in for, Angel?" he asks through gritted teeth.

My brain is rapidly trying to piece things together.

"Don't move and close your eyes," Apollo hisses as the black metal snake coils itself around my ankle.

"Is it a bomb?" I ask as my body shakes with fear. Taking a calming breath, I will myself to be still.

"No. It's a tracker but also bites like a snake, emitting a deadly poison. If the poison does not kill you, the pain surely will. It will scan your eye to confirm its target, so keep them closed.

"Now," he takes a steady breath, "who have you pissed off? This type of technology is illegal, which worries me. This is heavy stuff, underground stuff."

I grit my teeth, wondering what I can tell him that will not get me into trouble. Queen Irena? Did Laura set me up today? She was mad at me this morning, saying she will be my worst nightmare.

"Shit," he groans.

"What?!"

"Company." I feel his hand on my waist tighten. "Keep your eyes closed."

I hear footfalls to my left, and fear seeps into every pore. I can feel Apollo tense around me, and I can hear him drawing a knife. This is not good.

"Apollo," I whisper in question. "I'm sorry," I say, not knowing what else to do. I'm panicking.

A voice I have never heard before speaks. "Well, this is surprising, to say the least."

Apollo shifts slightly. "I assume you already know what grave offense you're committing to the House of Garthorn and House of Galleon. I will go easy on you if you call off the drone."

I hear laughter.

"Who sent you?" Apollo growls.

"The great Apollo of Garthorn, at my mercy. I am actually surprised I was able to catch you off your guard. Though," he pauses, "I don't blame you. She is quite distracting."

"Call off the drone."

"I'm afraid I do not take orders from you," he says easily.

I hear Apollo curse. "Who the hell sent you?"

"Unfortunately, I am not here for you, but for the impostor in front of you. It seems the House of Garthorn was infiltrated. Compromised, I'd say.

"And from the looks of it, she has you wrapped around her little finger. I'm impressed."

I can feel Apollo's questioning stare on me.

"Don't listen to him, Apollo," I whisper with my eyes closed.

Suddenly I hear a distant scream and know without a doubt it's Laura. Alarms in my head start ringing. She is not that good of an actor. That was a scream produced by pure, authentic fear.

Adrenaline starts pounding in my bloodstream. If Laura is screaming, then this is worse than I thought. I was about to tell Apollo Laura set this up out of jealousy, but now I am confused.

What is going on?!

"Who sent me is not your concern, Apollo. I am just here for the women, and we will be on our way," comes the man's firm request. "Apollo, this is in your best interest."

"My best interest?" Apollo asks with mockery. His voice is dark and threatening. "Very thoughtful of you. I will remember when I spill your blood."

"She can open her eyes. I deactivated it already," the man's voice says. I open them right as I feel Apollo react.

"Don't!" Apollo yells, but too late.

Apollo, with quick reflexes, grabs the snake before its fangs sink into my ankle but only to puncture Apollo's forearm.

"Apollo!"

I'm such an idiot!

He tosses the snake a hundred feet, and I see two red dots forming. Blood trickles out of them as Apollo falls to his knees with a gasp, grabbing the wound. ~This is all my fault!~

"Apollo!" I scream as tears stream down my cheeks. No, this is not happening! Not happening…

He's going to die.

This. Is. Not. Happening.

I see men surround me, but all I can see is the anguish on Apollo's face. "Apollo!"

He looks up at me, dark eyes glittering. I see his pain as he says, "Angel, anything you want to tell me before they t-take you?" I can see the veins in his neck protruding.

I feel a strong arm on me, and I blurt, "Apollo, forgive me! Queen Irena! She's a witch—"

Blackness overtakes me.

***

My head.

Bleeding hearts.

I roll to the left and feel my temples pound in furry.

"Are you awake, human?" I hear Mort at my side. "She is waking up, and from what I can tell from the body scan, she will be fine. Fractured collarbone, the brutes, but it will heal.

"Laura has a broken arm, but Leenie said she will be fine as well. She set Laura's arm a few hours ago."

I open my eyes to see Mort typing and blinking.

"Uh-huh. Right, I thought so too. This is bad, but fixable. Well, I like to be positive most of the time."

"Mort," I say.

She looks up at me and exhales. "Finally! She's awake. I'll talk to you in a second."

"What happened?" I say and try to sit up, feeling pain in my shoulder. I take in my surroundings and see that I'm in a tiny bedchamber.

Am I in a space pod? It looks very concerning with all the shiny metal and slanted lines. I steady myself and focus, going through my brain's filing cabinet.

Oh…

Shit…

"Apollo!" I yell, feeling dread seep into every bone in my body. "Mort, what's happening?! Where are we, and where's Apollo?

"Why did I open my eyes?! I'm such a moron! It was just instinct—I was not thinking at my highest level! That was an amateur move."

Mort places a hand on my leg. "There, there." She continues, "More than likely they would have overpowered you guys anyway. They had some pretty big guns, from what I saw.

"Apollo is good, but I don't think he's bulletproof. So, a few things to touch base on. The House of Galleon is waging war with the House of Garthorn."

My mouth drops open, and my heart jumps to high speed. "Come again?" I whisper.

"Apollo is on his deathbed, and it's a lot of finger-pointing at this point." Mort shakes her head.

"What?!" I scream, my voice breaking. "Mort, you better explain before I freak out."

My heart is pounding so fast I feel lightheaded.

"Apollo is very ill, being poisoned and all, terrible stuff. I can't get a lot of details because it's against code T-9, but I can just get basic information.

"Apollo and Tarren were blamed for the Galleon Princess's abduction. Apollo, when he was still conscious, spat in Queen Irena's face and called her filthy names.

"That did not go over well with the King, and he vowed that if his daughters were not returned, he would have Apollo's head. Naturally, House of Garthorn is defending their soon-to-be king's honor."

"No," I whisper.

212

"Oh yeah, that's just the tip of the iceberg. Then the queen laughed like one of those evil witches and said not to worry. The poison will kill him."

"We have to do something!"

Mort nods. "Well, that's tricky because you are currently being held hostage to be sold into slavery."

The color drains from my face.

"I know. Pierce is beside himself right now."

"Sold into slavery?" I squeak. "Sex slavery?"

"Probably."

"Mort, I will not be a sex slave," I hiss, tears welling in my eyes.

"You can exit the game if you wish, but you will never see Apollo again." Mort gives me a sad look and shrugs. "I told you there is bad blood here."

"Will Apollo die?"

Mort is typing again. "It's hard to say. Apollo seems like a fellow who does not give up easily, so I think there is a chance. I think vengeance alone might keep him alive.

"From what I hear, Apollo has never shown so much fury. Some worry that the beast within him will take him over from the unhealthy rage he displayed."

She shook her head. "Too much power for a mere human, if you ask me. I will get an update soon on his health from Pierce."

I squeeze my eyes shut. "There's nothing Pierce can do?" I ask, praying there is something, anything.

"He is working on it."

We hear voices, and Mort jumps up and shapeshifts into a butterfly within seconds. The large latch opens with a suction sound, and a man walks in.

The man is tall and, surprisingly, not as ugly as I assumed.

He has jet black hair and a beard, with silver rings in his ears. He is dressed in nice black clothing and a large gun on his hip. His chocolate brown eyes survey me, and I tense.

"So you're the woman that has two kingdoms at odds," he says, and sits next to me on the small cot.

"No," I say as I feel myself shake. "When you take a princess, this sort of thing happens, or did no one tell you that before you decided to abduct us?"

He laughs. "Sharp tongue." He smiles at me, and I shiver. "I would have slapped you for that comment, but I need you looking your best. I have some high bidders. Very exciting."

"Queen Irena paid you to do this? Why her own daughter, then?"

He looked like he was thinking in a mocking way. "Queen Irena, you say? What a worthless bitch—had one job to do and fucked everything up. Well," he winks at me, "I guess I have you to blame for that one."

I take a breath, trying to scoot back on the bed. "How did I ruin your plans? Or do I even want to know?"

"Well, let's just say that Princess Laura was supposed to be married to Apollo, and that was Irena's sole job.

"You were supposed to be killed long ago when Apollo was apparently showing interest in you. Any distraction was supposed to be taken care of immediately by Irena.

"Princess Laura seemed like she would be easily manipulated through mind control, thus giving me all power over her.

"Of course, Apollo would be killed after their child was born, but now that can't happen because of you. Now we will take Garthorn by force instead of the nice way."

"Apollo is dying. How are you going to get his child?" I ask, seething.

214

His jaw flexes, and he looks like he is keeping his anger in check. "I am working on that part. He was never supposed to get bitten—you were!" He surprises me by yelling, his face reddening.

I flinch. "What is the point if he dies?"

"There is a lot that I can benefit from taking over Garthorn. I am the rightful heir, in fact.

"The Garthorn family stole this land from my family long ago, and now I'm taking it back," he says, with a smile and a simple shrug.

"Who are you that you can do that?"

"Powerful—keep that in mind." He winks at me.

A man comes running in, clearly out of breath. "My Lord?"

The man sighs in frustration. "Speak."

"I just received word that Apollo has flatlined, my lord."

"Fuck!" he yells, and punches the wall so hard it makes a dent.

"No!" I scream. "Apollo's dead?!"

This is not possible!

Tears fall down my face as I try to keep it together.

"My Lord, he is still alive but in a coma state. It might take months before he wakes if he ever does," he says with a pinched expression.

The man rubs a hand down his face and turns to him. "Our plan is still the same, and if he ever wakes, it will be a bonus. All we need is his sperm, not his brain."

I don't realize I am crying until he has me around the neck, telling me to shut up. I think he slaps me, but I can't tell.

It feels like my world has just crashed and burned, and it's all because of me. It was my fault he was bitten.

215

I feel no pain when I am tossed around like a rag doll.

It's like voices talking when you're underwater, tears making my vision seem as though I really am sinking into the dark abyss.

What have I done?

CHAPTER 21

How long has it been? Three days or four? Surely it has not been five.

I rest my head on the back of the steel wall and feel every bump of the road. My short time being a pampered princess is now over. Seems like Fate really wants me to be a slave.

My hands are tied behind my back and my mouth is gagged because I would not stop yelling at the top of my lungs like a lunatic. I now regret that. I feel like choking on this dirty cloth; God only knows where it's been.

I am sweaty and exhausted. I glance around my metal jail and curse my bad luck. I can tell we are somewhere tropical. The humidity is like being wrapped in a wet, muggy blanket.

I am numb mentally and have been since I was taken. I feel defeated.

I don't know what kind of transportation these people have, but apparently, we are not in Kansas anymore. It took three days of air flight to get to this God-forsaken place.

Their technology is quite bizarre—fantastical, actually. But I am in no mood to admire anything, my brain rejecting anything that might make me somewhat happy.

I really do not know what's keeping me here. The anticipation that Apollo will pull out of his coma?

It's been four days with little recovery. Apollo's brain activity is in full decline, according to Ivy's update at the castle. He will soon be in ~veggie status~.

Mort is out scouting, trying to find out all of the information she can, hatching an escape plan with help from Pierce. Apparently, Laura is in the same state as I am.

Two Galleon princesses are up for auction on the black market. It's the golden goose, apparently.

Meanwhile, Fairy Godmother Inc. is having a little freakout. Apollo's sudden fall is not only messing up my dreams, but theirs.

I squeeze my eyes shut and will away the tears. We have three weeks left, and Apollo is in a freaking coma! He might not even remember me if he wakes up.

I stomp my feet and give a muffled moan while trying not to activate my gag reflex. I can't wait to get back and expose that bitch Irena.

I feel my body jump and jilt as I am pulled to the left. We are turning and slowing down, most likely arriving at our destination of doom.

The main commander, named Baulk Sel, informs me that I will take part in beauty rituals to boost my value. The large auction takes place in three days and much is to be done.

My black eye is healing nicely, and my broken collarbone will mend. Mort says that this auction is a very big deal, like the Olympics of sex trafficking. Makes me sick to my stomach just thinking about it.

Where is Liam Neeson when you need him because mine's in a coma.

The door to my little jail on wheels opens and I hear men shouting, making me flinch. I'm dragged out, and as the blinding sunlight hits me, I quickly take in my surroundings.

Men with obnoxious looking weapons are everywhere, but what I am not expecting to see is the most stunning beachside compound. This is like a drug lord's dream, owning a palace fit for a king.

My heart is pounding. This will be a nightmare to escape from.

There is a lot of wealth and money here, and something tells me that this is all under the radar, or tainted blood in high places, if you know what I mean.

I wonder if this planet has its own version of the dark, tainted souls of the Illuminati.

The cloth is yanked out of my mouth and tossed aside by one of the men in black. I swallow and cough, my mouth feeling like a desert.

I glance to my left and see Laura being hauled out of a similar-looking compartment looking exactly how I feel.

My eyes widen when I spot a long line of women who are chained together and being led into the compound. The guards appear to be abnormally large with creepy looking black masks on.

I shiver, fear taking over my body. I am normally not a nervous person, but these guys are quite disturbing. One walks up to me, and the skin under the mask appears burned. Red and angry.

I have my lifelines, I remind myself and take a deep breath.

"Move, Princess!" a man shouts behind me, making me jump.

I am walking now, following the long line of women, when sadness overtakes me. Some of these women are young, too young. They do not have the luxury of having lifelines—this is their real life.

Maybe, if nothing else, Pierce can score me a grenade that I can throw into a

219

room full of the rich, evil bastards.

We are taken into the grand marble entrance and led down multiple towering hallways. It's not until we get about six flights of stairs down that I get really scared.

Everywhere I look is either marble or golden accents, giving this exotic place a feeling of immense wealth.

I swallow as I am thrown into a surprisingly lovely room with Laura of all people. But hey, misery loves the company, and I would rather be with her than by myself.

I think I throw up a bit in my mouth at that horrid thought. Laura will take getting used to.

I quickly survey the room, which has several different, very spa-like beauty stations. A large hot tub-like bath is to the far right of the room, taking up a lot of space.

There are several weird beds with creams, muds, masks, and a massive station for hair and makeup. I take a breath. Like show ponies, they will make us nice for the picking.

I hear Laura make a sobbing noise and glance at her. She is also surveying the room, her arms crossed over her body like she is holding herself.

"We will get out of here," I say quietly.

She looks at me. "What for?"

"Well, I, for one, do not want to get sold to a crusty old man with a fetish for whips and chains.

"~50 Shades~ is only hot because he is an attractive billionaire. Otherwise, it would be a top story for ~Dateline Tonight~ titled, 'Nasty Pervert on the Loose.'"

I see her mouth twitch before her RBF sets in.

She grunts. "We can just use our lifelines. This is not real life, you know."

"Maybe not, but there are women here for whom this is very real. If anything,
220

maybe we can help them," I say, and plop down on a cream sofa, trying to stay as positive as possible.

She rolls her eyes and wipes a tear. "So much for a happily-ever-after. Apollo is going to die, and we can do nothing about it. Yay, Fairy Godmother Inc." She waves her hands mockingly.

I look down and don't say anything, pain twisting in my chest. Right then, Mort and Leenie shapeshift in front of us. I jump up and wait for them to speak, heart pounding.

Mort and Leenie start talking at once, then they both shoot the other a murderous glance. Leenie holds up her hand and speaks, making Mort roll her eyes.

"We don't have much time, so we need to go over some very crucial things—"

"We might have a way of escape and," Mort pauses with a smile, "a way to save Apollo!"

I gasp. "For real?!"

Laura's eyes go wide.

Leenie fixes her black hair into a low pony. "We have three main powerhouses at the bidding in three days.

"You need to catch the eye of one in particular, for he has major ties to one of the most famous healers in the realm. A healer who can cleanse Apollo's blood of the poison and save his life.

"Pierce will provide payment for this, for the sake of the company. He just received clearance."

Mort looks relieved and says, "Thank goodness for that. Pierce had to pull some serious strings. This man is older but filthy rich and has a castle in the north next to Mont Gallow.

"His name is Lord Eltson of Oria. The great healer lives in his castle by the name Merva the Great." She pauses.

"He loves a woman who can put on an act, like dancing. He's a major pervert, unfortunately. Viola, you worked at a strip joint right?"

Laura raises a brow and gives me a look.

"Hey," I hold up my hand, "I was never a stripper, Mort!" I shoot her a look for her bad choice in words.

"But I have watched them and maybe tried a few little moves. Only for the sake of working out, though. It's kinda a thing now." Why is my face reddening? I have done nothing wrong!

"Right," Laura says.

I frown at her — the prude.

"I will try and find out what he likes in more detail, but for now focus on being a sexy dancer," Leenie says very seriously.

Laura and I giggle at her choice of words—~sexy dancer—~with her weird accent. Laura stops suddenly as if realizing we both thought the same thing was funny.

"Just because I'm not a ~ stripper~ does not mean I can't dance," Laura says as if mildly offended, looking at her nails.

Is she serious?

"I will gladly let you dance for the old fart." I laugh.

"You both will, it will increase our odds," Leenie says, and walks over to the window.

Mort shifts weight on her feet and starts blinking. "Okay, next subject, the man we must avoid. Well, we must avoid them all, but this one in particular is Lord Eltson's biggest competition.

"Not to mention they do not get along with each other. He is dangerous and controls most of the underground market. He goes by the name Black Siron—a horrible human, from what I'm reading.

"So we have to get Eltson to outbid Black Siron. It will be tricky, but not impossible. I am hoping at least one of you will get Eltson because Black Siron usually only buys one female in that price range."

"Can't I just offer myself for free to Eltson?" I ask, feeling hopeful that we can bypass this whole auction thing.

Mort shakes her head. "You're being sold for money."

"Oh, right." I take a shaky breath.

~Here we go again.~ Not a dull moment.

"You're positive this healer will help Apollo?" I ask.

Mort sighs. "It's our only hope."

***

My hair is pulled, washed, oiled, painted, steamed, and I lose track of whatever else after the two-hour mud bath. Now I must make my way to sector 3 to get my body and my ~hoo-ha~ waxed.

I'm super excited about this one. I feel like a cat with its ears back.

I want to hiss at the big fat lady who keeps knocking me upside the head every chance she gets. Saying I am not dancing correctly and tilting my head enough, which is a lie. She just wants a reason to beat me.

I will have to talk to Pierce about how we can uncover this horrid place. I've already seen one girl get hauled off because she would not expose her breasts to the commander.

I walk past a large window that overlooks the ocean and gasp, Laura coming to stand beside me with the same expression of concern. There is a massive black ship docked, and when I say huge, I mean it.

It looks like a possessed pirate ship on steroids that would have Freddy Krueger nervous to board. Freddy would say,~ "Fuck that shit~." That's how intimidating the vessel is.

I shiver.

"You think this is Black Siron? Mort said he is arriving today with a few others."

She nods. "Leenie showed me his sign, which is a black raven or something."

The large flag on the ship is definitely a black bird of some sort. "I think that is a safe bet," I whisper.

"Eltson had already arrived."

I take a deep breath. "Dance class tonight again, makes me want to barf."

"Me too," Laura agrees.

"Is that him?" I point.

Laura looks behind her then back out the window with a squint. "Oh, dear Lord," she moans.

She is right. I see Black Siron being greeted by a whole fleet of people as if he is king. He is tall and muscular, broad shoulders dwarfing most men—save for Apollo.

Shit. He does not look like a man to cross; his black attire gives him a daunting appearance.

I would even go as far as to say the man is exceptionally handsome save for his face, which is half covered by a black Zorro-looking mask. I can see his black hair and bronzed skin due to his shirt's open neck.

I instantly feel sick. This man is all that is power. I just pray he does not fancy me—I can see him being ruthless. An evil man with the devil's own looks is beyond bad news.

I just wished I had a shotgun. I'd bust out of here like Rambo.

"I just got really nervous," Laura whispers.

"Lifelines."

She shakes her head and huffs. "Apollo is in love with you."

I look at her in shock.

She sighs and rolls her eyes. "Everyone can see it, even me." She looks at me and shrugs. "It is what it is." Laura is defeated, her prime ego deflated.

I still have nothing to say to her.

Laura faintly smiles and walks away.

What just happened?

I feel a pang of sadness for Laura, seeing the vulnerability in her blue eyes.

I glance out the window again and see Siren being led inside the complex with the stride of a man who gets what he wants.

A shiver slides down my spine.

This mission is just getting harder and harder by the minute.

CHAPTER 22

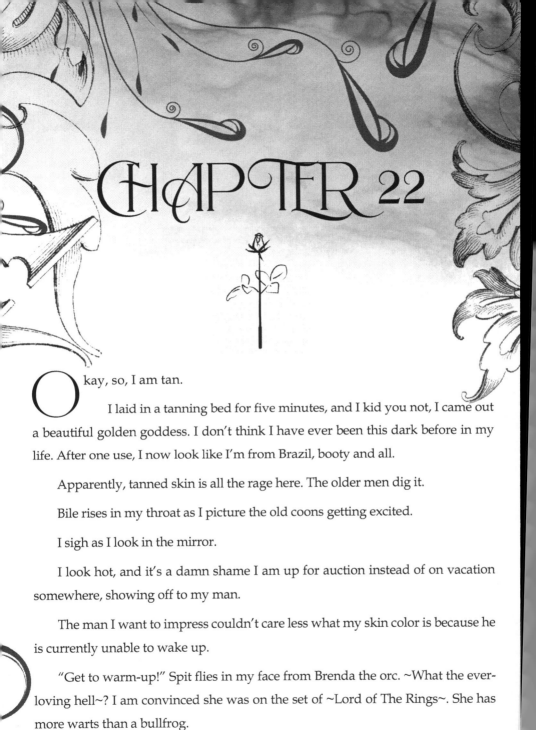

Okay, so, I am tan.

I laid in a tanning bed for five minutes, and I kid you not, I came out a beautiful golden goddess. I don't think I have ever been this dark before in my life. After one use, I now look like I'm from Brazil, booty and all.

Apparently, tanned skin is all the rage here. The older men dig it.

Bile rises in my throat as I picture the old coons getting excited.

I sigh as I look in the mirror.

I look hot, and it's a damn shame I am up for auction instead of on vacation somewhere, showing off to my man.

The man I want to impress couldn't care less what my skin color is because he is currently unable to wake up.

"Get to warm-up!" Spit flies in my face from Brenda the orc. ~What the ever-loving hell~? I am convinced she was on the set of ~Lord of The Rings~. She has more warts than a bullfrog.

I give her an I-will-slit-your-throat-given-the-chance smile and make my way to where all the women are lined up waiting for their turn to entice the bidders. Or be killed.

Everyone is trying to stay positive. I hear some giggling and frown in confusion when I spot a group of girls peeking through the curtains at the large round stage. Have they lost their minds? Maybe.

This is anything but a good time, and I actually feel sick. I saw a few girls hysterically crying earlier when the highest bidder bought them.

If nothing else, I will try to shut this down. Pierce said that this needs to get stopped to tip the scales above 50 percent on the Fairy Godmother graphs. This slavery ring is out of hand, clearly.

I grab onto a pole and lazily swing around it, wishing I was somewhere else. This fantasy just became a nightmare in a hurry.

We all look like harem girls in our scandalous belly dancer outfits with jewels and bangles. I glance at myself in the mirror and cringe.

I picked the most understated outfit, but the opposite happened.

There were tons of vibrant colors and fabrics, so I went with the muted tan color. I tried to find the ugliest color, but when I put it on, it just gave the appearance of me being naked.

The tan is shimmering and transparent in places, accenting my tan body perfectly. The damn thing is gorgeous, to my utter horror.

I tried to switch, but the orc would not let me.

"You will have everyone bidding on you," Laura says behind me.

I glance back and eye her outfit choice. Sky blue silk, very pretty with her blonde hair. "Excuse me. You look like an innocent princess. I think men like this thrive with that sort of look."

She cringes. "Shit. Maybe the red would have been a better choice."

"Well, we are supposed to look good, right? We have to get Eltson to bid on

HEIR OF THE BEAST

us." I take a breath and feel dread overcome me.

She laughs, and I raise a brow. "You look like you're naked."

I try not to laugh and cover my mouth with my hand.

"Is this transparent?" Laura grabs some airy fabric, still giggling.

I close my eyes and cringe. "At this point, I am not sure. I think this color is called shameless."

"At least the main parts are still a mystery." She is laughing harder now.

I am laughing now and shake my head. "Here I thought I was picking the modest one. Our luck sucks."

"Well, just don't spread your legs." That sends her off into another laughing frenzy as she holds her stomach.

I wipe a tear. "Oh, laugh it up. You look like a prudish ballerina that needs to be taken to the dark side by Grandpa Farts," I deadpan.

We are laughing so hard, and I'm not even sure if the things we are saying are even funny. I don't think they are, in fact. I think we both just lost our minds.

"Silence!"

We both clamp our mouths shut, and I hear Laura snorting through her muffled laughter. Brenda looks murderous, so I think quickly.

"Forgive us, this is just all very overwhelming." Which is the truth. I need to wipe this stupid grin off my face before I get punched in the nose. Laura's snorting isn't helping.

She snarls, "The blonde princess is up next, you are ten minutes out. No funny business out there, or there will be punishments." She eyes us both, then leaves.

That is sobering, actually.

Laura takes a breath and looks at me. "I might be leaving the game after this. If Eltson does not pick me, there is no reason for me to stay as a slave in this place."

I look down. "You could be wrong about Apollo."

"I'm not." She shrugs.

This is weird, but I am feeling very depressed at the thought of her leaving. In the past few days, I have seen another side of Laura. She is just very misunderstood, and I never gave her a chance before.

I look away, willing my tears to stop, my eyes cramping. I feel her arms come around me as tears trickle down my face. I hug her back and say nothing. A friendship is formed, a bond that can never be broken.

It's hard to explain the feeling of loss and loneliness at the thought of her leaving.

I hear Laura sniff, and she lets go with a weak smile. "Be strong. Apollo is worth it."

I nod, wiping my eyes. "Nothing will be in vain as long as you do the bend and snap out there," I joke, and try to pull myself together.

She rolls her eyes and grins. "Of course, there will be stunned silence after."

I laugh.

She laughs weakly.

Then I see her leaving. I take a shaky breath and realize Apollo's life depends on this, and I need to give my best performance no matter how horrified I am.

I close my eyes and pray that Eltson picks Laura, because I really do not want to see her leave just yet. I've never had a real friend in all my life, and I found one in the least likely of places.

I walk to where the stage is and peek through the curtains like the other girls were earlier. I shiver, hoping every male here dies a horrid death.

Laura is dancing gracefully but a little stiff, probably due to nerves. My heart goes out to her, to all these women. I'm seeing bids come in, and I suck in a breath.

My eyes scan the secret compartments where the bidders do their dark deeds.

It reminds me of the movie ~Taken~, except for the fact that this seems more circus-like, with all the dancing and whatnot.

I see Eltson's bidding booth. He is clothed in royal blue riches. The man is even being fanned by slaves he probably just bought. Disgusting.

He seems very interested in Laura, though, whispering a lot to his male advisers and pointing.

A bid is in.

He bid on her!

I nearly squeak in delight, but keep my mouth shut. ~Atta girl.~ We will make him pay later, but for now, this is great news.

I see Laura bend down then snap back up like a well-trained whip. My mouth hangs open. Laura just did the bend 'n snap! I think the planet shifted from its awesomeness.

She turns slightly toward the curtains where I am at and winks! I nearly laugh out loud, which is priceless. That made my day, my week. I can't believe she did that, and shockingly she made it look good.

She is not going home yet.

She is escorted off the stage to her highest bidder, who is Eltson. I close my eyes, thanking my lucky stars. Now, if I can just get Eltson to bid on me, I will not be alone.

I scan the bidding booths, and I am assuming the ones on the lower levels are the high rollers.

Black Siron's booth is all silver and red with men sitting around him. I squint, seeing him casually reclined in his seat like he isn't just about to destroy someone's life.

"I pray that he picks me," says a girl to my left.

I didn't even know she was standing there. "Excuse me?"

"Black Siron. I saw him up close and nearly passed out, never seen a man so alive," she says quietly.

"He could beat you to a bloody pulp."

She looks down. "He may, and he may not."

I frown at her. What choice did she have, though? If I were picking the lesser of two evils, I may want him to pick me too.

I glance back and note even from this distance he seems very gifted in the looks department. I can see the dark tattoos coming out of his neckline, and his forearms are covered like sleeves.

Shining silver rings and earrings catch the dim light, making him seem like a dark lord of the under realm.

Makes me wonder why a man like him must buy a female anyway. I would assume they would all fall at his feet.

Maybe he likes the thought of owning someone, which makes me sick.

I get elbowed in the back. "You're up!"

This lady.

I try to squash the nerves flying in my stomach and walk out, seeing eyes on me everywhere.

I am barefoot, my feet sliding on the slick surface of the round stage. It's a lot bigger when you're out here, and a lot more intimidating.

Seductive music starts with strong violin tones and smooth piano notes that mesh together romantically. I close my eyes and take a deep breath. ~This is for you, Apollo~.

I start with my hips then let my arms and hands flow as I spin once then twice. I feel a sadness in my movements, and in every sway of my body I can feel the weight of the world.

I can hear bids already, but I keep dancing until my five minutes are up.

231

I find the pole and use precision and upper body strength. I swing around it like a seductive ballerina, toes pointed gracefully. I am not dancing crudely but expertly, with elegant, beautiful lines.

I climb up the pole and spin down as my legs split like a seasoned ice skater twirling with grace. And before you worry, I am wearing silk panties. I am not exposing the goods to these goons.

I am surprised how fluidly I'm dancing despite my situation.

I fling my head back as I spin again, and I happen to see Black Siron standing, which almost makes me fall off the pole. Is he bidding on me?!

~Shit.~

I glance over to Eltson and he is standing as well, and then it dawns on me. They are in a bidding war.

My heart picks up a beat, praying Eltson does not give in and back down. I need to keep his interest, or I will do Apollo no good being bought by Siron.

I dance a little harder, spin a little faster, arch my back, and flip my hair with a little more passion.

By the time I stop, I'm sweaty and out of breath.

I feel eyes and whispers everywhere.

They're probably wondering why I am dancing with this much vigor. I keep my head down, not able to bring myself to look at these monsters. The bidding is still on and going higher.

I glance up with a frown, and I see Black Siron with his arms crossed over his chest in a powerful stance. He gives another bid, and the whole place quiets.

I glance around in question, still breathing hard. Then it dawns on me that the horrid man bid an insane amount that no one wants to compete with.

Eltson is furious and leaves immediately as his advisers follow him from his booth. I start to panic, almost like I am a scared deer caught in headlights.

232

Wait, that's not what's supposed to happen.

I don't know what possesses me, but I take off the stage and run like hell.

I don't know where I am going, but it does not take me long to get caught by Black Siron's people. I am kicking and screaming as they restrain me, hands once again being tied behind my back.

Angry tears fall.

I need to talk to Mort and Pierce to get me out of this ASAP.

Lifeline time.

I glance up again and gasp. Siron is standing right in front of me and my whole body tenses. He is tall and muscular like Apollo, making me immediately on edge. Will he slap me?

I flinch when he raises a hand, but all he does is smooth the hair out of my face. My heart is pounding as I watch him, bracing myself for anything.

His black hair is long, and his even darker eyes gaze at me through his mask. It's hard to make out his facial features, but I would assume they are handsome. His smooth jaw and lips are the only features I can see.

The man is like a dark god, all power and control. A shiver runs down my spine as he continues to gaze at me with intensity.

He nods to the man standing behind me, and he hands Black Siron a pen and paper, making me curious. ~What is going on?~

Siron starts writing, and after a few seconds, he hands the paper to me to read. I frown as my trembling hand takes the paper. How odd.

~I do my homework, little one. Apollo will have to come through me to get to you. You are mine. The sooner you realize that, the easier it will be for you. Though it does not seem like Apollo will be coming anytime soon.~

I swallow and glance up in confusion. Can he not talk?! How strange.

I glare at him and lean forward, ignoring the fact that he smells better than average, I'll give him that. Probably uses insanely expensive soap.

"Apollo will recover, and he will come for me."

He laughs, the breathy sound making my skin tingle. I watch him, also noting that I heard a sound when he laughed. So he isn't mute, then?

Siron waves his hand, and I'm taken away immediately. My kicking and screaming does nothing but exhaust me, and then I realize I am being taken to their dark ghost ship.

Something tells me that this is about to get bumpy.

I mentally strap on my seatbelt.

CHAPTER 23

I am tied to a steel pole on the lower deck of the ship of the Underworld. I would not be surprised if Hades resides somewhere on this massive ship.

The sky is dark and angry like the vessel I'm on. The wind has picked up and is currently blowing my hair around my face in the most irritating manner.

The water makes me nervous, dark and monstrous like it's alive, hungry for human souls to devour.

Now, I know this sounds bad, but in all honesty, it has been a couple of hours since anyone has touched or talked to me. It's the strangest thing.

I even have a dark cloak draped around my shoulders to shield my scandalous body from hungry male stares.

This could be a lot worse.

I am watching men run everywhere, doing this and that like the devil is on their heels. Whatever they're planning, they're doing it in a hurry, and it makes me anxious.

I hope a storm is not moving in.

"Princess, the Black Siron asks if ye' would like to get more comfortable?"

I flinch as I glance at a small man with kind blue eyes. He is dressed in all black and has a dark patch over one eye.

Is this a trick question? Like, if I say yes, will I get thrown into the black sea with the shark-man-pigs? Lipers? Whatever they're called.

"I mean you no harm, my lady."

What in the ever-loving-mind-game is this?!

I take a breath, trying to gauge his kindness. "I would like to be untied," I say meekly, then flinch when he moves toward me.

I sit tensely as he takes out a knife from his boot and cuts my ties with quick efficiency. I don't realize I'm holding my breath until he steps away. I rub my wrists and nod at him.

"Thank you."

He nods.

I stare at him, unsure of what to say. "What now?"

He turns and shouts something at a couple of men then glances back at me.

"You may sit out here as long as you stay out of the way of our men. When you are feeling tired, come find me, and I will show you to your room."

"My room?"

"Yes, we are having it prepared for you." He tilts his head at me. "Master Siron wants you to be very comfortable."

"Does he now?" I say, almost to myself.

"Give him a chance, princess." And with that he leaves — to go tend to other more important matters, I'm sure.

I think my mouth is hanging open. I glance around the deck, and not once does any man on this ship even glance my way. It's as if I am invisible.

Standing, I meekly make my way to the side of the vessel and glance over the edge. I can smell the salt from the water and the mist the wind brings.

We are high up, and I feel like I can see for miles. Miles of black waters.

A wave of nerves flash through my body, and I feel sick.

Is this Siron guy trying to win me over? Why would he do that? Unless he wants to lower my guard to take advantage of me, make me pay for my naive nature.

I rub a hand down my face, confusion clouding my brain. I need to talk to Mort fast and find out what in the heck is going on here.

I am doing Apollo no good being on Siron's ship. I only have one month left, for Pete's sake!

With that, I set out to find that old man and tell him I would love to go to my room, away from all this madness.

I am almost run over by several men, yelling at me to get my "~sweet ass"~ out of the way. I think I hear a "~sugar tits"~ from someone to my left, but I can't be sure.

I make my way to the upper deck, which is massive, and I find the main navigation platform. I'm shaking, but I try to hide it. I am way out of my comfort zone here.

~Life begins at the end of your comfort zone~, I remind myself. Pull yourself together, woman.

I nearly jump out of my skin. ~It's him~.

Siron is there wearing all black with his face almost covered. He is a towering figure, scary as hell.

My heart rate   jumps to life even though I order myself to act calmly. I want to back up slowly, but he already sees me.

Double shit.

He stops what he is doing to stare at me, and an army of gooseflesh litters my skin. The man is intimidating.

He makes some hand movements to the men standing around him, then he makes his way toward me, his black overcoat flapping behind him in the wind.

My heart is pounding so hard I think I might pass out in front of everyone. I take a deep breath as he stops in front of me, making me look down, not wanting to make eye contact with someone like him.

I feel his hand touch my chin and lift it up to meet his black gaze. I can tell his eyes are searching my face, and all I can do is stare back.

"What do you want with me?" I blurt, unable to keep silent. I jerk my chin out of his hand with newfound defiance.

Easy, Nelly.

He smiles, then glances out over the ship to the ocean. I can only see his lips, and I will admit they are nice, white teeth as well. Just an observation. He is a bit of a mystery.

Siron then pulls out a notepad and writes for a few seconds, then hands it to me.

I take it with trembling fingers and read it.

~Do you know sign language?~

I glance up and answer with clipped tones. "No."

He nods and takes back the paper to write again.

~Then you will have to bear with me~.

I see it, then nod up at him. I guess he can't talk, which is weird because I thought I heard him laugh. Maybe he is only able to make small sounds?

He shows me another note.

~Are you searching for your room? Or me?~

"Room," I say too fast. He has lovely handwriting, very odd for a cutthroat individual. But these guys do not seem uneducated — in fact, quite the opposite.

"Why are you being," I pause, "nice to me?" I speak loudly like he is slow. I wince and bite my lip.

He is expressionless as he writes, then hands me the note.

~My little dancer, I can hear your lovely voice just fine.~

I blush. Of course he can, I know, I'm an idiot. "I'm sorry," I say sheepishly.

He watches me for a few unnerving seconds, then writes again before handing me the paper.

~You are beautiful, and I am nice to beautiful things.~

I resist rolling my eyes. It is hard because they want to disappear clear back into my skull like I am possessed. "Lucky me."

He takes a few seconds to respond, then hands me the paper~.~

~You sound ungrateful. Would you like me to tie you to my bed then? Or maybe you can dance for me later?~

I suck in a breath as I read. "No, I am not ungrateful. Thank you for showing me kindness."

I'm breathing hard in panic, and I am really striking out on being street smart. I need to save the attitude because this could get ugly in a hurry.

I think I see him grin, but it's gone so fast I might be seeing things. I take another breath. "May I go to my room?" I need to get away from him STAT.

I see him studying me, and it makes me squirm. This guy has a very penetrating stare that seems to unravel my sense of calm. I just want to jump out of my skin. I need some Xanax pronto.

He writes then flips the paper around so I can see~.~

~I will have Marcus show you to your quarters. I will fetch you for dinner

in a few hours. I WANT your company.~

I swallow and nod. Mercy, he wrote ~want~ in caps, and that makes my heart palpitate.

He turns and whistles loud through his teeth, gaining everyone's attention. Quick sign language happens, and the older man I talked to before nods and comes running at me.

"Of course, Your Grace." He bows to Siron and then turns to me. "This way, princess."

I am rushed off the platform, feeling his stare on me. I don't like it. It's too much too soon. I need to get off this boat ASAP.

Siron is being nice now but for how long? I can sense his desire like a second skin. I am running out of time. "Marcus, is it?"

"Yes, princess. Ye may follow me to yer room."

I follow him inside the large ship's cabin and through many hallways until we stop at a metal door with yellow lights. I turn toward him and bite my lip. "Can you help me?"

His head jerks toward me in shock. "Ye are Siron's now. He will move heaven and hell to keep you. It's best ye accept yer fate."

I squeeze my eyes shut. "I can't!" I lower my voice and look around. "I can't. I am in love with another. Prince Apollo of Garthorn!"

He opens the door and lets me walk past him; angry tears cloud my eyes. He gives a heavy sigh and pauses at the door.

"I am sorry. Yer gown for tonight is hanging in the wardrobe. Please do not upset Siron. Ye will not like it. Keep him on yer good side, princess."

He shuts the door, and I start hitting the metal wall repeatedly. With ragged breaths, I glance around the beautiful chamber and grit my teeth.

It is adorned with yellow and grays, very girly, with lace and satin fabrics. A

240

lot of wealth here, especially for a room on a scary pirate ship.

~This could be so much worse,~ I remind myself.

Movement catches my eye as I see a white butterfly. "Mort!" I hiss.

She transforms in front of me and falls onto the bed, looking exhausted. "I was lost. That's all you need to know." She takes a breath. "We have much to talk about."

I sit next to her and nod. "I'm in deep shit, aren't I?"

Mort looks at me with a frown. "Deep shit? I don't think so," she murmurs, then looks at my feet.

I close my eyes. "It's an expression, Mort. It means I'm in trouble."

"Oh." She nods. "Yes, you are in deep shit. So, a few things we must touch base on. Apollo is still in a coma, and he is running out of time. He might die at any point."

I gasp and squeeze my eyes shut. "What a nightmare." I can feel the pain in my chest. I don't want to lose him. I have started to fall in love with him, if I am not already. He can't die—he just can't!

"Yes, well, Pierce is freaking out because Siron is someone he was not counting on. Siron is planning on overtaking Eltson's ship."

"What?!"

"If that happens, then Laura will not reach the healer in time, and Apollo will die," she says, and looks down.

We sit in silence. That's why all the crew members were running around like their heads were cut off. They were preparing for battle.

"Mort, Apollo can't die. It's my fault he was bitten." I will tears back, but a couple escape.

"Can you persuade Siron ~not ~to take over Eltson's ship? They plan on connecting with them early tomorrow morning."

I curse. "I am having dinner with the brute tonight." I glance at Mort. "What do you know about him? It might help when I talk to him tonight. Well, he can't talk, he is mute. That's about all I know."

Mort is typing. "Yes, I saw that. Strange because he was not always like that, from my records. I think he is sick actually, having to sit down from exhaustion, resting a lot."

"Huh," I say, deep in thought.

"Pierce is unsure what happened to him, maybe something to do with all of his battles. Voice box removed, maybe? Torture here is bad."

I cringe.

"I wonder," Mort says with a frown. "Do you think Siron is overtaking Eltson to gain access to the healer as well? The man seems to be in high demand."

My eyes brighten, and I sit up straighter. "That would be a blessing in disguise! I can do some digging tonight. If not, maybe I can even convince him he needs to see this man."

"It's all we got at this point." Mort walks over to the wardrobe and opens it up. She whistles and pulls out a golden gown, fit for an Egyptian queen.

"Not as good as Pierce, but this Siron guy does not spare any expense."

I take a shaky breath as my eyes gaze at the shimmering fabric. Looks like I have to put on my acting face, yet again.

~This is all for you, Apollo.~

CHAPTER 24

"You look really good, but Pierce is adjusting the ass area," Mort says as she motions me to spin.

"What!?" I shriek. "I do not want this guy to hump my leg! My boobs are already hanging out, making me very uncomfortable." I look at my ass, and it looks fine. What is Pierce trying to do, get me raped?!

"There is a method to Pierce's madness. He does not tell me everything, you know. So sometimes I'm just as clueless as you are. I have just learned to trust him," Mort says, and shrugs.

I close my eyes for a few seconds and then nod. "If I have to use a lifeline because of this, I will knee him in the balls."

Mort laughs and snorts.

I start to spin and feel the material tighten in certain places, making me nervous. The golden fabric is a long evening gown like one would see in old Hollywood, but more medieval.

The dipping neckline is my biggest worry. My ass is now on display and my breasts are presented as if I am a work of art. And I can also feel that my hair is tamed and less frizzy.

Only Pierce.

I hear a knock on the door and Mort is gone in a flash. I run to grab my dark cloak and put it on before they open the door.

"Princess, Master Siron awaits your presence."

I nod to a portly man and follow him through more hallways until we finally reach a large dining hall.

The dining corridor is cold and barren—metal everywhere with sharp lines and yellow flickering lights running the floor. It isn't ugly, quite the opposite, but it is extremely intimidating.

This ship is very scary from the outside, but very spacelike on the inside. Strange.

A long, steel table gleams in the middle of the room with two placements on one end. A server comes out carrying what I assume is a bottle of red wine.

He motions for me to take a seat just as the door opens again and Siron steps in, making me freeze. He has a black cane that he's putting most of his weight on.

He shoos away the server, and in moments we are the only ones left in the room. He looks impeccable in black finery and wearing a more elegant mask.

I wonder why he wears a mask. Maybe he is badly scarred from battle.

His shoulders pull tightly on the sharp black dinner coat. I can see his dark hair combed back nicely and I cannot deny the man is gifted in the looks department.

That is all I will say about that. He probably has an ego the size of this ship and a black heart to fill his large body.

I realize I am just standing here staring at him like a lunatic.

He takes a hand out of his pocket and pulls out a chair for me. I shiver, not wanting to move closer to him. But nothing is worse than showing your fear in front of a man, so I raise my chin and walk toward him.

I go to sit down but feel his hand as he stops me. It rests on my shoulders, pulling off the large overcoat.

I tense, having forgotten that I was wearing the damn thing. Double damn. I feel the coat slide off, and I do not make eye contact but quickly sit down, ignoring my wild pulse.

Siron sits to my left, and I stare straight ahead, biting my lip. He leans his cane against the table and sits back in his chair. I need a strategy, but my brain isn't working at the speed I need it to.

I feel him watching me, but I will not look. He moves, leaning over to pour me a tall glass of red wine, the sound filling the quiet room. ~Fine.~

I reach for it and down the entire glass, not caring how I come across. My situation can't get any worse, so I might as well feel less tense about it.

I place the glass down on the table, resisting a cringe over the bitterness, and glance at him. I see his lips form a slight grin as he leans over to refill my glass, never taking his gaze from me.

I can feel the wine pooling in my empty belly and coursing its way through my body. I relax and feel a tad less afraid.

Siron takes out a notepad and starts writing. He glances back up to me and shows me his form of speech.

~Don't be so scared of me, little dancer. Relax.~

I huff. "Have you seen yourself?" The wine is making me very toasty and brave. "You are very…intimidating."

He nods and writes again.

~Apollo is also a large man, yet you want him?~

Just the mere mention of Apollo makes my gut tighten.

"Apollo is an honorable man, much different. You have a very dark reputation.

245

You ruin women's lives by kidnapping them or buying them like objects. It's disgusting."

Careful, Viola.

Siron tilts his head at me and smiles, displaying white, even teeth. He looks down then leans over to drink his wine in one gulp. He writes in a messy, almost angry scribble.

~Can't argue with that. By the way, you are breathtaking. I knew that color would make you look like a queen. I want you to dance for me again.~

I bite my lip and narrow my eyes at him. "You're punishing me for being ungrateful? I am sorry." I pause as I take a nervous breath. "I have a temper."

I hear a breathy laugh and I shiver, unable to stop it. I am not sure what I'm reacting to besides the obvious.

I mean, he looks like a sexy Zorro on steroids, I'll give him that, but he is an evil creature that makes my skin crawl.

He writes again and slides the paper to me, his glittering gaze watching me.

~I like your fire, but I'd like to taste it instead of witness it.~

I swallow, not sure what to say to that. I need to turn the tables fast or he will have me for dessert. "Why can't you talk?"

He seems shocked, then leans back in his chair and studies me before writing. Siron slides me the paper as I lean in to see.

~A curious thing you are. I cannot speak because my voice box was damaged in battle. And I wear a mask because I wish to keep my identity a mystery. It has kept me safe thus far, my little dancer.~

~Now, where were we?~

I try and ignore his sexual energy, mentally kicking myself. "Have you ever thought about seeing a healer?" I feel there is more he is not telling me as I glance at his cane.

He shrugs.

I pick my words carefully. "I wanted Eltson to win my bid because I wanted to meet the great healer there. Merva the Great. I thought perhaps he could heal Apollo, before you won the bid.

"Maybe you also would like to seek him out?" I slightly glance up at him to gauge his reaction.

He leans forward and starts writing, glancing up at me then continuing. After a few seconds, he pushes the paper to me.

~Do you love him? Because if you do, I might have to kill him.~

I gasp. My heart is pounding, not expecting that reaction.

He is writing again, then finally slides the paper to me. ~I can see the way you react to me, little dancer. I am very observant. Even if you want to deny it.~

~Your snake eyes dilate when you look at me, and I can hear your pulse hammering against your smooth skin. I know what would happen if I were to touch you.~

As if on cue, my heart rate heightens, and my cheeks flush. I am so angry that I want to scratch his eyes out. "May I leave?" I whisper harshly.

Just then, the door opens, and I am being served food. I am not hungry, and the thought of this man thinking I am attracted to him beyond the physical is insane.

He probably thinks every woman has this reaction to him, and it makes me sick. I look at my plate with steak and veggies. It smells good, but I am so angry that it's making my stomach feel nauseous.

Siron motions for me to eat.

I stare back at him.

He writes, then slides the paper to me, his gaze hard on me. ~Eat or I will feed you the food myself.~

Do people flip each other off here? My middle finger is twitching, but I tap

247

down the insane urge and pick up my fork, stabbing broccoli. I take a bite, then glare up at him.

He is watching my mouth, and a slight smile pulls at his perfect lips. He is writing again with a smirk on his face. ~I want to see your eyes when I feed you. I am curious.~

I swallow with a frown. Excuse me?

He cuts a piece of steak and scoots his chair back, making me alarmed. I immediately go into panic mode when he slides his chair closer to me and pulls my chair toward him with his foot.

Now I am right in front of him, practically in between his legs. I can't breathe, and he leans forward, giving me a very close view of him.

I can't help but notice that he smells clean and wild.

He quickly grabs the notepad with his free hand and scribbles on it.

~Open your mouth.~

I barely open my mouth, and his gaze seems to light on fire. This man's intensity is scaring me on so many levels.

He grins as he puts the steak to my lips and nudges my mouth wider, slightly rubbing the salty meat over my lips before giving it to me. He sits back and watches me with those black eyes.

Why do I feel violated?

"What are you trying to prove?" I hiss. I need him to back up and give me space; being this close to him is making me mental. "I think it's safe to say you unsettle me. Probably like most people when they are around you."

Siron just watches me like he can see something most can't. I don't like that. I am not even sure what he is at this point.

He sits up, bringing his large body even closer, and grabs his pad to start writing. He pauses and glances at me, his gaze moving over my body then to my legs in between his muscular thighs.

~Just breathe~, I tell myself.

He starts writing again and hands it to me. I take it with shaking hands and I see that it does not go unnoticed. Seems like nothing goes unnoticed by this guy.

~*You enjoy your meal. Your eyes are very telling, my dancer, and I got the answer I was seeking. I will bid you a good night.*~

I frown up at him as he watches me read the note.

Siron laughs, the sound breathy, tilting his head slightly.

I grit my teeth and ignore how his mouth looks when he smiles. ~Stop it~.

He grabs my hand and brings it to his mouth, his hot lips lingering on my skin as he closes his eyes. I am tense and bite my lip, watching him breathe in my skin like I am some sort of goddess.

I am not sure how to process this man. He suddenly stands and leans down over me to reach for the notepad to scribble on it before he turns to leave with his cane.

I am so confused.

After he leaves, I just sit here in silence, trying to process my emotions. I glance over to the note that he left and read it.

~*Don't look so sad to see me leave. Enjoy yourself.*~

He's joking, right?!

Does he think I am pining for him? I sit there in silent fury. That man is a mind ninja. Or he is completely delusional.

What did he see in my eyes? Anger? Did he mistake that for lust or longing? I sure hope not.

I'm probably not going to sleep very well tonight.

***

"Tell me what's bugging you, human."

I get dressed in some medieval-looking gown that is chocolate brown and cream lace. Quite pretty actually.

The corset is a little tight for my boobs, but it fits well enough that Pierce does not have to adjust it. I start braiding my hair in thought.

Siron got a lucky guess on my size, or his last prisoner was my size. I wonder how many women wore this dress before me. I can already feel my anger boiling.

"Human?"

I glance at her. "Sorry, this Siron guy is on my last nerve."

Mort nods. "He has me very curious as well. I think he is very sick. I heard some crew members saying he was involved with a witch. When he broke up with her, she cursed him with a deadly virus."

I frown. "Really?" I think about that. "I can actually see that happening. He's kind of a playboy."

"Yes, he is a very attractive human like Apollo."

I shoot her a glance. "Do not compare him to Apollo."

She laughs and holds up her hands. "Okay, calm down. I think Black Siron is seeking out the healer. Pierce thinks he is going to hold Eltson hostage in return for healing power."

"That's perfect," I say. "So how are we going to get the healer back to Apollo?" A thought occurs to me—I have not asked about his health today. "How is Apollo?"

Mort sighs. "The same. Pierce has gotten clearance to pay the healer what he asks for. Probably virgin blood and unicorns' horns."

I nod. "We can do this, Mort. We can save him."

"Damn right we will."

I walk out onto the main deck and spend a few hours soaking up the sun. No one bothers me, and I am assuming its orders from the Black Siron.

There are men fishing, and I can't help but be intrigued by their devices. Maybe it's boredom, but I want to try it for myself.

I walk up to a large man who looks like he has a bow, but it's attached to other nets and metal contraptions. "Is it easy?"

He pauses and turns to look at me. His red beard and blue eyes remind of a Scottish highlander. I see his eyes glance up to the upper decks, probably searching for the warden. ~Eye roll.~

"Lass, if you catch a fish, I will be the one dancing for you."

I hear a few snickers behind me and a smile. "Deal."

He glances up again and shrugs. "If you're here, might as well put you to work. We have a lot of mouths to feed in this crew, so get to work, lassie."

He winks at me and hands me his large fishing contraption that smells like dead fish. Strange. The Scottish men in this world talk the same as on Earth. Parallel universes, mirroring each other.

"I am bored to tears. I will be delighted."

The next hour consists of me ~not~ catching any fish whatsoever. This is hard, not like shooting arrows at all. I let out a grunt of frustration and stomp my foot.

I blame my bad attitude on my inability to have patience. I could in no way defuse a bomb. I'd get pissed and end up headbutting the bomb and blowing my own head off.

I try again and hear laughs when I shoot the hook only for it to pitifully slosh in the black sea waters. "Are you kidding me?"

The laughter dies, and I hear someone approaching. I curse because I know what that sound is—a ~cane.~ I don't turn around. Instead, I try again. What's he going to do? Throw me overboard?

I pause. He totally could. I lower my fishing bow and turn around to stare at his imposing figure.

I suck in a little breath, only because I have never seen him in this state of undress, and in the general sense, like any female, it gives me a slight pause.

Less than a slight pause — we are talking about a split second in time.

I can still only see his mouth, but he has a billowy, unbuttoned black shirt on, exposing his golden chest. I huff — of course he is super ripped. With an ego like that, it's a must.

I wonder if he wears a mask because he thinks he is ugly — save for his mouth, that is. That's kind of sad. God-like body and a pizza face? A true crime, if you ask me.

He tilts his head at me, reminding me that I am just staring at him like I'm struck by how hot he is. ~Please, don't flatter yourself, Zorro.~ "Does the Black Siron need anything from me?"

That's PG.

~Only~ PG.

He nods to my fishing rod and flicks his hand to keep doing what I was doing. It's hard to tell with his bulky mask, but I think I see amusement in his gaze.

Huh, so the evil bastard has a sense of humor. How sweet.

I huff again and try to catch a fish, and fail yet again. The salty wind is antagonizing me, taunting me into breaking this shitty fishing device over my knee.

I grit my teeth and raise the bow again, and that's when I feel him behind me. I freeze.

I feel his arm come around me and guide my arms into a different position ever-so-gently. Then I feel his hands low on my hips, applying pressure to make me change my footing.

My heart is pounding, and I can feel his breath on my neck as he points to a metal latch.

I don't understand, so he leans into me to reach for the latch and flips it, causing it to lock. My eyes widen. No wonder I did have any power. A surge of adrenaline pounds through me, and I retake aim.

He comes to stand next to me and points at the waves and looks back at me. He is motioning me to ~wait~. He then points to the sky then back down to the waves, telling me to look...closer?

"You want me to look closer?"

He tilts his head like, ~kind of.~ He makes a fish movement with his hand and points to the waves, then the sky. Then shakes his head no, ~not good~.

"What?" I ask, getting frustrated. "No fish now?"

He nods ~yes~ with a grin.

I fight a grin as well—him demonstrating a fish was only slightly humorous.

He motions for me to shoot anyway with a shrug. I take a breath again and aim when I see him move to stand next to me, touching my hips again.

I adjust my footing as my pulse starts hammering in my neck like an ax murderer trying to break through the door. Siron points to the latch I almost forgot about, and I flip it, giving me power.

I am an expert on aim, being one of my Fairy Godmother traits. I target the waves. The shot pierces through the water like a bullet.

I scream and jump up and down like I am twelve with Taylor Swift tickets. I immediately stop, and I can feel my face redden as I notice eyes on me. Awesome.

But I glance over to Siron to see him smiling with the big redheaded brute.

"Siron, never did I see anyone get that excited over catching fish," the man bellows. "Maybe you should show her some more chores to do! She is very easily excitable." He winks at Siron.

I roll my eyes and toss the fishing bow at the red-haired man. "Thanks for ~NOT~ showing me the latch on the bow."

Siron signs to the man, and he nods, running off before I can punch him in the face. I glance back to the dark pirate and watch him pull a notepad out. So, he keeps one handy in case he must talk to me.

Siron leans his cane on a pole then starts to write, the wind making his shirt billow out. ~Just an observation~. He looks up at me and shows me the note.

~Tomorrow I can show you how to ensnare a big catch at the right time. I will not join you for dinner this eve. I have much to prepare for, and I am needed.~

I read it and nod. So I will not be in this leech's presence tonight. Perfect, Heaven sent.

"You don't have to trouble yourself on my account, I can get someone else to show me. I might as well be useful around here."

He walks up to me, and I tense. Siron shakes his head ~no~ and starts writing again, faster this time. He shows me the note.

~I will be the only one to show you, little dancer. I will not have my men distracted by your innocent charms. Clear?~

I can sense his negative energy. He is very serious. "Clear."

He takes a bow in front of me, and his eyes slowly slide over my body before he leaves with his cane. I shiver, feeling like he touched me, when clearly, he didn't.

I have a feeling I will not sleep well tonight — again.

CHAPTER 25

Apparently, Eltson is currently trying to outrun us.

It's not going to happen though. Mort says Black Siron's ship is much faster. I am super happy though; this experience has not been bad at all. Quite the opposite, weirdly enough.

Here I thought I was bought into some dark, twisted, sex slavery ring, but I have been treated like gold here.

It's very confusing because I am here relaxing like a queen on my fancy bed listening to Mort chew gummy bears. Not a pleasant sound. A lot of swishing and sloshing.

"Where did you get those?"

She looks up at me from her desk in the corner of our small room. "Pierce."

"He just gives you candy randomly?" I ask with a frown.

She rolls her eyes. "Not randomly, just when he feels bad. Earlier when I was scouting, I took a wrong turn and got caught in a room I was not supposed to be in."

I sit up and stare at her. "What room?"

"It's not a big deal."

"Well, it warranted gummy bears."

She shrugs, ignoring me.

"Just tell me, I'm bored to tears."

She sighs like I'm annoying. Mort looks like she is reliving something vile all of a sudden, her face losing some color.

"The chamber pot room. The man shut the door and I could not escape. I just had to flutter around until he was done with his...business."

I'm laughing before my brain can even process what she said.

"It's not funny, human," Mort hisses, cheeks red.

I fall against the bed, her angry face making me laugh harder. "You eat those gummy bears, you deserve them." I snort into my pillow.

Mort chews as she glares at me. "Being serious now—it has been three days since you saw Siron?"

I wipe my eyes and think on that. "I thought it was longer than that, but yeah."

She looks thoughtful. "What is with everyone being on the verge of death?"

"You think he is on the verge of death?"

Mort pops more gummies in her mouth. "Could be. That ex-girlfriend must have been very angry with him, nasty curse. The men on the ship are scared she will start coming after them.

"But wouldn't it be awesome if that Siron prick died? You would be free if he did, making getting back to Apollo easier."

I chew on my lip. "Yeah," I say, and take a breath. I get up, ready to get out of this room, feeling very claustrophobic all the sudden. "Mort, I will be back. Please watch where you're flying, for Pete's sake."

I can almost hear her rolling her eyes.

I wander aimlessly, nowhere in particular, just letting my heart lead the way. I laugh. My heart cannot be trusted, it tends to get me into lots of trouble.

I wonder why Siron has not sought me out. I thought I was bought as a sex object. Not that I'm complaining—just confused, is all. Maybe the man ~is~ very ill. He could be dead right now for all I know.

It's probably what he deserves. All his bad deeds must have caught up with him.

What is done in the dark is always brought to the light, or so the girls at the strip joint always claimed. I believe them too—you should have seen their faces, very serious.

But that doesn't stop me from wandering hallways I have never been through.

One of my many faults will always be curiosity. Which is why I signed the Fairy Godmother contract in the first place—I could not die in this life without knowing.

I think it's been an hour of me wandering with little luck. Why do I want to find him? Not sure—curiosity, I am guessing.

I wander back into their library, if you want to call it that. Study? It is one of the cozier rooms, which means the couches are not metal. They have black velvet cushions, which is way better than steel on your butt.

I take a random book off the bookshelf and plop down, gazing at the cover. It's some dictionary that looks fabulously boring. I'm not sure if I have enough patience for this.

I am too lazy to get up and look for another, my mind and body exhausted. My head falls back against the cushion, deep in thought.

It's crazy to think about where I started in all of this and now where I am at. What a ride it's been, for lack of better words. This has not been the Disney movie

I envisioned.

That's when I hear his cane, and for a split second, I get excited—no, I get ~surprised~.

It's not excitement. It's my boredom making me think crazy thoughts. I calm myself and take a breath as I listen. I hear him pause as he enters the room, probably seeing me.

Did he not want to see me? Strange.

"I can leave," I say, feeling his presence behind me.

I hear him continue to walk into the room, then I see him as he sits right across from me. He is wearing a tight, black shirt which makes him look larger than life. The dark villain.

I look away for a second, not wanting my brain to go to places I don't want it to. "I was just leaving."

Siron leans forward and grabs the book out of my hand with a frown.

I blush. "I just picked a random one."

He slightly grins and gets up, walking with his cane to the bookshelf. Skimming his long fingers over some novels, he finds the one he is searching for.

Siron walks back over to me and sits on the same couch as me, tossing the book onto my lap.

I swallow, not expecting him to sit next to me. "What is this? How to enslave people?"

His expression does not change as I look down at it.

I try not to smile, but it's hard. I close my eyes as I fight the grin that threatens my person. From the cover of this book, it is obviously a romance, and somewhere inside me, I can't believe how sweet the gesture is.

I take a steady breath as I look back at him. "Thank you, this sounds much better." ~Damn it.~ I grin at him and ask, "This yours?"

His eyes sparkle as he takes out a notepad from his pocket. Why does even that seem endearing? I need to get off this ship and away from him ASAP. I am losing my freaking mind. Cabin fever?

He writes, then looks back to me, showing me.

~Please tell no one. It'll ruin me.~

I laugh out loud. Holy mother of Mike, this cutthroat pirate is joking with me. "Whose is it really?" Probably belongs to one of his many female slaves.

He writes again then sighs as he hands me back the note.

~My chief's wife. Bloody irritating for a cutthroat and evil individual to have this sort of blasphemous material.~

I laugh again and can't seem to wipe the smile from my face. I look away because he is staring at me like he wants to dissect me or something.

I can smell him and it's not something I want to comment on. The fresh scent is nothing groundbreaking. Tons of men shower regularly and use great smelling soap.

Congratulations, you're not disgusting. Not worth a medal. Mega eye roll.

He hands me a note and I glance at it.

~My dancer, were you looking for me?~

My cheeks heat and I try to play it off. "No!" I stare again at his narrowed eyes.

"Well, I was just a little curious about your health, seeing how you're in charge here. I want to know what my future looks like."

I glance at him, then to his full lips. The color looks fine. I mean, they look healthy, not cold and blueish like a dead person. They have a nice creamy hue…I look away, feeling like I am the twilight zone.

I squeeze my eyes shut, telling myself to be normal.~ Please~, be normal. "So, how ~is~ your health?" I ask, then look at him with, I'm hoping, a normal expression.

My eyes might be too overly wide, though it's hard to tell.

~Hi, my name is Awkward. What's yours?~

He tilts his head at me like he is studying me. I hate when he does that, like he's trying to see into my soul. He leans back on the couch, displaying his wide girth—not god-like in any way.

Siron finally starts writing, then places the note on my thigh—~upper~ thigh.

I stare at the note on my beautiful emerald gown with gold lining. It was brought to me today, and I wonder if he picked it out or if it was just a random thing. Random, most likely.

I feel like it's hot in here, my hormones must be all whacked out. Nothing three margaritas wouldn't fix though. Just saying.

I looked around, wondering if they have tequila on this ship.

Focus.

I pick up the note and read it~.

My health is not your concern. I will say that you look a little pale, I hope you do not get seasick. If you are feeling that way my staff will be here to aid you.~

~But you should be happy to know I will release you once we make landfall.~

My head jerks toward his in shock.

He just stares back at me, dark eyes glittering.

"Why?" I don't mean to sound so upset, because I'm not. This could not have worked out more perfectly. I nod and smile, feeling a little lost. What's giving me pause? Why does my chest feel tight?

He is writing, and I watch him—dark tattoos gracing his golden skin, tight black shirt, Zorro mask, and shining black hair.

I curse.

I just need to see Apollo again. I almost feel tears welling in my eyes, my confusion is so frustrating.

If I was a physiologist, I'd probably say the sudden fall of Apollo impacted me emotionally and this is normal. Feelings of attachment are to be expected. It's how you're dealing with this sudden trauma.

I glance at him and realize he has been watching me while my inner battle is going on.

He slowly hands me the note, and I look. ~I see so much sorrow in your lovely eyes. Is this for Apollo? Do you not like my gift of freedom to you?~

I take a shaky breath. "Honestly?" I whisper. "I don't know."

Please don't cry.

He hands me another note.

~If you love him, then go to him.~

I look at him angrily. "Why are you so nice? I thought you were this feared monster!" Why am I yelling?! I am losing my shit, and I don't know why. Is Aunt Flow making an early trip to see me? Perfect!

He looks down and starts to write, pausing every few seconds like he is at a loss for words. I take another shaky breath and realize I could be having a panic attack. This whole experience it a lot to take in.

First off, I am on this weird planet trying to make Apollo fall in love with me, then BOOM he is almost dead.

Then I get this weird mind-fuck and get bought by this mega-sexy bad boy that is turning out to be the biggest teddy bear! ~Shit~. Tears are streaming down my face. I hate this.

I feel him grab my arm and jerk me toward him. My small body is now in his large lap. I stop crying.

261

I've never been this close to him before. I can feel his body heat and rock-hard muscle under me, and it makes me lightheaded.

Guilt fills me instantly. I am cheating on Apollo, it occurs to me — who is on his deathbed, for crying out loud!

Siron grabs me and pulls me to him, my head nuzzling his smooth neck. I feel more tears streaming down my cheeks as his arms encircle me tightly.

I feel his energy engulf me fully, and I never want him to let me go. Absolute insanity.

I can't do this.

This is so wrong on so many levels.

I pull back and try to get out of his arms, but he holds me still. I look at him, and he hands me a note, his dark gaze intense.

~Tell me what hurts you.~

"I can't," I sob.

He tilts his head and expels a breath.

"Why are you being nice to me? Why do you seem different? Why aren't you mean and cruel? You are not making sense to me right now," I moan in misery.

He adjusts himself so he can pull out his notepad to write. He writes quickly, glancing up at me every so often. I wish I could see under the mask.

Siron shows me the note.

~I still might be all the things you ask about, but circumstances have changed. I am dying, little dancer, and maybe I'd like to do something right for once.~

"What?! Why is every man I care about dying?" I scream. "What the hell is happening?!"

His eyes widen.

I clamp my mouth shut, heart pounding. Did I just admit to caring about him? Shit. I push off him and run from the room like a lunatic. Class-A crazy.

And the award for the best insane performance goes to…Viola!

Standing ovation.

I need therapy, a shrink, or maybe I will check myself into the nutty house, I'm sure they have one of those here. Insanity is common among humans everywhere.

I am not sure how I make it back to my room without a mental breakdown in the hallway for everyone to witness. I lay on my bed and scream into my pillow, kicking and punching the soft mattress.

Then the tears come, slow and brutal, like slow embers. I need to pull my shit together. I have never been this emotional before.

"Where have you been?!" Mort is suddenly in the room. "They are gaining on Eltson's ship and are closing in fast!"

I jerk up and sniff, wiping my eyes quickly.

"Are you crying?"

"No."

She snorts. "Looks like you are. Anyway, Laura is on the ship and apparently has not had the time of leisure as we had. The man Eltson is a real bastard apparently—she had to use a lifeline."

"Is she okay?" I ask, genuinely concerned, sniffing slightly. I guess not every captor is like Black Siron. I squeeze my eyes shut—~don't you dare cry, you cheap hooker.~

I put myself down because it will toughen me up. It's proven to work, or so I was told by the head stripper at the club. I give myself a shake and get up, taking a calming breath.

I got this.

No, I don't.

Yes, I do.

No.

Yes.

No.

"Human? You okay?" Mort asks with a raised brow.

"Mort," I take another breath and grit my teeth, "how is Apollo?"

She frowns. "I think the same, no new updates are logged."

I nod and try to re-braid my hair—step one in getting my shit together. "So what do we do now?"

"We can go up and see the action until they say differently, I guess. You need to tell Siron that we need to save the other princess.

"Laura needs to be out of harm's way or she might have to be ejected from the game altogether. Personally speaking, I think she is over this.

"Eltson came to her completely naked, wanting to play torture games—hence the lifeline."

I shiver. "That's bad."

Mort nods.

I take a deep breath and finish with my hair. "Okay, I'm going up."

I can hear shouts and screams already. I make my way to the top deck and see total chaos, cannons being loaded, men with dangerous-looking weapons aimed and ready.

I hear an ear-splitting sound and realize that we are in combat. My heart is pounding as I try to locate a bow.

I can shoot better than anyone on this ship—well, save for the fishing bow that I never got to shoot with Siron. I need to think fast and collected, not letting emotions rule my actions.

I run up to the red-haired highlander, kicking myself for not catching his name. "I need a bow!"

He looks at me like I've lost my mind. "Go below deck, lass, are you crazy?!"

"I can shoot!"

He pushes me out of the way and barks orders to the other men. Double damn.

I glance up and see Siron shouting commands while carrying a long, deadly blade on the deck above me, no cane in sight. I wonder if he is hurting, exerting himself like this.

As if he could sense my stare, our gazes clash, and I can sense his panic like a ton of bricks. Like a child caught with scissors in a running stance.

I will reflect on this later, but right now, he is making his way to me, jumping over this and that like a seasoned athlete running to the finish line. No signs of him being disabled.

He waves his arm for me to go below deck like a crazy person. He stops in front of me, entirely out of breath. His large chest moves up and down as his dark gaze sears me.

"I need a bow! I can shoot better than anyone here!" I yell over another loud crash. I think my right ear is humming.

He closes his eyes and shakes his head ~no~.

"Siron, trust me!"

He angrily shakes his head ~no~ again, then points to the door — ~or he will carry me~. He mimes that he will pick me up over his shoulder.

He is counting down from five like I'm a toddler, making me mental.

"Don't you dare!"

Within seconds I am heaved over his shoulder, my ass in the air. I try kicking and screaming but it is a lost effort.

He puts me down in the library, dropping me on the couch. My hair covers my face so I can't see him through the heavy mess of my hair.

"Siron!" I scream through angry tears.

I feel him pulling my hair away from my face until I see him. He grabs my face in his hands and his lips descend on mine.

I am frozen.

I feel the impact clear down to my toes, my heart in sudden shatters. He pulls back abruptly, and I bring my hand to my lips to try and feel the contact. ~He kissed me~.

Siron closes his eyes like he is angry and leaves me there on the couch with my erratic thoughts.

I'm not sure how long I sit there until I hear Mort screaming my name.

"Viola! What is wrong with you?!" Mort is in front of my face.

I look up at her, my badass self finally emerging after long thoughts of confusion and self-pity. "I need a briefing, Mort. Cut all the bullshit! I know I have been acting weird."

She takes a second, then says, "We are being overpowered. Siron is hurt, and I fear this could go south! It can't go south, that will only lessen our chances."

I stand up and hold out my hand, eyes narrowed. "Give me one badass motherfucking bow."

Mort's eyes widen, then she smiles, typing away. "Glad to have you back, human."

CHAPTER 26

"Mort," I say as we make our way up toward the lower deck, "I need you to shapeshift into a nondescript man in case I need help. This is going to be a full-blown, Rambo-style exit scene."

I strap my bows and equipment to me and tuck a knife in my boot for good measure. A loud explosion violently shakes the ship, making me slam against the wall. "Shit!"

"How's this?" Mort asks, now standing six feet tall as a rugged man.

My eyes widen as I take her cutthroat appearance. "Perfect, Mort. Impressive." I pause with a grin as I look at her pants, not being able to help my immaturity. "Does…it feel weird?"

"Does ~what~ feel weird?"

"You know…" I nod to her pants with a wide-eyed look.

"No, I don't."

"Are you serious? You don't know what I'm talking about? Because sometimes I'm not sure if you're joking," I say with annoyance.

"Joking about what?"

I stare at her. "A penis, Mort. A male penis," I deadpan.

Mort's man features contort into surprise then disgust. "I do not have a human penis — gross."

A burst of laughter escapes me. "What?!" I cover my mouth to gain control of my amusement. "What do you have then?!"

Mort looks pissed, making me laugh harder. "I still have a vagina, human."

My eyes widen, bulge even. "Mort," I take a breath, "you have just transformed yourself into the foulest female in history."

Mort tries to be angry, but it's not working. Laughter bubbles out of her throat, sounding very man-like.

We both have a moment of pure laughter until another explosion rocks the ship, bringing us back to our urgent situation.

"Okay," I say, becoming very serious. "Cover me, ugly man-woman."

"On it."

As soon as we make it outside, I can see how bad it really is. Eltson's men are everywhere, the two ships side-by-side. Eltson's men are thankfully wearing blue, making them an easy target.

I glance up at the top deck and see Siron fighting with the highlander, outnumbered by far.

Siron is bleeding from one arm and fighting with the other. He will not last long like this, not with his health in rapid decline.

~Hold on, Momma's coming.~

"Pierce has upgraded your focus, free of charge. He says...make it rain?!" Mort yells behind me with a frown, looking up into the sky. "I don't think you have the ability to make it rain!"

"Oh yes, I do." Smiling, I close my eyes and feel electric currents flowing through me like a river of lava. I can hear my heart beating loud in my head as I take a calming breath, adrenaline pumping.

I open my eyes, and everything is moving in a slower time. All color is muted save for the slightest hints and highlights. With a dark grin, I take aim at the man Siron is currently fighting.

My arrow flies like a scream fills the night. Dead on, straight through the heart. I don't have time to see the shock on Siron's face.

I fire off one, two, three, four, five, six more arrows within seconds, all hitting their mark. I start to walk, and my eyes focus on an explosion, the mushroom cloud rising slowly into the sky, almost beautifully.

I see men charging at me, but they are moving so slowly it's laughable. I raise my bow and hit each one of them with lethal accuracy, my heart rate rising.

The pounding becomes louder and harder the longer I stay like this. I am running out of energy fast.

I fire off arrows at the unsuspecting enemy, hitting more and more men, the shock showing on their faces as the arrows impale them.

I take a slow, labored breath. I can only do this a short while apparently before I feel like I want to die. I glance back at Siron and he is watching me with a horrified expression.

Siron is probably wondering what in the hell I am, just like Apollo.

I raise my bow and pierce a few more men before I fall to my knees in dizziness. My head is swimming in a tornado of lights and colors.

Now I know what it feels like to shotgun a bottle of Skol vodka on an empty stomach.

Sounds come crashing back in real time as I moan on my knees. ~Do not throw up, please.~ Another explosion sounds to my left, making my brain ring loud.

~Must keep going.~

I slowly stand up and pull out more arrows, but this time I do not have my slow-motion power. Does not matter, I am still an amazing shot.

I feel Mort grab my arm and jerk me to the left so hard I almost fall back to my knees. My eyes widen—I almost just got stabbed by a swinging sword.

~Huh.~

"Human! Get your wits together," Mort hisses as we hide behind a metal wall.

"I'm fine," I say, head pounding.

"Your bow is backward."

I look down and curse. "Oh, right, shit."

Mort's manly features turn into surprise, and she glances around the corner. "Nice shooting though. I think you gave Siron's men the advantage. The enemy is fleeing!"

"Really?!" I say, excited that this worked. "Can you see Laura on the other ship?"

Mort is typing for a few seconds. "She is on the deck being held captive, it states," she says, and looks up at me.

"I can sniper."

Mort pulls me to the right and points. "There, do you see her?"

It takes me a second, but yes, I do. Laura is crying, with a long blade held to her neck as Siron and his men slowly approach. Not good. She'd better be ready to yell for her lifeline if need be.

"He is going to slit her throat."

"Then you'd better take aim."

Without much thought, I step out into the open and pull my bow back to full capacity. I let out a slow breath and calm my body as I home in on her captor. She is far away — this is a risky shot.

"Shoot," Mort hisses.

"I can't, I don't have a clean shot. This is not a gun, Mort." I am sweating. The man's yelling at Siron's men in some different language as he jerks Laura around. "Fuck."

"Can we get behind him?"

I lower the bow and nod. "That way."

We both sprint down to the lower deck so we are in a better position to get a clean hit, though it does not make it any less risky. There is smoke everywhere and he could move, or I could impale them both like a skewer.

"We need to hurry, human."

The man is violently screaming, drawing blood at her neck from his recklessness. "Oh, not good," I hiss, sweat running down my forehead.

Without a second's thought, I fire an arrow too far to his left, missing my mark completely.

"You missed!" Mort's mouth is hanging open.

I know. But it made him move from the shock. A decoy. Diversion. Now I have a clear shot of his chest and I take it.

The surprise on his face as the silver arrow penetrates his chest, inches from Laura's shoulder, is priceless. Though I don't think he will save any money on his Geico insurance, because he's dead.

Mort's man-body hugs me. "You did it!"

I smile. Siron grabs Laura, who is bawling her eyes out hysterically, holding her bloody neck. We did it, though! I drop my bow and run toward them, up to the stairs to the top deck.

Siron's men are taking the remaining crew as captives as we speak. As I come in sight, most of the crew pauses and turns to stare at me in awe.

Or horror. Maybe thinking I am a witch or something—I don't blame them.

"Laura!"

Through her sobs, she turns her face away from Siron and sees me. "S-sister?" she asks meekly, eyes puffy. When she sees it's me, she pushes off Siron to embrace me.

"Are you okay?!"

Laura sobs and wipes her nose. "Yes, thank goodness you're a sound shot. What the hell took you so long?"

I stare at her.

She laughs and gives me another hug. "Kidding, nice work."

Siron is watching us with a frown.

Laura stiffens. "Double crap," she whispers. "I forgot about him. Do we need to be worried?"

I look at her and shake my head. "No."

She frowns at me in question.

I can't answer as Siron walks up to us with his arms crossed over his chest, his bicep still looking badly injured. I can see Laura eyeing him up and down—with curiosity, most likely.

He signs to his men, who take Laura, the men assuring her they mean no harm. She looks back at me in terror, but I nod that ~it's okay.~

I am left with Siron staring at me intently.

I fidget with my skirt as my heart pounds. I must break the silence. "I told you I was a good shot."

He lets out a loud breath and rubs a hand down his neck.

The red-haired highlander walks up to us. "Siron, I have never seen a female shoot like that," he says, and eyes me. "Are you thinking what I am thinking?" His assessing gaze is not friendly.

Siron signs to him and the highlander does not like what he is being told, leaving with a loud cursing, shooting me a glare. Siron looks back at me with the same knee-buckling expression in his eyes.

I can't see his face, but I assume it's less than pleased. He nods for me to walk with a quick jerk of his neck.

"Where?"

He grabs my hand and pulls me along rather violently. For the first time, I get a little scared around him.

He brings me down long hallways and I think we are going to the library again, but he takes a sharp left into a smaller room. He shuts the door and I back up against a desk, not sure what's happening.

"What are you doing?"

He just stares at me, breathing heavily.

"I will not tell you anything," I say, knowing what he wants to know. I'm playing with fire here. He could change on me in a split second. I brace myself, willing to use a lifeline. I should keep my mouth shut.

His jaw clenches as his dark gaze sears me. I can feel his energy. He is holding back, the veins in his neck bulging.

"I mean no harm," I whisper.

He turns his head like he can't stand the sight of me, his body language showing he is barely holding on to whatever restraint he has left.

Siron glances back to me and whips out his notepad, scribbling words. He hands me the note and I take it with shaking fingers.

~I feel pity for Apollo. Such lies from the lips of an angel.~

"I'm not lying. But I can understand what this looks like." I swallow, realizing I look like a trained killer.

He writes again, then hands me the paper.

~Be warned. You will be closely watched now. Until the time I release you. Lay low if you know what's good for you. You're lucky I do not lock you up for your deception.~

He turns to leave.

"I saved your life!"

I bite my lip.

He turns around so fast that I gasp, hand on my throat as I am now against the wall. His lips are next to my ear, and I hear him whisper,

"~Which is why you're still alive."~

Siron leaves me there.

I'm still shaking.

I hug myself, feeling empty inside. He used his voice, and the harsh whisper impacted me to the core.

The man hates me, that is clear. When he kissed me earlier, it must have been just out of confusion.

I touch my lips. It's best this way.

CHAPTER 27

Laura rubs her forehead and curses. "I do not trust Siron, or anyone in this world for that matter. How do we know we will be able to talk to this supposed healer in time to save Apollo?"

I sniff and do not say anything. We both lounge on my bed like queens, having been locked in our rooms since the raid.

From what his men say we should be making landfall tomorrow, then he will take the healer captive. Siron still has hope that he will cure whatever the black magic is that's killing him.

Pierce already confirmed that Apollo would be healed. All we must do is get him alone and buy his healing skills, or something like that.

I have not been in the right state of mind since Siron entered my life—forced himself into my life.

I only have three more weeks left. That's not long.

I can't wait to leave this place and see Apollo again—alive. I just need to see him again and fast. My heart hurts for him. This mess is all my fault and I must stay clear of mind and fix it.

I need to get away from Siron's energy, for he is sucking the life out of me. We don't have to worry about an escape because Siron said he'd release me—us. "He will release us."

I can feel her eyes on me. "You actually believe that crap? He is rumored to be an extremely evil man." She sits up a bit. "Have you seen him without his mask on? Is he scary? Super ugly? Deformed?"

"No, he never takes it off, but I doubt he's deformed."

"Shame he does not then," she murmurs, and falls back.

"Why?"

Laura giggles and looks at me. "Evil aside, that man is damn sexy." She waves her hand and licks her lips. "They don't make men like that back home."

I try not to smile. They don't make men like ~Apollo~ back home. "I have not noticed." I hear Mort snort in the corner, and I ignore her. Mort knows nothing.

"Yeah right. You have been in his presence for a while now. He's like Jason Momoa: sexy, but better. He's not an actor, but the real thing, ya know?

"You see though, I always fall for the bad boy. It's my problem in real life. I just need a good boy. I need dating help."

"Yeah," I say, bored with this topic.

She looks over to Leenie who is pretending to sleep, but one eye keeps opening. "Leenie, can I have a one-night stand with sexy Siron? Not against the rules, right?"

"Might as well." Leenie shrugs.

Mort laughs.

Laura's face brightens and she glances at me. "And you are sure this guy is not what he seems? I don't want to have to use a lifeline again if he starts to beat me or something."

I am not angry.

Nope.

I feel fine.

"Yes, but he can't talk." Or at least I don't think he can. He did whisper in my ear, but I think that was because I angered him so bad. The man hates me, that is a ~fact~ now.

Laura should go for it. I bet he'd be pretty good in bed. Not amazing, but good enough to make it worth it.

"He can't talk, huh? Why is that even sexier? I bet he has killer expressions then — like, panty-dropping expressions. Maybe I can get him to take off his mask."

"I don't think that is a good idea," I say, facing her.

"Why? You have hunky Apollo."

I take a second. ~Why?~ "Because if you bang him and he decides he likes you, he will not want to let you go. We need to be released."

"No, ~you~ do." She looks thoughtful. "Leenie, if I fall in love, do I get to stay? Even if it is not Apollo? Because bitch over here took him." She winks at me.

Leenie opens an eye and nods. "Actually, you can, if the main objective is met. If the main objective is met, anything is possible."

"Really?!"

"Really?" I say, shocked, sitting up.

"Interesting." Laura looks like she just stole the crown jewels. She glances at me. "What?" she says with a laugh. "He's hot, and why not save two men at the same time? Fairy Godmother Inc. will love us."

"If he's into you, I guess."

She laughs, looking offended. "You're telling me he has not tried to get with you once? I mean, he did pay a pretty penny for you, which is weird. It's also weird that he has not so much as got to second base.

"So maybe he's not into ~you like he thought."

Touché.

"He's sick, Laura, thankfully. I do not want to cheat on Apollo because this guy has nice abs. So does Apollo, ~news flash~. I doubt that's what the doctor ordered for him.

"Wild monkey sex is a must when you're dying?" I deadpan. Oh yeah, and he thinks I am a trained killer and does not trust me as far as he can see. Nope, just a ~Disney Love Agent~.

Yeah, I don't think he will buy that one.

"Right." She looks thoughtful. "Worth a shot I guess," she says with a feline look. "My time here is almost up and I want to get something positive out of it."

"He views me as a threat from that nice little performance of insane archery."

"That was impressive, I don't blame him. That might have been a little too much to stay under the radar." She looks at me. "I would have been so pissed if you shot me, though." She raises a brow. "Risky shot."

"Yeah," I say, and get up from the lush bed. "Lucky for you, Pierce made me a badass."

Laura rolls over and sighs. "I can sing like an angel, not that anyone gives a flying shit. It definitely didn't land me Apollo."

Mort laughs hard at that. "Flying shit."

Laura glances at Mort. "Your agent is weird."

"Understatement of the century," I say under my breath.

The door opens and Mort and Leenie are gone in a flash. There are a lot of men telling us what to do.

They're treating me differently than before. They stare a lot like I'm some alien—well, I guess I am. I get it and understand it. No more Mr. Nice Guy from Siron, I guess.

I'm actually glad. I want him to treat me like trash. It will allow me to shake this weird thing I have for him—this curiosity.

It's nothing more than that, and on some level maybe it's because he reminds me of Apollo. I think it's the arrogance, the male dominance that's almost irresistible to any female.

Nothing more than biological.

They say we can go on deck for a short while before dinner to celebrate the good news that they're in contact with Minerva the Great and he has agreed to Siron's terms on Eltson's release.

His men are being held captive somewhere in the lower levels of the ship. For the first time I am excited.

I can see Apollo soon. He's not dead and I can save him.

I smile, and Laura sees me and rolls her eyes, saying I'm too mushy for her. Not sure how she knew I was thinking about Apollo but ~whatevs~.

I glance down at my brown gown and take a breath. I did not want to stand out in the rich-colored gowns that were available.

My hair is in a low bun, and I tried my hardest to cover my cleavage but failed. The dresses are made to show off female assets, no doubt.

I look at Laura and grin. She is in a rose gown, looking radiant. Good, let her have her fun.

I only need Pierce again once Apollo is better. And I want to avoid seeing Siron or drawing any more attention to myself.

Time to get my priorities in line. Fairy Godmother Inc. depends on me, and me alone.

We are led to the upper deck to get fresh air, and to take in the dark beauty of

HEIR OF THE BEAST

the open sea. It's terrifying and stunning at the same time.

The wind whips tiny hairs out of my tight bun as I rest my hands in the metal rail. Closing my eyes and taking in a deep breath, the salty air refreshes my soul.

This experience is truly amazing no matter what happens.

I can hear Laura laughing and it makes me smile. She is something else, and I am glad she is my friend now. It's crazy how fast things can change here. I hope she finds what she is looking for here.

Maybe they will let her stay if Apollo is saved? Maybe everyone has the option to stay if they choose. I'll have to ask Mort about that later.

I see large waves as far as the eye can see. The massive ship moves up and down with each hard collision.

I turn and see the crew cleaning the ship from the recent battle, the bloodshed being washed away as if it never happened.

I killed men here.

A shiver slithers down my back. ~Don't think about that,~ they were bad men.

Laura is enjoying the shirtless men as they work to clean themselves and the ship. I can tell by her high-pitched laugh that she is excited.

I freeze.

Siron is sitting on a tall chair as he removes his torn black shirt to reveal a bloodied bicep and other bulging flesh. My cheeks heat to dangerous levels.

Are all these men built like gods? What do they feed the babies here, for the love of Pete and Mike and any other name I can think of?!

It's like their muscles are made from titanium—bulletproof. Great genetics. I look at his dark tattoos and raven hair and take a breath. Too bad he is a pirate and an unsavory soul.

I look away, not wanting to draw attention to myself by staring.

That's the last thing I need.

I need to get off this damn ship. I close my eyes again and focus on calming my breathing.

I'm not sure how long I stand here staring out into the sea before I feel a presence beside me. I don't look because I know who it is.

Bleeding hearts.

I see his large, tanned hands grip the rail like me as I continue staring forward. Why is the man seeking me out? I can tell he is looking at me. My skin is tingling, and I feel almost naked, exposed.

I grit my teeth and look to my right as our gaze's clash, the black stare piercing me. I wish I could see his face. It's very frustrating.

He steps closer to me, making my body tense.

I think I'm glaring at him.

Siron tilts his head and pulls out his notepad. He writes while looking up at me then hands me the note. ~Miss me? ~it reads.

Miss me?! Very arrogant, and I thought we were fighting. "No." I glance away.

I know he's writing again, and I wish my skin would stop buzzing. He hands me a note and I take it, though I don't want to.

~Liar,~ it says.

I jerk my head in his direction. "Liar?" I ignore the slight grin on his lips. He is wearing body armor, thank goodness, and is not bare-chested. Is he flirting with me? Trying to make up? How strange.

"You're taunting me. Why?"

I see his eyes lower to my breasts and my cheeks heat. He's not even hiding it. I look away and ignore that his black hair is braided down his back like a native warrior.

It's not hot at all.

Nope.

I feel him nudge me again with a note and I snatch it.

~Do you want me or Apollo? The choice is yours. Choose wisely,~ it says.

I almost gasp. I look at him, and he is serious, the smile gone. My heart is pounding out of my chest. Why would he ask me this? He knows my answer. He knows I do not like him like that!

He thinks I am a spy or something and still he is asking me this? I can feel my cheeks heat and my anger is rising. He hands me another note and I look down, not wanting to take it.

Siron puts it into my hand, and I glance at it, chest rising and falling.

~Your eyes have fire in them when you look at me, ~it says.

I take a slow breath. "Yes, they do." I pause. "Because I am angry all the time." I step back. "Apollo. I choose Apollo."

I turn and leave. This is ridiculous. The rage inside me is on the verge of boiling.

The audacity of this man. First he says I can go, and now he's asking if I want to stay? I don't even know what to make of it. I'm confused by him.

I keep walking.

~Where the hell am I going?~ I look around the hallway I just entered and curse. I'm lost. How long was I walking in justified anger?

I glance back, and he is right behind me, making me gasp. I back up against the metal wall and hold my hands up.

"What do you want from me?" I feel like that's a dumb question seeing how he bought me for sexual reasons, but I feel like there is something deeper here.

He is writing, looking upset, his jaw flexing.

I take the paper with shaking fingers.

~I want the truth, little dancer, and I will kiss you to get it. I want to prove to you that you are in denial, ~it says.

I don't think my heart could beat any harder, and I brace myself as he grabs me around the waist. ~Be a cold fish, be a cold fish. ~Don't smell the clean scent of him. Ignore how exotic he appears.

Do cold fishes feel like they are being engulfed in flames? Maybe after they're dead and tossed on the grill.

I'm being thrown into fire while I'm still alive.

His hands are applying pressure on my hips as he pulls me closer, my breasts now pressed to his hard chest. I feel faint and all I can see are his perfect lips.

"Don't kiss me," I whisper, feeling my eyes water.

He leans into my ear, and I shiver. "Then tell your eyes to stop begging me to," he barely whispers.

I squeeze my eyes shut.

His lips are now on my neck, and I moan, or sigh, or express my distaste. I hope.

I feel my body humming, tingling, a warmth spreading in my lower regions as his tongue tastes me. I try not to make a sound, but my vocal cords are not communicating with my brain.

The moment his lips take mine I am gone. He is devouring me almost to a point where I cannot breathe. His tongue plunges into my mouth and I am at his mercy. I cannot get enough of him.

Our mouths are combating in a heated and dangerous dance. I am breaking the rules, but my body will not stop. I can't stop. I can't. ~I want him.~

He seems familiar even though I have not seen all of his face. I have not known him long, but I can't contain this desire. It's almost as if I know his mouth already.

We are losing control.

I can feel his desire shift, and now it's turned desperate, frantic, ~wild~. I am pressed hard against the wall as his mouth breaks away from my swollen lips.

He scorches a trail down my neck, making me grip him harder. I am panting, grabbing at his dark hair, anything I can get my hands on. His mouth is on my cleavage, pulling me up to ravish me better.

Oh mercy. The man has passion, and he is almost scaring me with it. Our hearts are beating together, our breathing harsh and rapid.

I grab his mask and rip it off, wanting to see all of him.

He seizes me instantly and flips me around so I'm facing the wall. I can feel the hardness of him and the heat coming from his body. ~Bad move.~

"Not allowed," comes his harsh whisper.

I hear him moving while one arm braces me to the wall. He must be putting on his mask again, which makes me livid. "Why can't I see? I don't care if you're scarred," I hiss.

Siron flips me back around, and he is breathing hard, his large chest rising and falling. He is writing now, and I wait patiently, trying to get my brain waves back in sync.

What have I done? I have really cheated on Apollo this time, haven't I? It makes me sick to my stomach.

There is something about Siron that draws me to him, something safe and familiar.

Stupid, I know.

He hands me the paper.

~*You deny what you feel now?*~

I feel my eyes cramp, and I look away. "Yes," I whisper.

I can hear a hiss come from his mouth, and then he writes again. He hands me the paper after a few heartbeats, and I take it, dreading what it says.

~I thought you'd say that. Who do you work for? ~it reads.

I look at him. "Take off your mask, and I will tell you."

Will I?

I might have lied.

He just stares at me, then closes his eyes and clenches his jaw.

"Why won't you show me?" I ask, swallowing the lump in my throat.

He takes the note in my hand and writes on the back. He hands me the note and I read it, my heart in my throat.

~What will Apollo think when he finds out your heart is not his anymore? His woman in love with another man.~

"Go to hell."

He tilts his head at me and clicks his tongue. He is writing, and I am barely able to stand here and watch, I would have slapped him if he was not wearing a mask. I am not in love with Siron. ~Cocky bastard.~

He hands me the note with a smile.

~See you at dinner. Save some of that fire for later. I have quite the appetite.~

"In your dreams," I hiss.

I've always wanted to say that.

He turns back to me and winks, and then he is gone.

I notice that he is favoring one leg and that he seems to be very wary. I don't care. I wonder if our little make-out session hurt him, making me feel a little less guilty.

I let out a scream and stomp my foot, clenching my fists. I just lit the barn on fire this time and threw on some gasoline for good measure. I close my eyes, wondering what I will tell Apollo. Tell him nothing?

~I'm sorry Apollo, I was a little confused and made out with the Black Siron and it meant nothing. There might have been a little tongue action, but that's it. Swear.~

~Oh? What's that? You hate me? Perfect.~

That will not go over well.

How could Apollo want someone like me once he finds out? He will be devastated, rethinking whatever he feels for me.

"Viola!"

It's Laura, making me relax a little. She walks up to me with wide eyes. I frown at her in question. "Is everything okay?"

She stares at me and laughs. "I cannot believe it." She shakes her head. "Black Siron is in love with you, and you like him back! How in the hell did you manage that?"

I pale. "I don't know what you're talking about," I say lamely, heart pounding.

Laura puts her hands on her hips. "You are in a major pickle, lady."

I squeeze my eyes shut. "Shit," I hiss.

"Does Pierce know?"

"I don't think so, but who knows at this point. I could have destroyed our mission," I say, feeling sick.

"You had Apollo. Now, I get that this guy is crazy hot, but you had Apollo. How did you let yourself fall for an evil man?" Her eyes are wide and disbelieving.

"I don't know," I whisper. "I don't think I fell for him. I still love Apollo."

"Girl, you cannot have them both, this does not work that way," she says, and clicks her tongue and shakes her head.

"Something is different with Siron, and I can't figure it out," I moan in misery. "He reminds me of Apollo, if you want to know the truth."

Laura frowns at me and chews her lip. "They are definitely not alike. Maybe in the physical sense, I guess. They both have very similar builds now that I think on it.

"But this guy can't even talk! How did he sweet-talk you?" She holds her finger up. "Pun intended."

"I don't know, Laura," I whine. "What are we going to do?"

"Well, be prepared to get your ass chewed out by Pierce Charming."

"Do you think they have tequila on this ship?" I really need to know.

"They'd better."

CHAPTER 28

"Pierce already knows." Mort grins and pops her gum. I don't even want to know what she did to deserve that gum.

Laura glances at me with a frown. I look at Mort and take a deep breath, finding my inner calm. "You're telling me that Pierce knows about my...little love triangle?"

Double damn.

Mort holds up her finger and glances at us both. "Who didn't know is really the question here." She snorts and leans back in her chair. "Leenie, you knew right?"

"Yup."

Mort nods at my shocked expression. "Pierce told me to trust him, and to stay out of it." She chuckles and examines her plain nails. "We are trained agents, we know everything. Nothing gets by me."

Leenie scowls at Mort. "I thought Pierce told you?"

Mort's eyes widened and she snorts. "No."

Leenie levels her a ~RIIIGHT~ expression.

I close my eyes. "What did Pierce say?" I need words of wisdom, some sort of sign on what I must do. Too much male testosterone—my brain is malfunctioning.

"Well." Mort sits up, "let me ask." She types and blinks, scowling. "Hi, Mort here. Yeah, I know you know it's me. Uh-huh, right. Well, she is really confused, and very out of control at this point."

"Hey," I say with a frown. "I am not out of control, ~Mort~."

Well. Maybe. Probably.

Still never found that tequila.

"Right." Mort is typing and nodding.

"What's he saying?" Laura asks. "That threesomes are not permitted?" She laughs, snorting into her hand.

I roll my eyes.

Right?

"Well," Mort glances at me, "Pierce says just go with the flow. Do what feels right."

That makes Laura laugh harder.

"Do what feels right?" I repeat.

Mort shrugs. "Yeah. He said it might help to get Siron's mask off though. Maybe he is really ugly and that will help with your decision."

"That is very vain of Pierce."

Mort shrugs again. "That was my idea."

Leenie is also typing. "Okay, we will be making landfall shortly, about two hours out. Let's get to the healer then decide what to do from there."

We all nod.

Laura frowns and falls back down on the bed. "Now that you scored both of the hot alpha-men, how am I going to get laid? Very selfish of you."

289

***

I take a deep breath and walk out onto the large deck. My stomach is in knots. Laura went up about an hour ago and our agents left as well, to scout the area for any impending danger.

My nerves kept me down here, feeling like I am drowning. I still have my dilemma and I feel guilt eating me alive, tearing up my soul piece by piece.

How could I do this to Apollo?

I shiver.

I am a horrible person, not worthy of his love. I must tell Apollo what I have done, and I know it will break his heart. He will be confused, angry, and hurt.

My eyes start to cramp, and I take another breath, not wanting to give in to my emotions.

Right now, I need to be strong and cure Apollo, he deserves that. Then we can work out this mess I have found myself in.

My black hair is braided down my back save for a few strands that Laura pulled out for me. My gown is a lovely   pale green and white. Very medieval with a hint of the twenty-first century.

The style here is breathtaking. Pierce took in the bustline, much to my horror. That's the last thing I need right now. Sometimes I am not sure what Pierce is thinking—he can't play both sides here.

But I am too emotionally exhausted to put up a fight. I'll just let Charming do what he wants. I am already in way too deep.

I smile. Laura has been so supportive, and I could not imagine doing this without her.

There are plenty of handsome warrior-like men on this ship and she is in

~Laura-heaven, ~as she puts it. One with an eye patch and a large beard seems to be catching her eye.

He is very manly. Not even sure how she can see his face with all that facial hair. I can tell his body is perfect, like a lot of the men here…not to name ~any~ names. ~Ehem.~

But Laura is laughing, being herself. Completely different from when she first arrived. I can see why the man seems to be smitten with her. Good for her — at least someone is not emotionally destroyed.

If I can win Apollo back, maybe Laura can stay here with him? Even though the man is a cutthroat.

I look down with dread. The chances that Apollo will take me back are very slim — slim to none. I grit my teeth and walk, nodding to a few men.

The massive deck is full of pirate-looking warriors running here and there, probably getting ready to make landfall. I walk up to the rail, and in the distance I can see a large mountain.

I take a shaky breath and pray everything goes as planned.

We are finally here.

I look to my left and I can see Siron on the top deck like some god-like creature. Dark, tanned skin with his Native American-like black braid and tattoos.

His arms are exposed showing his bulging biceps. I think if he clapped his hands, he would create a quake with the impact.

He is wearing black armor with weapons strapped to him, making him appear dangerous, powerful, unnaturally…alluring to the female gender.

"Stop," I hiss to myself.

I look away and I can already sense that he has noticed me, making the hairs on my neck stand on end. I shiver, my body humming with anticipation.

All of these are not good reactions to confide to Apollo. I bite my lip and grit my teeth.

Why is Siron so... What's the word I'm looking for? Apollo-like. I can sense very similar qualities in them which is why I think I am having trouble.

I stiffen as I sense him behind me.

My whole body tingles.

"This is it. You can be cured and then you will release me," I say, trying to sound as indifferent as possible.

I feel his hand on my waist as he turns me. I look everywhere but his face, not wanting to jump into the tornado just yet.

My goodness, the man smells good. So good. It's like wild scent that can make a woman's brain malfunction.

I look up and tense. He looks so savage, his dark gaze trapping me as he starts to write.

He hands me the note.

~You look beautiful.~

I wanted to slap him. This is why I am messed up, confused, and sexually frustrated. Yes, very frustrated. He is too nice, too suave! He must know what he is doing.

I can see it in the glitter in his gaze. Siron knows what he is doing to me and will probably not stop anytime soon.

"Thank you. And you look like you are feeling...okay."

He smiles and looks out over the rail at the approaching land.

I did not see Siron all day yesterday. I thought we were to have dinner, but that never happened.

I thought it was because he was becoming very ill and physically could not. But he looks okay now, confusing me a little.

"Are you still going to let me go?"

Siron glances at me and expels a breath. He starts writing and slowly hands me the paper. I take the paper like I couldn't care less. Meh.

~You think Apollo will take you back after your heart's betrayal? Would you like me to take you downstairs again to remind you that you are mine?~

I lift my chin and ignore the nerves flashing through my body. "I was just projecting what I feel for Apollo onto you. It's because I miss him."

That was cold.

I can see he does not like that. His jaw flexes. He takes a minute, then grabs another paper and starts writing.

~By all means. I will release you.~

I bite my lip and glance up at him, not expecting that. "Thank you," I whisper.

He chuckles to himself and bows in my direction.

Why does he find this funny?

"Are you being truthful?"

He nods.

Siron tilts his head and writes more, then hands me the paper.

~I do not lie, my dancer.~

"What's funny then?"

He shrugs, making the muscles in his arms flex. Siron starts writing, taking his time, a smile on his perfect lips as he finally hands me the note. His eyes seem to sear me to the spot.

~I can sense, almost taste, how turned on you are by being next to me. Your eyes dilate and your breathing escalates. Not to mention I can see your hard nipples whenever I am near.~

~It's taking a lot of control on my part not to consume the passion I see in

your eyes. But I will honor the lie you tell yourself. Go back to Apollo. If he will even take you back.~

I suck in a harsh breath and my cheeks heat like my head is ready to engulf into flames. I go to speak but nothing comes out.

I can see the smirk on his lips as his gaze lowers to my breasts, and I feel naked instantly.

I am shaking with some emotion that I cannot describe. Anger, confusion, ~desire~, rage…

He leans down, making me tense. I am frozen. I feel his hot breath when he whispers in my ear, "Let me know if you change your mind."Siron turns and whistles, alerting everyone we have arrived.

Then he is gone.

My vision is tunneling.

I see bodies moving around me, but I can't seem to think clearly. I am so screwed. I will be in pain no matter what man I choose.

I cannot win.

So very tragic.

CHAPTER 29

"Keep alert," I hear a man say behind me.

I watch numbly as we are anchored, and Siron's men set out for the capture of the great healer. ~This nightmare is almost over~, I keep telling myself.

Eltson's life depends on Siron being healed, a worthy ransom for the aid of his personal miracle worker. It is still dangerous from what Mort was telling me before we arrived onshore.

I have a nervous feeling in the pit of my stomach. Apparently, we will be staying on the island of Mora Veil. It's a very small island, but very rich and off the radar.

It's like a vacation destination, from what I'm told. A destination for the corrupt, a place to cleanse a dirty soul. Eltson's wealth is vast, buying him an island and a towering castle.

I take a breath and glance around the tropical island. I still do not feel good about it, but that could just be my own guilt clouding my instincts.

I will have to face Apollo soon, and I am dreading it like the plague.

My legs are wobbly, still feeling like the ocean swaying under my feet. A wave of dizziness clouds my vision before it rights itself.

It seems like forever before carriages and horses come to fetch us. The massive carriages have yellow glowing lights around them, like space carriages from the future.

It really is awesome to see another world's technology that is so different from our own.

I take another breath as my eyes take in the scenery. The beach is stunning, and the towering mountains in the distance remind me of Mount Olympus. Home of the Greek gods.

Like Apollo.

"Let's go," Laura says beside me, and picks up her light blue dress to walk, "before some vicious tribe pops out of the trees to kill us."

~Really?~

"Did the ransom work then?" I glance at Laura. Siron left about an hour before everyone else, so who knows what is happening right now. I guess they struck a deal then?

"I have no clue, I can only assume," she says as we are led into a plush carriage.

The ride is bumpy, making my stomach even more upset than it already is.

"I really like him."

I glance at her and frown. It takes a moment for my brain to work. "Who?"

She grins, looking like a feline. "Well, if you have not noticed, I have been hanging around a certain someone."

My eyes brighten up as I think. "The hairy man?"

She bursts into laughter. "I like it, ~and~ I can tell he is very handsome under all of that manly facial hair. He's a great kisser."

I just stare at her. "Kisser?"

"Girl, you're not the only one who can have fun here."

I laugh, placing my hand over my mouth. At least someone is winning here. Too bad he is not the prince in question. I'm sure Laura would not fall for two men. What a nightmare.

"What's his name?"

"He won't tell me."

"What? Why?"

She shrugs and giggles. "He said he would soon."

Well, that is odd. "Why on Earth would he keep that from you?"

"I think he is just being mysterious."

I raise a brow. "A cutthroat pirate? Being romantically mysterious?"

She frowned at me.

"That's," I pause with a grin, "a little out of character. But what do I know?" I sigh and glance out the window. "I wouldn't take any advice from me."

~Do the opposite of anything I say or do.~

There is silence. "Well, I did think it was odd."

I look at her. "I'm sure it's nothing."

"It could be something."

Great, now I'm making her paranoid.

Laura leans forward. "I actually think this whole Siron being a ruthless pirate thing is bullshit."

She continues with a pointed look, "We have been treated like queens, Viola. This man is supposed to be feared beyond imagination."

"I know."

"It does not add up."

I nod. "We need to talk to Mort and Leenie."

"Agreed."

"Another thing," I say. "What do you think all of the other girls are doing while Apollo is in a coma?" Even saying that makes me sad, guilt filling up my thoughts.

"Probably falling in love with other men…getting laid. I don't know." She shrugs.

I nod with a chuckle.

"Destiny likes that butcher's son," I remind her.

"He's hot. I saw him."

I nod and glance out the window again.

Laura bites her lip. "Do you think he is some horrid outlaw, and that's why he won't tell me his name? Has he killed hundreds of innocent men?"

I stare at her. "It's possible. But he treats you good?"

She nods.

"Then I don't know. You will have to ask, I guess. Pry it out of him. At least he can talk," I say, and grin at her.

She laughs. "A small win."

We arrive at a large palace of white stone with gold accents; large pillars grace the entrance of the three-story entry. Like everything, it is stunning.

Men lead a handful of us into a lovely sitting room with men I do not recognize. Laura's manly man with no name walks up to the foreign men in white and gold finery.

They speak in a language I do not understand. but they are shaking hands and conversing as though they've known each other for a long time. Laura and I sit on the couch and wait patiently.

My heart is hammering. I just need to get to the healer and get back to Apollo before it's too late.

I have this insane sense of urgency. I don't even know if Apollo is still alive. I feel a wave of panic at that thought, willing the butterflies away.

Positive thinking.

It feels like forever before we are finally led to a room to freshen up in. I need to know if Siron was successful in getting healed. I need that medicine yesterday.

"Mort here." She is suddenly beside us, making Laura yelp.

I get up from the soft bed. "Mort! Talk to me."

"So, I think everything is going to plan, for once. Siron, from what I hear, has already received his first round of treatments for his ailments. He should be a healthy man in no time, according to Pierce."

She continues, "You need to track him down. We need that cure for Apollo, or we are going to lose him. We do not have time to spare."

I can feel my pulse hammering in my neck. "Where is he?"

Mort grins. "Follow me."

***

I follow the little white butterfly down long hallways.

We are sneaking, though no one told us we could not leave the room they placed us in. I just want to be sure I am not seized and taken back. I need to talk to Siron desperately.

"Hurry, Mort," I hiss. Butterflies are not the quickest bugs. It's rather frustrating waiting for Mort to make up her mind which way to go.

We finally stop in front of a large door and Mort does not fly further. This must be it. "Through here?"

Mort appears in front of me. "Be quick. Piece told me this is the recovery and spa wing. It's through this door and to your left."

Mort is gone.

I close my eyes and pray Siron will be reasonable.

Please let him help me.

I walk through the door and smell earthy smells. It's not unpleasant. The only thing missing is the Indian spa music.

I go through and see an opening to my left—a small room with an arched entry. The room is steamy, almost like a wet sauna, but not as intense.

I walk slowly, cautiously. I would hate to barge into this room and have weird men in here and not Siron. I shiver. That would be very awkward.

~This is not where I parked my car~, I would say, and run away.

I suck in a breath as I inch further inside. It's then I see the one and only Siron laying on a bed with only a towel covering his trim waist.

My face heats instantly.

This might be a bad idea, and I should have just waited until he was feeling better. I go to turn around then think better of it. ~Don't be a coward.~

I hope he is not dead.

I walk up to him slowly and notice his deep skin color looks very healthy. His bare chest is glistening from crystal-like water droplets, making my mouth dry up.

I notice that he is still wearing his black mask, shocking me. I wonder if he ever takes it off. How strange—maybe he is scarred.

The slow rise and fall of his chest assures me that he is living and breathing, not a Greek statue in the process of being sculpted.

Each ripple and dip of his muscle seems like a work of art, perfectly smooth and hard at the same time. I bite my lip as I start at his perfect mouth.

I reach for his mask, knowing this might be my only chance. Just a little peek.

His hand snatches mine, making me scream. He sits up so fast I do not register that I'm now pinned underneath him.

My heart is beating so hard I think I will have a heart attack at any moment. "Siron," I breathe. "Let me go."

I can see his eyes almost look confused as he stares at me.

"Ursula?"

I frown.

He is breathing hard as his dark gaze pins me.

The pressure and heat from his body is making it hard to focus. "Yes. Though you don't usually call me that?"

I can tell he is frowning, his chest rising and falling quickly.

I try to move, but he is not budging. Taking a slow breath, I try to stay calm, keeping my voice level. "I really hope this healer didn't do anything weird to you."

"What in the fuck are you talking about?" he hisses.

Immediately I am alarmed.

This is not good.

"Siron," I gently say. "Let me go, you're hurting me."

"You have two seconds to tell me what's going on, Angel," he says in a smooth voice.

I know that voice.

My heart is drumming against my neck. I feel lightheaded.

"What did you just call me?"

Another voice from behind us commands, "Easy. Get off her."

Siron stiffens and glances back.

The man is the hairy, bearded pirate. He is now standing right beside us, gently prying Siron's hands from my wrists. "That's it, nice and easy."

I am about to freak out at any second, but I keep my cool until I am freed. "What is going on?" I whisper, shaking.

The bearded man sighs loudly. "Nice to see you again, my lady. Forgive me for all the deception and disguise."

My eyes widen, the voice hitting my memory. It's not gruff anymore, but smooth and elegant. He takes off his eye patch and my breathing escalates as I try to register anything coherent.

"Tarren, at your service."

I pale. "What?" I barely say.

He looks very apologetic as he nods to Siron. "Looks like our prince has come back to reality," he quietly murmurs. "Take off the mask."

I can barely hear over the rushing in my ears. Siron looks at me and something flashes in his gaze as he takes off his mask.

I scream.

Because I'm staring at a dark ~Apollo~.

~What in the ever-loving shit?~

I pass out, I think, because everything goes blissfully dark.

CHAPTER 30

A miracle, or the worst deception?

"How?" I whisper.

Laura's eyes are wide, almost protruding, as she hugs her knees. "Blindsided."

I lay on a plush bed with Mort, Leenie, and Laura staring at me. I take a slow breath, trying to slow my heart rate down.

When I saw him, it was like a shock to my system. My soul left my body for a split second then came back.

"Did Pierce know all along?" I ask Mort.

Mort glances at Leenie. "I believe he did."

"Why in the hell didn't he say anything, Mort?" I sit up, feeling almost betrayed, hurt, ~stupid~.

Mort looks innocent as she visibly swallows. "I do not know, but if I were to guess, I'm guessing that it would have to do with Fairy Godmother rules.

"Until you find out for yourself, Pierce can only nudge you. He cannot under any circumstances interfere with Fate. Pierce cannot give you information such as this unless you find out for yourself."

"Awesome," I say, and grit my teeth. "This whole time it was freaking Apollo. How embarrassing."

Laura shakes her head and clicks her tongue. "But he looked so different with that dark hair and bad-boy getup. I guess the mask just gave the illusion of someone else.

"I mean, in hindsight, I can see it now. Same body type and arrogance, I suppose. And I guess he still had those weird black eyes, but I just thought it was because he was evil or something.

"And, usually, people with dark coloring have dark eyes." She glances at me with a shrug. "I didn't know, Viola. Do not feel bad. Your eyes saw what you wanted them to see, and you saw a cutthroat killer."

She sighs and pats my leg.

"I should have known," I admit. I should have known it was Apollo's lips, hands, body, and soul, but I didn't. That makes me feel horrible and confused.

Taking a calming breath, I glance at my hands. I was so obsessed with getting back to Apollo that I missed the most obvious thing right in front of me. My guilt clouded what was so apparent.

Laura snorts. "You were not the only one who was duped."

"Tarren," I say.

Mort snorts too. "Now that was a great disguise. I had no idea. He was really hairy." Mort's eyes are wide as she glances at Leenie. "Did you?"

"No," she clips out, looking bored. "Didn't care enough to notice."

Laura huffs, pulling her long blond hair to the side. "I am not sure if I'm mad or not. I can't decide."

A knock on the door makes us all tense.

Mort and Leenie are gone in a flash.

Laura gets up to go to the door and I hold my breath. I am not sure if I am ready to see Apollo just yet.

I need to get my feelings and emotions in order. I don't want to see him when I am an emotional mess.

I tense as the door opens, revealing Tarren, clean and shaven. Relief washes over me. He looks handsome, the same dashing Tarren that I thought was a rugged pirate.

I can't see Laura's face, but I can tell something is passing between them. My heart is in my chest. He is saying something to her, something I can't quite make out, though it is not my business.

I turn and pretend to examine my fingernails.

~I'd kill for a mani/pedi.~

I peek over my shoulder and see them embracing, her head buried in his neck. At that moment I smile, a warmth spreading through me like honey.

Laura thought she was falling in love with a cutthroat pirate when it was the noble Tarren in disguise.

I am so happy for her, because truthfully, I was a little nervous about the cutthroat pirate guy being her lover.

Fate knows what it's doing.

That scenario would probably never repeat itself in a million years.

Tarren lifts his head and glances at me, and I hold my breath. "Tarren," I say.

He takes Laura's hand and leads her over to where I am, never taking his gaze from me. Tarren sits in the chair next to the bed and inhales. When he tilts his head at me, he reminds me of Apollo.

"Are you okay?" he asks.

I stare at him.

Tarren nods. "Apollo is cured," he says carefully, and he glances at Laura then back to me.

"That's great news," I breathe, my hands twisting my pale green gown. No matter what I'm feeling, that is wonderful news. It feels like a weight lifted off my shoulders.

"Let me clear some things up for you. Apollo is a very strong man, not easily taken down by a drone's poison. But it did affect him mentally—profoundly, actually." He pauses.

"When you both were taken, Apollo was extremely ill, but still able to function on pure stubbornness.

"We found out about Irena's deception and demanded she tell us what was happening, to put it nicely. It was at that point when Apollo started showing signs of not being himself."

"The poison," I say.

Tarren nods. "He would turn dark, not remembering what he did. Blackouts would happen, scaring everyone. That's when I knew we were racing against the clock.

"Apollo would not break down physically first, but mentally. The beast within was emerging."

"Oh my," Laura murmurs. "That actually makes sense. I always thought Apollo was different—supernaturally weird, even." She shot me a glance. "In a good way."

I try not to smile.

Tarren leans back in the chair. "Yes, we were all very nervous, not knowing how long we had. So, we faked Apollo's coma and devised a plan to rescue you both.

"We did not want anyone thinking Apollo would come after you. I advised that Apollo should stay out of it, with him being so unpredictable, but he was not having it.

"We intercepted Black Siron's ship and made quite the bargain with them. A king's ransom to let us go as them so as to not raise the alarm, in a nutshell." He grins.

"I still can't believe we were able to pull it off in that short of time. Apollo wanted to be Siron, not wanting anyone else to have you.

"His mind didn't understand that this was all a ploy, fake. It was almost like he didn't comprehend — his awareness not working properly. He would get lost in the ploy as if it were real.

"At one point he would remember, then the next he would not. Then he lost his voice right before we got to you and that's when his mind took a dangerous turn.

"The poison took a stronger hold of him the more time passed. He was competing with himself, not realizing that he was Apollo and vice versa."

I am stunned, not sure what to say. I don't know what I was thinking but it was not this. Honestly, in this foreign world, I did not know what the hell was going on.

"It's starting to make more sense. But why didn't you just tell me?" My heart goes out to Apollo, realizing now how hard it must have been. He still came for me even though he was so sick in the worst way.

"He made me promise not to. He didn't want you knowing how messed up in the head he was. And at the time I thought it might be best if you didn't know anything until he was healed.

"I was sure you would avoid him like the plague, but I was wrong, I guess. You were drawn together no matter what."

I can feel my face heat. "Yes, well, he was not exactly the mean killer I thought him to be."

That's because he was Apollo.

~Mega eye roll.~

"Yes, he would come back to himself occasionally. He was so angry that you were falling in love with Siron. He was jealous of his own self, in a sense." Tarren locks eyes with me.

"I had to be the one to calm him down. It was not pretty. I received a broken eye socket, hence the eye patch. He was a beast, unable to process that you would kiss another man."

"That is not fair," I whisper.

"That is manipulation." Laura's voice is angry. "Definitely not her fault."

Tarren holds up his hands. "Ladies, Apollo was not himself. I realize this, and now he does as well."

I swallow, wondering how Apollo must have taken the news. "Did he remember everything?"

"Yes."

~Shit.~

"I need to see him," I say.

He nods then glances down as if he doesn't know what to say.

"What?" My heart palpitates.

"He still needs to recover."

I can see Laura looking at me.

"He's sick still?" I ask.

Tarren looks up at me. "He's angry with you."

I gasp, my skin feeling hot. "Why?"

~But then I knew what Tarren would say.~

"He believes you both are the cause of this deception and he told me to tell you that he wants nothing to do with you." He quickly adds at my gasp, "Until you come clean.

"He said your deception almost cost him and the citizens of Garthorn their lives." Tarren's face reddens. "He's really angry, so much so that he sent me here instead of himself."

My mouth is hanging open. "That piece of shit."

Tarren's eyes widen.

"That arrogant devil can't come and tell me himself?" I mutter to myself as my blood boils.

Tarren looks to Laura for help, but she just lifts her chin.

Bitch code.

I stand up. "Where is he?"

"That is not wise, my lady."

Laura walks up to Tarren, saying slowly and firmly, "Tell her where he is. This is not your battle, Tarren."

He exhales and glances at me, then finally mutters, "He HAS   been a royal pain in the ass. Go get him then." He winks at me.

I fight a grin. Apollo will not pull a temper tantrum after everything I have been through. I have a plan to bring that boy to his knees.

***

"Mort,"

"Yes, human."

I am powerwalking to Apollo's quarters after Tarren gave me directions. I am beyond over this. "We need to make a pit stop, code red."

trying to keep up with me as she walks. "Code red?"

m happy that Eltson is treating the Garthorn Royal Army with open arms.
e more Garthorn ships arrived today — that would be enough to make anyone
ap their pants.

Eltson's men do not have a choice but to be very hospitable. Especially after
the knowledge of the sex trade got out.

"I need Pierce."

"Take the door on your next right."

We enter a small sitting room, thankful that it is empty. I am breathing
hard, my adrenaline pounding through my veins. "I need a killer dress — or
undergarments — whatever."

She is typing and blinking faster than normal. "Oh. I have an update."

"What?" I say, impatient. I just need to see Apollo — like, right now.

"Apollo is attending a party right now. He is not in his room." Mort looks up
at me. "It's something Eltson put on to keep Apollo and the Garthorn royals happy
until they leave at first light."

"What?!" I shriek.

Mort is still typing. "Pierce says go to the party. Act like you are not there to
see him. Play your cat-and-mouse game, then go in for the kill."

I suddenly grin. "Pierce, you dirty dog." I take a breath. "Is Laura going?"

Mort rolls her eyes. "No, I think she is mating with Tarren."

"Gross," I say. "It's not called mating, Mort. She is making love, hooking up,
getting laid."

She frowns. "Mammals on Earth mate. I read that."

"Yeah, for animals, Mort."

She stares at me.

"Never mind, just tell Pierce to make me a killer gown. It's okay that I attend, right?" I try not to panic.

"Oh yes, there are a ton of women here. Have you seen how big this place is?" she asks while typing.

~Oh perfect.~

~I bet they are having a heyday with Apollo.~

I close my eyes and curse. Why do I feel so panicky? I think I just need to see him and talk to him to make sure we're okay. ~Gosh,~ I sound like a lovesick moron.

"Pierce already has a red gown in stock he wants to use, he just needs to adjust it to your size. He says five minutes. He has ten people working overtime on it," Mort confirms.

"Awesome," I say, pacing around. "Hurry, hurry," I say to myself.

"Oh! I got something for you."

I glance at Mort with an eyebrow raise. "Well, it's from Laura."

"What?"

Two large drinks appear in her hand. "Tequila drink—from Pierce at Laura's request."

I laugh, covering my mouth, feeling so touched. "This is amazing," I say, and take one, gazing at it like it's the Holy Grail. "I really needed this." I laugh. It tastes amazing—a refreshing margarita.

I hear a choking sound.

"This tastes really bad," Mort says with a grimace, and puts her drink down with a shiver.

"It's delicious, Mort," I purr as I drink more, feeling its calming warmth. "It has alcohol in it, that's probably what you're not liking."

ɔt want to see Mort drunk right now.

ɛed her.

Drinking my lovely margarita, I wait, loving that I feel so much calmer. Stress gone like the wind. ~Thank you, Laura~. "Ready?"

Mort types more, then nods. "Ready."

I spin like Cinderella. I know the drill. My green gown transforms into a ravishing ruby ballgown. I gasp, my hands feeling the satin fabric that seems to be spun from pure hellfire.

"Oh," I murmur as I feel the V-dipping neckline and tight waist. The rich fabric flows out at the hips like glistening rubies.

Mort starts clapping.

I feel my hair and I can tell Pierce did an updo fit for a queen. "Mirror," I breathe.

Mort shows me a hand mirror and I laugh, covering my mouth. I look stunning. The ruby of my lips matches my gown flawlessly. I am seduction personified.

My raven hair is glossy and piled high on my head, elegantly accenting my long neck.

"Tell Pierce this is incredible." I glance at my smooth skin, my high cheekbones highlighted by a dark blush. My eyes are classic and sultry, making my discolored gaze seem to glow.

I feel devious, cunning, confident, ~sexy.~

"Now go get him! Bring this mission to an end. No one does it like Pierce." Mort gives me a nod like a soldier.

If this doesn't work, nothing will.

Before I leave, I glance back. "When can I tell him, Mort?"

Mort sighs. "Not until the twelfth hour of the day before the mission ends. A week and a half."

I squeeze my eyes shut. "That's going to be an issue."

Mort doesn't say anything, and I leave with a heavy heart.

I walk alone, my ruby skirts flowing around me with each careful step. The hallways are dimly lit, creating an eerie effect. I shiver. I can hear my red heels and my deep breathing, heart pounding.

This could turn out bad or good. A wave of nervousness washes over me when I near the great room.

It's not as big as a ballroom, but still large enough to hold a hundred people. It seems more intimate. The light is very low, romantic even, mysterious.

It's perfect.

I walk in and feel the hairs on my skin stand on end. Eyes are on me. My body tingles and my stomach tightens. I take a breath and saunter through the crowd.

~I'm just here for a drink~, I tell myself. A server comes up to me when I reach the far end of the room, asking me if I would like champagne.

~Yes.~

I have tunnel vision. People swarm everywhere, women in lovely gowns and men in their finery. I feel hopeless, a sadness overcoming me.

I take a sip and pretend to feel nothing, wondering if Apollo is even here. Hopefully he did not decide to leave.

I start to scan the room, needing to know if I'm wasting my time. Everywhere I secretly examine I do not see Apollo, and that's when I start to doubt my decision in coming here.

I dodge men's advances and make my way to an outdoor garden area, the tropical air drifting in.

I freeze.

I stand in the doorway and see Apollo's magnificent form faced away from me. His hands are resting on the balcony rail with his head hung low. He looks very upset, and I can probably guess why.

I shouldn't feel a happy thrill that he's not having fun with twenty-plus women around him. I pray he is in the same agony that I am.

As if he can sense me, he slowly turns around, and the expression on his face when he sees me is nothing short of shock. Disbelief.

Something raw and intense flickers in his deep gaze.

My knees want to give out. The full impact of seeing him without his mask on makes me want to groan, swoon, and fan my flushed face.

Apollo is gorgeous. His hair is still dark but shorter, in a messy, sexy-as-hell man bun. One loose ringlet has escaped the unruly confines of his tie.

He is dark beauty.

Lethal on so many levels.

I can see his skin and a little upper chest; his dark shirt is undone in an almost messy fashion. Like he could give two shits how he looks. Which is even hotter in my opinion.

Not to mention his shirt is loosely tucked into his trim hips, showing off his powerful thighs and ~bulge.~

I look away to regain my wits.

~Take a breath.~

~Don't hyperventilate.~

When I glance back, I notice that he is taking me in like I was him. The fire in his eyes is borderline unnatural.

He pushes off the balcony and walks up to me slowly, like a stalking predator. His chest is rising and falling, and I can see the veins in his neck, jaw tense.

314

I swallow and look up at him, incredibly nervous. He stops mere breaths from me, and I can't look away, though I try. I am shaking, senses on overdrive.

I feel my eyes sting with emotion, and I make a small sound.

His glittering gaze moves over my face, to my lips, then down to the swell of my breasts. He is breathing hard. The tension is so thick I can almost taste it, choke on it.

Apollo reaches for my hand and gently brings it to his hot lips, eyes locked on mine. I suck in a harsh breath when I feel his tongue swirl over my inner wrist.

He kisses each finger so softly I think I might die from the torture. The low lighting on his face gives him a wicked appeal, dangerous. This man is capable of very bad things, naughty things.

"Dance with me," he whispers.

I do not have a voice.

He tilts his head and takes my hand, pulling me. Apollo pulls me to the dimly lit dance floor, which is very crowded.

But I don't see any of them.

A melody similar to "Moonlight Sonata" rings loudly in the air, intensifying our intangible chemistry. The sound is dark and sensual, transforming, manifesting something quite powerful.

His hand on my lower back presses me to him, his hot mouth tracing down my long neck, barely touching his tongue there. We are moving, swaying slowly, gracefully, as he kisses my shoulder.

My eyes fall closed, and a moan escapes my lips.

There is no need for words.

I can hear him loud and clear.

Apollo spins me, and his hands are everywhere they shouldn't be in an elegant dance. I catch a glimpse of his eyes in the dim lighting and a thrill explodes in my body.

He has a dark grin playing on his lips as his movements become more demanding. He jerks me up against his body and dips me aggressively.

Luckily, I am a great dancer, and I adapt to him, feeling the passion, the dark desire burning off him.

I faintly realize Apollo is a brilliant dancer — a ~sexy ~dancer.

His lips scorch a burning trail down my neck to the valley between my breasts, licking and softly sucking. I feel him smile against me and heat swarms in my belly.

He pulls me back up and we spin together, his lower hand pressing and molding my ass to him. More strands of hair escape into Apollo's face making him even sexier than ever.

I am smoldering, burning embers.

With one breath of air, I will ignite.

His lips are on my neck, my body pressing to his most scandalously. I can feel the hard muscle under his clothes and the heat of his body.

He leans back and grabs my face with his calloused hand. He stares down at me with an intensity that takes my breath away. His lips crush to mine, groaning into me.

This kiss is different. It is profound.

I feel a tear stream down my cheek as his mouth devours mine. I can barely catch a breath for he is kissing me so furiously. It's almost as if the kiss is punishing me, bruising me.

We stop dancing in the middle of the dance floor, my hands cupping his face as we kiss, our lips pouring into one another. The ground falls away, reality falls away.

He is everything to me, I realize.

Apollo bends down and scoops me up, still moving his lips over mine. He holds me close and whispers in my ear, "~Want a private dance?"~

Shivers explode all over my body, and I can barely breathe. He whisks me away, not letting me escape his tight grasp.

I grin into his neck. Looks like years working in a strip joint will shockingly pay off.

For the first time ever, I thank my bad life choices.

CHAPTER 31

I stare at him, and he stares at me.

My pulse is hammering against my neck, my breathing shallow and fast.

He carries me to his king suite. There is a massive bed in the middle of the dimly lit room, I faintly note through my brain haze.

This is happening?

This could turn south if he starts asking me questions. The lust haze could clear and make way for doubt.

"Who made your dress?" His voice is husky and hot.

The dreaded questions.

But the dress is killer.

I can play hardball too. I am not going to let this go south.

Smiling, I tilt my head at him like he always does to me. I can be coy and tempting just as well as he can. Seduction can go many ways. I can feel him putting up some walls which I will break down.

Time to step out of my comfort zone.

"Do you like it?" I ask as innocently as possible, doing a slight spin for him. "I think red is a confident color."

He watches me, almost unsure how to take my sudden mood change. "Are you confident, then?" His voice is soft and harsh at the same time.

I give a throaty laugh. "~Oh,~ very," I purr.

He closes his eyes for a moment then he pins me. "You know why I'm upset."

I can still hear the music through the walls. His room is very close to the Great Hall.

"Stop the questions and dance with me," I say with a grin that I know made men in the past do stupid things. I start swaying my hips, the champagne giving me some bold moves.

I close my eyes, thanking my lucky stars I have perfect rhythm. I start humming a song that is ~NOT ~of this world, just to add to the playfulness.

What song? "Close" by Nick Jonas.

Legit song.

I have a decent voice and I'm just barely mouthing the tune. I wonder if this world has heard anything close to pop music.

"What are you singing?" he asks in a low voice, black eyes glittering. He's probably never heard that style of singing.

It's seductive.

I laugh and shrug. "You like it?" I can hold a tune well. I actually impress myself. If he doubts me being from this world, this might confirm it.

I reach up and start taking pins out of my hair, still swaying with my imaginary song. My glossy hair falls down my back, and I give it a shake before I resume my seductive singing, humming.

Apollo looks intense and on ~fire.~

His chest is rising and falling, mouth hanging slightly open.

I smile and lock eyes with him, swaying.

Apollo runs a hand down his face like he doesn't know what to do with himself. His gaze travels down the length of me. The man is on the edge. Just a couple more pushes and he's mine.

I hum as I walk over to the massive four-poster bed. I test out the sturdiness of the columns and deem them durable. I sing suddenly and glance back at him, giving him a catlike grin.

This is a lot of fun, seducing the sexiest man alive.

"You're trying to seduce me?" he asks, wiping his mouth.

I bite my lip and grab onto the post, casually swinging around it. "Never would I think it." That makes me smile at him clearly being uncomfortable in the best way.

This is working better than I thought, and I've just started.

Adrenaline pounds in my veins at his predatory expression as he watches me, his hands grasping a dresser, knuckles white. That will only hold him for so long. I beam to myself.

Pierce hooked it up for me. I can feel garters under my dress which I do not think is custom here. I think Pierce gave me some Earthly fashion to take down Apollo.

"It won't work." His voice is husky. "I want you to tell me who the hell you are."

Not working?

I almost giggle.

~Silly man.~

F.R.BLACK

This dress is way too ballgown-y to swing around a pole and not have an epic fail. My hands slowly move over my breasts and down to my waist, circling around to my back.

I doubt girls are this bold here ~ever.~

Apollo makes a harsh noise, but I delightfully ignore him. No going back after this. He has not seen anything yet. I'm about to rock his world.

I'm not wearing a bra, so I will be dancing topless with my thong and garter. My pulse is beating so fast I can barely hear myself think.

Which is good—no thinking, just reacting.

I start to unzip my dress and open my eyes, locking them with his, slightly licking my ruby lips. He gives me a warning look—~don't do it~. I don't stop and he takes a slow step toward me as if to scare me into stopping.

"Angel," he hisses, pleads. "Don't."

Not a chance.

I turn around and let the dress fall to the ground, shimmying out of it, giving him a view of my tone, apple bottom. I bend over, and I can hear his sharp intake of breath as I step out of the confines of the gown.

I flip up seductively, my long hair touching my ass. I start moving my hand over my sensitive skin, feeling like I am about to ignite. Moments tick by as I take a steady breath.

My garters are ruby red with glossy black fishnets. ~Oh my~. They are more risqué than I thought. I hadn't been able to see them before this, only feel them.

Don't cower now.

It is as if time stands still. Heartbeats go by. I cover my breasts and slowly turn around, leaning on the bedpost behind me, moving hypnotically.

Apollo's hand is covering his mouth like he is frozen solid, not moving a muscle. The only way I know he is not a statue is the rise and fall of his chest. He

321

looks like he is about to hyperventilate.

~So thrilling!~

He drops his hand, leaving his mouth hanging open. Apollo's glittering gaze meets mine and a dark smile suddenly spreads over his lips. My skin tingles and my stomach tightens in response.

I lower in my movements then back up again, back pressing to the poster.

"Drop your arms, ~now,"~ he orders in a harsh whisper, licking his lips.

I bite my lip, noticing the bulge in his pants has grown three times its size.

~Checkmate, Apollo.~

I drop my arms, giving him a full view of my glorious C-cup girls. My nipples are tight, and my skin is on fire, flushed. I move before Apollo can pounce on me, not able to look him in the eyes just yet.

I can feel his energy escalating, making me a little apprehensive.

I grab the pole and climb up it, moving and rocking my hips, then sliding down, spreading my legs. I am very flexible and limber, something I'm sure is shocking Apollo.

A bold move indeed.

I was going to dance more for him, but in an instant, I am pinned to the wall, hands over my head.

I gasp when I feel him devour my neck then my breasts, yanking me up to give him better access. I moan, scream, pant, squirm as he sucks my nipples.

He is out for revenge.

My wrists are pinned above me, and I am at his mercy.

He finally lets go of my hands and grabs my ass, grinding against me while he sucks and kisses me everywhere he can: my neck, chin, shoulder, earlobe — before lifting me up again to torture my breasts.

Apollo   is a storm, barely giving me time to react or breathe. I moan his name and then desperately grab at his shirt. "Off!" I pant.

His dark gaze glitters as he removes his shirt with one violent pull.

~Holy moly.~

~Apollo is like a superhero, muscles flexing and shifting.~

Instant skin on skin, my breasts pressed to his hard, muscled chest. The sensation is overwhelming, especially when I can feel him ripping my thong in half with a dark grin.

My lower region is on fire, and my mind is in a delicious haze as I feel his hand start to work me ~there~.

I come so hard and fast that I scream—and he's ~barely~ touched me, for crying out loud. This man is just too much sexiness for me to handle. A mere little human versus a god-like creature.

My lady bits are dazed and confused, like the moment you wake up in a hospital bed with doctors leaning over you with a bright light.

I hear him chuckle and the sound is the hottest thing I have ever heard. "I am going to torture you all night," he threatens in my ear, sending an instant thrill down my spine. "Do you want it?"

"Yes," I breathe.

He slaps my ass then throws me on the bed only to pounce on me, taking my legs and spreading them aggressively.

I should not be surprised at his fervor. I must have been driving him mad for this amount of heated passion.

I sit up as our lips collide, his mouth dominating mine. His tongue thrusts into mine, and I can feel his teeth, biting and sucking in a fiery frenzy. I am gasping for air.

He jerks my head back by pulling my hair, kissing down my neck, biting, licking, sucking. I gasp, feeling perspiration dotting my body.

I have~ never~ been with a man with an ounce of whatever Apollo is producing. This man's sexual appetite is breaking the scale.

I grab for his pants, wanting all of Apollo desperately. He growls in my ear and lets me frantically remove his pants. My eyes widen when his pants are removed.

Apollo in all his glory. Adonis, unnaturally glorious. His erection is huge and ready. I am mesmerized for a moment as I take him in my hungry gaze.

I lean up and slowly grab the hot length of him, hearing him hiss in delight. I have so much power now, the mighty Apollo pleading with me, begging me to use my mouth.

And I do, enjoying every minute of torturing him, pleasing him.

He groans and fists my hair, sending a thrill down my spine. I speed up my pace, tasting him, feeling the heat. He is delicious, just like I thought.

He pulls back with a jolt.

"Enough, ~Angel~," he rasps, and pulls me off him, pinning me on the bed again. Apollo is a dominant creature, and it's extremely hot.

~Too hot, heady.~

He moves, and his mouth devours me down ~there ~and brings me to many climaxes that I can barely withstand. I am screaming for mercy, but he does not stop.

I am in a daze, sensations taking over my mind and soul.

I feel like I have run a marathon.

Once again, his lips are on mine, but his touch is soft this time. Soft and ~loving~,   imprinting on me. I feel him, his heart and soul, and I need all of it.

There is no way I'm walking away from this not being wholly changed and affected forever.

"Apollo," I breathe.

I feel so much emotion.

Apollo gazes down at me as he penetrates me, making me gasp. He takes me hard and fast, bracing over me as he pumps to a delicious rhythm.

I didn't think he would fit, but it would seem that I am a perfect fit.

After that moment, all I can remember is him kissing me as my world ignites into a bonfire. With each thrust of his hips, I'm being further and further claimed by him.

I'm spinning with pleasure when I feel him tense, spilling himself into me. We both are spent, and he falls on top of me, breathing hard, kissing my neck, cupping my face.

"I'm falling in love with you," I blurt, heart pounding.

He tenses and lifts to look at me, dark eyes are intense. "Falling?" he asks with a sudden boyish smile. He clicks his tongue.

I just stare at him, biting my lip.

He sighs and lifts himself up to stare down at me. "After round two, you'd better ~know~ you love me."

The dark look in his gaze promises naughty things to come.

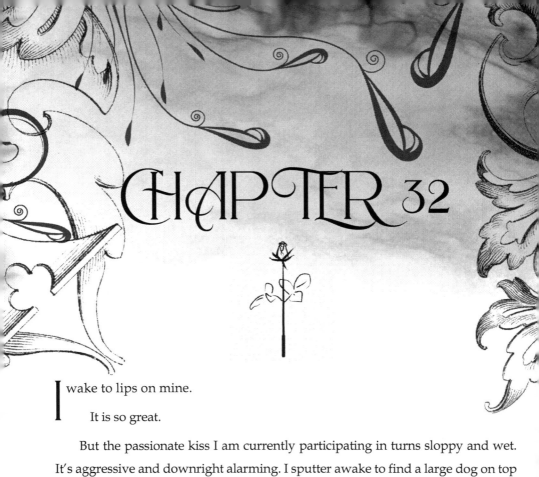

CHAPTER 32

I wake to lips on mine.

It is so great.

But the passionate kiss I am currently participating in turns sloppy and wet. It's aggressive and downright alarming. I sputter awake to find a large dog on top of me, licking my face.

"Ahh!" I scream as the canine jumps off the bed and disappears through an open door to my left. My heart is beating fast as I sit there, trying to piece together my brain.

I was making out with a dog, not Apollo. Think I saw that scenario in a movie once, and I am just fortunate enough to experience it in real life. That just happened. I will take that experience to the grave.

I wipe my mouth, cringing.

Glancing next to me I can see the spot is empty…~empty~. I look around the room and shiver, flashes of last night flickering in my memory.

Legs tangled together, sweat, hot kisses, moaning, nails scratching, my hands pinned above my head, Apollo's head between my legs.

My face heats.

Placing my hand on my forehead, I fan myself.

That was a night that will go down in history. How many times did we have sex? Four? Five? Apollo was relentless, his stamina overpowering mine.

I picture him now, naked with his golden body over mine. I grin like a schoolgirl, feeling butterflies in the pit of my stomach.

"What are you thinking about?"

I jump, seeing Apollo in the doorway. His hair is wet, dark ringlets combed back from his face, and a towel is hanging low on his hips. ~Holy...mother...of... Mike.~

Dark eyes intense, his tattooed bicep looks sinful. He looks naughty — a man mothers warn their sweet, innocent daughters about.

Apollo after a shower should be outlawed.

I swallow.

~I like — er — want to have sex, my name is girl~, is my intelligent thought.

His gaze lowers to my breasts and I remember I am still naked save for my garters. I pull the crisp sheets up and blush furiously.

I need a mirror. I must look like the girl from ~The Exorcist~ — hair tangled, mascara-stained eyes. I curse and shrug, praying I looked halfway decent.

"I was just thinking...Did you see a dog?"

Looking back, Apollo nods. "Yes, he took off with my shirt, not sure how he got in here."

Smart dog.

I laugh and our eyes clash.

~I did not make out with a dog.~

~He knows nothing.~

Apollo walks over to me and sits on the bed, his large frame dwarfing mine. I can smell the clean scent of him and it's driving me wild inside. Stay cool. Stay cool.

"We need to talk."

I sigh and hold the sheet to me, feeling very vulnerable. "Yes, we do." I look down, not sure how to handle this.

Apollo lifts my chin with his hand, making me look at him. "Who are you, Angel? Let's start there."

"How many days until we are back in Garthorn?"

He frowns. "Five."

"I will tell you in eight days. Please, give me a little more time," I plead, seeing the flex of his jaw.

He expels a breath. "Are you in trouble? We are dealing with Irena and her witchcraft. She will be on trial next month."

Relief flashes through me. "Wonderful news. But no, I am no threat, and I do not think I am in trouble."

~Freaking rules.~

He lifts and sits more in front of me. "Then why can't you tell me now?"

I squeeze my eyes shut. "You will understand when I tell you. It's very complicated." I bite my lip. "So complicated, but you have to just trust me."

When I open my eyes, Apollo is studying me, seeing right through me. He looks down and sighs. "Eight days and no longer, if that's my only option."

He reaches for me and scoots me closer, hands on my thighs. His fingers toy with the garter under the sheet and he looks up at me. "What are these?" His voice lowers.

I take a breath. "Where I'm from," I say carefully, "men really like them. It's called a garter."

"Where you're from. You're giving me little hints?"

I blush. "Yes."

"Men like them, you say? Men saw you in these?" His gaze is unblinking. Serious.

"No. Just in general."

I can see the muscle in his forearm relax. Apollo does not seem like the sharing type, more of the ~touch-my-woman-and-I'll-slit-your-throat~ type.

Apollo's hand is slowly massaging my thigh. "Speaking of other men…you fell in love with Siron."

"Which was you," I point out.

"You didn't know that."

"Apparently, neither did you," I say. "How are you feeling?"

"I'm fine," he says. "Which one would you have picked?"

This is really bothering him, I can tell.

I expel a breath. "Both."

He raises a brow. "It troubles me that you would give your heart to another."

"Apollo, it was you. If you came to me in different disguises, I would probably fall in love with every single one of them," I admit. "You are irresistible to me."

That seems to do the trick.

Apollo pushes me down on the bed and leans over me, his wet hair tickling my shoulder. It seems lighter, like the dye is washing out. The heavy weight of his body makes my skin tingle, his body's heat engulfing me.

"I know you are not from here. I've known that for a long time." His lips kiss my shoulder.

"I want to care, to be angry, to demand you tell me right now. But I find that I don't care as I should. I am almost dreading it."

"You are dreading it?"

"I do not want you to tell me something that will affect how I feel about you," he admits.

I swallow, praying that he will be understanding, or I will be devastated. For the first time, I am having panicked thoughts that he will not take what I have to say with ease. It scares me.

"Because I have never felt this way about a woman. It's as if I was struck by lightning when I saw you. I tried to fight it, but I could not." He looks at me with a devious grin.

"I could not take my eyes from your torn dress that first day. Your skin was wet, and I could see your nipples through the material. I can remember almost forgetting how to talk, which has never happened.

"The rushing in my ears when you gave me your first defiant stare. I wanted to taste that fire." His tongue swirls on my skin and lowers his voice.

"I wanted to fuck you so bad it hurt. I think I've dreamed of you every night since, naked in my bed like this. I thought I was losing my sanity. It was so out of character for me.

"It was like you poisoned me, and you were the only cure." He pauses to suck on my skin. "You didn't put a spell on me, did you?"

I think he's really asking, which makes me laugh. "No, I did not." ~Though my dressmaker is on point~.

My pulse is hammering at the things he is saying. I had no idea. I guess Pierce was right when he said Apollo liked the shipwrecked outfit.

Apollo admitting this to me makes this so real. We both are in this way too deep to have this blow up in our faces. I have so much emotion inside me that it frightens me.

He moves the sheet, and his large hand finds my flat belly, slowly massaging it. I really wish I had a mirror right about now. I'm feeling a little self-conscious at the moment.

Though, when he looks at me, it's like I'm the prettiest woman on the planet.

I feel his hand near the underside of my breast, making me tense, skin tingling.

"I want you, Angel."

"I want you too," I barely say.

Apollo tilts his head at me and takes a breath, his muscled chest rising. "I want you as my wife." He cups my heavy breast, squeezing it.

"Yes," I moan, all I can get out.

Apollo groans as he pinches my nipple. "You are so gorgeous. Never have I seen a woman swinging on a pole as you did. I want more of it."

I open my eyes and look at him, breathing hard as he massages my breasts. "Are you sure you can handle it?" I pant.

He squeezes my nipple hard.

I yelp and jump up, laughing, moving to the other side of the bed. "Stay away, I can't think when you do that."

Apollo grins and adjusts his towel. "You're naked. I can't get that out of my head."

"You asked me to marry you. Focus," I say with a laugh.

"I believe you already knew that, Angel. I want to marry you in eight days," he says.

Fear washes over me.

After I tell him.

Apollo tilts his head. "How does that sound?"

I try to calm my nerves. "Perfect," I whisper.

"I don't want to lose you." He grabs my legs with one reach and yanks me back to him. I gasp when he has me pinned again.

"When I was Siron, I thought I'd lost you to another man. It made me go to dark places. I never want to feel that again."

"Well," I say, loving the smell of him, his golden skin so tantalizing, "as long as you do not plan on being someone else again, that should not happen."

His head leans down and he kisses my neck like he can't help it.

"Are you going to do something about the sex trade?"

He leans up and nods. "It's a heavy process, but when we get back, I will gather our allies to take them down.

"Galleon wanted to wage war with us until they found out about Irena's betrayal to your father. They will want to take out whoever abducted his daughters, you have my word on that."

I closed my eyes, seeing all those innocent girls. "Thank goodness."

In one second, the bedsheets are ripped off me, and Apollo covers my body with his.

"Apollo!" I shriek, laughing. My legs are spread, wrapped around his waist. Skin on skin, if you get my meaning. My face heats.

He groans, grinding his hips.

My body ignites.

"I can't get enough of you. But I have to eat. I'm hungry," he rasps. "Starving, actually."

"You're hungry?" I ask, confused. We did have high activity all night with no nourishment. Apollo is a large man.

"Yes, for breakfast." He leans back and grins. Apollo suddenly grabs my thighs, yanking them over his shoulders. His head is now between my legs as the realization hits me.

I gasp, jolting with pleasure. It seems surreal. My vision swims as I feel his scorching hot mouth devour me.

We are supposed to leave at first light.

I think we might be a little late this morning.

CHAPTER 33

We left a few days ago. The journey feels long when one has a veil of guilt hanging over them.

Dread sinks into every pore of my body.

These are the final days—it's almost over.

I am happy and smiling on the outside, but on the inside, I am screaming. I feel sick, nervousness taking me hostage. I can't sleep and I can barely eat, feeling my doom approaching.

Apollo seems overjoyed. I'm sure the scales on the Fairy Godmother radar are above 50 percent now.

The evil is dropping. People are starting to thrive, the blanket of evil lifted due to the capture of Irena and her dark army.

~Will Apollo still want me?~ is the burning question.

I squeeze my eyes shut and take a steady breath. I mean, men in the past have taken the information well and have had ~happily-ever-afters~. Apollo could be the same.

I think he will take it well enough, but I'm just not sure. Apollo could feel played, betrayed in a sense, like my love was just an act. I hope not.

He might not even believe me. I'm sure Fairy Godmother Inc. will have to give me something to prove to him that I am who I say I am, and not a lunatic.

I gaze out over the ocean as we near land ahead.

I feel arms circle around my waist, making me tense, then I sigh when I feel his lips on my neck. "What has you scowling?" Apollo whispers.

I smile, hiding my inner panic. "Nothing, just glad to get off this ship."

"Are you nervous?"

I look at him. "About?"

"Our engagement announcement in two days," he says with a pointed look. Apollo nuzzles my neck, breathing me in.

I swallow.

He is having the engagement party on the same day that I will tell him my big secret. Why would he do that? That just puts even more pressure on me. Maybe Pierce has a gentle way I can tell him.

~Seven women are here from another planet. They were beamed here in hopes to win your dark, wayward heart, so you wouldn't fuck everything up for the rest of the universe.~

Yeah. I'm sure he will take that well.

"Tell me, Angel."

I shake my head and force a laugh, spinning around to face him. "Nothing is wrong," I murmur, and raise on my tiptoes to kiss him. Yum. He is delicious, smelling of fresh air and soap.

He kisses me back and slightly bites my lip, smiling into me. "You know, you can just tell me your secret now. You're making me nervous that I'm not going to like it."

I suck in a breath. "I can't tell you, ~yet~."

"Yes, I am aware. You keep saying that, but you also have been closed off from me since leaving. It pains me to see the agony in your eyes."

I close my eyes and force a smile. "I just hope you're understanding."

He tilts his head at me. "You say you mean me no harm. You say you come in peace, and that you pose no bodily harm to anyone. So why would I not be understanding? How bad can it be?"

"Well…It's a little bizarre."

Apollo raises a brow and looks thoughtful. "You have something bizarre to tell me?" He is smiling now. "Were you raised by wolves? You're really a mystical fairy?"

He levels me a hard stare. "You were once a man?"

My eyes widen in shock. "No!" I smack him on his bicep.

He laughs and shrugs. "You're making me wonder the worst."

"No, I am all female." That's the only thing I'm certain of at this point.

He grabs me, his hands smoothing over my ass. "Oh, I know you're all female, Angel. Just teasing you."

I moan when he kisses me again, hot lips moving over mine, dark eyes glittering. He pulls back and bops me on the nose.

"I must go. I will find you later. Your father wants to meet immediately. I can't imagine why," he says with a wink.

Gosh, he is so handsome.

I watch him leave with a sick feeling.

Here we go.

***

I am greeted like I'm some celebrity.

My father hugs me and cries, telling me how sorry he is for Irena. I am escorted by tons of guards like I carry the crown jewels.

To be honest, it's all a blur. All I can think about is how I am going to tell Apollo. I hug myself, feeling lost.

This is too perfect.

This is a true fantasy come to life.

~The calm before the storm.~ That saying scares me, knowing its truth.

This could all come crashing down in a couple of days. I can't let myself be happy until I know Apollo will be okay with me being an agent of Fairy Godmother Inc.

I get to my beautiful room only to gasp.

~Pierce.~

"Pierce," I breathe.

Mort is suddenly beside him.

He looks impeccable in a pin-striped suit, fitted perfectly. Of course, Pierce would have fashionable clothing. The man is all that is elegant and the best clothing designer in all the universe.

"Take a breath."

I take a breath and say nothing, shocked to see him here.

He leans against the wall with his hand stylishly resting in his pocket like he is in an Armani ad.

"This is your ~End Game~ briefing, and I am happy to say we have done it. The Fairy Godmother is thrilled. She knew it was you all along." He points at me.

I frown. "How? And it's not over yet."

He grins and I think his teeth sparkle. "True, you still have one more obstacle.

337

How did she know it was you? Your rare eye color."

He nods to the chair next to the window. "You might want to sit for this."

Dread sinks in.

Coming from Pierce, that is never good.

I find the chair and numbly sit.

Pierce glances at Mort then back to me. "You are the lost daughter of Galleon."

I snort. "Yeah, I think I know that by now."

He shakes his head. "No, the ~real ~one."

I stare at him.

I laugh and smile. ~This guy~.

Pierce smiles too. "I am being serious."

"Wait." I stand. "What are you talking about?"

"Sit."

I sit, panic welling in my chest.

"This is quite rare. It's only happened once before, in fact, but our Fairy Godmother knew immediately." He continues, "You fell through a portal as a small child, sent by Irena's black arts.

"And Fate brought you back to your rightful place. Pretty amazing, if you ask me. This job never ceases to mystify me."

I am breathing hard.

No way.

Not possible.

"You are not from Earth, but from here. Your supposedly heartless mother never left you in Texas. You were wrongly banished," he says. "You were found by the fire department and put into foster homes."

338

"I don't believe it."

"I have your DNA. Your biological father is the King of Galleon. We did not need to fake anything." He tosses some papers on the desk with a wink. "Read it if you want."

"You could have faked them."

He laughs. "No reason to fake them, there would be no reason for us to lie." He leans against the wall.

"Trust me, I do not have time to make up fake scenarios such as this. That is not what we are about, and I think you know that."

I glance at the papers that confirm my hysteria. "How?"

"Irena should have just killed you." He smiles. "Glad she didn't, but looks like Fate had other plans for you. You were destined to come back."

Mort says, "That, I was not expecting."

That means the King is my ~real~ father.

Emotion stings my eyes. I'm not sure how to deal with this information. I have a family? Family is so foreign to me, never having had one. I feel a tear stream down my cheek. "This is a lot."

I feel dizzy.

Pierce nods. "You're a tough kid, you'll get through it." He winks at me. "This is very good news for you—someone without a family now has a real one." Pierce smiles and walks over to me.

"And now we have to talk about your last day here. I do not have a lot of time for I must see every girl here still.

"If you win Apollo's heart in the end, the other females have the choice to stay or go. It's our little ~thank you~ for their participation.

"It's a surprise in the end for them, if you will. They do not know this until I talk to them."

I wipe another tear, feeling like I am in the twilight zone. "There is a lot resting on me then."

"A lot — so don't mess up."

I blink at him.

"All contestants will meet at dawn by the South Shore. This is not negotiable, by the way. Our Fairy Godmother ship will leave after first light, which is roughly seven o'clock.

"All the contestants will be aboard, including you. The only way you may get off is by Apollo coming for you." He continues, "If he is too late, then the magic ends. Game over."

I swallow, feeling my nerves take flight. "How am I to convince him?"

He nods and pulls something out of a blue velvet case. "This is called the ~Darling Medallion~." Pierce holds up the most beautiful necklace I have ever seen.

It is a diamond heart necklace, with a large cobalt crystal center. It sparkles and glimmers like tropical water in the bright sunlight.

"It's beautiful," I breathe.

"You are now a Fairy Godmother ~Darling~, which is a high honor. This necklace is your gift for winning the competition — if you can convince Apollo, that is.

"You shall wear it with pride. This medallion can never be broken, and it allows you to get in touch with Fairy Godmother Inc. if the need should arise."

"You still keep in contact with all of the winners?"

"Yes, we are very fond of our Darlings. You have a lifelong relationship with us. We are family here, and we never abandon anyone.

"Did I mention we have a killer Christmas party that all Darlings are invited to? Though last year the Sexy-Santa elf set Cinderella's dress on fire.

"No joke. Elves cannot drink whiskey — they burp fire, as it turns out."

My eyes widen in shock.

Unbelievable.

I shake my head. "How does this necklace help me with Apollo?"

"When the time is right, let him touch it." Pierce continues, "This will give him a very real vision of who we are and that you are telling the truth. It's a very ~convincing~ vision, and he will not doubt you."

I bite my lip, then nod, and I take the necklace from Pierce. It shimmers and sparkles, the weight of it making me feel as though it will shatter if I drop it. He helps me clasp it around my neck.

"I have faith Apollo will come for you."

I pray he is right.

"Otherwise, we are all out of the business."

CHAPTER 34

I take a shaky breath.

This is it.

This is where it all will all begin or end.

"Pierce says this will be the last dress he makes you," Mort says as she types and blinks. "He also says it's been an honor."

~My engagement dress~.

I grab the Darling necklace that hangs around my neck and squeeze it. It's finally time. I am to be escorted soon.

April, Destiny, Ivy, and Laura came to me earlier, wishing me good luck. They all have found a home here except for Cherie, but that's okay. She has had the time of her life apparently — no regrets.

I have not seen April my entire journey here, being a slave and all. But when I saw her, she appeared wild and free, a far cry from when I first met her as a timid little pixie girl.

She was so happy for me, saying that it was meant to be. Pierce had told them about me being from here all along, the real lost princess. This place is where it all began for me. Fate has taken me back.

Destiny is in love with a very handsome man and seems happy. Ivy has also come to love it here. I forgot that the girls were all living their experiences here as well. I was not the only one who came out on top.

Which is why I need to win Apollo over today.

"Tell Pierce the honor is mine."

A tinge of sadness washes over me. I will miss him, and especially Mort. I give myself a shake not wanting to think about that yet.

I start to spin, not needing Mort to tell me. My skin tingles and sparkles flicker around me.

This never gets old.

I gasp, skin feeling hot. I glance down and just stare. I am now in Cinderella blue, a shimmering gown that must have rivaled hers. My hands touch the magical fabric and I sigh, feeling like a goddess.

It's gorgeous, like everything Pierce makes. The off-the-shoulder neckline exposes me just enough to seduce and tantalize.

I feel my hair. The raven locks twist and twirl down my back, shimmering as if enchanted. "Mirror," I breathe.

Mort holds a mirror out in front of me, and I suck in a breath.

"Pierce really wants you to have the best chance." Mort grins.

I glance at her and I raise a brow. "That sounds a little vain, but I will take it. If this does not work, then nothing would have worked."

I touch my full lips, a glistening nude. My lashes are sooty black, contrasting with a pearlized eyeshadow. I look angelic.

"I don't think you can look prettier than that," she agrees.

"Thanks, Mort."

"No problem, human."

I suddenly hug her, making Mort gasp. Her stiff body slowly relaxes, then she hugs me back with a fierce hold. We embrace it for a little while before I pull back.

I can feel my eyes cramp with tears, but I will them back into my eyes. I can't say anything to her or I will cry, and I think she knows this.

She nods at me, then I turn to leave right as the knock on my door comes.

They're here to escort me to the ballroom, where I will meet up with Apollo. The announcement has already been made this morning.

I can see the guards' eyes widen when they see me which gives me a little more confidence.

The long walk to the ballroom seems like it takes an eternity. My skirts swish and glitter as I walk, trying to calm my breathing.

I round the last corner and see Apollo talking to a group of men, faced away from me.

His hair is back to normal, its platinum ringlets escaping the confines of his tie. He is dressed in sleek Garthorn finery, metals and sashes of cobalt blue on top of stark black.

My heart flutters every time—the man's beauty will always hold me hostage.

His wide shoulders turn, a laugh playing on his lips.

Apollo sees me and my breathing hitches.

The smile on his lips slowly disappears as his dark gaze takes me in. Then our gazes clash and I am lost, swimming in the dark abyss that is his eyes.

His mouth drops open and the tilt of his head makes my stomach twist.

He walks over to me, never taking his dark gaze from me. Grabbing my hand, Apollo kisses it like it's the first time we are making contact. My heart constricts.

The feel of his gentle touch has me undone.

"You, my dear, look like a goddess. Is that your secret, then?" he asks in a low voice.

I close my eyes and nod. "It is."

"The way you look tonight, I'm actually not sure if you're being serious or not." He pulls me close where I can feel the heat of his body.

"You mesmerize me. I find that it is hard to breathe when I'm near you. I feel like you are not real."

~Not real.~

I cringe.

"Can I tell you my secret now?" I whisper, needing to get this off my chest.

"After a dance and champagne. There's no rush, Angel," Apollo insists, as he pulls my arm without waiting for an answer.

We enter the ballroom, and everyone cheers for us. I smile, on the verge of a panic attack. I just let Apollo lead me, praying I do not fall and die from heart failure.

Tunnel vision.

We dance as everyone watches us in awe.

He spins me around the Gothic ballroom. The feel of his hands on me makes everything else fall away for a split second. My gown glitters and sparkles like diamonds in the low lighting.

Finally, the dance is over. I feel like everything just happened in a blink of an eye. Maybe I'm not ready. Doesn't matter if I'm not ready, it must happen.

It's time.

Apollo leads me to the gardens, the cool night air kissing my flushed face. Each heartbeat echoes in my mind. My fingers feel numb.

I sit on a stone bench as he stands, walking around as if he can't sit still.

"All right, what weird things are you going to tell me?"

My heart is pounding loudly as I take a steady breath. Time to rip off the band-aid. "I am not from here," I say.

Apollo side-glances at me then raises a brow. "I gathered that, Angel."

I nod. "Right. Well, I am not from this planet."

"Come again?"

"I am not from this planet, Apollo. I was sent here on a mission with five other girls, a mission that involved you," I blurt out, and redden. That might have not sounded the best.

He just stares at me with an ~are-you-crazy~ frown.

"I know what you're thinking—"

"No, you don't, trust me."

I can feel his anger start to rise.

"I explained that really badly, but you didn't let me finish."

Apollo expels a breath. "I could probably agree with that assessment." He holds up his hand, silencing me. "You are from another planet? Are you trying to play me for a fool? After everything, we went through?"

"No!" I yell, standing up. "I am from a different planet. It's called Earth. You wanted the damn truth and here it is!"

"Earth? So you're not Ursula, the lost princess of Galleon?" he asks, chest rising and falling.

"Well, actually, yes I am," I say quickly. "Stay with me, it gets complicated.

"Irena banished me through a portal when I was four years old, and I landed on a planet called Earth. That's why I never had a memory of my young childhood. I did not know this until a few days ago."

346

He laughs.

I laugh as well, but in more of an insane way.

~The Darling Medallion.~

Thank goodness. "Apollo," I say over his laughter, "touch this. It will make you understand what I am poorly trying to tell you."

"You want me to touch your sparkly necklace?" He chuckles again. "And here I thought you were going to tell me the truth, not some insane tale of time travel."

"Touch it."

I'm starting to panic.

Apollo's jaw tenses and he slowly walks over to me, humor gone. "What are you trying to do to me?"

I grab his hand and put it on my crystal. Instantly Apollo's eyes glaze over and close as if someone put a spell on him.

I stand there with my pulse hammering like a fire dancer. I keep his hand on my necklace as I see his eyeballs moving around under his lids.

I close my eyes and plead, begging that this will work.

~Please.~

I am not sure how much time passes, but when he opens his eyes, I see the sheer shock. He is breathing hard, yanking his hand away from me.

"I can see why..." He pauses like he is regaining his breath. "Why you had trouble explaining it."

I feel tears in my eyes. "Are you angry with me?"

He laughs and looks up into the sky as if seeking divine help. "Am I angry with you? I am not sure how to answer that."

"What is going through your head?"

"That Pierce guy is very strange, we both can agree on that," Apollo says, more to himself. "I can't believe they sent three fleets to try and snag me."

"Please don't be angry."

Apollo glances at me and I can't tell how this is going to go. "You're leaving tomorrow morning? With the other girls?"

Fear creeps into every pore. "If you do not want me, then yes," I whisper.

Apollo drags a hand down his face. "Now the dresses make perfect sense." He gives me a crude stare. "He did this one perfectly." He nods to my gown.

I feel a tear stream down my cheek.

"Is anything about you real?"

I sniff, feeling like I am losing him. "Yes, everything else."

Apollo nods and is quiet.

"I love you, Apollo," I whisper.

I can see him tense at that. "Are you paid to say that, Angel?" He looks at me, pain in his gaze.

"Absolutely not, Apollo. We are not forced to fall in love. It is our choice. You are not forced either.

"Without Fairy Godmother Inc., I would have never met you. I would never have known what I was missing out on.

"When I say I love you, it comes from my heart, my soul. Fate brought me here, and I am grateful," I say, and wipe a tear.

"I was born here, Apollo. This is my home. All my life I have felt out of place and never knew why, and finally I am back where it all began."

Apollo gazes up into the sky and exhales.

"Say something," I whisper.

"How long do I have?"

I squeeze my eyes shut. "Until dawn. On the South Shore."

"And Laura?"

"She will be leaving as well." I continue, "Without our commitment, no one will benefit."

Apollo looks at me, arms crossed over his large chest. "But she has to tell him too?"

"It's not required. Only me, apparently."

"Tarren must know."

I wipe another tear. It seems I can't control them anymore. "I'm sure she will."

"Or I will."

I just stare at him. "Do you love me, Apollo?"

"I am not sure I can answer that," he admits in a low voice. "I am going to leave and clear my thoughts. Please, go in and enjoy the party."

He turns to leave.

"Apollo!" More tears stream down my face.

He turns to look at me with pain in his eyes.

"Will you come for me tomorrow?"

"Time will tell, Angel."

And he leaves me there, weeping uncontrollably. I know one thing: I will not sleep a wink tonight. My worst fear has come true.

But what did I expect? I don't know how much Pierce revealed to him from the Darling Medallion. It's a lot to digest.

I just hope Apollo does not make the worst decision of his life, because there are no second chances.

I do love Apollo Augustus Garthorn. He must see that he loves me too, despite everything.

In just twelve hours.

CHAPTER 35

O nly one will stand at the end of it all.

"Are you ready?"

I glance at Mort in the early morning darkness. "I think I am going to throw up, to be honest." I am in a dark cloak, my hair braided down my back. My nerves are making me sick.

Mort takes a deep breath. "No matter what happens today…we did our best." She pats me on the shoulder. "There, there."

I smile at her.

"Mort, I will miss you terribly," I say with a breath. "Whenever I see a white butterfly, I will always think of you." I smile through watery eyes.

Mort wipes a tear. "That makes me emotional."

I laugh.

She sniffs and I grab her, hugging her. "Let's go." I kiss her head and we both make our way to the South Shore.

I walk outside and see all the girls in dark cloaks, each one of them getting into a carriage. The air feels heavy, the tension thick with uncertainty.

I am sure Fairy Godmother Inc. is providing escape and transportation. On the side of the vehicles, I can see the Fairy Godmother crest.

Laura comes up to me, face pale. "How are you doing?"

I shrug, shivering in the crisp morning air. "As good as I can."

"I have a bad feeling."

My stomach drops. "Why?!" I can feel the storm coming, brewing, like a lightning strike to my heart.

Laura pulls me into a carriage that's not occupied yet. We both get in and shut the door, leaving us in the moonlit darkness. "Tarren just left me."

I swallow, feeling sick. "And?"

She begins again, "Apollo was not himself last night, according to Tarren. He got trashed and told Tarren everything. Tarren came to my room demanding answers, super pissed."

She continues, "I don't think Apollo has fully healed yet. Something is wrong."

"From the poison?"

Of course, from the poison. Something that I caused.

Laura sniffs. "Yes, the recovery process is not overnight."

"I don't understand."

Laura is not making sense. She'd better start making fucking sense before I freak out.

I take a breath, ordering myself to calm down.

"Apollo was extremely hurt and angry last night and till the wee hours of the morning, I think. Tarren is very concerned that he is not thinking clearly."

I look down to my hands fisted into my cloak.

"He's not coming," I whisper.

The realization hits me like a ton of bricks. Laura stares at me, then looks out the window, at a loss for words.

"He's not coming," I say, louder.

I can see tears stream down her face. "I had to tell Tarren goodbye." She takes an intake of air. "It killed me, Viola." Her voice is broken.

"Apollo. Can Tarren help?"

She looks at me and shrugs. "Tarren did say Apollo ~is ~madly in love with you, and that's why his brain is having a hard time processing this. Well, because of what mental state he was in.

"So, when he became drunk, it's like his brain short-circuited."

"We have to go back, Laura," I say in a panic. "When Apollo realizes what he has done, he will never forgive himself."

"He could still show up," she offers with a small smile.

I shake my head. "When Apollo gets like this, he is determined."

"He still can show up."

"We have to go back." My voice catches and breaks. "This can't be the end."

~Don't let this be the end.~

Tears stream down my face.

"We can't go back."

"Are you sure?"

Laura wipes her face and nods. "I already tried."

Our carriage stops.

We are already here?!

The door opens and Mort and Leenie are there.

"We have to go." Mort smiles. "I'm sure everything will work out. It's nearly dawn."

I walk out and I feel like I am moving in slow motion. Sounds and details are barely being registered in my mind. I watch as Pierce walks toward me in his long wool coat flapping in the wind.

I can see the other girls being ushered onto a very fairy-tale style ship. Its golden and white wood gives it an enchanting elegance. I am in no mood to appreciate it.

I do not want to get on that.

When Pierce walks up to me, he reminds me of Chris Harrison from ~The Bachelor~, telling me this will be the last rose given out.

Pierce looks down at me. "How are you doing, kid?"

I say nothing, feeling my emotions too close to the top.

He glances at his watch then out toward the direction of the castle, as if Apollo will be showing up any minute. I can't look.

"You know, the other girls really did an amazing job at taking down Irena's evil forces. I believe April and Ivy were on their last lifeline."

He continues as he stares out into the distance, "I didn't think they could do it, but they did."

"Why are you telling me this?"

"Because" — he pauses — "if Apollo by some chance does not show, the scales are still borderline to where we will not lose Fairy Godmother Inc."

I look up at him. "That's wonderful news," I whisper, meaning it. "Do you think Apollo is not coming then?" I can feel little bits of my world falling away.

Pierce's blond hair blows in the wind as he stands quietly. "He only has ten minutes left before I must get you in the ship."

"Ten minutes," I breathe. "That's not long enough! He's not going to make it, Pierce!"

Pierce's face is that of stone as he gazes toward the castle. "I wish I had an answer for you. You did your best. That's all you can do."

"Pierce!" I scream, feeling like this is becoming too real. "It's not good enough. Will you let me go to him? He is not himself."

"I know he is not, which makes this extremely unfair. These are not my rules. Once the ship leaves, that's it.

"I worried this would happen and tried to buy you more time, but I got denied by the council," he admits.

"No," I say.

Little pieces of me are crumbling away. Gone with the wind.

I am the girl at the end of ~The Bachelor~ who does not get the ring.

"I'm not leaving without him, Pierce," I tell him, pleading with my eyes. Can't he see how I'm hurting?! He must do something!

Pierce does not say anything and looks in the direction of the castle. "Unfortunately, that's impossible."

I glance to the ship and see the girls in tears, hugging each other.

This is not happening.

"It's time, I'm afraid."

"No!" I scream. I turn to look back to the towering castle in the far distance. "Apollo! Damn you!" I wipe the hot tears streaming down my face. "Apollo!"

I feel Pierce pulling me.

"Let go!" I try to push him off me. "I am not leaving without him!"

He pulls me into his embrace, surprisingly strong. His arms hold me tightly as I thrash. I look up into his eyes, vision blurred.

"I was born here, why can't I stay?" I desperately try this tactic. "I don't want this to be the end."

"It does not matter, I'm afraid." I can see the pain in his expression.

"Pierce, I can't leave him."

He glances toward the Castle of Garthorn, then closes his eyes, jaw flexing. "If you do not leave with me, you will be transferred out. I am so sorry."

I am crying, delirious with pain.

I can feel Mort hugging me from behind and it makes me cry harder.

I feel Pierce pick me up, and I just bury my face into his wool coat, not wanting to take one more breath.

I numbly feel for my Darling necklace and rip it off, throwing it. Maybe Apollo will find it and realize what a mistake he's made.

Apollo Augustus Garthorn the Fifth just made the biggest mistake of his life.

***

~New Orleans~

The sound of heartbreak is complete ~silence.~

My bathroom is steamy from the hot bath I am soaking in. A week has passed, and it feels like a lifetime, the pain ever-present. A distant memory that seems more like a dream, a nightmare.

I slowly lift my leg out of the steamy tub filled with red rose petals. Yes, rose petals—how fitting. My skin is smooth and perfect. But who cares? I don't. Nothing matters to me anymore.

Little water droplets fall off my leg, breaking the sound of silence.

~Drip, drip, drip.~

Fairy Godmother offers therapy for their contestants who lose.

I laugh rudely.

~Give me a break.~

I am just going to stay in this bath for the rest of my life. I slip under the rose-filled water, feeling weightless, tranquil. I just want to stay like this forever, insubstantial.

My eyes cramp but I have no tears left. I am just numb.

I   wonder   what Apollo thought when he came to his senses. Is he broken like I am? Will he never forgive himself?

What did he do when he came to the South Shore and saw I was gone? Did he cry? Scream? Or did he not care at all, actually thankful I was gone?

I will never know, unfortunately.

I break the surface of the water, gasping for air.

A knock at the door makes me jump.

I am still, hoping the person leaves as I listen. It could be Laura—she said she was going to bring pizza and ice cream. She is just as hurt as I am.

The knocking again.

~Damn,~ this person must know I'm home. If it's Laura she will not leave until I open the door.

Cursing, I get out of my serene ~depression~ bath. I grab my black robe and hear the knocking again, a little more forceful this time. I try to towel dry my hair.

"Coming!" I yell, irritated.

I am getting water everywhere.

I walk out of the bathroom and through my living room, water dripping off my legs. I hope it's not FedEx or my landlord.

I unlock the door and open it.

I scream, my hand over my mouth.

I am frozen.

I am staring at a man who looks just like Apollo. A god-like human is currently standing in front of me. He is wearing a fitted leather jacket and tight, dark jeans showcasing his muscular form.

I am confused.

I might need therapy after all.

"Angel," he breathes in a husky voice.

I can't move.

"How?" I barely say. Am I hallucinating?!

He holds up my Darling necklace.

"Apollo…" I think I say.

His blonde hair is tied back, and his dark gaze sears me. "May I come in?"

"Come in?"

I am dazed.

He tilts his head. "Yes. I would love to come in. I had to move heaven and hell to get here." He smiles at me, and it makes my brain malfunction. "So I am coming in whether you like it or not."

Joy explodes inside my chest, so much sensation and disbelief. "Did you get molested on your way over here?" My eyes are wide, probably bulging.

He raises a brow, his black gaze moving over me. "Can I touch you?"

"Yes," I say.

I am suddenly in his large embrace, his male scent making me dizzy. Tears flow down my face, I am crying, and I can't stop.

"I am so sorry, Angel," I hear him whisper into my wet hair.

"I don't care, you're here now," I breathe into his neck. "I don't know how, but you're here." I sob.

He lifts back to look at me, eyes watery, impacting me to the core.

"I love you with everything that I have, and I am not going anywhere." His large hands are on my face, wiping away tears. "I'm sorry I took so long, but I made it."

I now know the true definition of happiness.

~Of true love.~

CHAPTER 36

He is here, ~really here~.

In New Orleans.

"Apollo," I whisper as he holds my face, his penetrating stare making my skin tingle.

"Viola, is it?" He smiles down at me.

"Angel." I laugh. "I like Angel."

He nods with a sexy grin and glances around the room for the first time, raising a brow. After a few minutes, he runs a hand down his smooth face. "Your living quarters give me anxiety, I will admit."

My eyes widen and I laugh. "What? Why?" I glance around the room too.

Apollo leaves me and takes in my small living room with red and white floral couches. It's not great, but cute, and I find myself blushing.

He is so larger than life that he makes the room feel even smaller. It's almost laughable. He exhales and glances back to me, that black gaze seeing too much.

"I could have kicked in your door in seconds. It's not safe for a girl who looks like you."

He continues with his hands on his hips, his black leather jacket pulling on his thick biceps, "There is a man living on the first floor of this house, I'm sure you're aware of that?"

"Most men are not built like a superhero." I roll my eyes. "And yes, he is harmless. A true gentleman," I say in my proper voice, still in shock that he is standing in my small living room.

I forgot how gorgeous he is. Well, I didn't forget, I was just willing myself to erase his image so I could function in life.

He tilts his head at me. "There's no such thing as a gentleman, just a patient wolf. Remember that."

I laugh at that. "So, you're not a gentleman?"

His gaze narrows on me. "I think you know the answer to that, Angel."

Goosebumps litter my body and I pull on my robe, feeling a wave of nervousness. "How did you get here?"

He walks over to me and grabs my hand, pulling me toward the couch. He sits down and takes up the whole love seat, but it doesn't matter because he pulls me on his lap.

I realize I am still wet and naked under the black robe. I quickly bring my legs to the side, blushing. I don't think he noticed, though, and I sit on him princess-style.

Only a week has gone by, and I feel out of my element with him. It's like if Thor just decided to show up and have tea with me on my couch. Very unnatural.

I feel like I am out of breath, still in a state of surprise. In his world it was different, but here on Earth, he looks more superhero-ish than ever. Out of place.

I bite my lip. I can't believe someone like him is in love with me. I mean, I still have my Fairy Godmother physical gifts, but I can't shake how nervous I feel.

I'm good though.

360

~Act normal.~

"So, how did you get here?"

"You're wet, and you smell like roses," he says. I can feel his hand tracing circles on my hip.

I take a breath, telling myself not to throw the robe off and tell him to take me. ~Down, girl. Down~. "I was in a bath when you knocked."

My depression red-rose bath.

Apollo's expression does not change as he glances in the direction of the bathroom. A strained silence passes between us, and I clear my throat.

"So how did you get here?" Does my voice sound higher?

"You were in a bath?"

"Yes," I barely say.

He shifts under me making me grab onto his shoulders. "Are you trying to tell me you're naked?"

I think my face turns cherry red and I smile. "Well, I didn't take a bath with clothes on."

Apollo nods, then grins, looking down. "I'm sorry, Angel. I will try to focus," he murmurs. "I just missed you, everything about you. You must have been so hurt by me."

He glances up at me and my heart squeezes.

"Why didn't you come?"

"I convinced myself you were lying in my drunk state. In hindsight, I can't believe I was able to do that. I admit that I was hurt by what I saw when I touched your necklace, and I just lost it.

"I didn't think you were leaving, so I called your bluff. I just thought it was another one of your tall tales, I suppose. I was a complete idiot. A fool," he admits, jaw flexing.

"Tarren came running in that morning yelling at me, and I still didn't believe it. He said you and Laura were gone forever." He takes a breath.

"I remember standing there when the realization hit me. I called your bluff and I lost. I ordered the Garthorn army to comb the land to make sure you were not trying to escape me.

"Though even that didn't make sense because you said you loved me. After two days I started to panic, and I went to the South Shore. I went there and fell to my knees, praying for a miracle."

I felt my eyes sting, listening to him.

"My knee hit your necklace, the magical one you made me touch. So I grabbed it and I held onto it tightly, asking if anyone heard me. I must have pleaded for hours."

I leaned into him, kissing his warm skin, inhaling his neck. My heart throbs. "And then what?"

Apollo wraps his arms around me tighter. The smell of his scent and his leather jacket should be bottled and sold.

"I was transported to the Fairy Godmother headquarters."

"Wow," I breathe.

I can feel him smile. "I had to stand in front of the Universal Jury, far beyond Fairy Godmother Inc., and plead my case. It took three days before they made the decision to let me come get you."

"What did you tell them?" I whisper in awe.

He looks at me. "That this is a woman I cannot live without, and that I would give my life for her if the need arose. Most of all, that I fucked up.

"I told them you were born in Delorith and they would be committing a grave injustice if they denied me. Take that and spread it over three days. It was brutal,

362

but so worth it."

Apollo looks at me. "All of the girls now have the chance to return if they so wish it. Pierce made sure of that."

I wipe a tear and look up. "I can't believe you did all of that for me. I am so happy." I laugh. "Laura will freak out."

Apollo instantly leans up and kisses me hard, hands holding my face. The taste of his lips makes a swarm of butterflies take flight in my stomach. His mouth is hot and passionate.

"Delicious," he groans in my mouth, and deepens the kiss, sweeping in his tongue. He is a drug, an amazing kisser.

"We are supposed to leave for the Fairy Godmother's office immediately," he breathes between our lips. "They stressed that time is of the essence."

He molds his mouth to mine with more wild tongue action. This man can do astounding things with his tongue, I remember.

"I was advised to not touch you until we made it back," he smiles against my mouth, "but you're naked, so…"

I squeal as Apollo picks me up and carries me to the wall, making my legs wrap around his hips.

Adrenaline pounds through my veins when I feel his mouth suctioning hard to my neck, his hands sliding under my robe and gripping my ass.

My hands are in his glorious platinum hair, ringlets everywhere. ~Sexy as hell~. He lifts his head and the dark, passionate look in his gaze leaves me breathless.

I am the luckiest girl in the universe.

He touches me ~there~, and I close my eyes in bliss, my world spinning. "Look at me," he groans, and licks his lips, dark eyes glittering.

Apollo smiles when I look at him while his fingers are now deep within me, moving with precision, the pace accelerating. I can't even think of words, my mind is mush.

"I am going to make you scream, Angel."

And boy do I. I think poor Johnny downstairs will be reaching for his earplugs. Explosions fire off in my body. I am overheating.

He yanks off my robe, ~thankfully.~ I am so hot, I might pass out. "Apollo." I beg for something, and I want it right now. I feel his mouth everywhere. His hand unzipping his pants makes me excited.

He pins me harder against the wall when I feel the hot length of him enter me with one fast plunge. I gasp and hold on—MERCY.

I don't even recognize my own voice. He is pumping into me so fast that I can barely register anything but mind-blowing pleasure. I just hang on for dear life, moving my hips with his.

I feel his mouth on my breasts, neck, shoulder, jawline, and lips. It's like a whirlwind. We are hot and heavy. I don't know where he begins, and I end. I have heard that saying before and now I understand it fully.

There is something so erotic about me being completely naked and him fully clothed. I hear him whisper harshly into my neck as he thrusts harder. Endearments come from his lips and my heart is full.

And then it happens.

My ovaries explode.

~Kidding~, but we both come together, and it is ~magnificent.~

I feel a heavy wave of dizziness as Apollo lowers me to the ground, kissing my hair. "I love you, Angel."

My legs are shaking and my brain running on overdrive, but I hear him say it,

"Wait till I get you back home. We need to build your stamina," Apollo says in a husky voice full of dark promises.

"Now, let's get you dressed and ready before the Fairy Godmother turns us into mice." He pauses with a frown. "She really did say that...and she was not smiling."

I laugh.

~I love him.~

CHAPTER 37

I sigh as I watch Apollo from my room, sitting on my floral couch, deep in thought.

He removed his leather coat due to the warm weather and is now sporting a charcoal gray, V-neck tee that shows off his muscled torso.

Tattoos are visible on his arms and upper chest, making me shiver.

I wonder what's going through his head. That beautiful frown on his face gives me pause. That detached stare makes me curious.

"Penny for your thoughts?"

He looks at me and his eyes go round as saucers. "Where are the rest of your clothes?"

I look down at my short jean shorts with a high waist, paired with an off-the-shoulder white blouse. I look killer. But this must be a shock for Apollo, coming from a world that is very formal.

He stands up, eyes devouring me. "I do not understand this world. It leaves very little to the imagination."

I laugh. "What were you thinking of?"

"You."

I frown. "Good or bad?"

"Let's walk and talk." He winks at me, smacking my ass as I pass him. "I can't believe men in this world are able to function with their women wearing such things. I can almost see your ass in this."

I feel him grab me there, seemingly unable to keep his hands off me, making me laugh.

"It's just the style, people here are used to it," I say, and look back, seeing him still eyeing my body from behind like I am naked. "So, what were you thinking?"

We make it outside on the busy streets and I turn again to wait for him to catch up. He is purposely walking slow. "Apollo?"

He looks up at me with confusion, making me laugh again. These shorts seem to have him mystified. "I asked about what you were thinking?"

Apollo grins and grabs my hand, bringing it to his lips. "I was wondering if you will be happy with me, or if you will miss this crazy place."

Apollo's eyes widen when a dude with a green mohawk walks by in a dog collar and Gothic clothing.

I chuckle into his muscled arm. His face is priceless.

"Apollo, I will be very happy with you, you can trust me. I know we have had our issues, but I have nothing left to hide.

"Honestly though," I kiss his warm shoulder, never wanting to let go, "I don't care where I am at as long as I'm with you."

He looks down at me, a blond ringlet falling free. "No more secrets between us, Angel."

"Agreed." I pull his arm so he will lean down, kissing his soft lips. ~Yum.~ "People are taking your picture." I giggle in his mouth.

He glances up and sees a few camera phones aimed at us.

"They probably think you're some celebrity or a fitness model," I say, and grab his arm tighter. ~He is mine, ladies~.

Apollo glances down at me. "I'm pretty sure you in those shorts are causing the fuss. I am having a hard time watching these men staring at your legs without losing my temper."

I smile~. I disagree.~

Apollo is unnaturally hot. It does not take a genius to see that. "Where are we going?"

"Over here."

I falter just a bit. It's where this all started. Where Cherie and I first saw Pierce standing there with his amused smirk.

That day forever changed my life.

I look to my left and see Mrs. Martinez, the Burrito Lady, and I freeze. Longing crashes through me.

This woman makes the best burritos in all the universe, I'll place money on it. She carries a large cooler full of tinfoil-wrapped, steaming-hot, green chili burritos.

"Apollo!" I say, dragging his arm with me, startling him. "Have you ever had a burrito?!" I need to contain my excitement. I glance back to him, pulling him harder.

He looks confused as he follows me.

I am about to rock his world.

We walk up to her, and I say, "Mrs. Martinez!"

She glances up to us and a wide smile spreads over her face, wrinkles softening her dark eyes. "My Viola, I was wondering what happened to you!" She gives me a tight hug.

After a few moments, her eyes drift over to Apollo, and they widen. She says something in Spanish and laughs, elbowing my side, giving me a wink.

Apollo raises an eyebrow at me as I glance toward her. "He," I say loudly, pointing to Apollo, "has never had a ~burrito~!"

I say it like it is a sin breaking one of the Ten Commandments.

She does the sign of the cross on her chest and mutters something under her breath. She immediately opens the cooler and a cloud of delicious stream rises followed by the best smelling Mexican food.

My mouth waters and I grin at Apollo's curious expression, his abnormal eyes glittering with mirth.

Apollo's a big boy. I bet he can put down some food.

I try to pay her, but she waves my hand away, giving us both a heavy, wrapped burrito. I say thank you and give her a kiss, knowing that this will be the last time I will eat one of her burritos.

I glance at Apollo as we walk toward the Fairy Godmother Inc. door and stop. "Open it like this and take a bite," I command, doing the same.

"We are very late, but this smells very good," he says, and takes a large bite.

After seconds of me holding my breath, waiting for any reaction that would tell me that this is the best food he has ever eaten, he closes his eyes with an expression of bliss.

"What in the fuck is this?" he says as he covers his mouth.

I take a bite, hot green chili coursing through my mouth like a storm of ecstasy. "I know, right?!"

"It's insane."

"Out of this world."

"Sorcery."

"I might orgasm."

Apollo nods. "I won't judge."

"Oh my gosh, did you get a chunk of beef and cheese?" I whimper.

He does not say anything as he finishes his last bite and wipes his mouth. "That was wonderful, thank you for that." He looks mystified.

I laugh and give him my last half, which he gladly takes with enthusiasm. We both stand there wiping our faces, and I crack up, leaning in to give him a kiss.

He hugs me tight, his hands roaming over me.

"We'd better go," I say, feeling excited.

"Ladies first." He holds the door open, his hand still gripping mine like he doesn't want to let go.

We walk up the staircase and push open the metal door to see the same elegant office that I first saw and remember. Cheers and claps erupt when we enter fully, seeing Laura and the rest of the girls who want to return.

Laura runs up to me and hugs me, then scolds Apollo, saying, "~About time!~"

I glance past Laura to see Pierce, Mort, Leenie, and the Fairy Godmother all staring at us. My heart constricts. I thought I would never see them again.

The room quiets.

Zora walks up to us in a white, fifties-style dress, and I swallow, feeling nervous. She looks beautiful with her perfect face and a high bun.

"You both are cutting it close," she condemns with an eyebrow raise.

I close my eyes, knowing it is my fault. I will leave out the steamy apartment incident, they can't prove anything there.

"I'm so sorry. That's my fault. I saw Mrs. Martinez outside and I thought... just one last time."

Zora's eyes widen as she grabs the necklace at her neck, looking back to Pierce.

370

"Mrs. Martinez."

Pierce lets out a breath and checks his watch, looking troubled. Everyone exchanges looks, confusing me. I shift uncomfortably as I glance at Apollo.

Zora shrugs at Pierce. "I could eat a chicken burrito before I leave to the seventh gate."

"We don't always have to be on time," Pierce agrees, as everyone in the office chimes in with eagerness.

I place a hand over my mouth to contain my amusement and relief that I am not in trouble. I guess everyone knows about the magical burritos.

I hear Laura from my left. "I'll take one for the road, Pierce, please."

"I second that," Mort says.

"All right, let's make this fast!" Pierce says and takes out a notepad. "Orders, please! Speak now or forever hold your peace." Pierce points at Apollo. "You want another, big guy?"

Apollo looks at me with an amused smirk. "Give me two. I think I need to take one back and study it for our cloning facilities."

Pierce nods. "Never a normal day at Fairy Godmother Inc., that's for damn sure."

***

~In the briefing room~

I will say goodbye to Earth forever, and it does not bother me because I am staring at the most seductive, ~dark~ eyes. Apollo walks around me and clasps the Darling necklace around my neck.

Pierce walks up to me with a grin. "I get to make your wedding gown, my dear. It will be my honor. And do tell me when you're with child, I am quite good at sending great baby clothes."

I hug Pierce fiercely, knowing that he is such a special person. Apollo and I did not use protection, so the idea that I might be pregnant could be very true.

A surge of delight courses through me when thinking about having a child with bouncing blond ringlets. I look at Apollo and I can see that he may be having similar thoughts.

He squeezes my hand and I feel butterflies in my chest.

This is a ~happily-ever-after.~

I feel my eyes gloss over.

"I have never seen two people glowing as much as you two." Pierce laughs. "You will all be missed, but rest assured, we all get together at the annual Fairy Godmother Christmas party.

"Think of it as a company Christmas party. You will always be a part of our family. And yes, we celebrate Christmas. Every world has something similar, trust me. Every world needs saving.

"The big man upstairs likes us a lot." He winks.

"I can't wait," I say, feeling Apollo rubbing my wrist. I look at Apollo. "Do you have Christmas on Delorith?"

"Yes." He moves his head to the side. "We call it something a little different."

Pierce nods. "Isn't it Savioright Day?"

"Yes," Apollo agrees.

"There are a few worlds that don't, but most do, anyway." He claps his hands. "When you both are ready, step into the pod and press the blue button. I will bid you both farewell, until we meet again."

When he leaves, I glance down at my lovely pale green gown and smile up at Apollo. "This is it."

"This is it, Angel."

I frown up at him. "How's your head? Will this be okay for you?"

"I will be fine." He kisses my forehead. "I should be back to full health. I only experience head pain occasionally. No more confusing thoughts.

"I had one more treatment before I came, and I am feeling back to normal."

"I am so sorry."

He laughs. "Angel, I would have died for you."

I close my eyes at that, then feel his lips on mine, the kiss turning passionate as his mouth moves over mine. I lift my head. "Tarren will be so happy Laura is coming back."

"Yes, that will save our relationship. He was devastated," Apollo admits.

"Am I pregnant?" I take his hand and put it on my stomach.

"I hope so, but if not, you will be soon," he says with a dark glimmer. I laugh as we make our way into the pod.

I take a breath and grab his hand. "Let's push it together."

"I love you."

He grabs my chin and kisses me right as we both push the button.

***

"That, my friends, is a ~happily-ever-after~," says the Fairy Godmother with a wink, and a generous bite of her burrito.

CHAPTER 38

"Laura, you fat hooker!" I say as I waddle. "Wait for me!" I can hear her laughing as she turns to face me, her large tummy draped in shimmering emerald green.

She eyes me with a raised brow. "If you start getting contractions from all your swaying and squawking, Apollo will be very upset."

I wave my hand. "Pish-posh."

Yes, we both are eight months pregnant and ~no~, it was not planned. I am two weeks ahead of her though, which is why I almost didn't make it to the Fairy Godmother Christmas party.

We've just arrived, and the men have gone to see about hanging up our cloaks.

I am wearing a deep-scarlet gown with glittering diamonds under my bustline. It's a stunning piece that Apollo surprised me with. My raven hair is piled high on my head with glittering pins.

"Hold on," I pause, out of breath, and smile at passing people in reindeer hats. "Okay, we can go now."

"Wow, this place is massive," she says in awe. "And so festive."

Fairy Godmother Headquarters is a sight to see. I am not sure how big this place is, seeing how we were beamed here—and yes, it was safe for the baby.

I can hear loud Christmas music emitting from the main hall and it sounds like a rocking time. Silver and blue Christmas decor is draped everywhere, making the grand place look like a winter wonderland.

Everything seems to sparkle and twinkle, like it's right out of a fantasy. There are tons of beautiful people here, elves running everywhere, and female servers dressed as slutty snowmen.

And I look like a water buffalo.

"You look stunning," Apollo whispers in my ear, seeming to read my mind. I turn to see Apollo looking insanely handsome in his black tux, made by Pierce.

He wanted to try out some new clothing and Apollo is such a great specimen. This man looks like every woman's fantasy.

His glorious hair is tied back despite my wanting it down. Let me say this: When his hair is down, it gives me instant hot flashes. His dark eyes glitter down at me, his expression making my body tingle.

"And you, sir, look handsome," I say, grinning up at him.

He rolls his eyes. "Tell me something I don't know."

I hit his arm and laugh. "Funny."

Apollo winks at me. "How are you feeling?" His large hands smooth over my belly. "Is she kicking?"

"I am feeling good," I say, and grab his hands to feel more toward the under part of my belly. "Here, do you feel it?"

Apollo looks down as he waits for a kick, then smiles at me. "She will be a feisty one, like her mother."

I laugh as he leans down to kiss me, filling my heart. This past year has been

---

bliss with him—he is truly an amazing man.

It took a little getting used to, living in a castle and being called the Queen of Garthorn. But my favorite thing about my new life is my family and friends, something that I have never had before.

I am gushing, feeling so lucky. I know it's corny, mushy stuff, but I cannot wait to spend the rest of my life with him, to see our kids grow and thrive.

Though I am not sure what we will say when they ask us how we met. That might be our teensy-weensy little secret.

Tarren walks up to us and pats Apollo on the back, looking dashing as well. "I've just seen people with green skin, scared the hell out of me in the bathroom."

Apollo raises an eyebrow. "My wife scared the hell out of me last night with green skin, in the bathroom." He gives me a pointed look.

I roll my eyes. "It was a face mask."

Laura grabs my arm and points into the Great Hall. "I see Pierce and Zora."

I look through the throng of people and see Pierce in a white and blue tux and a Santa hat, looking perfect, laughing at what someone said. The life of the party.

We all walk into the hall and see a giant Christmas tree the size of a two-story building. It's a breathtaking glittering blue and silver with tiny hints of purple. The festive music blares and laughter rings in the air.

A waiter came up to us in a white tux and a Santa hat. "Can I interest you in some of these?"

What's ~these~?

We all lean over and look at the tray carrying what looks like baby poop on a cracker. I cover my nose, nausea swimming in my belly.

We all pass politely as I try to get my stomach under control. Apollo gives me a pitying look.

"There is lots of food over there that I can see. I'll go and get you some," he offers.

"No, I'm fine."

Apollo shakes his head, a grin pulling at his mouth. "No way, Angel. I've seen you when you're hungry and it scares me."

Tarren is listening, and they both agree that the pregnant women need to gorge themselves, apparently. Laura shifts. "Let's find a place to sit before my ankles swell."

I nod, waddling over to a ton of beautiful tables with white glittering chairs. We find an empty table and sit, sighing with relief.

"Look at this place, it's enormous!" I say, and laugh.

"Look at all of the hot people," she says, looking around with a wide stare. "I wonder if all these people were once on missions."

"I bet a lot of them were."

Pierce's voice startles us. "There are my two pregnant mamas!"

"Pierce!" we both say, and try to stand up.

"No, no!" He laughs. "Stay seated. I do not want to deliver a baby tonight—I am in my favorite suit."

Laura and I exchange ~yeah, right~ looks.

He sits down at the table and is all smiles. "I cannot believe you both are having girls—and pregnant at the same time, no less."

We both laugh and agree.

"Well, before you leave, I have gifts for you both." Pierce beams.

"That's so sweet! This place is amazing, by the way," I say, meaning it.

"Isn't it though?" he agrees, and flags a waiter for another drink.

"Where is Mort? I have to say hi to her," I ask, looking around.

"Oh." Pierce sighs and points at the stage at the far end of the hall. "She's been at the karaoke all evening. Apparently she's drunk off champagne.

"She really likes the bubbles. I had to hear all about the bubbles for twenty minutes." He looks pained.

I place a hand over my mouth to stifle a laugh. "Is she singing to someone?"

I see Mort looking like her cute Sailor Moon self and wearing some sort of large Grinch hat that is about to fall off. Oh dear.

"Yes," Pierce confirms as he squints in her direction. "I think that's Phil from accounting."

"I think he looks uncomfortable," Laura says with a raised eyebrow.

"Most likely. I'll grab her in a minute." Pierce laughs. "Wait, too late, she sees us."

Mort beelines it for us with a big smile and champagne in hand, hat fallen off somewhere. "My human!" she slurs, and wraps her arms around me.

"Mort!" I laugh. "That was some nice singing up there."

"Yeah, I just gave what the audience wanted." She stumbles to the left.

"Have a seat, Mort," Pierce says.

"I'll be back. I have to tell Phil how I feeeeel." Then she is gone.

Pierce winces. "She will regret that. She despises that guy."

I laugh. Only Mort.

Apollo and Tarren arrive with plates of food like we weigh two-hundred pounds. Now that I think about it, we might. But who cares. It looks and smells delicious.

Pierce stands and shakes hands with the men.

"Thank you. I hope some of this is for you?" I smile as Apollo sits next to me.

"Just a little." He winks.

Pierce takes a sip of his drink. "I'll let you guys eat. I have to prepare for our next mission."

I take a bite of shrimp and bacon with zero guilt. "What's this mission?"

Pierce leans forward. "A hard one. So hard, in fact, that we have just gotten clearance that if we fail, it will not count against us."

Apollo clicks his tongue. "I feel sorry for the man in question."

I kick him under the table. "How? He super evil?"

"It's not that. It's quite complicated. I am dealing with a race of people who think of themselves superior to anyone who is not them," he says with another drink.

"Can't you just make the agents their race then?"

"No, because that's the problem. Fairy Godmother thinks they need to be put in their place by a human. Their ego needs altering. They have this whole ~Hunger Games~ thing going on there that needs to be fixed."

"~Hunger Games~?" Laura frowns. "I love that movie."

"Not if you're in it," Pierce says. "I'm scared too many lifelines will be used to complete the mission. I am asking for more, but I am not confident the council will agree."

He reaches for some shrimp off my plate. "I'm going to personally find a girl myself. I need a girl who will not back down and has an ego to match theirs.

"I get to throw a wild card in with Fate's picking. So that's fun," he says, chewing.

Laura laughs. "Find a celebrity."

"Right." He nods, pointing at her. "I just have to find one that is willing to do it, and I've got a week to pull it off." He points at the shrimp. "Those are legit."

"That's exciting though," I say, wishing I could get updates on the mission. "Will you tell me how it goes?"

"Of course." Pierce winks and stands up. "Don't forget to take pics in the funny picture booth." He bows and leaves in a hurry.

Apollo kisses my neck. "I would hate to have his job."

I look at him. "I think he loves it though."

I am just hoping whoever he picks knows what she is getting herself into.

It's one hell of a ride.

~But oh-so worth it.~

Please Follow me on Patreon and Facebook!!

https://www.patreon.com/user?u=41187078

https://www.facebook.com/F.R.BLACK123/

IF YOU ENJOYED THIS BOOK

PLEASE LEAVE A REVIEW AND TELL ME WHAT

YOU THOUGHT!

A VERY SPECIAL THANKS, HOLLY QUINN AND BARA, FOR EDITING MY

WORK AND MAKING IT SPARKLE!

Made in the USA
Columbia, SC
06 July 2025

60401124R00211